THE SAMARITAN

THE SAMARITAN

CHAZ BRENCHLEY

St. Martin's Press
New York

For information, address St. Martin's Press, 175 Fifth Avenue, New York, N.Y. 10010.

Library of Congress Cataloging-in-Publication Data

Brenchley, Chaz.
The samaritan / by Chaz Brenchley.
p. cm.
ISBN 0-312-01813-4
I. Title.
PR6052.R38S2 1988
823′.914—dc 19 87-38238
CIP

First published in Great Britain by Hodder & Stoughton Limited.
First U.S. Edition
10 9 8 7 6 5 4 3 2 1

For Carol Smith.

For her collection.

Contents

Part One

Violent Delights

1 Here's Looking at You

– as you go down to the river. It's a good night for a walk, clear and cold, under a sky of gravel-sharp stars. A skittish wind stirs your hair, plays with the litter around you, light-footed as a kitten or a lover. The orange glow of the street-lamps twists things disturbingly out of their true colour – but no, let's not be didactic about this. The colour you see is the true colour, for you and for that moment; and it doesn't disturb you to see a red car paled to a dirty white. There are no absolutes. Everything has a thousand faces, and every face is real.

Inside your bag, something shifts with a cold sound as you turn into the road beside the river. You smile, and heft the bag in your hand, feeling the weight of it.

There are benches along the quayside; and he's waiting on one of them, as he promised. He sits hunched and alone, staring out over the water, almost in the shadow of the bridge.

He glances up as you get closer. He's a young man, probably in his early twenties. His hair hangs limply to his shoulders, and his cheeks look half-molten in the alien light. Acne, perhaps – the vicious kind that comes with adolescence and stays till middle-age.

"Hullo," he says dully, knowing you, his voice flat and bitter, a salt plain with no water. "Thanks for coming."

You nod, and drop the bag beside the bench. It settles heavily, and you smile again, thinking of hooks, and of rope. Chain would perhaps have been better; but there was none in the garage, and you were in a hurry. Next time, perhaps – though next time, of course, it will be different.

You sit down beside the boy, murmuring something about the river, and the night. He only grunts in reply, but that's all right. This is a game you've played many times, and you know the rules. There's more than one way to open a conversation, and one of the best is to say nothing.

Waiting, you watch the boy as he lights a cigarette with shaking hands. He's thin, harsh-edged against the city's glow, coarse-featured and afraid. You look at his wrists, slender like a woman's; at his bony shoulders; at his neck, jutting out of an upturned collar. You count imaginary vertebrae between your fingers, like a rosary.

It would be so simple, so laughably simple. You could reach out, grip him so, twist thus – and it would be done. You could do it for him, as you did it for . . . as you did it, once before.

But let him talk, there's no hurry. And there's no need to be so quick yourself. You've learned that. All roads lead to Rome; so what does it matter, if some of them are slower and less easy? It means nothing in the end. How could it?

So you sit back, ready to listen; but your mind is playing already with rope, and with hooks; and your eyes are straying to the iron girders of the bridge above . . .

2 *Bloody Paradise*

As always, she slept like a child, foetal under the covers. Fenner lifted the duvet back to watch her, smiling at the curled fist with its thumb suspiciously near her mouth.

He lay still for a long time, propped up on one elbow, just looking. A slow finger of sunlight pushed its way through the gap in the curtains to lie across Tina's shoulder, edging towards the tangled darkness of her hair. Her skin twitched gently; and Fenner shivered, thinking suddenly of the thousand ridiculous, impossible things that went on every second beneath that secretive surface, all the chemical and biological reactions that together made a human being. Thinking how easily something could go wrong – what a fragile and treacherous thing a body was.

And sleep was strange, too. You never worried for yourself, but it was frightening sometimes to see it in someone you loved. To watch and wonder what it was that kept their uninhabited bodies still breathing, when they'd let the reins slip so far . . .

Almost, Fenner reached out to shake her and call her back;

but he stopped himself just as his hand touched her shoulder, skin on skin, still warm where the sunlight had passed. Not yet. He needed time alone, to think. He didn't understand what he was doing here, in bed with a girl half his age; there was no logic to it. His life had stopped making very much sense two years ago, but this was the most senseless thing of all . . .

Tina stirred, and that stray beam of sunlight brushed across her face. She frowned slightly, and her eyes opened.

"Morning."

Tina blinked up at him. "Is it? Oh good."

She rolled onto her back and stretched out, eyes closed, grunting with pleasure as she eased kinked muscles. Fenner grinned, feeling a tension slide away.

"What's good about it being morning?"

"I'm not getting up till the afternoon." She smiled at him. "Which means I've got plenty of time to help you out with that erection of yours, and still get in a couple of hours' more sleep on top."

Fenner could feel an explosive bubble of laughter swelling in his chest, looking for a way out. "How did you know I had an erection, you awful brat? Considering I'm lying on it?"

"You always do in the mornings," she said sweetly. "Fucking randy bugger, you are. Now do you want to do something about it, or are you just going to lie there until it goes away?"

The next time Fenner woke, he was alone. The other side of the bed was still warm, though, and he could hear Tina moving around the flat. He lay still, watching a couple of flies hunt each other across the ceiling; and a few minutes later she came in, chewing a knuckle thoughtfully.

"What's up?" Fenner asked, recognising the symptoms.

"Fenner, are you conscious yet? I want to talk to you."

He sat up, holding out an arm to her. She perched on the edge of the bed and took his hand in both of hers, turning it palm-uppermost and began to trace the lines with a finger.

"I've just been through the post," she started hesitantly. "There's a couple for you, that look pretty boring. And I had one from my mother, usual great long what-d'you-call-it, screed, I haven't read it yet . . ."

"But?"

"But there was one from the solicitors, too. Probate's been granted, and all the forms and stuff are ready. I only have to sign some papers, and Auntie's cottage is all mine."

"It's about time." Fenner squeezed her hand gently. "I'm glad, love. What are you going to do, be an absentee landlady? You'll make a fortune from the tourists, in summer."

"No. I don't want to let it."

"Why not? It's the best thing, surely. It'd be stupid to have it sitting empty most of the year, and I'd hate to see you sell it. You don't need the money that urgently. And anyway, I've never been to Wales."

"No, you don't understand," Tina said, almost desperately. "I want to go and *live* in it."

"Oh. I see." He pulled his hand free and turned away, reaching towards his cigarettes to cover the movement. Anything, not to let her see his face.

"Ohhh . . ." There was a groan of frustration behind him, before she grabbed him round the throat and jerked him back onto the duvet.

"*Us*, stupid," Tina hissed in his ear. "Us. You and me. Two of us. Together. Get it?"

"What? But . . ." For a minute, Fenner didn't move; then he disentangled himself carefully and got to his feet. "It's no good, I can't think like this. Why don't you get dressed? I'll go and make breakfast."

Fenner was turning the sausages under the grill when she came through ten minutes later. She was barefoot, wearing jeans and a baggy sweatshirt, with a nervous edge to her that made her look younger than ever to his eyes. She came across to him, and slipped her arms round his waist; he waited till she glanced up, and kissed her gently. She stood passively under his lips for a moment, then twisted away.

"You'll burn the sausages."

"Damn the sausages."

Fenner pulled the pan out from under the grill and dropped it onto the stove with a clatter. He rubbed Tina's shoulder through the sweatshirt, keeping his other arm firmly around her.

"Come on. Tell me."

Her head nestled against him, one black curl tickling the

corner of his mouth. "You. You're going to say no, aren't you? And I want you there. I *need* you, Paul."

It was perhaps the fourth time she'd called him by his given name, in as many months. Fenner felt something jerk deep inside him, and swallowed quickly.

"I'm sorry, Tina, but – hell, it wouldn't work, that's all."

"Why not?" Her mood shifted again, like a yacht tacking into the wind; her voice was challenging now, almost electric. She pulled away from him, going to the table to slice bread. Fenner winced, seeing the loaf tear as she hacked at it.

"Take it easy, love. You'll have a finger off."

Tina tossed a glare at him, then looked down at her handiwork and giggled reluctantly. "It's not very straight, is it? Still, it'll do to wedge a door open. It's not very fresh either." She slid that first slice off the breadboard and began to cut another, more carefully. "Why not?" she repeated. "Trot out your excuses, Fenner my lad. I'll shoot 'em down like clay pigeons."

Fenner kept his eyes on his hands, as he pricked the sausages. "One, I'm forty years old. Which is twice your age."

Tina snorted. "Ridiculous. *And* untrue. You're thirty-nine, and I'm twenty-one. And what the hell does it matter, anyway?" she demanded, suddenly furious. "I love you, right? I'd love you if you were eighty. It doesn't make any difference to us. It's just other people, isn't it? Let them say what they like, I don't care."

"You might start caring, if it started happening. And it would, in a village. People whispering behind your back, watching you from doorways . . ."

A contemptuous shrug answered him. Fenner sighed, and went on. "Two. You can't take a degree long-distance, so we'd have to leave it for a year anyway, till after your finals."

"No, we won't. I'm chucking the course at the end of term."

"The hell you are!"

"I am too." She gestured at him with the breadknife. "Listen, Fenner darling, has it ever occurred to you to wonder why I wanted a degree in the first place? Doing this course was just an interesting way of getting through another three years, while I tried to decide what I wanted to do with my life. And now I've decided. I want to live with you in a little cottage in Wales, growing onions and keeping chickens. And painting, sure; but I'm not going to stop painting, just because I quit this course. I don't need a bit of paper to tell me that I know how to draw."

"What about money?" he grunted.

"That's your share of the partnership. I'm providing the cottage, you provide the cash. We won't need much, anyway; I want to be self-sufficient, as much as possible."

Fenner split the sausages silently between two plates. Tina came up behind him, and he felt her hands circling his waist, her cheek rubbing against his shoulder-blade. "*Please*, Fenner?" she whispered. "Look, it'll be okay, I promise. It'll be good for you too, you can write that novel you're always talking about. There won't be all the distractions, out in the country, you'll be able to get down to it properly . . ."

"I don't know, love," he said helplessly, knowing two things – both what he wanted, and what he didn't dare accept. "I tried being married once before, and I made a godawful mess of that. And an even worse mess of myself, afterwards." He hugged her gently, in lieu of the thanks that she wouldn't let him utter.

"Who said anything about getting married, dopey? I'm talking about living in sin."

"Yeah, but it comes to the same thing in the end."

"Doesn't have to." She freed one hand to pick up a sausage and began to eat, crunching it thoughtfully. Fenner growled, deep in his throat; Tina smiled, and dropped the last inch of the sausage into his open mouth.

"I'll tell you what, then, I'll make a bargain with you," she said, licking her fingers while he chewed. "I'll ask the university to give me a year out, and we'll give it a trial, eh? Then if it doesn't work, we can always come back again and pick up the threads here. Hell, you could even keep this place on, if you wanted. You can afford it; and that way, we'd have a place to come back to for weekends. Keep up with people." She smiled up at him casually, but her voice was pleading. "How's about it, guy?"

Fenner shook his head slowly. "We can't just jump into something this big, Tina. You've got to give me time to think about it."

"Think? What's to think about? Here I am offering you bloody Paradise, and you carry on like it was Gethsemane.

Sometimes I wonder why I bother with you, Fenner, really I do." She grinned, and dug her fist into his stomach. "Then I remember what you're like in bed, and suddenly it's all so clear . . . Look, I'll give you two days, okay? I won't even talk about it, promise. A forty-eight hour moratorium, while Fenner thinks."

He nodded silently. Tina pulled his head down to hers and kissed him, with no hurry and a good deal of concentration.

"Immoral persuasion," she explained. "I'm going to whisper things into your ear while you're asleep, too – like in 'Brave New World'. Come on, let's eat. Bags me first with the ketchup, there's only a dribble left."

The ringing of the telephone jolted Fenner free of the thoughts which had been playing hopscotch in his head all afternoon. Tina answered it, and came back scowling. "It's for you, Fenner. Inspector Malone."

Pleasure and surprise, salted with amusement; Fenner took a liberty, and ruffled Tina's hair as he passed. Mike Malone and he had been friends for many years, and they'd shared too much to let that friendship go. But equally, there was too much between them for Tina to find it easy to accept him. She held Malone to be largely responsible for the mess Fenner had been in when she'd found him, and it seemed that nothing could stop her prickling every time their paths crossed. In the end it had proved easier for the two men simply to let their friendship lie fallow for a while. Fenner in any case had been wholly absorbed in finding new patterns and a new focus for his life, and he'd barely noticed Mike's absence from it; there'd be room to fit him in somewhere, as and when.

And the when was now, four or five months on, and from Tina's expression sooner than was comfortable; but he wasn't going to let her bully him any more. There was no purpose to it now, he didn't need it. So he grinned, and ruffled her hair, and went to talk to his friend.

The telephone was on Fenner's desk in the spare bedroom, which served as a study for him and an occasional studio for Tina, when she wanted to work at home. He slid a sketchbook and a pile of pens off his chair, sat down and picked up the receiver.

"Mike, hi. Long time. What's new?"

There was a brief silence at the other end of the line. Then: "Don't you know?"

"No. What is it?"

"Another murder. Messy one, makes it look like our old pal again. Pick up an evening paper, they've got the story; but listen, what I'd like, can I talk it through with you tonight? Say down the Victoria, at six?"

Fenner hesitated, seeing rows of grinning faces across a bar-top, endless rows of bottles eternally running dry, eternally filling themselves again. He shook his head sharply to break up the images. "Yeah, sure, Mike. I'll be there."

"Good. Thanks, Paul. See you then."

Fenner hung up, already shuffling words around in his mind, looking for the best way of telling Tina.

3 *Auld Lang Syne*

Predictably, Tina was furious. She stormed at Fenner, cursing Malone and himself alternately. Finally, though, when he shrugged and said he was going anyway, she turned icily quiet, said that of course it was his own affair, and went into the study with a book. Fenner was half-inclined to follow her, but held himself back; that would be too great a betrayal of his own independence, and hers. And she had to learn to trust him sometime.

He collected his jacket and his cigarettes, called goodbye through the closed study door, and went down the stairs and out into bright sunlight.

His neighbour was sitting in the open doorway of her own flat, knitting and listening to the radio.

" 'Evening, Diana," he said, as she glanced up. "Not *more* bedsocks, surely?"

She laughed. "Paul Fenner, if you say another word about my bedsocks, I'll double your rent. As it happens, this is a bed-jacket."

"A *what*? Honestly, Di, I swear you wear more clothes in bed than you do out."

"It's where I do most of my reading," Diana said placidly. "And I get cold, if I haven't something to put around my shoulders."

"Pernicious habit, reading in bed. What you need is some nice warm male distraction."

"Were you volunteering?"

Fenner sighed. "Ah, if I were only free!"

"You mean I'd have to negotiate with Tina."

"That's it. And I warn you now, she drives a hard bargain. See you later, Di; I've got to run now, I've got a date."

Diana's rich voice chased him up the hill, but he didn't catch the words. His mind was shifting gear already, sliding down into old and familiar paths. Somewhat to Fenner's consternation, it felt a lot like coming home.

Even if Mike hadn't phoned, one glance at the evening's billboards would have sent Fenner into the first newsagent he came to, for a local paper. The *Evening News* fliers shrieked at him from every corner, with all the hysteria of a disregarded prophet and the voice of his own particular past.

BODY FOUND HANGING UNDER BRIDGE

and

TYNESIDE BUTCHER – HIS FIFTH VICTIM?

Fenner frowned; a simple hanging didn't seem like the Butcher's style. But he bought a paper and read through the story as he walked, trusting other pedestrians to get out of his way.

A young man's body was found early this morning, swinging from the Tyne Bridge. The body was hanging from two ropes, equipped with steel hooks. The cause of death is still uncertain, but a murder inquiry has been launched.

The victim was Peter Adams (23), an unemployed graduate from Newcastle Polytechnic. He lived in Blyth Road, Fenham. Relatives have been informed.

Chief Superintendent Alan Warley, who is heading the inquiry, has appealed to the public for help. "We need to know where this boy went last night, who he spoke to, what he did. We're particularly interested in anyone who thinks they may have seen him in town, in the quayside area, sometime after midnight."

This is the fourth bizarre killing in the city, in the last three years. But are they all the work of the same psychotic killer, the man they call the Butcher? Chief Superintendent Warley refused to speculate; but all the evidence points that way.

The Butcher's previous victims were . . .

Fenner skimmed hastily through the rest of the report; he of all people didn't need a summary of the Butcher's career so far, and he knew that the paper could have nothing more useful to discuss. Nobody saw the Butcher at work, nobody heard him, he never left so much as a scuffed footprint or a cigarette-end behind. The police could find no reason for any of the deaths, and no connection between them. They couldn't even say for sure that there was just one Butcher; for all they knew, it could have been four different people. Each of the killings was different; but each was so bizarre, it was easier to assume that there was one mind behind them all. Easier, and infinitely more comfortable to postulate just one psychopath loose in the city.

The wind was warm and heavy, pushing at Fenner's back, nudging him like a dog. He glanced over his shoulder at the smudged charcoal line of cloud that lay on the horizon, giving a limit to the sky. It's going to thunder, he thought; then chuckled quietly to himself. Fenner the weather-prophet. Not a likely role, or a convincing one. Like Fenner the writer, or Fenner the drop-out, living in a cottage in the Welsh hills . . .?

Futures arrayed themselves before him, railway lines running parallel for a space, then curling away from each other like the threads of a fraying rope. Futures with Tina and without, in Wales, in Newcastle, other places. Success or failure, long life or an early death – all of them dependent on the decisions he made now. His life lay in his own hands, malleable and uncertain. It was almost frightening to be given so much control over his own destiny, after a lifetime of doing what other people said. He kept looking for a *deus ex machina*, a voice from the heavens, a finger pointing and a quiet command . . .

Fenner started, as a rusty green Cortina shot past inches away from him, and an angry Geordie voice yelled something indistinguishable. He jumped back onto the pavement, grinning. So much for being in control. It all came down to accident, in the end.

He turned right, and a few minutes' walk brought him to the Victoria, a small nineteenth-century hotel standing like an island on the corner of a modern housing estate.

The interior of the bar was in keeping with the rest of the building, dark wood and red-shaded lamps, leather-covered benches. Malone was sitting in their old corner, with a pint and a large Scotch in front of him. Fenner nodded across the room, then stopped dead as he registered the whisky. Malone never touched spirits, he remembered; and he remembered just how long it was since they'd been in touch, how far he'd come . . .

So he went to the bar, and ordered a tomato juice.

"Gone a bit prissy, haven't you?" Malone said, as Fenner joined him. "Drinking Bloody Marys, yet. And never mind poor old Malone, who sacrificed half a month's salary to get you a whisky."

"Sorry, Mike, but you could have saved your money. This is straight tomato; I don't drink any more. Sixteen weeks, and counting."

"Yeah? Congratulations. That makes your second divorce this year." Malone tilted his glass towards Fenner, in a mock salute that didn't hold a trace of mockery.

"Thanks."

They talked for a while as old friends do, saying as much with silence as with words. Eventually, Fenner lit a fresh cigarette and tapped the evening paper, where it was sticking out of his jacket pocket.

"What about this, then? Is it the same guy again?"

"Sure to be." Malone nodded. "At least, it's as sure as anything else we know about the bastard, which is not a lot. I can tell you one thing, though; he reads newspapers."

"Meaning?"

"He's picked up on that stupid 'Butcher' tag. Used real butcher's tools this time." His lip curled distastefully. "Meat-hooks. You know, what they hang the pigs from, in the back of the vans? Only this butcher's meat wasn't dead yet."

"Oh, Christ." Fenner drew deeply on his cigarette, to give his hands something to do, to keep them away from the whisky. He'd purposely left it there, as a little test of will; but suddenly he regretted it. "You mean that boy was *alive* when he was hung up there?"

"So the doctor says. We managed to keep it out of the papers for today, at least, but I don't suppose that'll last. It's the sickest thing I've ever come across, Paul. Those hooks were pushed through the kid's ribs, into his lungs; then the ropes were fixed under the bridge, and he was left to swing on 'em. The doctor reckons he took twenty minutes to die."

"Time?"

"About one in the morning. Give or take."

"And nobody heard him? He must've been screaming fit to bust, if he didn't pass out first."

"Gagged," Malone said. "Very efficiently gagged – enough to keep him quiet, not enough to choke him. Didn't want him to die too soon."

Fenner thought for a minute. "But surely someone must've seen something? A guy hanging someone else off a bridge isn't exactly inconspicuous."

"No – but this fella's not exactly stupid, either. He worked from *under* the bridge: climbed up in the shadows, looped the ropes over a girder, then dropped down and hauled away. With one big fish on his hook." Malone's large, coarse-looking hand clenched around his glass till the knuckles showed white, impotent and trembling.

"Take it easy, Mike."

"Yeah. Sorry. I just – they don't usually get to me, but this guy . . ."

Fenner nodded. He didn't feel it so much himself, now that he was no longer involved; but he remembered the white-hot fury that used to sweep through him unexpectedly when he had been, leaving him shaking and weak with reaction. It was the senselessness of it that touched them so deeply. Ordinary killing, murder with some kind of motive behind it, they could understand; but apparently random, reasonless slaughter was something else entirely. And then there was the simple downright cruelty of the deaths, the feeling that the killer had stood there laughing as his victims died; and that cut deeper still, cut worst of all.

"Okay," said Fenner, "but how can I help? I'm on the outside now."

"I know." Malone brushed that aside with one emphatic gesture. "But you were right there in the middle with the early ones, right? And you can't have put every stray thought into your reports. I want to talk them all over with you, and stir the new ones in, and see if you can't come up with something we've missed. There's got to be a link somewhere."

"How do you know?" Fenner asked mildly. "Maybe this guy really does pick 'em at random. Maybe he stands on street corners at midnight and takes the first that comes along."

"Yeah, maybe he does – but even there it's a connection, right? We're talking about people who go for walks alone, after midnight. So let's talk, Paul. It's got to be worth trying, at least."

Two hours later, Malone gave up with a despairing shrug.

"Nothing," he said. "Just *nothing*!"

"Well, I'll keep thinking," Fenner promised doubtfully, "but I honestly don't hold out much hope. Your best chance is just to wait till he makes a mistake, it seems to me."

"This little sweetheart doesn't make mistakes." Malone drained his fourth pint, then got to his feet abruptly. "I'd better be off; Susan will've been looking for me this last hour. Can I give you a lift home?"

"No, thanks," Fenner said slowly. "I've got some thinking of my own to do, and it's better here, away from the flat."

"Right. I'll see you around, then, Paul. G'night."

"'Night, Mike. And – say hullo to Susan for me. For auld lang syne."

The whisky still sat untouched in the centre of the table, amber touched by red fire where it reflected the wall-lights. Fenner folded his hands and looked at it, conducting a neat, civilised debate with himself. Should he drink it, or shouldn't he?

The arguments became long and involved; eventually he shook his head free of them, and settled simply for looking. It was a beautiful thing, a glass of whisky – glass and contents resolving into something far greater than either, a sheer pleasure to look at. A thing of beauty, he thought, is a joy forever; similarly, a cat may look at a king. Likewise and therefore he, Fenner, would look at this glass of whisky.

Outside, thunder crashed. Fenner quirked an eyebrow; he had been right after all. Right about the thunder. He glanced at the window, to see the first of the rain hit and wash down the dirty glass. Not that it would make it any cleaner; Newcastle rain was dirty too. Like the city. Like the people in the city, people who could hang a boy on meat-hooks and leave him swinging under a bridge . . .

His gaze shifted back to the whisky, which seemed to have inched a little closer. Almost as if it wanted to be drunk. And why not? That was what it was for, being drunk; and there had been a time when it had seemed as though that was what Fenner was for, too. Being drunk. It might be good to be drunk again, just once, for old time's sake. Auld lang syne. Good to get away for a while, away from the city and men with meat-hook minds, away from Tina and her eternal vigilance, her silent suspicions . . .

And then a hand flailed across the table, sending the glass smashing into the wall. Fenner looked up to see Tina glaring down at him, soaked to the skin, her face livid.

"You bastard!" she hissed. "You *promised* . . ."

"I didn't touch it, Tina," he protested mildly. "Cross my heart. Mike had bought it for me before I got here; and I just sat and looked at it all evening. Smell my breath, if you don't believe me. Nothing but tomato-juice and cigarettes, I swear."

He pulled her down beside him. She touched his face lightly with wet fingers, then leant forward to kiss him hesitantly, almost nervously.

"All right," she muttered. "I'm sorry. But – oh, God, Fenner, I was so *scared*! You were gone for ages, and I knew I couldn't trust that bastard Malone not to get at you about it, so I came down in the end, and when I . . . when I saw you sitting here with the whisky, and you looking like you were half gone already, I . . ."

The rest was lost, as she buried her head in his shoulder. Fenner cradled the wet hair tenderly, startled beyond words. He'd never seen Tina cry, not once, not even during the first hard weeks when she'd bullied and pleaded and used every other trick in the book to stop him drinking. She'd never cried till now, when the fight was over.

He waited until the slim shoulders had stopped shaking beneath his hands. Then, sliding a finger under her chin, he lifted her face up and kissed her gently.

"Listen, bright-eyes," he murmured, "I love you, but you

mustn't call Mike Malone a bastard, okay? He's my friend."

She snorted. "What kind of a friend is it that takes an alcoholic to a pub for a chat?"

"He didn't know I'd stopped," Fenner said. "I haven't seen him for a long time, remember. And anyway, I'm a reformed alcoholic."

"That's just lip-service. You're still a goddam wino underneath, you always will be." Her fists tightened helplessly on the lapels of his jacket. "Hell, Fenner, what am I going to do with you?"

Suddenly, that was the easiest question in the world to answer. Fenner touched his lips to her cool forehead, and told her.

"I think you'd better take me to Wales, don't you?"

4 *Moral Duties*

Up early after a bad night, Fenner sat at the kitchen table alternately smoking and coughing. A padded envelope lay in front of him, unopened.

It was still unopened an hour later, when Tina came in yawning.

"Whassup?" she grunted, sliding her fingers through his hair. "I'm the one with the early lecture. What are you doing out of bed?"

"Asthma," he shrugged. "Couldn't sleep."

"Bad?"

"Not much fun."

"Why didn't you wake me up, then?" she scowled, as she filled the kettle.

"What for? You can't breathe for me. Now shut up and pass me the scissors. We're celebrating."

"Scissors?" She hunted them out of a drawer, then peered over his shoulder at the package, reading the return address on the label. "Hey, is this it?"

"I think so. Why don't you open it and see?"

The envelope had been closed with a dozen staples. Tina forced them open, put her hand in and drew out a short letter and a glossy paperback.

"Wow," she said, staring at the cover. "Doesn't it look different, on a real book?"

Fenner considered it. "You know, it's not such a bad face, at that. Though I reckon it looks better on me."

Tina snorted. "If you go in for realism, I suppose. The lived-in look. They painted out half the lines. And the bags under your eyes."

"If I have bags under my eyes, it's because you keep me awake half the night, you rapacious female." His hands settled on her waist, the thumbs fretting against her hip-bones.

Tina squirmed, laughing. "Look who's talking . . ."

Her arms found their way round his neck, and they fell into one of those embraces which seem so natural to long-time lovers, who have forgotten that it was ever awkward to fit your body to someone else's.

"If you're that short on sleep," she continued comfortably against his neck, "don't you think we ought to go back to bed for a bit?"

"I thought you had an early lecture?"

"Mmm – but there are times when it becomes not only a virtue but a moral duty to cut a lecture. Nothing shakes a professor more than a roomful of empty desks. It's good for their souls. And anyway," her lips brushing his skin as she spoke, "I thought you said we were celebrating."

"I was thinking more of coffee, and drinking each other's healths."

"Stuff that," Tina said. "It's not every day a girl gets the chance to go to bed with a famous writer."

"Yes it is, idiot."

Tina grinned. "Look, are you coming, or are you not? Because if not, I think you . . ."

But Fenner was already taking her by the wrist and tugging her out of the room, leaving the end of that sentence abandoned in the kitchen, with the steaming kettle.

They made slow, lingering love in the morning sunlight, and slept, and woke to make love again. At some point during those endlessly-stretched hours, a perspective shifted, so that sex wasn't simply a pleasure and a physical declaration of love; it became truly a celebration, of something more than the first copy of a published book.

And afterwards, with their bodies lying sprawled and all but abandoned on the bed, the ringing of the telephone seemed almost as dirty an intrusion as a camera-lens would have been.

"Leave it," Tina muttered, her eyes not even opening.

"Better not." Fenner rolled away from her and shambled unsteadily through to the study, feeling something like a puppet-master, operating his body long-distance.

"Yeah, hullo?" He took the telephone over to the window and stood unconcernedly naked, looking down into the back alley. A stray alsatian was nosing among the dustbins, while a pack of Asian boys played soccer between two gates, and their sisters stood watching beneath a telegraph pole. A cat slept on the concrete in the centre of Fenner's yard, seemingly the focus for all the sunlight.

"Can I speak to Paul Fenner, please?" A man's voice, pleasant but business-like; no one Fenner knew.

"Yeah, this is me."

"Good. My name's Jackson, Mr Fenner. I work for the *Evening News*."

It was as though a trip-switch had flicked over in Fenner's mind. Nothing about him had changed; but everything was different.

"Yes?"

"It's about your book. We had a packet from your publisher this morning, advertising blurb and a copy for review; and my editors would like to do a feature on you. Would you be willing to give us an interview?"

"Well, I'll tell you what it is. You people weren't exactly my best friends during the trial and so forth; in fact, you gave me shit. No, don't interrupt; just read the book, you'll get the point. And alcoholics tend not to be too generous to the people who shove them over the edge."

"It'll be a straight interview," Jackson said earnestly. "Whatever you say, just printed verbatim. Along with a summary of the trial and the book, of course. But . . ."

"But nothing," said Fenner. "You know as well as I do that no interview is ever straight. It's not what you say, it's the way you present it – the bits about my sinister smile and my chain-smoking, and the silent woman who watches you with blank eyes from a corner. Those are all quotes, by the way. And there's a different woman now, but the rest is much the same."

"Does that mean you won't see me?"

"I didn't say that. I wish I could, but my publisher would slay me, if I turned you down. She spent half a lunchtime telling me how large a market we could have in this area, if it was exploited properly. So I'll give you an interview, on one condition."

The inevitable wariness crept into Jackson's voice. "What's the condition, Mr Fenner?"

"That I see and approve copy before it goes in. And I don't just mean a verbal agreement, that your editor can override. I want an absolute veto on the whole article, and I want it in writing."

"I'll have to consult my editors about that," Jackson said cautiously.

"Sure, consult away – but I don't want to hear another word from you until you've got a signed bit of paper in your hands. Goodbye, Mr Jackson."

He hung up, and turned to find Tina in the doorway, holding out his bathrobe and shaking her head in mock reproof. "Honestly, Fenner! Think of the neighbours!"

"I was thinking of the neighbours. Diana'd be delighted." He pulled the robe on. "Talking of which, why don't we take her out somewhere tonight? We might as well go mad."

"Okay, but it's my treat, right? I'm proud of you, fella. Not about the book, so much – I mean, I am, of course I am, but not sort of urgently proud any more. I'm just impressed, the way you didn't slam your fist right down the telephone line and into that reporter's throat."

Fenner smiled. "I didn't recognise the name, which helped. I'm pretty sure he wasn't one of the pack around at the trial. Don't worry; once I've got that veto, I'll be able to handle him."

"Maybe so; but I'm going to be there when he talks to you. And if he tries to get nasty, I'll stub a cigarette out in his ear. That'll stop him."

They dressed and went downstairs to show Diana the book and check that she was free for dinner in the evening; and found her packing a small trowel in her handbag, and checking a bus timetable.

"Where are you off to?" Tina demanded.

"Gilsland."

"What's that, some kind of pleasure park? Flamingoes and stuff?"

Standing behind Tina, Fenner put his arms round her and squeezed gently. "It's a village, over towards Carlisle. Di's husband is buried in the churchyard there."

"Oh." Tina bit her lip, said, "Sorry, Di. Didn't know. Put my foot in it again, didn't I?"

"It's all right, dear." Diana smiled calmly. "Only I like to go out there every now and then, and keep it looking nice. I owe Jem that much, at least. I'd better run, though, I can catch the bus at the top of the road, and it goes in ten minutes."

"No need for that," Tina said quickly. "We can drive you there. Can't we, fella?"

She tilted her head back, and rubbed it against Fenner's cheek. He smiled into her dark eyes, and said, "Yes. Of course we can."

"Good, then. And no arguments," as Diana opened her mouth to protest. "We've got nothing planned, and I really fancy a day out. We're celebrating anyway, Fenner's book came this morning. We'll leave you for a bit and go exploring, if you want to be alone there . . ."

"If I want to talk to my husband's ghost, you mean?" Diana laughed softly. "I wouldn't know what to say. It's been twelve years now, almost thirteen. I don't even miss him any more."

You're still counting, Fenner thought. And kissed Tina's hair as she stirred, and held her closer.

They drove to the village, found the church, stood beside the grave while Diana weeded and watered. Listened, while she talked.

"It was the squadron that wanted him buried here. There are a couple of other RAF graves scattered around, you'll find them if you look. He was stationed at Spadeadam, you see? That's north of here, through that forest we saw . . . It's the middle of nowhere really, only the one road leading up to it. That's how poor Jem was killed, he was walking up to the base one night and he was hit by some drunken corporal in a six-tonner. Stupid, really . . ."

"I expect you're glad he's buried so close, though," Tina said. "At least you can come and visit. I mean, if he'd been stationed down in Cornwall or somewhere . . ."

Diana shook her head. "You've got it the wrong way round, dear. I only live in Newcastle because of Jem being here. I don't want to haunt his grave, I'm not that morbid; but it wouldn't have felt right, just to go off and leave him here. I had to stay somewhere close."

Later they drove to Hadrian's Wall, and walked a little; and they ended up eating in a pub close by, while Diana talked about her life since Jem's death, how she'd scraped by on an RAF pension until her parents had died. They'd left her enough to buy some cheap flats in Newcastle, and do them up; and she managed quite comfortably now, letting them to students.

"And layabouts like Fenner," Tina said cheerfully, ducking as he swatted at her.

"There aren't many like Paul." Diana's voice had a distant quality to it, as if she were still remembering her Jem, reliving the time they'd had together; but her words were immediate and genuine. "I'd hold onto him if I were you, Tina."

"Oh, I intend to. Both hands. Teeth too, if he struggles."

Fenner smiled. "I won't struggle."

5 *Ghosts*

THE WHOLE TRUTH

by Andrew Jackson

Last year Paul Fenner's name was in everyone's newspaper, if not on everyone's tongue. He was interviewed on television, and both cheered and abused in the street. He was also paid a great deal of money for his story, by a national newspaper.

Now, months after the fuss had died down, Paul Fenner is telling the story again, in his own words. He has written a book, called simply MORAN, giving his own personal account of the events leading up to the arrest and trial of the infamous MP turned gun-runner. But what this book also gives us is a portrait of a policeman operating under intolerable strain. And what can happen when he finally gives way . . .

Fenner was born in Northumberland and spent his childhood in Hexham, where his father was a policeman. The young Paul was captivated by Sergeant Fenner's tales of life in the force; and as soon as he was old enough, he enrolled at the Police Training College at Hendon.

Once his training was complete, he came back to the North-East and settled in Newcastle as a police constable. His superiors soon took notice of his enthusiasm, his intelligence and imagination; he won early promotion, and was encouraged to transfer to CID. Once there, he worked his way up from detective-constable to Inspector; he married an attractive local girl, Susan Armstrong; and his future seemed assured.

Four years later, though, his life was in ruins. His marriage had collapsed, and Susan was now living with his colleague and friend, Inspector Mike Malone. Fenner's drinking, which had always been heavy, was out of control; and suddenly he found himself at the centre of a nationwide scandal which wrecked his career and might easily have put him in jail.

Fenner still lives in Newcastle, in the small flat he took when he split up from his wife two years ago. They were divorced in January. At the age of thirty-nine he is a lean, active man, a heavy smoker who seems always to be looking round for a drink that isn't there.

I asked him first why he had written this book; hadn't he had enough media coverage already?

"More than enough. If any one newspaper had told the truth about me, I would have been happy to let things lie. But in the end I got fed up with the endless stream of lies and disinformation; I felt I had a right to tell the story from my side."

But hadn't he done that already, in the press? There was a series of articles that appeared under his name.

"That—! They paid me £20,000 for my name and peddled the worst garbage of the lot. I didn't have any control. It was that more than anything that made me decide to write my own book."

MORAN is a very honest book. Fenner freely admits his own alcoholism, and states that he was drunk when he arrested Albert Moran. "I'd been sitting in the car for six hours, watching an empty house," he recalled. "It was bitterly cold, and I'd been taking nips from a bottle of Scotch all day. When I saw Moran arrive, and knew that luck was on our side at last, I drained the bottle before I got out of the car."

Then came the incident that was made so much of, in court as well as in the press. Moran offered Fenner a large bribe, to let him slip away; and Fenner saw red. "I went berserk," he said calmly. "They tell me I broke three of his ribs, and I know I knocked some teeth out. I've still got one somewhere, for a souvenir. That wasn't mentioned in court," he added with a grin.

I asked him how he felt now, looking back at it. "That's a stupid question. What do you want me to say? I don't regret it, there's no point. It happened. And it can't happen again; I'm no longer a policeman, and I no longer drink. All you can say is that having been through it, I know something more about myself. I know I'm a person who gets dangerously violent if I'm grossly insulted when I'm grossly drunk. Nowadays that information is of very little use to me, so I don't think about it much."

Fenner's book provides some fascinating insights into the wheeling and dealing that went on out of the public's eye, to keep Fenner himself out of the dock. In the end, a deal was struck: Moran wasn't charged with attempted bribery, and Fenner wasn't charged with assault. "I don't think it would have come to court anyway," he shrugged. "There were no witnesses except Moran, and he was terrified of me."

Fenner seems to go out of his way to present himself as a hard man, who can take knocks and come back fighting; and I think that's a true picture. But it's not the whole truth. There's another side to him, a gentler, more romantic side which doesn't show in the tough style of the book. MORAN ends with Fenner's resignation from the force, a bitter man who's slowly drinking himself to death. A few months later, he met and fell in love with an attractive twenty-one year old art student, Tina Blake. Throughout the interview she sat beside him on the sofa, silent and watchful. Fenner glanced at her constantly, looking for approval or support or reassurance – or possibly just looking. He maintains that he'd be dead by now, if it wasn't for her: that it was her strength more than his own which finally stopped him drinking.

"She's my criterion," he says simply, and she smiles.

Paul Fenner has written an open, moving, honest book, the picture of a tormented, unhappy man; but that man is not today's Paul Fenner. He and Tina will be leaving Newcastle soon, moving to a cottage in North Wales. He talks about it as an exile might talk about his homeland. He's not running away from his ghosts; he's bidding them farewell, and moving on.

MORAN is published by Colophon Paperbacks, at £3.50

6 *Remember, Remember*

– which of course you do. That's what's important, after all – far more important than the doing. It's been said before, that an action isn't complete until it's been looked back on, and savoured, and cherished. It's true, you've proved it. The doing is a sudden, sharp blessing, to shiver you and bring you up; but it ends as suddenly, however careful you are. Like a cable snapping, or like a caller hanging up, leaving you with nothing in your hands, no way to reach after them. It could bring you crashing down again, if there weren't the memory to cling to, to glide home along. And memories are forever, they're always there, always ready for you. Doors that can't be locked.

So you remember them all,

(all except the first time, the bad time. That one still blisters and burns when you touch it. Don't think about it. Not now. These are the good times now)

you keep them in your head like candles in a chapel, nightlights in the daylight, your dark burning glory. They are your talismans, tokens of your strength; they proclaim you, crying "He has done this, and this!" to a weaker world.

Bring them out and line them up.

Impress us.

After the first (and a long time after), the next was the old one, the aching one. Remember?

You found her in a car-park, waiting with the endless patience of the dead at heart. There were no cars, except your own; you parked at the further end and walked back to where she was standing, your feet crossing all those neat white lines, pointless at this hour, marking nothing but time.

"You're very young," she says bitterly, accusing. "Youngster. What do you know?"

You know she is an old woman, sour and useless. One foot in the grave.

"I know you need help," you say.

"Help!" she snorts. And looks away, into the darkness. It's always dark when they call for you. These are the moths, the ones who hide from light and cry because they cannot find a candle.

"There's nothing left for me," she says suddenly. "Dust and ashes. Dust and ashes."

"Tell me about it," you say. "Tell me what's wrong."

"Why?" she asks harshly. "What for? You offer me water, and it turns to dust in my mouth. Dust and ashes."

"What does that mean?" you ask; and she laughs.

"It means I am old, you little fool. Older than you can imagine. Look at me. What do you see?"

You see something less even than it claims to be, something that moves with no strength, withered from the roots. You try to find a name for it, and stumble between crone and husk. She is a leaf that has reached her true autumn, and should fall.

"I see a human being," you say.

"Liar."

Spittle flecks the corners of her mouth – but surely not saliva. Nothing so fresh. She wipes away the sour juices with a fine handkerchief, and laughs.

At herself, at you – who knows? Not you, certainly. All you know is the need to choke that laughter at its source, and restore the night's velvet. This hag cuts at it, more than you can bear.

And she wastes what remains of her life, hating it; and she would waste her death too, going into it alone and private.

So you reach out for it, furious and hungry.

Your hands close on her neck, feeling the skin loose and folded, the fleshless throat unprotected. Your thumbs press savagely in. She gapes and croaks, mouth flapping, arms waving a weak protest.

But you have done this before; and closing your eyes won't close out the memory. It reaches for you, rushes at you, plunging like horses; and you curse, and throw the hag down as your fingers slick with sweat. You rub your hands across your face, telling yourself that you can't smell blood, there is no blood, can't taste the warm iron of it in your mouth . . .

Calmer, you look down at the hag, flopping like a landed fish at your feet. Her breath is shredded to rags and tatters in her rattling throat. She might die anyway, but you can't just leave her, you have to be sure. And you don't want to leave her, anyway. You want to do it.

"Dust and ashes," you murmur, smiling. Let it be dust and ashes, then.

You go to your car, and fetch the spare gallon of petrol from the boot.

You unscrew the cap of the plastic container, and pour the whole gallon onto the woman's coat and skirt and skin. She pushes herself up onto her hands and tries to crawl away. You strike a match, and toss it onto her back.

Somehow her ruined throat finds voice enough to scream once, cracked and strange, as the flames explode across her face. Then she falls, and sobs, and rolls on the tarmac, and burns.

When she is still, you walk to your car and drive slowly through the city, every street-lamp flickering to fire as you pass, every black rubbish-bag a charred and blackened hag.

And the taste of sweet water was in your mouth, and all the stars were singing.

Remember?

7 *When the Party's Over*

"Fenner, when are we going?"

He took a cigarette from her pack and lit it slowly. "When do you want to go?"

"Soon. It's almost two months now, since we said; and we haven't done a thing about it, hardly."

"I haven't been delaying on purpose, love. I just wasn't in any hurry, once I was sure what I wanted."

"It's all right," she said, "I know that. But term's over and my year out is all fixed up, and my feet are starting to itch. There's nothing to keep us here now."

"Okay, fair enough. Let's do it, then." Fenner thought for a moment. "How's about July – the weekend after your birthday? Make it really special. And that'd give you time to spend a few days with your parents, before we go. You said they'd be down at Robin Hood's Bay all summer."

"Yeah, I'd like that. D'you want to come too?"

"No, thanks. Something tells me I wouldn't be altogether welcome." Tina's parents had objected to Fenner right from the start, and meeting him later hadn't changed their views; he knew that when they looked at him, all they saw was labels: *violent, notorious, alcoholic, old enough to be her father*. No middle-class couple was going to be happy seeing their daughter mixed up with labels like that; and if they couldn't see past the labels, he had no way to change their attitudes and saw no point in trying. "And I could use a little time on my own, to try and sort things out a bit."

"Okay, fella." She accepted it easily; and that was a part of her wonder for Fenner, how she understood his need to be alone, and to work at a relationship that to her seemed as natural as breathing.

He smiled at her, and said, "I'll phone a couple of removal firms, shall I, and get some estimates for shifting us down?"

"No, leave that to me. We won't be taking that much with us, if you're keeping the flat on at this end; and I've got friends at college with a van." She spoke absently, her mind clearly on something else. Fenner said nothing; and a minute later she went on, "we'll have to have a party, Fenner. With my birthday *and* us going away, we couldn't not."

He didn't think he had moved at all; but when he looked down, he saw Tina gently removing a crushed and broken cigarette from his clenched fist.

"Nothing to get in a panic about," she said softly. "You'll be fine. With a flatful of friends, do you think anyone's going to let you near a drink? Even if you wanted to?"

He didn't respond, he couldn't. She took his hand and unfolded the stiff fingers, one by one.

"Look," she said, "if you can make it through a heavy session in a pub, you can make it through a party. And you've got to do it sometime."

"Have I?"

"Well, no, I suppose you could go on running for the rest of your life, just in case; but the further you run, the more likely you are to trip over."

"Bitch," he said, smiling. "What's that supposed to mean, anyway? I think you got your semantics in a twist."

"Sounds uncomfortable." She scratched the palm of his hand lightly with a fingernail. "But I think it means we're having a party."

Fenner was sorting papers in the study, tossing ten into a rubbish-bag for every one that went into a file. Tina came through with a torn envelope in her hand.

"Here."

"What's this, can I chuck it?"

"No, you can't!" She snatched it back indignantly. "That's my invitation list for the party. You can add who you like – or cross 'em off. Don't forget we each have a veto."

"Fat lot of good a veto is to me," he said, scanning the list. "I don't know a quarter of these people. I think you're ashamed of me, Tina. You never let me meet your friends."

"That's right. Wouldn't be seen dead with you." Tina rumpled his hair, then turned to go.

"Hang on a sec." Fenner picked up a pen, and scribbled on the bottom of the list. "I can't think of anyone else I want, except these two. But if you're going to use your veto, use it now."

Under Tina's list, he had written *Mike and Susan*. Tina looked at it, and her face went very still.

"No, that's fine," she said in a careful, controlled voice.

"Just don't expect you to talk to them, eh?" Fenner said, deliberately attacking her acquiescence.

"You got it, fella."

"Pest."

"Well, for God's sake," she snapped, suddenly explosive, "what the hell do you expect? She was your wife, he was supposed to be your best friend; and they fucked you up good and proper, between them. You were in such a stinking mess, when I found you . . ."

"You can't blame them for what I did to myself. And if Susan hadn't left me, we wouldn't be here now."

"You don't know that. And it's not the point, anyway." She scowled, then shifted ground slightly. "How come you're so keen to have them round? I didn't know you were even talking to Susan."

"I'm not – I haven't seen her since the divorce. I just think that's gone on long enough. Strikes me that now's the time to build a few bridges."

"Let's be civilised, you mean? All good friends together?"

"That's right. Think you can manage it?"

She glared at him; then her lips twitched into a reluctant smile. "Oh, damn you, Fenner. You're too good to live, you are. But all right, I'll try. Just for you."

"Thanks, love. I appreciate it. And I'll let you into a secret, shall I? You might even like Susan, if you want to let yourself. She's got a lot going for her."

She shrugged, and smiled, and left. Fenner turned back to his desk, riffled through the file of letters he'd put aside for saving, then deposited them all in the rubbish-bag with a gesture of mute eloquence.

The night of the party, Fenner felt almost a stranger in his own home, displaced along with all the familiarities that made it his. Its particular smells had been driven out by a fog of smoke, its private and secret sounds by music so heavy it seemed to drift down with gravity, to lie in layers above the carpet and trickle slowly down the stairs and out of the open door to the street.

The geography was different too. His regular routes from one room to another had vanished when the furniture was moved. Previously he could find his way round in the dark, with no trouble; now, with the dim lighting that Tina insisted was *de rigeur* for any party of quality, he could barely move without stumbling over a glass, or an ashtray, or a body.

There were people everywhere – people dancing in the living-room, people talking in the kitchen; they were kissing on the stairs and singing in the street, and God only knew what was going on in the bedroom or the study.

He poured himself another tomato-juice and added Worcester sauce, wondering where Tina was in this chaos. It was far more her party than his; most of the faces were strange to him, and he felt a need to be with her in order to justify his own presence here. Stupid, of course, in his own home: but there seemed to be no one around over twenty-five, and the young are an exclusive clan.

They weren't unfriendly; indeed, as he squeezed past the crowd in the kitchen, someone handed him the butt-end of a joint, with a muttered, "You want to finish that? I'm bushed."

But it was the friendliness of locals to a stranger, natives to an alien ambassador; he didn't belong, and his only real access to them was through Tina.

He drew heavily on the joint as he made his way across the living-room, slipping almost unnoticed between the dancers. The music pulsed through his body and mind, almost tempting him to join them. He took another drag, but the smoke was bitter and oily now; it had burned down almost to the cardboard roach, and what little was left was too unpleasant to be worth smoking. He dropped it into an empty beer-can, hearing it hiss sullenly as he went on and out into the hall.

When he checked, the closed bedroom door hid nothing more exotic than a debate, apparently on the social relevance of plastic bicycles. No sign of Tina, either there or in the poker school in the study; so he went on down the stairs, inching carefully past three sprawling couples.

The party had spilled a long way into the street, overrunning half a dozen low walls and concrete flower-tubs. Tina was perched on the window-sill, talking to two girls. One was tall and blonde, the other shorter, her dark hair cropped like a boy's, wearing immaculate evening tails.

"Fenner. Hi." Tina moved up and patted the sill beside her. "Come and sit down, I've been keeping it warm for you."

"It's all right, I'll just lean, thanks." He propped himself up against the wall and took out his cigarettes, handing the pack round. Tina took one, the other two didn't.

"Fenner, these are the people who're driving us down to the cottage. The scruffy one's Georgina Hughes" – the tall blonde raised her glass to him and smiled – "and this is Jude. Judith Eliot."

"Hullo." She looked him up and down, and said, "So what do we call you? Fenner, or what?"

"Just Paul." Tina had taken his surname, for her exclusive use. It was a romantic gesture, he knew; but it meant something to both of them, so they might as well indulge it.

"I like the penguin suit," he said, trying to avoid asking the inevitable party questions: what do you do, what do you want to do, where did you meet Tina . . .

"She only wears it to show me up." Georgina smiled, relaxed and confident in simple jeans and T-shirt.

"She doesn't," Fenner said, knowing that she knew it, but wanting to say it anyway.

"There's charming, now." Jude looked at him sardonically, while Georgina laughed. "Does he make toast too?"

"No, he burns it." Tina hooked her fingers into Fenner's belt and pulled him closer. "Don't you, sweetheart?"

"Always."

"Typical man," Jude said. "Gives you cancer, burnt toast does. He'll have you in your grave before you're forty."

"Oh, I don't eat it. We save it up to feed the pigeons with. Come back in a year, and there'll be carcinomatous pigeons dropping dead all along the West Road. Pigeon pie, for the cost of half a pound of frozen pastry. Long range planning, see."

"We won't be here in a year," Fenner reminded her gently.

"So we're providing a charity. Feeding the poor." She put her feet up on the window-sill, leaning back against Fenner for support. "I'm an absolute saint at heart. Besides, I hate frozen pastry."

Georgina put her glass down on the wall beside her; Jude picked it up and emptied it. Georgina smiled.

"There's plenty more upstairs," Fenner said.

"No, it's all right," Jude said. "We'd better be going. We only looked in to see Tina."

"Don't be silly." Tina swung her feet down and stood up abruptly. "The night's hardly started yet."

"Tell that to the buses."

"Sod the buses. Fenner'll drive you home."

"No, it's all right. Honest. I've got a job in the morning, anyway."

"Stay an hour, at least. You'll be safe with Fenner, he's not drinking . . ."

"Actually, darling," Georgina said, getting to her feet and

stretching lazily, "what Jude's trying not to say is that she's got the hots for me, and she can't *wait* to get me home and tear the clothes off my back. Compris?"

"Si, comprendo. Sluggy bastards, the pair of you. Have fun."

She hugged them both, and watched them walk up the road arm in arm.

Fenner hesitated, then said, "Um, did they mean it? About going home to screw?"

Tina shrugged. "I expect so. I wouldn't know, really, would I? But they do, if that's what you're getting at."

"Yeah, that's what I'm getting at."

She glanced up at him. "Fenner, if you say one word about it being a shame and a waste, two such pretty girls and all, I'll murder you, I promise. Or maybe I'll just tell Jude and let her loose on you, she'd do it better than me."

"I'll bet. I wasn't going to, though. At least, I don't think so. I might've thought it, a bit."

"It was written all over your face."

"Well. They are pretty." He shot her a sideways glance. "Does that put your nose out of joint?"

She tested it with one finger. "No. But honestly, Fenner, you're like a kid with his face pressed up against the glass. You'll be asking me what they get up to in bed, next."

"No, I won't. Don't need to. I saw a dirty movie once. Swedish. *Very* erotic."

"Filthy pig."

A door opened, milk-bottles touched and sang softly.

"Hullo, you two."

"Diana! Hi."

"Don't tell me you're on the run from your own party, you spineless creatures."

"Not really. Just having a breather." Fenner gestured at his own open door. "Are you sure you won't come up for a bit? It's quite an education, watching the young at play."

"Yeah, come on, Di, you'd enjoy it."

"Dressed like this?" She was wearing a long quilted dressing-gown over a cotton night-dress; when she moved, Fenner caught a glimpse of the famous bed-socks on her feet. "I'm not getting changed again, just to come and be deafened by music I don't understand, and shouted at by reds in the bedroom. I know what student parties are like, I've had them overhead for the last ten years."

"Is it that bad?" Tina asked worriedly. "I mean, they'll quiet down a bit if I ask them."

"Bless you, no. Not to worry. It doesn't disturb me. I don't sleep much anyway; I'll probably outlast the lot of you tonight. I'll be reading till three or four in the morning, and getting up again at eight."

"That doesn't sound enough to me," Tina frowned.

"It's all my body wants nowadays. Old age catching up with me, I expect. But you get back to your party, the pair of you, and don't fret about me. Goodnight, now."

The door closed behind her, and Tina shuddered theatrically. "Four hours' sleep a night? How can she? It's not healthy!"

"Healthy enough, if that's all she wants. We don't all need ten hours, like some people I could mention."

"I don't need them, I just like them. You wouldn't begrudge me my simple pleasures, would you?"

"Not so long as I get to share them."

A car came slowly down the hill, stopped opposite the flat. Fenner lifted a hand in greeting, as Mike and Susan got out. Mike had a bottle in his hand.

"Oh, help . . ." That was Tina, beside him, slipping her hand into his.

"Relax," Fenner murmured. "The war's over, remember? This is peacetime. Reconciliation."

"Yeah, but it was still them turned you into an alky. Her."

"No, it wasn't. It was me."

And then there was no time to talk any more. Mike reached them first, smiling with only a trace of anxiety, holding the bottle out as an offering. To Tina.

"This is for you," he said awkwardly. "I reckon I owe you more, for looking after Paul the way you have; but . . ."

Tina shrugged, looked embarrassed, looked down at the bottle – and finally smiled. "Well, don't tell him, Mike, but it's been a pleasure. Mostly."

"My fan." Fenner grinned down at her. "Why don't you take Mike upstairs and get him a drink? I'll bring Susan up in a minute, I'd like a word with her first."

"Sure. Come on in, Mike – but do me a favour, eh? Forget you're a policeman, just for tonight?"

"No problem," Mike assured her, following her inside.

Fenner turned back to the street, where Susan was standing on the pavement, watching him with quiet, careful eyes. Her blonde hair was cut differently, shorter and more fashionable, and her clothes were new; but the greater change showed in her face and body. Despite the tensions of the moment, she looked and moved like a woman at peace with her world and herself, happy in a way Fenner hadn't seen since the early days of their marriage. He remembered the last time he had seen her, when they had met in her solicitor's office to discuss details of the divorce; he remembered the hunched shoulders and the face pinched in so tightly on itself, and wanted to say a hundred different things; and couldn't think of any way to say them, so simply said hullo.

Her lips twitched into a smile. "Hullo. How are you?"

"Good. Very good."

"Mike said you weren't drinking any more?"

"That's right."

"I'm glad, Paul. Truly."

"I know." Their smiles came easier now, as each recognised in the other a reflection of their own contentment. "You're looking well."

"Mmm." The acknowledgment stretched into a gentle hum, and Fenner laughed.

"Fancy a drink, then? I'll fetch it, if you don't want to face the mob just yet."

"I'd like a tonic water, if you've got it. Or fruit-juice. No alcohol."

"You don't have to keep off it for my sake."

"I'm not. Drinking makes me feel sick at the moment, that's all." Her eyes sparkled with secrets, and the desire to tell them. Fenner found a conclusion, and jumped to it.

"Are you pregnant, Susan?"

"So my doctor assures me."

"I don't have to ask if you're pleased about it," Fenner chuckled. "You look as smug as a saint after her first miracle." He put his hands on her shoulders and kissed her lightly. "Congratulations."

"Thanks, Paul." She glanced in through the open door,

then looked up at him curiously. "I suppose that was your Tina, who stole my husband away?"

"Yes, that was my Tina. Want to meet her?"

"Mmm. But does she want to meet me? I thought she scuttled away a bit fast."

"Yeah, maybe. But there's only one way to get over that. Want to chance it?"

"Yes. Once more unto the breach, and all that." She slipped her arm through his, and smiled suddenly. "This is nice, Paul. Being able to talk to you again."

"Right." He squeezed her arm in agreement, and led her inside.

"What about this Wales thing, though, Paul?" Malone said, above the babble of twenty urgent voices. "Seriously? Can you really see yourself keeping goats and chickens, and brewing nettle wine and all the rest of it? I never noticed you showing any interest in so much as a pot-plant, up to now."

"No, Tina's the one on the self-sufficiency kick. I'll help out, but it won't worry me if it doesn't work. We're not short of money. I'll be happy just to be shot of this place. I've been here too long, the city's gone sour on me."

"What the hell are you going to do, though, if you're not ploughing the fields and scattering? You'll be bored out of your mind, son. Guaranteed."

"Not me, Dad. I'll work. I want to do another book, just to find out if the first was a fluke or not."

"Yeah? What about?"

"I don't know, haven't a clue. Maybe a novel. I'd like to do that."

"I'll tell you something else you could do," Malone said. "A book about the Butcher. There'll be a flood of them when we finally run him down; but if you started on it now, you'd be well ahead of the field. You know the case inside out to start with, you worked on it yourself, and you've still got friends on the inside. You couldn't miss."

"No, I probably couldn't. If I just wanted money."

"It'd be more than that, Paul. I know most of the real-life shockers are only pulp, but they don't have to be. You didn't do MORAN for the money, did you?"

"No. I don't think so."

"Right. So why not work the same way on this? It could be

a really important book. Apart from anything else, a sideways look from you might help us see where we've gone wrong this time, which could be right handy when the next psychopath turns up."

"Keep trying, and you'll talk me into it. I don't know if I could cope, though. It's such a foul case, I was glad when they pulled me off it; I don't particularly fancy plunging right back into all the details again. And I'd probably have to meet the guy himself, if you catch him. Try to find out what makes him tick."

"When, not if. But I could fix a meeting."

"Sure you could – but the question is, do I want to meet him? I don't know, Mike. If there's one thing that makes me feel I'm well shot of the force, it's that case. I think I'd like to stay shot of it, and try something new."

"Well, it's your decision. But think about it. Me, I'd like to see a book written by someone who's pretty much on our side, for a change."

The heavy rock had given way to a gentler music, and the dancing to quiet talking. Some people had left, a couple drifted off to sleep; the rest, the serious party-goers, were settling down to the next stage, breaking out hidden bottles of whisky or vodka and starting to look towards dawn.

Mike and Susan had long since gone, but Fenner was settled more comfortably with Tina's friends, now that alcohol and time had worn down the rough edges of their youth. He sat by the window, part of a small group talking about anything that occurred to them, and staying quiet in between.

Tina appeared, looking harassed.

"Fenner, love – cigarettes?" she muttered, running both hands through her tousled hair. "I'm half-gone, but Marie's having a crisis, and she's got to talk to someone. I don't mind, but I can't face it without tobacco."

Fenner groaned, and stood up. "Sorry, I'm out myself; I've been bumming them for the last hour. But you get back to your Good Samaritan act, or whatever it is. I'll nip up to the all-night garage. I could use some air anyway."

"Sure?"

"Sure."

"Oh, you're a lovely man." She hugged him briefly, then

yawned. "I think I'll make some coffee, while I'm through here. It'll keep me going through the true confessions. You want?"

"I most definitely want. I'll only be a couple of minutes."

He ran down the stairs and out into the night. Up onto the West Road, still jogging; but there he slowed to a walk, and finally to stillness. The city dropped away below him to the river, the familiar bridges lit like jewelled bands across the dark water. He knew this view at every time of day and night, in every season; it was the face of the beloved, dirty enough to be human, loved enough to keep him so through the bad time, before he met Tina.

It was the face he had denied, and meant to turn his back on.

It was beautiful tonight, warm under the hazy yellow of the street-lights – but, thank God, it was no part of him now. He saw the same face, and the same humanity; but his burden of love was gone, deliberately rejected. He looked, and knew he could leave with an easy heart.

Tina was another matter. The move had been her idea, and she truly wanted to go; but she was reaching out for a dream, rather than walking away from a reality. The difference in perspective might yet bring the whole adventure crashing down in ruins. Fenner had seen tonight how much a part of the city Tina still was. She was tied into it through a hundred friendships, where Fenner had only memories; and while he had been cutting as many links as he could, to leave free and unencumbered, Tina seemed to be reinforcing hers, wanting to be sure they would survive the separation.

Perhaps they would; perhaps hers was the best way, after all. The human way. He couldn't tell. Perhaps by keeping her friendships strong and secure, she would find them supporting her in Wales, keeping her going through the bad times and helping her to believe in the good. Or perhaps they would bring her running back inside a month, lonely and bored out of her mind without their bright company.

The only thing he was sure of was that it was her decision, and she had made it. All he could do was watch, and hope, and follow her.

8 What You Did to Katy

From the report of the post-mortem carried out on the body of Kathryn Holland, age 29, occupation telephonist:

> . . . The spike penetrated five centimetres below the xiphisternum, passed through the medial edge of the right crus of the diaphragm, and left the chest through the third intercostal space, posterially. The tip of the spike abutted against the anterior surface of the scapula, and seemed to have caused a comminuted fracture of the wing of the scapula. Both second and third ribs were fractured at the site of penetration. The insertions of latissimus dorsi and subscapularis were avulsed. The lung parenchyma were surprisingly undamaged. There was a longitudinal split of the aorta, which was full thickness and twelve centimetres in length. The right hemithorax was full of blood. The diaphragm was greatly bruised. The mode of death was exsanguination. The appearances suggest a high-velocity penetration injury, and that the body was suspended on the tip of the spike for five to seven hours before discovery.

– Or in other words, you impaled her.

She was waiting for you by the roadside; and together you walked down one of the steep paths that lead into the dene. It's a sweet place, this, a sudden valley turned to a great garden, slashing like a deep green living wound across the north side of the city. A place of lawns and rhododendrons, waterfalls and bridges, swans. A place to be beautiful in, and happy.

But she is bleak as the weather, bitter rain that snags your skin like gravel. Her voice jars at you, ugly words with an ugly insistence; and yet you deal with her kindly. Kindly by your lights, that is – but your world is harsh-lit, and cruel to shadows. And she is all shadow.

You meant to give her to the river in a slow offering; but the path you take leads you down past a half-demolished cottage, and in a skip outside, you see a rusting length of iron, sharp at one end. Part of an old fence, perhaps, or just a support for a washing-line. Who knows? Whatever it was made for, it can serve another purpose.

So you ask her to wait, while you pull it from the skip; and then you carry it down with you without explanation, to the burn at the valley bottom. She asks no questions.

Impatient now, with the rough iron biting at your hands even through heavy leather gloves, nevertheless you let her lead you along beside the water, until you reach the waterfall, and the rocks. There, you stoop for a stone; and casually, easily, you bring it down on her neck.

She crumples, as though there are no bones in her. You lay her out, put the jagged point of your pole a little below her ribs, and thrust steadily.

You would have taken it slowly, knowing no urgency and finding less pleasure in haste; but somehow, as you feel the first grating resistance of bone and see a dark stain touching the cotton of her dress, her eyes open like a lid onto darkness, and she draws a clumsy breath to scream with.

And you drive the spike sharply in, twisting and turning it while she flops and jerks like a fish on a gaffe; and with one movement you hoist her high, and drive the butt-end of the pole deep into a split in the rock, where it wedges and sticks fast.

And there you leave her for the morning to find, hanging above water, like a flag.

9 *Running Down*

"Let's not make a big thing of it," Tina had said. "We'll just get into the van and go. That's enough. No dramatic gestures, for God's sake."

But they had to say goodbye to Diana. And when they knocked, they found her red-eyed and pale, her smile weak and unconvincing.

"Di, what is it?" Tina demanded, laying a hand on her arm while Fenner hung back uncertainly. "You're not getting upset over us going, are you? We'll be back, often. Promise."

"No," she whispered. "No, it's not that. I'll miss you, of course, but . . ."

"What, then?"

"It's – just something I found. In the yard, this morning. It . . . Oh, it distressed me. But I'm all right now. Really."

"Like hell you are. What was it?"

"Just a cat. A dead cat. Silly, isn't it?" She fished for a handkerchief. "At my age, crying over a stray cat, for the love of Mike . . . But – well, it wasn't very pleasant. Kids, I suppose. You know how they hang around in the alleys all day. They must have grabbed it, and – and just thought it was funny, I suppose."

"Oh. Right. I get you." Tina hugged her gently. "What had they done to it, do you want to say?"

"The usual things. What you'd expect, I mean. Broken its legs, burnt it with matches, stuck things into its eyes."

"Little bastards."

"And then – and then they threw it into *my* back yard. I expect they thought that was funny, too, leaving it for someone else to find when they went to take the dustbins in, or hang out the washing. There were flies . . ."

"Poor Di. Don't think about it, love. The cat's dead, it's not hurting any more. It's over."

"I can't *help* thinking about it! And it's not over. The cat may be dead, but I'm not. And it's just – just knowing that there are people, right outside my house sometimes, people who *like* doing things like that . . ."

"I know, Di, it's horrid, but you can't do anything about it. You can't change the way they think. Forget it, that's all. It's all you can do, unless you actually catch them at it."

Forget it – or run away from it. Leave it behind. It's another answer, Fenner's answer. Dead cats, twisted and broken – or boys, swinging under bridges. It's the same thing, he thought; and almost smiled, hearing Jude revving the van's engine behind him. The door was open, and they were only a step away.

Diana blew her nose, and kissed Tina. Reached out a hand for Fenner, and kissed him too.

"Go on," she said. "Go. Don't mind me. Just get the hell out of here. And mind you look after yourselves, the pair of you."

"You too," Tina said. "Don't forget you're coming to stay,

when we're settled. I'll ring you as soon as the phone's connected."

"Do that. And send me a photo, I want to know what the cottage looks like."

They promised, and kissed her again; and climbed into the van, while she watched and waved. Fenner and Tina were sharing the front seat, while Jude drove and Georgina perched on a box behind. Fenner pulled the door shut, but the lock didn't catch.

"You have to slam it," Jude said watchfully. "Dead hard. Real macho stuff."

So Fenner slammed it, thinking that this should be symbolic; but in the end it wasn't, it was just a van door closing. Jude shoved the gear-stick forward and they pulled away from the kerb. "Let's not make a big thing of it," Tina had said; so Fenner said nothing. But his hands knotted themselves together in his lap; and his eyes fixed themselves on the cracked wing-mirror, where he could see a shrinking image of Diana. Still watching, and still waving.

He lifted a hand to his breast pocket, for his cigarettes; but Tina nudged him, and nodded towards a hand-written notice Sellotaped to the dashboard. 'If you want to smoke,' it said, 'you can get out and walk.'

He scowled. Tina reached up for the hand that still lay immobile against his chest. She pulled it down onto her lap, and squeezed.

"It's all right," she whispered. "Plenty of lay-bys between here and Wales. They'll stop, if we ask."

He nodded, and forced himself to relax. Of course they would; but he was damned if he would ask first. He'd wait for Tina . . .

"Put the radio on," Georgina said, after an hour or so. Jude nodded, and touched a switch. Speakers hidden in the doors filled the van with music, a rich soprano aria. Jude yelped, and reached for the dial.

"Don't," Georgina snapped. "Leave it."

"What? I'm not driving with this shit belting out at me."

"Then don't drive. I'll take it for a spell. But leave the music."

"Georgie, you know I hate this stuff!"

"And you know I love it. Listen, Jude, you're not turning it over to some bloody plastic disco station. I mean it," she added, as Jude's hand stayed static on the radio.

"Then we'll do without music." Jude hit the on/off switch, and the sound died.

No one spoke. Fenner couldn't see Georgina, in the back; but he glanced sideways at Jude, and saw her hands clench on the wheel as she edged out into the fast lane. The speedometer crawled up from fifty to sixty, sixty to sixty-five; and he wondered what the safety-limit for speed was, in an elderly Volkswagen.

Suddenly Georgina spoke again, her warm, mellow voice surprisingly acid. "Jude darling, you are of course quite entitled to risk your own life by driving just as foolishly as you like; and you know that my life is yours, to do what you want with. But don't you think it's a little hard to take a chance on Tina's and Paul's, especially when they're paying us for the privilege?"

For a moment, everyone was very still. Then Jude drew a slow, hissing breath, glanced in the mirror, jabbed at the indicator and swung over, across the inside lane to pull up on the verge. She slammed the handbrake on, threw off her seat-belt, opened the door and jumped out.

They watched her through the windscreen, as she vaulted the fence and walked off into a wide green field. Tina made a move to follow her, but Georgina stopped her with a hand on her shoulder.

"Just let her be, a few minutes. She'll be okay."

So they waited. After a minute, Fenner got out for a cigarette, and Tina joined him.

They leant against the side of the van, watching the small figure that was Jude wandering aimlessly across the grass. They saw her stoop, and straighten; move a pace or two, and stoop again. Then she turned to come back.

She climbed the fence more carefully this time, and came over to them cradling something in her hands. As she joined them, they saw that it was flowers. Daisies of some description, Fenner thought; but bigger than the city variety, and their hearts more golden.

Silently and solemnly, she handed them one each; then climbed into the van. Fenner moved to follow her, but Tina shook her head. "Finish your cigarette," she said. "Give them time."

He nodded, and tucked Jude's gift carefully into his lapel. "Say it with flowers, right?"

"Something like that. It's enough for us; but maybe not for them. Give 'em time."

And there was time for a second cigarette – Tina called it stoking up for the next stretch – before Georgina put her head out of the door.

"'S okay," she said. "Crying jag over. You can come in again now."

Both she and Jude had flowers in their hair.

Fishing out of curiosity among the papers heaped on the dashboard, Fenner found a pile of thin card bookmarks, all bearing the same legend, white on black:

Lonely? Desperate? Suicidal? Phone The Samaritans.

He fanned them out between his fingers, and glanced at Georgina, who'd taken over the driving.

"Who's been filching from the library, then?"

He'd noticed these bookmarks before, piles of them scattered by the checkout point.

"It's not filching," Jude said behind him, when Georgina only smiled. "We said we'd take a few and pass 'em around among our friends."

"You must have a strange collection of friends."

"Ha ha, very witty."

"Actually," Georgina said, sliding smoothly and calmly into the small space Jude left between breaths, "you'd be surprised how many people do call the Samaritans, at one time or another. People you know. I mean, I have."

"You, Georgie?" Even Tina was surprised.

"Straight up," said Jude. "Last year sometime. She could've talked to me, and she went and phoned some pig of a man instead."

"He wasn't a pig of a man," Georgina said mildly. "He helped, more than I'd bargained for. If I hadn't talked to him, I don't suppose I'd ever have got hitched up with that butch bitch in the back there."

"Stupid cow," Jude said affectionately. "Of course you would. You think I was going to let you go?"

"You'd have had a job stopping me. But anyway," she said, visibly picking up her thread again, "that's why we have the bookmarks. Take one, if you want."

"Not much use in Wales, is it? It's a Newcastle number."

"Yes, but it's a *telephone*, Fenner darling," Tina said. "You know, long-distance talking?" She took one of the bookmarks, folded it, slipped it into a hip pocket.

"Local would be cheaper. Not that I've any intention of using either one." If he wanted, he could remember days when he might have done; days when he came very close to it, even. But he'd always found alternatives: at first in the bottom of a bottle, and latterly in Tina. He laid his hand lightly on the back of her neck, to tell her that he had his own personal Samaritan, who didn't need phoning; by her smile, she knew it already.

"And it's more than just peddling bookmarks, too," Jude said a little later, as if she'd decided suddenly to tell a secret. "We're really quite dedicated, aren't we, Gina? At the moment we're helping out on the Rape Crisis line and Gay Switchboard, and come the autumn we're both going to train to be proper Samaritans. Me, I'm only doing it for purely selfish reasons, mind." Her voice dropped to a hoarse whisper. "It's the only way I can be sure that she doesn't go phoning up any more strange men. I've fixed it up with God; every time she phones the Sams, it'll be me who answers."

"I'll hang up."

"I'll call you back."

"You'll be too late, I'll have hanged myself by then. With black silk stockings, natch. And a strange cabalistic design painted in lipstick on my naked stomach. *Very* romantic."

"Damn it, there's nothing romantic about a hanged woman. I've seen them, you haven't." Fenner spoke very softly and very clearly, trying not to see in the windscreen a dim reflection of a body swinging below a bridge. That was behind him now; it wasn't fair that he should look ahead and still see it. He closed his eyes and rubbed them, the sound of skin on soft skin seeming oddly loud to him in the silent van.

"Can we stop soon?" Tina suggested. "It must be lunch-time by now. And I'm dying for a cigarette."

"Meaning that you think I ought to have one?" Fenner opened his eyes to glare at her, then chuckled. "Don't look so bloody cautious, girl. You're quite right."

"There's a pub coming up, if you can hang on ten minutes," Jude said, looking at the map. "We'll get food there, with any luck. And it's neatly halfway too. Good place to stop."

"Like a border post?" Fenner said. "Suits me. We can bid farewell to the city and toast our new lives, all with the same drink. Hell, I'll even buy the round to do it with."

"Fenner . . ."

"It's a custom," he said, grinning. "You always get customs at border posts, don't you? And anyway, I meant a round of fruit-juice. If I can't toast my own future in alcohol, I'm damned if the rest of you are going to."

10 Your Way

And then there was the man you met, who took you walking on the golf-course, high summer and the dead of night. The very dead, which is how you left him, mysteriously drowned in the middle of the fourteenth green, his lungs full of water and only the blood and bruises around his mouth to give a clue. Needing some sharp brain on the police force to remember that the sprinklers had been working all night against the drought, and to realise that a sprinkler-head could be forced into a man's mouth, that eventually he could drown even on that fine spray, if he had nothing else to breathe . . .

But enough of memories. They sustain you, yes; but you too could drown if you drink too deep. Let them lie a while. They're always there. Reliable. True friends.

You drive home late, and curse; some thoughtless animal has left their car in your place, in front of your house. Oh, if you were petty – how they would regret it, coming out in the morning to find tyres slashed and windscreen shattered, the instruments wrecked and the upholstery ruined . . .

But that's not your way, not the high way. You never were vindictive. Not like that.

So you drive round to the back, and park the car in the alley behind.

As you lock the car door, a shadow shifts behind a telegraph pole. Startled, you straighten up; something small and dark dashes into the light, and stops. Only a dog, the little black mongrel that haunts this alley. Smiling, you stoop for a stone; but instead of cowering and running in its normal fashion, tonight the dog attacks, rushing forward, teeth pearled by the moonlight.

It snaps at your hand, but its teeth only grate on the broken brick your fingers found. Before it can retreat, you snatch it up by the tail and hold it out at arm's length, swinging helplessly from side to side, yelping and whining alternately.

It's against all policy and all precaution, right on your doorstep like this; but after all, it's only a small thing, only a dog. No one will care.

So you swing it against the telegraph pole a couple of times, to silence it. Ribs snap audibly, like pencils. The dog whimpers like the wind across a bottle, hoarse and husky. You drop it, and stamp on its legs to stop it running.

And now the Swiss Army knife from your pocket, the right blade, a quick glance either way to be sure that the alley is empty and you are unobserved – no windows lit, no movement – and you stoop over the crying, dying thing, hearing it gulp at air.

It still has tongue, and eyes – but not for long.

And when that's done, while there's yet some thin mist of life clinging to the wreckage of a body, you wedge its tail between two garage doors and leave it dangling, for the children to find in the morning.

Part Two

Dreaming in Colour

11 *Soft and Certain*

"The bleating of the kid excites the tiger."

Right on cue, a tan-and-white kid tumbled out of the shed and ran up to butt at Fenner's knees, bleating excitedly. Tina smiled over her shoulder, while her hands went on tugging and squeezing in rhythm, sending jets of white milk noisily into the aluminium pail between her knees. The nanny-goat she was milking chewed on her cud as on some mind-numbing drug; her strange, slitted eyes stared fixedly into a dark corner of the shed.

"Hullo, tiger. Why aren't you working?"

"Stuck." Fenner bent to scratch behind the kid's ear. "How's the lad, then?"

"Monty? He's fine. Getting bigger every day." The steady stream of milk faltered, and died to a trickle. Tina pushed herself to her feet and hefted the bucket critically. "About half a pint more than yesterday, I reckon. Good girl, aren't you, Sylvia?" She slapped the nanny's flank and came out of the shed, bucket swinging in her hand.

"Who is Sylvia, what is she?" murmured Fenner.

"She's an old goat, of course. Hadn't you noticed?"

Tina slipped her arm through his, and they went into the kitchen together. He made coffee, while she filtered the milk; and she'd just finished when there was a quick rap on the open back door, and a man put his head in. He looked to be in his early fifties, with steel-grey hair and horn-rimmed glasses, and a round, fleshy face. His plump cheeks were heavily indented through having to accommodate a broad and apparently perpetual smile.

"May I come in?"

"Great skies above, it's Pastor Morgan!" Fenner leapt to his feet. "Come in, sir, come in! Sit, sit." He propelled the newcomer into his chair, then hissed at Tina. "Have you been talking after lights out again, girl?"

She shook her head. "Nor smoking in chapel. I expect you were swearing on the Sabbath."

Fenner smote himself upon the forehead, then went to the tall dresser and picked something off one of the shelves. He dropped to his knees, and shuffled across the stone floor to their visitor's feet.

"Bless me, father, for I have sinned."

"Wrong religion, old son," Tina advised; but all Fenner got was a chuckle, and a pat on the head.

"What is it now, then?"

Fenner opened his hands, to show two twisted lengths of metal. "I knackered your drill-bit."

"Forgive him, Father," Tina put in. "He knew not what he did."

"Now listen, you two. I don't mind you laughing at me; but I won't have you mocking my religion. It must stop. Is that understood?"

Fenner got to his feet, head hanging, the very image of a guilty schoolboy. "Yes, Padre."

"And for God's sake call me by my name!"

"You wash your mouth out!" Tina said in shocked tones. "Taking the Lord's name in vain, you were. We *heard* you."

Their guest spluttered vainly. Fenner made another coffee, and passed it over. "There you go, Alan."

"Thanks, now." He spooned sugar in deliberately, while Fenner rolled a cigarette. They smiled at each other, each man acknowledging his own particular vice, and enjoying it.

"So tell us, how runs the world with you?"

"Oh, well enough, well enough." The pastor smiled suddenly. "You will have heard, I take it, about the disturbance at Chapel on Sunday?"

Tina grinned. "Old Mr Jones calling Gareth Pugh a fornicator to his face, and saying he wasn't fit to read the lesson? Yes, Huw told us all about it."

"I'm just sorry I wasn't there," Fenner said. "But he didn't really say fornicator, did he?"

"Indeed he did. Old Mr Jones is very strong on terminology."

"He'd have to be." Fenner tapped ash into the sink. "But what does he say about us? That's what I want to know."

"Never you mind," Alan observed placidly. "Any remarks he makes to me are a private matter between the two of us – at least until he chooses to blurt them out *in* my chapel *on* a Sunday for the whole world to hear."

"You sound as if you enjoyed it," Tina accused.

"Ah, well, Gareth's face was a sight not to be missed. And poor Gwyn Roberts too, blushing in her pew like any schoolgirl. And her thirty-three this year. I was quite ashamed of her, being so transparent. However," he brushed all that aside with one chubby hand, "I am not here to gossip about those foolish people. Mrs Johns in the shop told me that you want to sell off some of your aunt's old furniture."

"Too right we do." Tina twitched the cigarette from Fenner's fingers, and inhaled deeply. "This place is furnished like a forties film-set. Agatha Christie, or something. Miss Marple would fit just lovely. We don't. There's no room for Fenner's legs, for one thing. So we're going to clear it out, and go all modern. Floor-cushions and Habitat."

"Oh dear, are you really?" He looked distressed, blinking around the room as though expecting all the furniture to be whisked away next moment, like a painted backdrop.

"Don't worry, it'll all be very tasteful," Fenner assured him. "Good elm and pine mostly, I fancy. The main trouble with what we've got now is that it's too fussy, and there's too much of it. The rooms here are so small, we've got to salvage as much space as we can."

"I'm sure – but it does seem a little, how to say it, wanton, to throw out such beautiful craftsmanship." His eye caressed the big dresser like a gentle hand, and Fenner laughed.

"I think that may stay, actually; it is at least practical. Come on, we'll show you what's definitely going. We haven't even thought about prices yet, but you can have first refusal on anything that takes your fancy."

"That's very kind, Paul. Thank you."

Crouching under the steep eaves in the back bedroom, Pastor Morgan touched loving fingers to a glass-fronted cabinet for which Fenner and Tina could find neither use nor place.

"If you have any sense in you," he said, "you'll have someone in to cast an expert eye over this little lot. Some of the pieces must be worth a packet. More's the pity."

"For crying out loud, Alan!" Tina's fingers twitched, as though she wanted to throttle him. "We *said* you could have first refusal. Friends come before dealers."

"Yes, but I can't hope to offer you what they're worth, so . . ."

"So you'd better make us an offer now, hadn't you? Before we find out what they're worth?"

"Oh, Tina, I can't do that. Good business comes before even friendship. Honest business, anyway." He stood up and went to the doorway, pausing for one last look, taking a reluctant farewell of the little cabinet. "I'm not talking about small amounts, you understand. Discount percentages, or that. Take that little cabinet; it's a genuine antique, that. I'd pay you as much as I could possibly afford, because I think it's beautiful; but a dealer will give you five or six times as much, and still sell it for a large profit. I can't rob you like that; so no. You get the dealers in first, and I'll see what's left, after."

"Fenner . . . ?"

Knowing what she was thinking, he grinned. "Not my business, sweetheart. It's your property, not mine. I'm just enjoying the battle."

"I bet you are. But if he turns violent, you'll have to sit on him while I run for the handcuffs."

Alan blinked. "Is this some private language you two are talking, or can anyone learn it?"

"Native dialect. You only pick it up after months of close contact; and getting that close would upset the elders of your chapel considerably. Not to mention your ageing mother."

While Fenner rambled, Tina hoisted the little cabinet off the floor and carried it across to Morgan. "Well, go on," she snapped. "Take it, will you? I'm not carrying it down to your blasted car for you."

"Tina—"

"Don't bother," she said, thrusting it into his arms. "It's a present, right?"

"No. I can't."

"You've got to." She smiled blandly. "'Cos if you don't, I shall just heft it right out of that window, see? So if you want to preserve this priceless piece of Britain's heritage . . ."

"You wouldn't." But his hands were already clutching it with the gentle strength of a father anxious not to hurt his child, but desperate not to let it fall.

"Here comes your young gossip-monger," Morgan said, glancing down the lane as he carried the cabinet out to his car.

A track-suited figure could be seen running steadily up the hill towards them. "I won't wait. If he's going to spread any more truths about my flock, I'd rather not have to confirm them."

He turned his car expertly and drove down towards the village, sounding his horn as he passed the runner and receiving an acknowledgment that was half wave and half salute.

Fenner and Tina waited at the gate; and a couple of minutes later the runner arrived, slowing gradually to a walk. He was a teenage boy, with the dark hair and the lean, wiry body of the true Celt.

"Hullo, Huw," Tina said. "Are you coming in?"

He shook his head. "No, I won't stop, ta. Only I met John the postman down at the bridge, and I said I'd bring these up to you, save him the time."

He pulled some letters from the pocket of his tracksuit, and handed them to Tina.

"*Diolch yn fawr, Huw bach*. Is that right?"

"Right enough." The lad grinned. "You need to work on the accent, though."

"Where are you off to, Huw?" Fenner asked, curious. There were no more cottages above theirs, only the long hill rising.

"Over to Llyncoed." He named the village in the next valley, some five miles away.

"What? *Running*? The boy's mad." Fenner turned to Tina with a gesture of despair.

She smiled. "No. He's not mad. Just young. I bet you'd have done the same for your first girlfriend."

"Ah! So that's it, is it, Huw?" The boy just grinned, embarrassed. "Is she pretty?"

"She's lovely." He said it soft and certain, and Fenner laughed.

"Go on then, kid. We won't keep you. But mind you bring her over sometime, eh?"

Huw nodded and ran off, falling easily into his stride again, tough legs pushing him up the lane. Fenner sighed, and shook his head.

"And him only sixteen . . . I can feel myself coming over all sentimental. But I still think he's mad. Me, I would've waited to catch the bus. Even at his age." He saw Tina's eyes skimming a postcard, and asked, "Who's that from, then?"

"Diana. She says we're half a dozen different kinds of beast for not going back the way we said, and she'll obviously have to wait till Domesday to see us if she leaves it to us, so she's decided to come here instead, and how about next weekend? She says to phone her and fix it up. Sound okay?"

"Sounds fine."

"Good. I'll give her a ring in a minute." Tina flicked the card with her fingers. "Her handwriting's awful, isn't it? All wobbly."

"Is it? It didn't used to be." Fenner took the card, and frowned. "She must've been in a hurry, or something. Or maybe she wrote it on the bus."

"'Spect so." Tina was checking the other mail. "One for you from Colophon, one from Her Majesty. And one for me, from Newcastle. Looks like Gina – I don't know anyone else who uses purple ink. Come on, let's go in. You show me where you're stuck with this silly book of yours, and I'll set you straight."

12 Bitter Whey

By the time they reached the station, light was already soaking up one quarter of the sky. Fenner locked the car from habit, and they walked hand in hand onto the deserted platform. A light in a building at the far end suggested there was at least one member of staff on duty, but they saw no sign of him.

"What I don't understand," Fenner said, sinking onto a bench and rubbing his hands across his face, "is why Diana wants to arrive at such an ungodly hour in the first place."

"She's coming on the sleeper. I told you that."

"Yes, but why? There must be perfectly decent trains during the day. Trains that'd get her here at a respectable hour. She could've got a connection onto the local line, too, and saved us coming all this way to meet her."

Tina shrugged, and sat down beside him. "I daresay she

could; but she didn't, so why worry about it? At least this way we get to see a bit more of her. I'll drive back to the village, if you're that tired."

"No, thanks."

"Why not?"

"Because you may be the light of my life and all the rest of it, and a liberated woman on top, but that doesn't alter the fact that you drive like a demented cuttlefish. And that's at the best of times, which five o'clock in the morning is not."

Tina snorted. "That sounds good, coming from a guy whose eyes are still gummed together."

Fenner grinned, pushed himself to his feet and walked to the edge of the platform. The line ran due east here, following the valley between two steep hills; looking through the pass, he could see the sky fading through all the blues to a bleached white on the horizon. As he watched, a line of fire appeared, almost liquid against the linen sky; and slowly, reluctantly, the sun rose into view.

"Listen," Tina said softly beside him, slipping her arm through his. "Isn't it beautiful? I never heard the dawn chorus before."

"Yes, you have. Don't you remember? The first night we met, at that crazy party of Carey's. We talked till dawn, and then you walked me home the long way, through the dene and over the moor. There were birds singing all around us."

"Ah. I must've had other things on my mind . . ."

She rubbed her cheek against his shoulder, and smiled up at him; and he said, "Tina, tell me something. Why me? I don't understand, I never did . . ."

" 'Cos you're tall and dark and sexy, of course. Why else?"

"Seriously."

She sighed, frowned, said, "I don't know, Paul. I just wanted you, that's all. It wasn't sex, or anything. Not at first. I even said that, remember? I said I wasn't asking to sleep with you."

"Mmm. You were very firm about that." He slipped his arm round her waist, and she chuckled happily.

"I meant it, too. I did. I just wanted to be involved, that was all. You needed someone, any fool could see that; and maybe I wanted to be needed. No, it was more than that, more specific – I wanted you to need me. You, specifically. You were so different from anyone else I knew – so much more real, in a way. With your divorce, and your drinking, and your poor face all used up, the way it was . . ." Her fingers brushed over the lines around his mouth, as if trying to rub them away. "Am I making any sense?"

"Plenty. But I still don't understand it." He caught her hand before it could move away, and touched his lips to the palm. He wanted to respond, to tell her something of what she had meant to him, and what she had come to mean; but suddenly there was a dark shape building on the silvered track, and points shifted with a harsh, mechanical clanking that shattered the mood.

"Here's the train."

They stepped back from the edge and waited, holding hands, while the diesel groaned slowly to a halt. Two men came out of the lighted building and stood talking to the driver through his open window; at the other end of the train, a wide door slid aside and a guard began to toss sacks down onto the platform.

"Maybe she missed it," Tina said worriedly, glancing from one end of the platform to the other, and back again.

"More likely she's still asleep. But we can't go knocking on every window, asking for Diana."

A minute later, just as Fenner was thinking of boarding the train and asking someone, one of the doors swung open.

"There she is," Tina said. "Come on."

But it was a steward who got out first, carrying a case. He set that down on the platform and turned back to the door, holding out a supporting arm. Tina shook her head.

"It can't be her," she said. "She'd never let anyone . . ."

Her voice died away, as a woman climbed slowly down from the carriage, leaning heavily on the steward's arm. She was stones lighter, and looked ten years older; but there was no question, it was Diana Trumbull.

Fenner ran down towards her, leaving Tina to follow more slowly.

As he reached her, Diana looked up and smiled at him, a thin, sick smile that shook him more than anything else about her. All the richness seemed to have fled from her, leaving her like milk that has been soured and skimmed and skimmed again, a curdled, bitter whey with no strength in it.

Fenner hesitated, then bent over to kiss her cheek, as he might have done for his mother or any ageing relative.

Perhaps it was only an acknowledgment that something had changed; but to him, it felt like a betrayal.

Tina joined them as he straightened up. She stared openly; then – as if desperately searching for something conventional to say, to avoid saying anything real – she stammered, "You – you've lost weight, Di."

Fenner winced. Diana blinked twice, opened her mouth – and laughed.

Her laugh at least was the same. A little faded, perhaps, but not directly touched by whatever it was that had wrecked her so. She took both Tina's hands in hers, and kissed her.

"Yes, dear – but don't ask me what diet I've been using. It's not recommended."

Fenner picked up her suitcase, and Diana linked arms with each of them as they made their way towards the exit. Fenner wondered at first if this was just the friendly gesture it seemed to be, or whether it was a way of covering her need for support; but her hand lay lightly on his forearm, and she seemed quite comfortable walking. He was aching to know what had happened to her, but he pushed all questions to the back of his mind, until Diana was ready herself to answer them.

When they reached the car, Tina held out her hand for the keys, and Fenner dropped them into it with as much of a grin as he could muster.

Tina deliberately took them the long way home, so that they came over the hill and down to the cottage from above. When they turned the last corner, the whole valley lay spread below them in the soft morning light. Diana caught her breath, and seemed not to let it out again until the car was parked and they were walking up the lane to their gate. Her eyes drifted slowly from the colourful, slightly messy garden to the cottage, looking almost self-consciously pretty with its bright gloss-work setting off the old stone walls and the lichen-stained tiles on the roof.

"Oh, you lucky, lucky children!" she murmured.

"What do you mean, children? Even Tina's been out of nappies for a year or two now; and you and me, Di, we're the same generation."

"No, we're not," Diana said flatly. "Granted I'm not much older than you in years, but I'm not sure we were ever the same generation. Certainly not any more. I'm too old even to dream of something like this." One wave of her hand took in the cottage, and the garden, and the land behind, and by implication their whole lifestyle. "And you're getting younger every day." Her voice died into a whisper, but both Fenner and Tina caught the words and the pain that lay behind them.

"Come on, Di, don't get morbid." Tina elbowed her way past Fenner and slipped an arm round their friend, pulling her on towards the door. "You're on holiday, remember? And you're not exactly old yet. I wouldn't let you be, even if you were. Besides, this may look dead pretty on the surface, but you know you wouldn't like it for keeps. You said it yourself, before we left. You said the country was all very well for the odd fortnight, but you'd hate to have to live in it."

"Oh, not to live, no," Diana said, almost smiling. "But I'm not talking about living. If I only had a place like this, just for a few months, I think I could be happy."

Her words dug a deep silence between them, more by their mood than meaning; then she shivered, and chased them with a brittle smile. "Still, 'thou shalt not covet thy neighbour's house'; and you were neighbours of mine for a long time, even if it wasn't long enough. Why don't you put the kettle on, Paul, while Tina shows me around? I'm dying for a cup of tea."

Tina took Diana's case from Fenner, letting her other hand brush his hip as their eyes met in a mute gesture, a promise of support; then she pushed the door open and led the way in.

Fenner followed the two women after a minute, worried and disturbed, trying to pin down something solid which would explain both Diana's appearance and her words. He could find nothing but a sense of threat, horror crouching behind a flimsy door.

Twenty minutes later they were sitting round the kitchen table, in a silence which should have been companionable but was only difficult. None of them could relax; whatever had changed Diana so hung heavily in the air between them, dark and massive. Fenner saw it as a great weight which a single word could bring crushing down upon them, promising destruction.

To give himself something to do with his hands, he reached

for the tobacco and papers. Tina's eyes flashed an appeal, so he rolled two and passed one across the table.

"I was hoping you might have given them up," Diana said bleakly.

Fenner shot her a surprised glance. "Does a crippled man throw away his crutch? And since when have you been a puritan, anyway? Or have you just fallen victim to all the propaganda?"

She shrugged. "Something like that, I suppose. I just don't like to see you hurting yourselves. There are enough ways of being hurt by other people, and things you can't control."

(Like hooks, Fenner thought, and men with shadow faces, men who work at night and laugh like spiders.)

"Oh, don't worry about us, Di," Tina said lightly. "We'll be okay. Only the good die young, right? Or those the gods love. Neither of which applies to us. Anyway, my grandad's smoked like a chimney all his life, and he's ninety next year."

"And your Aunt Gwensi smoked, and *she* was fifty-seven when she died," Fenner pointed out. "One swallow doesn't make a summer. We're not safe, love, so don't fool yourself."

"Safe? No," Diana said, dropping the words like lead shot into a pool. "But then, no one's exactly *safe*, are they? I've never smoked in my life, and I'm only forty-five, and I'm dying."

(And yes, thought Fenner, yes, of course, that's what it is. Why didn't I see? You're dying, and you're only forty-five.)

No one spoke, or moved. There were no questions left to ask, and nothing to say. Death was a razor, slicing the threads that bound their lives together, unpicking stitches to let all their comfortable securities fray slowly into the wind.

13 Lady Sings the Blues

Cancer is a word that kills words. It is the horror that scuttles at you from the shadows, sideways in its own proper motion, on thin legs like needles that tattoo fear across your face. It is the dark man who lies hidden beneath your bed, the hand that snatches at you from secret places. It's the chariot that Time rides when he's in a hurry. It's a vampire word that sucks you dry of laughter, turns the wine to vinegar, leaves you with nothing to say.

So they walked in silence along the shore that afternoon, going slow for her sake and trying not to show it. Tina strayed aimlessly across the sand, gathering shells and pebbles for no reason other than to look as though she wanted to. Fenner walked backwards much of the time, glancing quickly from one to the other, then turning his eyes upwards before either could meet his gaze. Gulls turned overhead in a chaos of feathers and wind, shadows against the pale sky.

Diana kept her eyes before her feet, stepping over driftwood and rocks. Every now and then she stopped, turning her back to the cliffs, staring out across the sea to where ships cut through the misted horizon.

They came to a stream that shaped a new path to the sea after every tide. Fenner jumped across, and turned to help Diana; but she didn't even see his offered hand. She was giving all her attention to the sea; and he wondered what words she might be hearing behind its song.

"In a real world," he said at last, "Tir na n'Og would be out there, and we'd all be climbing into a boat to find it. The land of the ever-young."

Tina straightened up with a razor-shell in her hand. "Some people call it America."

Fenner snorted. "The Americans call it America."

Diana broke away with a sudden movement, moving up the beach to sit on a half-buried rock. Fenner crossed the stream again, taking Tina's hand as they went to join her.

"I'm sorry," Diana said, with a helpless gesture. "I suppose I shouldn't have told you, really."

"That's nonsense. You had to tell us." Tina kicked at a pebble in the sand, digging it out with her toe. "We'd have been worried as hell, knowing there was something wrong and you not telling us what it was. At least, this way – well, we can't help, exactly, but at least we know. It wouldn't have been fair any other way."

"I'm beginning to think it wasn't fair to come at all. You're not exactly going to enjoy this week, are you? Sharing your house with a dying woman . . ."

"Diana! Stop it, will you? Just – just stop it, right?" Tina was almost shouting now, and almost crying. Fenner reached out to her, but she shrugged his hand off without even looking. "I mean, we're your *friends*, right? It's not just a word, it's something real – or it isn't anything at all. And if it's real, it can handle things like this. What the hell do you want us to do, anyway – not know a thing about it until one day we get a letter from a solicitor saying that we can't have the flat any more 'cos our landlady has – has *died*?" She barely hesitated before that last word, then slammed into it with all the force that she could. Diana sat very still for a minute, before reaching out a hand to her.

"You're right, Tina. You're quite right. I'm sorry, I didn't mean to . . ."

"'Course I'm right," Tina said with a sniff. "We love you, okay? So don't try and bloody run out on us, before you have to." Fenner saw their hands tighten until the knuckles showed white. Then Diana's arm started to tremble, and Tina pulled away.

"Fuck the lot of you," she said lightly, kissing Diana's cheek. "*I'm* going to dam that stream."

Tina splashed around with her jeans rolled up above her knees, getting sand on her clothes and in her hair as she built a wall of stones mortared with seaweed. Fenner and Diana sat quietly watching.

"You know what we must look like?" he said after a time. "Two proud parents keeping an eye on their prodigious offspring. I don't think I can stand it."

He kicked his sandals off, and bent over to roll up his trousers.

Diana chuckled faintly. "I do feel that way sometimes, just a little. As if I'd suddenly inherited a grown-up daughter, without all the hassles of helping her grow. It's nice. But . . ."

"But?"

"But I do wish I'd had children of my own. It's too late for me anyway, of course, even without . . . Oh, the cancer, blast it. Why can't I say it? But it rubs it in, knowing that I haven't got much longer. You can't help thinking about all the things you could have done, the chances you let slip . . . And the worst of it is that you're always aware of the chances you're *still* letting slip, the things you may never get a chance to do again, or do better. For instance, this may be the only chance I have to come and stay with you; and it's already spoiled, partly. There must have been a better way to break the news, but I missed it."

"Hell, no one ever does anything the best way, Di. You're still human; that's not going to change, just because you've been given a deadline, while the rest of us are still muddling along in a mist. I can see where it might bring things into sharper focus for you, but that's all." Fenner shrugged. "I just wish I could find some way to make things better for you. You wouldn't like to do something foolish, like junketing off on a world cruise, would you? If you fancy it, just say the word, and I'll come. We both will."

She smiled, and shook her head. "No thanks, Paul. It's sweet of you; but I don't want to find myself too far from a hospital any more. I'm not brave enough to face it without drugs and so forth. And I was never the adventurous type anyway. I would have liked to have been, I suppose; but as you say, I'm not going to change inside, simply because I'm dying. If I did do something like that, it'd just be bravado; under the surface I'd be feeling uncomfortable and insecure, and wishing I was back at home with my bedsocks and a good book."

"Hey, Fenner!" Tina was just too far away to overhear, and might not even have realised they were talking at all. "Come on, if you're coming! I want more rocks. There's some up by the cliff's edge, there."

He stood up, feeling his toes sinking into the dry, warm sand.

"Okay, Di? If I go?"

"Yes, of course. I'll be fine, just watching you two play. I'm really quite comfortable here, in this sunshine. That's one thing I'm going to do right this summer," she went on with a thin smile. "Such a tan, I shall have . . ."

They took Diana to a restaurant for dinner. Tina frowned, watching her refuse any vegetables and then simply pick at the sole she'd ordered.

"You ought to eat, Di," she said hesitantly. "I mean, you could at least try to fight it. People do, don't they? And they win. Spontaneous remission, they call it, but I'm sure it's all to do with your attitude."

Diana sighed. "So's my doctor. He keeps nagging me too. Good food and early nights, he says. I managed the early nights, because he gives me sleeping-pills to be sure; but if he wants me to eat, he can whistle for it. It's the pain-killers that take away my appetite, but I couldn't manage without them now."

"Is it very bad?"

"Oh, it's bad," she said. Then: "It's funny, but you have to learn to be honest with people, about things like that. I remember the third or fourth time I went to see my specialist – I knew what was wrong with me by then, he was just talking about treatments – and he asked me if I'd been having much pain. You know what I said? It was just automatic, the sort of thing you always say when people ask you things like that. I just shrugged my shoulders and said, 'I'll live.' And he sort of blinked, and I suddenly remembered that I wouldn't. I'm afraid I was a little hysterical," she added. "But he couldn't see the joke."

"I'm not surprised. Specialists are only grown-up medics, after all." And the expression on her face indicated Tina's view of medics, at whatever stage in their development. "But listen, Di, you've got to be straight with us, about what you want to do while you're here. We have got some sense, we won't try to drag you into things you can't possibly manage, like long hikes over the hills and stuff like that. But any time you're feeling bad, or just tired or anything, just say, won't you?"

"I will, pet. I promise."

"And you can tell us all the things you can still manage to eat, too," Fenner put in. "A little temptation might work wonders; so anything you fancy, just say. Right up to truffles and champagne."

She smiled. "Thanks, Paul. But I'm not allowed alcohol."

"Not even champagne?"

"Not with all these pills and potions I have to take."

"Right you are, then. No champagne. I'll just tell you jokes instead. I'm going to get you giggling somehow, I promise you that much. You're not leaving here until you look a hell of a lot better than you did when you arrived. Understood?"

Diana didn't say anything; but she saluted, with a half-mocking little gesture that she might have picked up from Tina.

Fenner returned the salute. "Carry on, sergeant. Which

reminds me." He gathered Tina in with his eye, but his attention was still turned towards Diana. "I was talking to Alan Morgan the other day, that's the village pastor, and he was saying that when he was doing his National Service, he came up against this career sergeant who . . ."

In the space of the next few days, Diana was introduced to Alan Morgan and others. She learned to milk a goat, established a pleasantly sentimental relationship with Monty the kid, and came as close to anyone ever had to the Red Baron, a half-wild ginger tom who had annexed the woodshed as his own particular territory. She sunbathed, and walked, and even swam a little; and she laughed rather more than Fenner had expected. While it was still obvious even to a stranger that she was a very ill woman, the bitter helplessness that had gripped her before seemed to recede a little, so that she could at least enjoy something of the present.

On the Friday of her visit, they drove to the nearest town on a shopping expedition. Tina and Fenner both had a list of items they couldn't get in the village, ranging from typewriter ribbons to a chain for Monty, who had taken to chewing through his tether. Diana wanted to find a few small presents, to take back to friends in the city.

"Not trinkets, though," she said. "None of your tourist rubbish. Let's face it, they won't be souvenirs of this holiday, will they? They'll be souvenirs of me."

They found a car-park on the edge of town, and walked in towards the centre. It was another gloriously hot day, and they did the shopping in easy stages, finding benches in the shade to rest on whenever Diana admitted the need.

"What about lunch?" Fenner suggested, as a clock struck one. "Myself, I could certainly eat; and Tina has the appetite of a house-martin."

"What's wrong with that?" Tina demanded, giggling. "Pretty small birds, house-martins. Or are you suggesting that I eat flies?"

"God forbid. But I read somewhere that house-martins have to eat five times their own body-weight every day . . ." He dodged quickly, grabbed her foot as it scythed past his waist and deposited her in a municipal flower-tub. "What about you, Di? Any particular fancy we can seduce your appetite with today?"

"You'll laugh," Diana said, "but what I'd really like is fish and chips, with a mug of tea to wash it down."

"Yeah!" Tina cheered her. "And I know just the place, too. Follow Auntie."

She led them through a twisting confusion of cobbled back-alleys, to a small cafe tucked between a barber's and a motorbike repair shop; but at the door she checked suddenly, and went back.

"What now?" Fenner asked, turning round curiously.

"Look." She pointed at a Yamaha 175, parked out in front of the repair shop. A sign on the seat said, 'RECONDITIONED. GUARANTEED. £200.'

"It's only five years old, too," Tina said, glancing at the registration. "Talk about cheap . . ."

"It's probably falling to bits inside."

"Not if it's guaranteed."

She crouched down to look at it more closely, and Fenner frowned. "You look serious."

"I am. Why not? It's a real bargain."

"Can you ride a bike?"

" 'Course! There was a boy I was going out with when I was a spotty teenager, who went in for motocross racing. I must've told you about that, Fenner? I got dead keen on it. Only then he dropped me when it turned out I was better than he was, and I was too broke to buy a bike of my own. But it'd be really useful to have one now. Let's face it, it'll be ages before I pass my test; and even then, one car between the two of us could make problems. But if I had a bike . . ."

"Can you afford it?"

"Once I get the money for all the furniture, sure." She glanced up at him. "You'd lend me, till then. Wouldn't you?"

"If you're sure you want it, yes."

She nodded, and straightened up. "Hang on a minute." As she disappeared into the shop, Fenner turned to Diana.

"Sorry, Di – looks like lunch'll have to wait a bit. There'll be no stopping her now. Are you okay?"

"I'm fine, yes." She chuckled, and he cocked an eyebrow.

"What's the joke?"

"I was just thinking how like Tina it is. To come down here for fish and chips, and end up buying a motorbike."

Tina came out then, with the shop manager in tow. She had keys in one hand and a crash-helmet in the other. "I'm just going to take it round town for a test," she explained airily. "I said I'd leave you two here as hostages."

"I wouldn't trust her," Fenner said gloomily to the grinning manager. "She's done this before, leaving friends as a guarantee and then abandoning them. You'll not see her again, you mark my words. And you'd never get two hundred quid for us. Lucky to sell us at twenty pound the pair . . ."

He might have gone on, but at that moment Tina kicked the egine into noisy life. She revved it a couple of times, shifted into gear and bumped slowly off over the cobbles.

Fenner and Diana waited outside, leaning against the alley wall with the sun in their faces and the stone cool against their backs. Diana's eyes were closed, with thin lines etched around her tight mouth.

"Trouble?"

"Not really. Just a twinge. More a reminder than anything else, a hint of what I've got to go back to." For a moment she let those words hang unsupported in the air between them; then she went on, "It's going to be bad, going back, Paul. There's no point pretending. It's helped a lot to be with you two, but going home on Monday is going to knock me right down again. It all looks so grey and hopeless when I'm alone, trailing between the flat and the hospital, with no one to talk to who understands, or even knows . . ."

"So don't go back," Fenner said simply, meaning it. "Stay with us. We can look after you. And there's a good hospital down the coast, so you're only an hour's drive from treatment in an emergency."

"That's really kind of you, Paul – but it wouldn't be fair, on either of you. I had to nurse my mother through her last illness, and I know what it's like. I couldn't ask you to do that."

"You didn't ask. I offered."

"All the same, no. You don't know . . ."

"You're forgetting, I was a policeman for fifteen years. I've seen everything, Di. I'm not going to turn faint and sickly, just because I have to look after a sick woman."

"No, but – Paul, do you imagine that I really want my friends to see me as I'll be in a few months' time? Or worse, to have to care for me? To clear up my vomit and bring me bedpans, and to wash a body that'll look worse than any concentration-camp victim? Do you suppose that's how I want to be remembered?" Her voice was low and hard, almost vicious, driving at him like a whip.

"It doesn't matter what you'd look like, Di. You'd still be you inside. That's all that's important."

"Not to me." She opened her eyes at last, and met his gaze directly. "I mean it, Paul. I don't want my friends anywhere near me, when I get like that."

"Okay, then. I won't press you."

(But if you think we're going to keep away just because you're not pretty any more, you've got us very wrong, Di my love. If you won't come to us, we'll come to you; and we'll be there right up to the end, to hold your hand and kiss you goodbye when you go.)

"That doesn't mean you can get all depressed again, just because we're not there," he said aloud. "We're only the other end of a telephone, for God's sake. Give us a ring if you start getting gloomy, and I'll administer some of my patent medicine. I'll keep half a dozen joke-books by the phone, ready to get you laughing."

She smiled. "You don't need books, you fool. But I will phone. I promise."

And then the alley was filled with noise, and Tina came racing back from the other direction, cocky and confident, brakes squealing as she stopped right in front of them.

"It's not going to last long if you treat it like that," Fenner commented acidly. She stuck her tongue out.

"That was just to impress you. I know what I'm doing. But get your cheque-book out, grandad. I want it."

14 The Worst Truth

It was a bad time for Diana, the day she left. There was no question of her coming to the window to wave, as the train pulled out; but they stood still and watched anyway, until the train had dwindled and been lost among the browns and khakis of the long valley.

"We'll have to go back. Soon." Tina spoke flatly. Fenner's face twitched slightly, but he said nothing. "Fenner, we've *got* to. We can't leave her on her own. Not like that."

"No. Of course not. But – not yet, eh?" Faced at last with an urgent need to go back, Fenner was having to confront the fact that he was almost scared to return to the city. The words themselves said it all: 'going back' meant slipping again into all the shadows of his past, all the horrors that he'd come to Wales to escape. It had been that unvoiced, virtually unrecognised fear that had kept them from making a visit during the summer; there had been excuses in plenty, clear and believable reasons for staying, but behind them all lay a superstitious dread of walking those streets again. He didn't actually believe that the city had power to tempt him back into the old paths, the ways of drink and danger; but safer not to put it to the test.

Still, there was an obligation now, a pressing claim that couldn't be ignored. And, too, there was the silent promise he had made to Diana, not to abandon her until the very last was over. Yes, they would go back; but not yet. Not quite yet.

Home again, Fenner rolled cigarettes while Tina shut the goats up for the night, and the chickens. When she came in, she kicked her sandals off at the door and came straight to him, sitting on his knee and burying her face in his neck.

He didn't know what to say or do, to comfort her; he had no experience, and his own distress was enough to cope with at the moment. Diana's going had finally unleashed all his grief and sorrow, and the pain of it was like a spring released, thin wire slashing and cutting all through him. So he knew how Tina felt; but he couldn't help. All he could do was hold her, and hope that that would be enough.

Eventually she moved, to rub her eyes and wet cheeks against his shoulder in a cat-like action that might have made him smile, another time.

"Sorry," she whispered.

He kissed her. "It's all right. I understand."

"No. No, you don't. It's not Di – or not just Di. That's bad enough, but . . ."

"What, then?"

"You. You'll be forty soon. That – that's only five years younger than Di. And she's *dying*, Fenner . . ."

"She's got special damage," he pointed out softly. "It's not automatic at forty-five."

"No, but it's *possible*. If it can happen to her . . ." She looked at him with the eyes of one who has finally realised the worst truth that lovers can ever know: that one of them must necessarily die before the other.

Fenner had come to terms with this long since; and having been through one divorce already, he was not inclined to look so far ahead. "If it comes to that," he said lightly, "you could get yourself knocked off that motorbike of yours, any day you fancy. Or a tree could fall on you, or Monty could trample you to death, or Alan Morgan could strangle you with a pair of black lace panties. I'll be careful, love; but there's not really that much you can do about it, except keep putting one foot in front of the other to make sure that you're still alive today, and things are looking good for tomorrow. And by the way," he went on, settling her more comfortably against his shoulder, "I rather resent the suggestion that I'm so geriatric I'm liable to give out at any moment."

"That wasn't what I meant. You know that." But her mouth was curling again at the corners, and Fenner could feel the tension ebbing out of her muscles. She sighed, and shifted her weight a fraction.

"Smoke?" he asked, reaching out carefully with one hand, not to disturb her.

A frown touched her face. "You said you'd be careful."

"Not that careful. You're not going to nag me into giving up, woman, so don't try. D'you want?"

"No. Yes. No, I'll just have a drag of yours."

"Sure."

But both cigarettes were smoked and shared, and the clock struck midnight, and still they sat there, needful of each other's stillness to remind them that there was a good life here, and they had found it. Happiness was a quicksilver thing, that could be touched but never held; and they both knew that they must grope half-blind for a while now, before they found it again.

"What about tomorrow?" Fenner asked, as the clock's chimes sliced like silver knives into the silence. "We did say we'd take Monty to the slaughterer's, but . . ."

Tina shuddered. "Not tomorrow. I don't care what we do, but not that."

"All right. How's about a mystery tour?" This meant sticking a pin at random into a map of Wales, and spending the day wherever it landed.

Tina nodded. "Okay. That'd be nice." She slid off Fenner's lap, and touched his cheek with her fingers. "I'm going to bed. But don't be long, eh?"

"I'll be right up. I promise."

And when he went up she was waiting for him, naked as her fears and hungry as the night. It was a slow drum they moved to, a winter drum, a sound from that season when survival is the only thing that counts and the only force that motivates. Survival deals only in moments, and makes no promises; but seasons change, its voice moves further off, its hand is not so heavy. The drummer left them at last, and the song their bodies sang shifted key and tempo; it had begun almost as a dirge, and ended almost as a paean.

And when it was ended they found some measure of peace, sleeping in a warm tangle under the quilt, as far away from the world as they could ever come.

The next morning, their mystery tour took them down into the Rhondda, to a small town made rich by coal and steel a hundred years before. Walking the streets at random, they ducked into a dark little antique shop to avoid a shower of rain. Tina vanished instantly into the back of the shop, to rummage through a rack of clothes; Fenner ran his eye along a shelf, caught sight of a dark, cylindrical shape and smiled. He lifted down a genuine top-hat, smothered with dust but otherwise in near-perfect condition. He brushed and blew the dust away, and perched it on top of his head.

Just then Tina whistled for him, soft but insistent. "Fenner, come here for a minute. You've got to see this."

She was holding something in both hands, long and straight, a cane or walking-stick.

"I've got the hat, you've got the cane," he said, tap-dancing towards her. "All we need now is the white tie and tails, and we'd be all set. Or one of us would, at any rate."

(White tie and tails. Yes, of course. Why hadn't he thought of that before?)

But as he approached, her right hand shot out suddenly, and a steel shaft gleamed in the shadows. Fenner came to a careful stop, as the sharp point pricked his chest.

"It's a real genuine sword-stick," Tina said enthusiastically, sliding the blade back into the body. "Look, there's sort of a safety-catch to stop it leaping apart at awkward moments, and . . ."

"Tina."

"Mmm? What?"

He took the sword-stick from her, and balanced the top-hat on the end of it. "How's about we buy them both, as a present for Jude? Put the final touches to that party gear of hers?"

"Fenner, you're a genius! She's a born exhibitionist, that girl. She'd love them."

"That's what I thought. That's settled, then – so long as the guy's not asking a fortune for them. I refuse to be conned, even for Jude's sake. Should we look around for something for Georgina, too?"

Tina shrugged. "Well, if we see anything. But she's not going to have hysterics if we don't. Gina'd be just as happy with a box of chocolates, she doesn't go much for fancy presents. I gave her this really nice embroidered blouse once; and the next time I saw it, it was on the back of a mutual friend and Gina was bumming around in her usual sweatshirts. It wasn't that she didn't like the blouse; but Carol had seen it and said how lovely it was, so Gina had just given it to her. She does that. If we bought her something special, as like as not it'd end up with a total stranger."

"Okay," Fenner said. "We'll just get her a box of Thornton's, when we go."

They drove back at sunset, with the dark stain of night seeming to creep up into the sky from the slag-heaps and the shadowed machinery at the pit-heads. Fenner kept his eyes on the road.

"Are you feeling any better now?" Tina asked quietly.

"Me? I'm fine, what are you talking about? It wasn't me who spent half the night crying."

"Don't try and feed me that macho bullshit, Fenner mate. You can't fool me. You'd have been crying too, if you could only remember how."

Which was true, twice over. Tears would have been a welcome relief last night, but for Fenner tears were a thing of the past. He had cried too often and too easily, when the drink was in him; and since then, he had never cried at all. It was a loss he regretted; tears seemed to prove a simpler path through sorrow, to take you flying over bad ground which the dry-eyed man had to slog through, foot by weary foot.

"Maybe you should teach me."

"Nah, you're too stupid. You have to be the sensitive type, like me."

"Sensitive? You're about as sensitive as a dead horse. Anyone with a nose like yours would've removed themselves from human society years ago, if they'd had any sensitivity to speak of . . ."

And as the banter grew ever more outrageously personal, each contrived to tell the other that they were back on a relatively even keel, still hurting but not drowning in it. Soon Fenner was driving one-handed, the other arm hanging round Tina's neck while she manipulated the gears.

The following week, Fenner walked into the village to do some shopping, leaving Tina painting in the garden. When he came back there was a strange, savage landscape unfinished on the easel, and Tina was standing in the middle of the garden path, hands in pockets, staring at her feet.

"Mike phoned," she said dully. "Mike Malone."

"What did he say? Or does he want me to ring him back?"

She shrugged. "I don't know. I suppose you'd better, he didn't tell me much. You'd get more out of him."

"About what?"

Her eyes came to meet his, empty as nut-shells, dry and shockingly passive.

"Diana's dead."

15 Red and Warm and Waking

Beat.
Beat.
Beat.

That drummer was back, voice of winter loud in his ear in late summer. Or was it just his own heart, cold and hard and heavy?

"Already?" he said; and felt a stab of guilt, as though he betrayed her by believing it, as though that made it true. He might have chosen to deny it or ignore it, even to pretend it had never been said; and that way Diana could have lived on, in his mind at least. People are only dead to those who know them dead. But it was too late now. The knowledge had been passed on like a baton, and his fingerprints were on it, a signature of acquiescence.

"Yes. But it wasn't the cancer. He said she was murdered."

"No." This time the denial was easy and obvious. Diana's gate into death had been chosen and specified in advance. He had schooled himself to that knowledge, and learned to accept it; but this was too much. For someone to pre-empt her own slow but steady progress into death, to force her on before she was ready . . . No. Diana couldn't go like that, he wouldn't *let* her go like that.

"That's what he said." Fenner wasn't sure whether Tina too was trying to disbelieve it, by accusing Mike of lying, or whether like Cleopatra she was blaming the messenger for the message; but her voice was flushed with a sudden anger.

"I'd better ring him. Did he say where he was?"

"CID."

It was impossible, the whole thing – but why else should Mike be involved, and phoning from the station? Unless he'd simply got his facts wrong, or misinterpreted the evidence. Maybe that was it. If he didn't know about the cancer . . .

Fenner turned back at the door, to see if Tina would follow; but she stood isolated on the grass, twisted in on herself, and he knew there would be no reaching her yet. So he went inside, and dialled the well-remembered number.

"CID."

He remembered the voice, too. "Mike Malone, please, Jenny. It's Paul Fenner here."

"Oh – yes, of course. Just a moment, Paul. I think he's expecting you . . ."

Fenner heard the murmur of voices, the clatter of a typewriter; then there was a click, as his call was switched through to Mike's office.

"Hullo, Paul."

"Mike, what is all this? Tina said you phoned her . . ."

"Yes. Diana Trumbull – your landlady, yes?" Mike ran on over the facts without waiting for confirmation. "She had the flat below yours. She's dead, Paul. She was murdered some time last night."

"Murder. You're sure about that? There were reasons why she might have . . ."

"Suicide? If you mean the cancer, yes, we know about that. But there's no question, Paul. It was murder."

"Tell me."

"It's messy. There's no point in—"

"Yes, there is. I want to know."

"For God's sake, Paul! Do I have to spell it out? She's the Butcher's latest, isn't that enough?"

Of course. He should have known. There are some things you can't run from. And he'd been tied in with the Butcher right from the beginning, he might have known he wouldn't escape this easily. But:

"No," he said quietly. "It's not enough. I want the lot, Mike."

"Well, get it from someone else, then."

"*Mike!*"

"Jesus. All right then, if you must. You know that old Roman temple out along the West Road, say quarter of a mile from your place?"

A few low walls, little more than foundations, inside a wooden fence. One big stone slab for the altar, and a couple of broken pillars. "Yes."

"She was found there. On the altar, naked. Slit from throat to groin, and all her innards pulled out, like some augurer's sacrifice. Or a carcass butchered. Very apt, really."

Dim and distant, as though the windows had been closed and sealed and double-glazed, Fenner heard an engine revving. Lifting his head from his hands, he looked out to see Tina astride her bike, dark curls blowing free as she raced away up the hill. She hadn't even bothered to pick up her crash-helmet from its shelf in the kitchen. Either she'd simply forgotten it in her grief, or – more likely, Fenner supposed – she'd deliberately not come into the cottage, to avoid meeting him. He could remember times during his marriage when there had been sorrows too great for sharing, when he'd been driven out and away from his wife, unable even to consider her needs in the face of his own. There is always a point where interdependence gives way, where people have to go off by themselves to work out their own ways through; and it looked as though Tina had reached that point, if she was dodging even the sight of him or the chance of having to say where she was going. If even his concern for her was too much for her to cope with . . .

"Take care, then," he whispered to the sound of her exhaust; and turned away from the window to face himself. She had broken and run long before he would have; this was perhaps the moment when he needed her most, to learn from her that there was still love and comfort in a sour world. But she had gone, and from his own experience he knew that chasing after her would be the worst choice he could make. She would come back when she was ready

(unless, like Diana, she met the hard edge of life out there, and overran it. It's a flat world, my masters, and too easy to slip over the side. And God, he wanted her here, safe with him, and the rest of the world shut out. There were too many people out there, and he didn't trust one of them)

and until then, he'd just have to manage alone. He could do it, he'd done it too often before. Though there had always been the whisky then, and that wasn't like being alone. Since he'd met Tina she'd always been there in a crisis, and she'd always been enough; he hadn't needed alcohol then, only her. But she'd left him this time, to cope by himself; and not to spite her or anything, and certainly not to blame her, because he did understand, he really did – but by Christ, he'd like a drink.

Nothing in the cottage, though, and the pub wouldn't be open yet. And he couldn't face a pub anyway, all those people, none of them Tina and none that he could trust. He just wanted to sit and be safe, here on home ground, and wait till Tina came back. So perhaps he wouldn't drink after all. Selfish, too, to give Tina more to upset her, a day like this. He'd just sit for a while, and think about it. And smoke. A cigarette, that was the thing. That'd help . . .

He sat in the kitchen, his body instinctively seeking sunlight while his mind ached with the chill of dead flesh on cold stone.

(Only the stone won't be grey any more, with the colours of sleep and silence. More vivid now, painted in slaughtercolour with this new offering, perhaps to wake some dark and bloody god for whom this Butcher is only a servant, preparing the way for his master. Blood seems black in time, but it's only

seeming. It's always red underneath. And you can scrub it off and scrub it off, but the stain's still there, red and warm and waking. Lady Macbeth knows that, and so do you.)

And after a time, as he rolled another with automatic fingers, there was a light tap on the back door and Huw came in, confident and smiling.

"Hullo, Paul. Only me." He dropped a light haversack onto a chair and went over to fill the kettle. "Tina out on the bike, then? Only she said I could have a lend of it, to run over and see Steph."

Fenner had hardly moved, only his eyes flickering once to the boy's face to see who it was; and he didn't reply.

"D'you reckon she'll be back soon? She said I could have it, definite, and I told Steph I'd be over, so she'll be waiting for me. Where's she gone, not far, is it?"

"For God's sake, Huw." Fenner spoke almost in a whisper, his eyes focused on the cigarette he held between two still fingers. "Not now. Not today. Go on the bloody bus."

"Had a row, have you, you and Tina?" He was chuckling, mocking lightly from the deceptive shelter of his own love; and a spasm of fury gripped Fenner, crushing the cigarette, turning his knuckles white

(white as Diana must have looked, what was left of her, with all her blood drained out across the cold rock)

and setting his hands shaking.

"Get out," he said, still in that low voice that nevertheless cut the air between them cleaner and harder than any shout. "Get the hell out."

"Oh." There was a pause, then a click as Huw turned the kettle off. "Right, then." He picked up his pack and went to the door.

"Huw."

"What?"

"I'm sorry. I didn't—" No, can't say that. He did mean it. But not like that. Just go away, that's all. "You'd better understand what's going on. Things may be a little messy here for a few days." It was better, slightly, once he started talking. Looking for the words, he could turn his mind away from the facts for a moment. But he still wanted Huw gone. "A friend of ours has been killed" – a good safe word, that. It says enough, but not too much, and with any luck he won't ask how – "and we're both pretty shook up, so . . ."

"Oh glory, Paul. That's terrible." Huw stood uncertainly in the doorway. "Is there anything I can do, or . . .?"

"No thanks, lad." Fenner gave him a thin smile, and reached for the tobacco again. "Just leave us be for a bit, eh? Just till we get ourselves straight again."

"Yes, of course. But – well, if there is anything, you will let me know?"

"Promise." Fenner nodded.

"Right. Goodbye, then. And don't, you know – " One hand flapped vaguely in the air, and Fenner's lips twitched.

"I'll try. Thanks, Huw. Cheers."

Hours passed, the earth turned, the sky lost its light; and still Fenner sat there, smoking, waiting. In his head, this crisis had turned into a test – not of their love, which didn't need testing, but of their relationship. When Tina did finally come back to wanting other people, would it be him that she wanted first? She had older friendships, built on different foundations; an impulse could have taken her even as far as Newcastle, if she wanted someone other than a lover and if Fenner couldn't fill both roles. So he waited: either for Tina or for a phone-call, from Jude perhaps or one of Tina's other friends, to say that she was there and staying for a while.

Always at the back of his mind was another possibility, a policeman at the door or a phone-call from a hospital, to say that Tina had had an accident, been taken ill, been sick, been raped, been killed, was dying, was dead, was found dead, was dead on arrival . . .

At last, as the old clock in the hall struck the quarter after midnight, the roar of a bike engine poured down the hill to fill the night, and Fenner's head. Stiff shadows swept across the garden in a sudden, brilliant light, and vanished with that light. The engine coughed, and was silent; and footsteps came down the path and round the cottage to the back door. Fenner didn't move, making no guesses and trusting neither instinct nor familiarity. Other people could drive a bike like hers, and walk like her; and he trusted no one except her. They might do this for a joke, send a policewoman on a motorbike, only to tell him that she was dead, dead, dead . . .

The door opened, and Tina came in.

He stood up, and she came to him like a moth to the light, her head pressing into his neck. The hair was cold, and the skin beneath colder still.

He brushed his lips across her forehead, and hugged her close. "You're freezing."

"You don't exactly need to tell me." Her fist had closed round the collar of his shirt, crushing it, pulling the shirt tight across his back. Gently he disengaged her fingers, then held the icy hand in his, willing warmth back into it.

"How've you been?" she asked, after a while.

"I'm all right." Now. "What about you, where did you go?"

"Up. Into the hills." She shrugged against him, a small, uncertain gesture. "I didn't go that far, on the bike. I walked miles, though. And I found a stream and threw stones into it, and . . . Oh, you know. The things you do, when you're alone." Her grip tightened on his hand. "I'm sorry I ran out on you, Fenner. I shouldn't have, it wasn't fair."

"It's all right. Don't worry about it. Do you want a coffee?"

"Yes. Please."

"You'll have to move, then."

"In a minute." She turned her face up to his, and kissed him. "That's for me." And then again, more slowly. "And that's for Diana. For loving her."

"Listen, though, Tina." They had discovered that they were hungry, and were sitting over large platefuls of scrambled eggs and mushrooms. Fenner turned the talk abruptly towards a decision that he had made – or that had made itself – sometime during that long day. "There's something I've got to tell you."

"Mmm? What is it?" Her eyes narrowed suspiciously. "Don't tell me you're pregnant again?"

"Only a little bit, miss. But seriously. I'm going to go back."

"Back?"

"To Newcastle."

Beat.

Tina swallowed, licked her lips, opened her mouth. "Fenner . . ."

"Not for good, stupid. But I've got to go."

"Why?"

He shrugged. "I could be very dramatic, and say that it's a debt I owe Diana. Because it's true, I do feel like that. But mostly I just want to nail that bastard."

"For Christ's sake, Fenner! You're not in the bloody police

any more, remember? You're a dropout now, writing a world-shattering masterpiece of modern fiction. I'd like to see him nailed too – but it's not your responsibility, any more than mine."

"Diana was my friend," he said quietly. "That makes it my responsibility. Doubly so, given my training and experience. I've got an inside line to the official investigation, through Mike Malone; and it might be very useful to them, to have someone snooping around independently. Some people won't talk to the police, but they will to a guy who stands them a drink in the pub. It's just logic, you see. I ought to be there, and I've got to go."

"No, Fenner, no. It's all wrong." Tina's anxiety showed in her body more than her face, as she ran a hand through her tangled hair and rubbed the other along the edge of the table, back and forth like a metronome. "It was being a policeman that started you drinking, remember? And it'll be worse than ever if you try to get back into all that now, with you being so tied up emotionally. It'd destroy you. And I need you in one piece."

"I'll be careful," he said. "I promise. But I've still got to go, love. I can't just sit here and twiddle my thumbs, while Diana's lying dead and her murderer's laughing. I may be able to help; and I have to try."

Tina chewed her lip for a minute; then she said, "Well, maybe. Let's talk about it in the morning. But I'll tell you one thing, mate. If you go, I'm going with you."

"Don't be silly. It'll only upset you, and there's nothing you can do to help."

"Oh, yeah? Listen, there are still a lot of people who'd talk to a girl more easily than a bloke. I could be really useful, I bet, if I tried. But even if I don't do a sodding thing. I'm still coming. You don't really think I'm going to trust you over there all by yourself, do you? 'Cos I'm not."

"Yes, but you *can't* come, Tina. We can't both go. Somebody's got to look after the livestock. And it wouldn't be a good idea just to leave the place empty, for any length of time."

"That's no hassle," Tina said. "What do you think friends are for? Huw'll keep an eye on everything for us, milk the goats and the rest of it. He'd do anything for me if I lent him my bike for the duration. That way he'd be able to get over and see Steph any time he liked. We could tell him to bring her back here, too; I expect they'd like somewhere to go, where they can be alone."

"Yeah, well, we'll talk about it in the morning." Fenner got slowly to his feet, and held out a hand. "Coming?"

She nodded, and stood up. His arm slipped easily round her waist, and he held her close for a moment, his lips touching her cheek in a brief salute. "Thanks for coming back."

"Thanks for being here, when I did."

Part Three

Going Back

Early sunlight dappled the road with the hedge's shadow. Fenner and Tina stood by the car, wondering if there was anything else they should be taking.

"I wish we knew how long," Tina said, drumming her fingers on the top of the open door.

"No way of telling. But we've still got a lot of stuff at the flat, remember."

"If it hasn't been burgled."

Smiles were thin this morning, connections were too easy. Burglars to murderers, their flat to Diana's – only a step down, and that step slippery with blood. But Fenner did his best, knowing that the effort was necessary. It was a long way back, in more than miles; and if they didn't take laughter with them, they were going to find precious little there.

"Come on," he said, walking round to the driver's side. "Let's go, eh?"

"Okay."

But still they hesitated, standing with their feet firm in Wales, in the good life: looking down into the valley, back across the garden to the cottage. And while each of them waited for the other to move, the sudden tongue of a motorbike smashed like a hammer against their stillness. Tina glanced up the lane, and said, "Huw. Coming to do the polite and introduce Steph before we go."

"Good."

Good to have someone to say goodbye to, to give them the impetus to go. The word would be a springboard, sending them on their way down and down, into a pool that looked as dark as blood, and as deep. Down and down; but at least they would be moving.

So they waited, until Huw pulled up on the verge behind the car. There was nothing flashy about the way he handled the bike; he was careful, methodical, obviously safe. Fenner grinned, suspecting that the caution sprang from Huw's concern for his passenger, rather than himself. She rode pillion with her arms wrapped tight around the boy's waist, her face hidden behind the visor of Tina's best helmet. Huw was wearing the old one, with the visor scratched and held together by Sellotape.

Tina frowned. "He won't be able to see a thing through that."

"You leave him be. He'll manage. And I bet he enjoys the sacrifice."

Another bad word, sacrifice, flicking him past the tight walls of his control

(cold flesh on dark-stained stone, fresh offering to a thirsty god)

and setting a shiver to run under his skin. But Huw was off the bike now, pulling the helmet off and helping the girl to unstrap hers. Lifting it clear like a crown, to let the sun play on long hair as pale as a flame in daylight, as straight and fine as silk.

Fenner whistled softly. "He's a good picker, our Huw."

"Or she is. But he said she was lovely."

Huw took her hand and led her forward, his eyes flicking from her face to theirs, and back to her again. There was a touch of nerves about his smile, almost embarrassment; and Fenner sympathised, remembering the awful task of introducing his first girl to friends of longer standing.

"Tina, Paul – this is Steph. We thought we'd just catch you, to see you off."

"You only caught us by a moment," he said easily, using their arrival to oil over his and Tina's reluctance. "I think we've got everything we need now, haven't we, Tina?"

"Yeah, sure," she said, catching his mood and going with it. "Have fun, you two. Just make yourselves at home, right? You've got our number at the flat, if anything happens."

They smiled and said their goodbyes, and a minute later Fenner was almost surprised to find himself already in the car with Tina beside him, the doors closed and the engine running, seat-belt firm across his chest and his hand on the gears.

"Go on, then," Tina said gently. "Wagons, roll."

He nodded, and put the car into gear.

Tina waved through the window, and Fenner sounded a rhythm on the horn. In the mirror he could see Huw and

Steph waving, until a turn in the lane took them out of his view.

Beside him, Tina giggled unexpectedly.

"What?" he asked, puzzled.

"I was just wondering how long it'll be before they find the Durex in the bedroom."

"There aren't any Durex in the bedroom."

"Yes, there are. I picked some up in town yesterday, and left them on the pillow."

"What the hell for?" He stared across at her, and she giggled again.

"What do you think, stupid? I don't know if those twc have actually started yet, but with a cottage to themselves and all the time in the world, I bet it won't be long before they do. And Huw's a sensible lad, but he might be a bit shy about buying his own. So I left him some."

Fenner was silent for a minute; then he began to laugh. "You're just a pimp, you are. Are you sure Steph's sixteen yet?"

"Who cares? We're not going to rat on them. And I'm all in favour of people screwing, so long as it makes them happy. Adults don't have any monopoly on happiness, however many laws they make to try to convince people that they do."

"Anarchist."

"You bet. *And* a pimp."

The slanging and the laughter died away, as the balance swung with the miles, and suddenly they were nearer to the city than the valley. Already they had passed the pub where, with Jude and Georgina, they had toasted their future. It was hard to be certain, but one of those fields on the right must be where Jude had picked the flowers, to make peace with; that one, Fenner decided, thinking that he recognised a wind-twisted tree.

"We'll have to go and see them," Tina said abruptly.

Fenner blinked. "Jude and Georgina?"

"Yes."

"We will do. Soon. But was I thinking aloud, or have you bugged my brain?"

"Don't need to. Some things are just bloody obvious. There might as well have been a signpost. CAUTION.

YOU ARE NOW ENTERING A NOSTALGIA ZONE. DO NOT LOOK AT THE FLOWERS."

When they reached the flat, Tina got out of the car first. Fenner followed her to the door, where she stood fidgeting with her bunch of keys.

"Look," she said. "That's Diana's spare, she left it with us, remember?"

"Yes, I remember." Tina was staring at the small brass key, hard enough to emblazon the zigzag pattern on her mind forever. Fenner put his hands on her shoulders and began to rub them gently, kneading taut muscles between his fingers. "We'll have to get used to it, sweetheart," he said. "She's going to be everywhere, for the next few days. If we're going to let it throw us, we might as well go home."

Tina dropped her head sideways, to rub her cheek against the back of his hand where it lay on her shoulder. "I can handle it," she whispered. "Just give me time."

She picked through the other keys on the ring, slid one into the lock on their own door and twisted it.

The steps ran up before them, dark and familiar, the air heavy with a summer's dust. The mat was covered with free papers and glossy advertisements. Tina put her foot across the threshold and poked at them with the toe of her trainers, like a swimmer testing the water.

"Welcome back to civilisation," she said softly.

"Let's not make a big thing of it." Fenner threw her own words back at her, from when they'd left the city. "Come on back to the car, we'll take some stuff up with us and save a trip."

They unloaded the car, then spent a time merely wandering around the flat, tasting the ambience that had once been so much a part of what they were, trying to discover what had changed, to make them feel so alien now.

Then they unpacked, slowly and methodically. Fenner made coffee, rolled himself a cigarette – then decided that roll-ups were wrong here, too much a part of his other life. He went up the road to the newsagent, and came back with a hundred Winston. He and Tina talked desultorily about friends they should visit and places they should go. They had something to eat, and coffee again; and still Fenner made no move even to let Mike Malone know that he was back in town.

Perhaps tomorrow would be soon enough – but tomorrow Diana would be another day dead, and the killer another day safer, as memories faded and evidence was lost.

Fenner scowled, and got to his feet.

"Going into the study, to phone Mike."

Tina nodded. "Tell him hullo from me, will you?"

Fenner rang the station, was put through to the special incident room, asked for Malone, was told to wait. Then:

"Malone." His voice was more than tired. World-weary, Fenner decided. As though he were sick to death of everything.

"Hi, Mike. Paul. You don't sound so good."

"Hullo." Malone showed no surprise. "If you're ringing for news, do us both a favour and save your phone bill, eh? There isn't any, and I don't think there will be. This fucker's just laughing at us."

"That's why I called." Now that it came to the point, Fenner was strangely shy of explaining. His offer to help might look like simple arrogance, or even a direct insult to the efficiency of the police force Fenner had left. "I want to talk to you, Mike – now, tonight, if possible. Where can we meet?"

"Are you back over here?"

"At the flat, yes. Come here if you like."

Malone chuckled, a laugh like a wisp of smoke, thin and tenuous. "Fat chance of that. I've got no time to socialise, Paul. Any time I'm not here, I'm in bed."

"It's not exactly social. Can you duck out for an hour, and meet me in a cafe?"

"We're supposed to eat in the canteen. But I might be able to work it. Half an hour, anyway. Where and when?"

Fenner came back into the living-room to find Tina aimlessly licking her finger and rubbing at dirt-marks on the window.

"Did you get through?"

"Yes, I'm meeting him at Tatties at nine o'clock."

"Oh. Right." She hesitated, then, "Look, Fenner love – would you mind if I went to see Jude and Georgina, while you're with him? I'm not trying to cut you out, we can see them together in a day or two. Have them round to dinner, or something. But I want someone to talk to tonight, I don't want to just sit here on my own, and . . ." She flapped a hand at the radio, the bookshelves, the emptiness.

"Of course I don't mind. Why should I? They're your friends." And yet, absurdly, he did mind. Duty was a cold thing, holding him and letting her run free. She could look for help, where Fenner could only offer it. It was her freedom, and her choice; and he resented it.

17 Questions

Tatties had changed, over the summer. It used to be a run-down, dirty little cafe with nothing to recommend it except the food, which was hot, plentiful and well-cooked. Now the interior had been glossed with chrome and smoked plastic panels, a bank of video games had been installed to attract a new generation of customers, and the food looked meagre, expensive and unappetising.

Fenner paid for a coffee at the counter and took it to the furthest corner in a bid to escape the machines and the attendant pack of leather-jacketed youngsters. He felt unreasonably irritated by their noise and laughter, by the persistent flashes and harsh bleeps of the machines, in fact by all the changes he could see. The old Tatties had been comfortably, cheerfully sordid, and he actively regretted its passing. *Fair is foul and foul is fair* – and that gave rise to another train of thought, as he wondered how fair the Butcher was. He probably looked much like anyone else, standard photofit, with every feature indexed and classifiable. It's not psychopaths who wear their hearts on their faces, only lovers and drunks. A clever psychopath is a politician, his whole life a mask designed to give him enough shadow to play in . . .

Soon he spotted Malone through the window, crossing the street towards the cafe door. Even from this distance and through glass, Fenner could see his friend's exhaustion. Mike walked as though he were hanging from a hook

(a sharp steel hook, a butcher's tool)

in the back of his neck, his head and shoulders dropping loosely forward, ready to fall if the string were cut. He watched his feet as if he didn't trust them.

He came in, and Fenner called to him. Malone made his way between the tables and fell into a chair with the abrupt gracelessness of a man who's not pretending anything. His skin was grey with fatigue, his eyes veined red.

"What do you want, Mike?"

"Food." Malone rubbed a hand across his face, and shook his head. "Something hot. I don't care what."

Fenner ordered, and Malone ate; and then it was time for talking. But Fenner let a silence fall between them, again feeling awkward, embarrassed, not knowing where to start. It was Malone who forced the issue, saying, "What's it all about, then, Paul? Not exactly social, you said – so what?"

Fenner concentrated on tapping every last loose flake of ash from the end of his cigarette. "I want to help," he said, almost idly. "Help you find the Butcher."

"For Christ's sake, Paul." It came after a pause, in a subdued groan rather than a shout. "I know how you must be feeling, but – hell, you should remember what the amateurs are like, when they fancy they can help. It's just nuisance."

"I'm not an amateur. Not in that sense. I've got as much experience as you have."

Mike snorted. "Experience – what's that? Counts for nothing, in a case like this. Look, shall I tell you what our brilliant and imaginative, our *experienced* police force is doing right now, to track the Butcher down? A house-to-house, that's what we're doing. With two hundred extra men brought in for the occasion, we're going round every bloody house, flat and bedsit in the city, interviewing every damn citizen. I'll tell you, you don't need a lot of experience to ask the same questions five hundred times a day. Or to fill out the answers on a form, or feed them into a computer. I'm spending all my time just cross-checking. If Pete says he was screwing Joe's wife on the night of the twelfth, does Joe's wife confirm this? And is she telling the truth? And if so, where the hell was Joe? That sort of thing, for a whole bloody city. I'm sorry, Paul, but there's no place for you."

"Not with the official side, no. Obviously not. But there must be something I can do. Snooping around on the sidelines, something."

"We don't know where the bloody sidelines are. No one's bothered to explain the rules of this game. One private sleuth isn't going to make any difference, Paul. Especially as you'd be working in the dark even more than we are."

"That's why I need you, Mike," Fenner said. "To lighten the darkness a bit."

"Me and Jesus Christ? You'd do better to rely on him. I can't give you access to the computer, or the briefing room."

"No, but you could keep me in touch. Privately."

"Waste of time, there'd be nothing to tell you. There's nothing to find, see. This bloke's so careful, so damn *clever* it's not true. The forensic boys have been over that bit of ground a dozen times, and the – uh, the flat, and . . ."

"Diana's flat?"

"Yes."

He remembered the key on Tina's ring. But forensics wouldn't have needed a spare, they would have had Diana's own. He thought of them working their slow way through the flat, looking at everything, sticking their scientific fingers into Diana's secrets, probing her drawers and scattering grey dust across her tidy shelves and surfaces . . .

"What did they find?"

Mike shrugged. "I told you, nothing. Nothing at the flat, and nothing at the temple. The ground's too dry even to register footprints, and he didn't do anything convenient, like treading where the blood had soaked the earth." Fenner winced, and Malone touched his arm lightly. "Sorry, Paul."

"It's okay. I should have thought of that myself." But he'd been too obsessed with images, blood on old stone and a sacrifice to more violent gods than Alan Morgan's biddable Jesus. He'd been thinking as a writer, not as a detective; and Mike knew it as well as he did. *Amateur*. "What's the main thrust behind the house-to-house? Are they looking for the Butcher himself, or just witnesses?"

"Either. Both. Anything." Mike scowled. "You know – maybe someone saw someone in the street late, or heard a door slam when their neighbour should've been in bed. Or maybe we'll find a contradiction somewhere, and break an alibi. Except no one's producing alibis at the moment, because we've got no one to accuse." He shrugged. "We'll pick up some petty thieves, but it'll take a miracle to turn up anything useful. But then that's all we've got left to hope for anyway. The Chief's taken to church-going, to try to improve our chances. Oh, and his image with the press."

Fenner smiled. "But not necessarily in that order, right?"

"Right."

"He's still not going to call in the Yard?"

"Not a chance," Mike said gloomily. "He's left it too late. He'd be crucified if he admitted now that he was out of his depth. All he can do is keep on bluffing, and wait for that miracle."

Fenner nodded. There were politics in the police force, as there were everywhere. And the rules of political survival stated that once you'd said publicly that you could solve a case without Scotland Yard's assistance, once you'd declared to the press that you and your team were as good as anything London had to offer, you had to stick to your guns and prove it. You couldn't back down three or four murders later, and admit that you couldn't cope.

"Will you, though, Mike?" he asked again. "Will you keep me in touch, if anything does come up?"

Mike sighed. "I suppose so, yeah. It can't do any harm. And maybe you're the Chief's miracle, after all."

"Me and Jesus Christ?"

"Something like that. I'd better not take a chance on it, anyway. I'll let you know what I can. But God knows what you think you can do. It's not a one-man show, this one." An expression of disgust touched his face briefly. "But then, God knows why you want to get involved at all. I know she was your landlady and so on, but still . . . Why don't you go back to your bloody typewriter, and leave us poor bastards to get on with it?"

"She was my friend," Fenner corrected mildly. "I can't just hide myself away and let my friends be murdered." Then, with an abrupt change of direction, "When did you last see Susan, Mike? See her properly, I mean? To spend time with, talk to, relax together?"

"I don't know. The night before they found Diana, I

suppose. Not since then. I only go home to sleep, nowadays, and I don't get much of that. It's bad, I know, with Susan pushing eight months now, but what can you do?" He stopped suddenly, frowning. "What's that got to do with the price of coal?"

"Turn round and take a look at yourself," Fenner urged. "There's a mirror just behind you. Go on, have a good look."

Puzzled, Malone glanced over his shoulder at his reflection. "Okay, so I'm not exactly spruce at the moment. So?"

"You're a wreck, man. You're not eating, you're not sleeping, you haven't seen your wife for days; you're pushing yourself as hard as you can go, as many hours as you can find in a day. And you're doing it for Diana, Mike – *and you didn't even know her*. I loved her. You think I can give her any less?"

"It's different," Malone said uncertainly. "It's my job."

"Mine, too." Fenner said it flatly, believing it. "I may not get paid for it any more, and I may have found other things to do since; but I've still got the soul of a copper. And this one's mine."

Malone nodded slowly. "Good luck to you, then. I won't argue any more." He looked at his watch, and stood up. "I'd better be getting back. I said half-nine, and it's after that now."

"I'll walk with you."

Coming out into the cool night, it was like leaving the dregs of the conversation behind on the wipe-clean table, with the dirty crockery and Fenner's dog-ends. Out here they could go back simply to being friends again, and Fenner took full advantage of it. "Tina said to say hullo."

"Did she? That's nice. Give her my best."

"Will do. How's Susan?"

"Thriving. Burgeoning. Memorising baby-care books, the last I saw."

"Does she know what she wants? Or doesn't she care?"

Mike chuckled. "Brain surgeon, novelist, Prime Minister – she'll be happy with anything, just so long as it's a girl."

"Yeah?" Fenner grinned back. "Tina'd be pleased."

"Go over and see her sometime, why don't you? The pair of you, I mean. She'd like that."

"Would she? Right, then. We'll do that."

The police station was a modern building, concrete and glass. Half its windows were dark, but there were still no blinds on the others; Fenner could see figures sitting or moving in every room with a light. He rehearsed them in his mind: that was CID, there was the forensic lab, and the fingerprints room, and . . .

Two car doors swung open as they paused on the steps, and a voice hailed them. "Inspector Malone! Just a minute, Inspector . . ."

Fenner had them tagged as press even before they were properly out of the car. No other profession could emulate that aura of bustling, earnest enquiry – not even the police.

"Anything for us, Inspector? Any developments?"

"Sorry, boys." Malone always adopted a hearty, rather patronising tone with journalists, Fenner remembered. It didn't sound so convincing tonight; there was an edge to it, as though the bluff exterior were being worn away, and they'd find nothing but sharp steel beneath. "No comment."

Rather to Fenner's surprise, they took him at his word, not badgering him any further; but one of the two was turning to Fenner, saying, "Mr Fenner, isn't it? My name's Jackson. You remember, I did a piece on you for the *Evening News*, earlier in the year."

"Yes." Fenner kept his voice carefully neutral. "I remember."

"Can I just ask you, are you back in town for good?"

"No. Just visiting. Seeing old friends." Fenner deliberately threw a glance at Mike, and a quick smile; but Jackson was quick.

"Nothing to do with this latest Butcher murder, then? If I've got this right, Mrs Trumbull's flat must have been directly below yours. I suppose you knew her quite well?"

"Quite well, yes. She was my landlady." Which Jackson probably already knew, so he might as well admit it straight away.

"And as I understand it, she visited Wales only a week or so ago. You moved to Wales yourself, didn't you? Can I ask—"

"Yes. She was staying with us."

"But you're only here to visit friends? Are you sure it doesn't have some more direct connection with Mrs

Trumbull's death? You were a policeman yourself, after all, you worked on the early Butcher cases . . ."

"Several of our friends here were also friends of Diana's." Fenner said softly. "I would have thought it was rather an obvious time to come over and see them, when they're feeling the same loss that we are. Now why don't you piss off and find yourself a story?"

Jackson grinned. "No offence, Mr Fenner," he said, "but I think I've found myself a front page."

18 A Front Page

The flat was dark and empty when Fenner reached it. Tina would be a long bus-ride away by now, running from solitude herself and leaving it for him. He had no right to complain, remembering that he had planned to come alone and leave her in Wales; but it made him restless and unsettled. He turned the radio on, spun the dial aimlessly and switched it off again. All the records and the stereo had gone to Wales with them; and in any case, he couldn't sit long enough to listen to music. He thought about cooking, but didn't want to eat. In the end, he picked up his jacket and went out again.

Almost without a conscious decision on his part, his feet turned west up the hill. He thought he was only walking; it wasn't until he reached the first DoE signpost that he realised where he was heading.

He followed the signs, and came to the fenced-off patch of ground where the temple lay, between two houses. It was strange to find an ancient monument in the centre of an up-market modern estate; stranger still that the only gap in the fence opened not onto the road but into a private garden. a small plaque on the garden gate said, *Access to Roman Temple through this gate.* Below this, a larger hand-painted notice was wired to the gate on a wooden board. *PLEASE close this gate behind you. People are living here!*

Fenner couldn't be troubled with passing through two gates and someone else's garden, when only a wooden fence separated the temple from the road. He vaulted over it, then stood motionless for a time, eyes fixed on the shadowed stones. It was too dark now to read the information board, but Fenner had little interest in that. The information he was after was on no public notice. Nor did he expect to find it here; he could see no sign of the police examination, but he knew they would have checked every pebble and every blade of grass. If they had come up with nothing, then there was nothing to be found. The stones knew the killer, and would never speak; Diana knew, and would never speak. Which left only the Butcher himself, or some stray witness who didn't realise the importance of whatever it was he or she had seen. Maybe the Chief was right after all, with his house-to-house; maybe all they could do was ask questions, and wait for that mixture of coincidence and luck which constitutes the modern miracle.

Fenner walked slowly in, towards the first ankle-high ridge of cut stone which marked where the temple's outer wall had stood. Inside it one great slab, carved and figured more by the rain than Roman hands, lay between the stubs of two broken pillars. It looked different in the dim light of the distant street-lamps, whiter than the other stones,

(when it should have looked darker, blood turned black, with its red heart hidden)

seeming almost to glisten as it drew the eye. Fenner was puzzled, that it should seem so much cleaner; but the clue was in the word. Cleaner. Of course, they couldn't leave it with the blood caking in the dips and runnels of the ancient altar. Someone must have come to scrub it clean,

(but you can scrub it off and scrub it off and the stain's still there, red and warm and waking)

taking the last traces of Diana from the world, the marks she had made when she was dying.

Fenner reached out tentatively to touch the dimpled surface of the stone. It even felt clean, disinfected, as though someone had tried to make it as perilous to life as a mortuary slab, thinking that a more fit memorial. Or a more fit place for the next sacrifice . . .

For there would be a next, of course. Another, and another. This man wouldn't stop until he was stopped. It wasn't enough, simply to wait for a miracle – nor even to hunt for one. Even if the house-to-house did turn up something useful, it might be months or even years before it was spotted and recognised for what it was; and that would be months or years too late for another victim, or two, or three.

Looking around him, Fenner wondered what on earth could have brought Diana here in the dead of night. Granted, she didn't sleep well; but she was much more one for bedsocks and a book than for early-hours walks through the city. Unless the killer had picked her up elsewhere, at her flat perhaps, and brought her here. But why should she come? She'd have no reason for driving around with a friend at that time, much less a stranger. Which was another thing. Was the Butcher a stranger to her? Hard to believe that she knew him, but someone must. He must have friends, or at least acquaintances, somewhere. No one lives entirely in a vacuum.

A dog barked, close at hand; and closer still, a car door slammed. Fenner looked back at the road to see a patrol car parked, and two uniformed men standing beside it, watching him. No one he knew. They came to the fence and climbed over, tense, silent figures that sent a kick of adrenaline into Fenner's system. Then he realised what was happening, and almost laughed aloud.

"Excuse me, sir," one of them said quietly. "We'd like to talk to you for a minute. Ask you some questions."

"Ask away." Fenner sat down casually on one of the pillar-stumps. "But it might save time if I give you some of the answers straight off. I suppose someone phoned from one of these houses, to say there was a suspicious figure hanging round in the temple, right? Right," he went on easily, seeing the acknowledgement in their faces. "Well, I'm not the Butcher, and I can prove it half a dozen ways if I have to. And I'm not a souvenir-hunter either, coming to take away a chip of stone or a slice of blood-soaked turf." As he spoke, he saw that there were several squares of turf missing around the altar. Removed by the police, he imagined – but whether for forensic purposes or simply for the sake of appearances he wasn't certain.

"Can I ask what you are doing here, then, sir?"

"Hard to say." Fenner groped for an easy way to put it,

something which would satisfy them; something true, but not the whole truth. Probing his own motives was painful enough, he didn't need interrogating. "Diana Trumbull was a friend of mine," he said at last. "I was out of town when she was killed, and I suppose I just wanted to see the place where she died." Good enough.

"A friend of yours?" The younger of the two policemen was looking distinctly interested. Obviously, if he couldn't bring in the Butcher, next best thing was a friend of the victim's who hadn't yet been questioned. A smaller feather in his regulation cap, but a feather none the less. "Could I have your name, please?"

"Paul Fenner," he said with a sigh. "*That* Paul Fenner."

"Christ." The oath came from the younger man; the other gestured him to silence. Fenner let it hang for a moment, then, "If you're wondering whether an alcoholic ex-DI could turn into a rabid killer, you might as well save your brain-cells, because the answer's no. I worked on this case myself, in the early days. And Mike Malone will give me a character reference. Tell him you talked to me, he'll be amused." And amusing Mike could become quite a priority, the state that man was in. Almost as much as amusing Diana had been. "Goodnight, now."

He turned and walked confidently away, without looking back. Vaulted the fence and strolled away up the street, knowing that they were staring after him. Didn't look back.

Didn't go home, either. There was nothing for him to do there, and his mind was too full to do nothing, almost as restless as his body. So he went walking, striding across the rough moorland that divided the west side of the city from the wealthier north. Mainly he was walking simply for the sake of it, relaxing into the steady rhythms that set the mind free to wander; but his direction was not entirely purposeless. On the far side of the moor he crossed a railway bridge, turned past the cinema and made his way to the street where Jude and Georgina had a flat.

He found the door with no trouble; but though Tina had said she wasn't trying to cut him out, she might still prefer him not to butt in tonight. So he moved down the street again to the corner, and hitched himself onto a low wall. He didn't mind waiting, and she'd probably be glad of company on the way home.

At around midnight, the flat door opened and Tina came out with Georgina. They stood chatting, while Fenner watched from the shadows; then Georgina noticed him at the corner, and nudged Tina. She turned and looked; and the two girls exchanged an anxious glance. Georgina put a hand on Tina's arm, shaking her head.

They hadn't recognised him, that was clear; even Tina couldn't identify a murky silhouette at a distance on a dark night. To them he was only a figure hanging round on a street corner, threateningly male. He approved the caution, even as he winced inwardly at the idea of Tina ever being frightened of him.

Moving slowly, he walked into the light of a street-lamp, and waved. The tension left both girls at the same moment, Georgina leaning back against the wall and running a hand through her wild hair while Tina made a small, explosive sound and came running down the street towards him.

"What the hell are you *doing*, playing Butcher or something?" Relief made her voice sharp with anger, but her hands were gentle, circling his waist and saying she was glad to see him.

"No. I just didn't know if you'd want me barging in. So I thought I'd wait."

"Bloody idiot." She smiled, resting her head on his shoulder. "It's nice to be met, though. Come and say hullo to Georgie."

She slipped her arm through his and led him back to the flat, where Georgina stood watching.

"She says I can say hullo," Fenner explained.

"Hullo," Georgina said amiably.

"Hi." He cocked his head questioningly. "Where's the small violent one?"

"Jude?" She grinned. "It's her turn to wear the halo tonight. She's on Observation Duty, down at the Sams." Fenner looked carefully blank, and Georgina went on, "The Samaritans, remember? We must have told you we were training with them. We're both official Helpers now – which means we get to sit and listen every now and then, and make the coffee while everyone else does the work."

"Sound fair enough to me."

"Yes, but we're horribly keen, darling. Can't wait to get in there and start talking people back off window-ledges." She broke off to glance at her watch. "If you're going for that bus, you'd better run."

"Don't need to now, I've got my bodyguard. We can walk back, over the moor." Tina grinned up at Fenner. "See? I was being terribly sensible. Jude's gone off with the van keys, so Gina couldn't drive me home. And I didn't fancy the moor on my own, somehow."

"Christ, no. You'd better bloody not." Too many dark hollows on the moor, far from the lit pathways. Pools of darkness a girl could be drowned in.

"Dead masterful he is, sometimes," she said, cuddling up to Fenner. "But men do have their uses."

"So they tell me."

Fenner felt detached and slightly confused, as if he were out of phase with them, and missing something. Then he smelt the alcohol on Tina's breath, and understood.

"Are you drunk?" he demanded, laughing.

"Mmm. And stoned. 'S nice."

"It seemed like the right thing to do," Georgina said easily.

"Yeah. It probably was." He looked from Tina to her friend, and nodded. "Thanks."

"My pleasure."

"And you can believe *that*," Tina said, giggling.

"Come on, brat. Home."

"Yes, boss."

They said goodnight and headed off towards the moor, Tina still gripping Fenner's arm.

When they got back, he propelled her gently but firmly through the flat to the bedroom. She sprawled on the bed, gazing up at him fiercely.

"I hope you're not proposing to put me to bed, like some blasted nanny," she said. "I'm not even drunk any more, just friendly."

"Call this friendly?" Fenner dodged one flying foot and snatched at the other, levering the shoe off. "I'll tell you what it is, though," he went on. "Putting you to bed is exactly what I intend to do. But unlike any nanny of my acquaintance, I'm planning to join you. And if you dare let all that wine put you to sleep before I've finished with you, I shall be *very* annoyed."

"Oh. Well, that's different." She stopped fighting him, nudging at his stomach with one bare foot while he worked on the other. "That's exceedingly different. I don't think there are the words to describe how different that is. But if you're proposing to take all my clothes off yourself, you'd better get rid of your own first. 'Cos I'm not moving from this bed; and it'd be a shame for you to have to get up again, once you've started rolling around with me."

He lifted an interested eyebrow. "Will undressing you involve a lot of rolling around?"

"I shall defend my panties," Tina said haughtily, "to the last breath in my body." And with a sudden grin, "I might even cross my legs. Then you'd be in trouble, Fenner mate."

He woke late the next morning, and alone. Tina was in the kitchen, eating toast and reading the local morning paper.

"Here." She tossed the paper over. "You'd better see this."

No offence, Mr Fenner, but I think I've found myself a front page. And Jackson had been right. There was an old photograph of himself and Mike leaving the station, several years back; and a banner headline. THE HUNT FOR THE BUTCHER – A NEW TWIST? The article that followed was pure speculation, from beginning to end; the only solid facts being that he was back in town, that he had been Diana's tenant and had lived above her, and that he had been seen with Malone. It wasn't much to build a front page on; but it was enough, and the assumptions Jackson had made came perilously close to the truth.

"It's not going to help your idea of snooping round incognito," Tina said.

"No. No, it's not."

"Sod it, Fenner, let's go home. We can't do any good here, it's hopeless."

"No," he said. "You go, if you want; it's not your job. But it is mine. I've got to try, at least."

19 *No Light, No Warmth*

And he did try. He knew that the slow machinery of a full-scale police investigation was testing all the orthodox pathways, and finding nothing but dead ends; so he set himself to work on the fringes, trying to find an approach – or a person – that had been overlooked. Every spare hour he spent in writing down what he could remember of the Butcher's previous kills, and then all he knew of Diana's life, trying to find some connection, however tenuous; but most of the time, he was out. He haunted pubs and clubs and meetings, everywhere that people gather and talk; he eavesdropped on private conversations and insinuated himself into them when he could, sifting every word he heard, his head aching with the effort of trying to identify anything which might take him forward. He believed fervently that someone somewhere must know something, though they almost certainly wouldn't know it for what it was. That was his task, to put his finger on a half-remembered shadow seen in a street or an odd noise in the night, something – however small – sufficiently out of the ordinary to stay in the mind. To put his finger on it, and say, "This is where we start."

Tina stayed with him. She was edgy and unhappy, making no secret of her unfaith; with every day that passed she was more sure that they were wasting their time. But she stayed; and she helped where she could. At Fenner's request, she wrote out her own account of Diana's life and habits, without reference to his, to give him another perspective and more material. She did the pub circuit separately, and talked to people in the streets and shops, speaking to neighbours she'd only smiled at before. Without Fenner's experience and training, she didn't really know what to listen for, and wasn't confident of spotting it when it came; but there was always the chance.

"And I've got to do *something*," she said. "I can't just sit and watch you sweat yourself to a shadow."

But they found nothing, heard nothing, came up with nothing.

"No surprise," Tina said two weeks later, when Fenner had come in disconsolate and depressed after yet another wasted evening. "We must've been pretty bloody arrogant to reckon that we could find something that a few hundred coppers had missed."

"It doesn't necessarily follow," Fenner said wearily. "They might not be looking in the right places."

"Yeah – but if they're not, then neither are we. And I'm all out of inspiration."

"What's that, another bloody hint that you want to go home?"

"If you like."

"Christ. That's all I've had from you, since the day we got here." It was as though simple savagery was the only emotion he had left, or the only weapon coarse enough for him to use. "I thought you were coming to help, but all you've done is whine. Why don't you just piss off, if that's the way you feel? I said you could, I don't know how many times; and it might be a damn sight easier for me without you hanging round my neck."

"I don't exactly need your permission to leave," Tina said acidly.

"Then why don't you go? Go back to your fucking goats, and leave me to get on with it."

Tina sat for a moment after Fenner had said it, as though it took that long for his words to reach her; then, without answering or even looking at him, she got to her feet and walked out of the room. He heard her feet on the stairs, quite slow and deliberate; and heard the front door slam behind her.

On the coffee-table in front of him was her bunch of keys. The quarrel was far too close for Fenner to see it clearly, or begin to imagine what it might have done to them; but the picture of Tina at the door without her keys came readily to his mind. He knew the pose, the frown, the irritable flare of the nostrils as she hammered on the door. But the cure for that was easy, too. He snatched up the keys and went after her, down the stairs and into the street.

There was no sign of her, though, up the hill or down. She must have moved quickly; something slashed at his eyes, sharp and stinging as hail on the wind, at the thought of Tina starting to run as the door slammed, Tina running from him.

Turning to go back in, he found that the door had swung shut behind him. His own keys were in his pocket, but Tina's were in his hand; he turned them over to find the one he wanted, and found another instead.

(Look. That's Diana's spare, she left it with us, remember?)

And maybe that was the answer – to dig, rather than scour. To stop looking through the city, and to look inside Diana's life instead. To look for signs of the Butcher in a place where they should shine like neon, rather than fading away into a city where everything was the colour of death.

Of course, the police would have gone through the flat already, careful as cats, checking everything for fingerprints and *raison d'être*, looking for anything that might be out of place. The smallest straw will show the wind's direction. But the police didn't know Diana, and they might not easily have recognised a wrongness that would strike her friends immediately.

Fenner held the small brass key in both hands, rubbing his thumbs against it as a superstitious man might rub a talisman; then he fitted it into the lock, twisted, and

(please, let there be something. An answer. Please?)

pushed open the door.

There are different degrees of silence, in an empty building. There are silences that are still warm and active, saying that someone was there only a moment ago, or a minute, or an hour or two. There are older, more weary silences that smell tired and bored, silences that have been waiting for days for something to fill them. There's a sleepy, companionable silence that might have settled in for weeks or years – the sort of silence that wraps itself around a visitor like water around a swimmer. You can move through it, but you can't change or destroy it in a moment; it is a silence that absorbs sound, reluctant to surrender.

And then there is the silence that is simply cold and hollow, that may have been newborn the moment before you met it or as old as a stone. It is the silence that beats with a regular rhythm, that dances to a winter drum, that smells hard and sharp and acrid; and it means nothing but death.

Fenner walked into Diana's flat as though he were following a glacier's trail into a place of no light and no warmth, with nothing but the sour smell of ice to guide him to the heart of that silence.

Standing quietly in the living-room, he tried to fall back into old habits long abandoned, to see through a policeman's eyes and filter what he saw for information.

As far as he could tell, there was nothing new among the pictures and ornaments in the room. Some china pieces were standing crooked, where presumably the police searchers had moved them. Diana would have straightened them automatically; Fenner half-reached to do so, then checked himself sharply. Tonight he was an investigator, looking only for facts. There was no place for sentiment.

One alcove was lined with bookshelves; and remembering Diana's habit of using any convenient scrap of paper for a marker, Fenner knew that he'd have to go through the pages of every book there, just in case. Just as he knew that the police would already have done so, and his time would almost certainly be nothing but wasted.

Where to start, though? Not there; the books were a minor concern at the moment. There were more likely places . . .

When the knock came, timid, barely more than a rattle of the letter-flap, Fenner was sitting in the hall by the telephone. He was doing nothing because there was nothing more to do here; and he might almost have been waiting for that knock, expecting it in the same way that an optimist always expects good luck without knowing when or how they'll meet it.

But this wasn't luck, good or bad; it was Tina, tired and cold, nerves twitching at her fingers and lips.

"I saw the light," she said. "I was scared, a bit; but then I didn't have my keys, and I remembered about hers, and I thought it had to be you. I'm glad, it would've been horrid if it was someone else . . ."

Fenner had completely forgotten their quarrel, in the intricate games of hunt-the-thimble he'd been playing with Diana's ghosts. He remembered it now as he might remember a scene from a play he'd watched last week or last year. It was dead, nothing, gone with the wind as far as he was concerned.

But not for Tina. With nothing to distract her, he knew exactly what she would have been doing. Walking blindly through the streets, playing it over and over inside her head, hating him and herself alternately until she was too exhausted to relive the emotions and fight it through yet again.

Now, though, her curiosity was overriding even that. She peered past him into the hall, and asked, "Why are you here, anyway?"

"Sniffing around. I should have done it weeks ago."

"Why, have you found something?"

"I'm not sure. It's probably just a dead end, like everything else, but . . ."

"What is it?"

He gestured her in and led the way back to the low telephone-table. "Look."

She reached to pick up the strip of thin card that was lying slantwise on the Yellow Pages. "It's one of those bookmarks, isn't it? For the Samaritans. Jude and Georgina had a bunch of them in the van."

Her eyes moved to meet his, and he smiled. "No," he said, "I don't think there's any connection there. Except Diana probably got hers at the same place, the library. But it was here by the phone, and she wouldn't have picked it up unless she was thinking of using it."

"I can't see Diana phoning the Samaritans."

"Can't you?" Fenner asked the question quietly, and let Tina work it out for herself.

"All right," she said. "She might have. If things were getting bad. If she was really depressed, she wouldn't want to drag us down with her. But I still don't see how it helps, that she might have been going to call them. I mean, we know she was feeling pretty low, we don't need this to tell us."

"Yes, but what if she *did* call them? What if it was just a day or two before she was murdered – or just an hour or two? She might have said something then, that would give us a clue. If she'd talked about the way she was living, the people she was seeing, the places she went. Any information would help, even if it's only background; and it could be a whole lot more."

Tina nodded thoughtfully. "So what are you going to do, get in touch with the Samaritans and ask?"

"I'd better phone Mike first. For all I know, they may have

thought of it themselves and chased it up already. In fact, they bloody well ought to have done; but they've taken her address book away, and all those scraps of paper she kept numbers on, and they left this here, so they may not have seen the possibility."

"Yeah, right. But I wouldn't phone Mike now, if I was you."

"Why not? Sooner the better."

"Not at three o'clock in the morning." She twisted her wrist round to show the face of her watch.

"Christ." He'd lost all touch of time here, with the clocks still and his mind so full. "You're right, I'll leave it till the morning. But . . ." It was Fenner's turn to shrug now, helpless as a whale caught between tide and tide. Leaving Diana's flat meant stepping back into his real life, the one he shared with Tina; and he didn't know where he stood there. That brief quarrel meant nothing to him now, but it must have been eating at Tina all night, building itself into something monstrous. He didn't even know how to talk about it, without seeming to make light of something that couldn't be so to her.

She hadn't touched him since he'd opened the door to her, not so much as an arm brushing against him in the passage. He was almost afraid to reach out to her, in case she pulled away. But if he was going to sleep tonight, he needed the comfort of her sleeping easy beside him. Remembering nights when they'd lain cold and sleepless together with an unfinished fight between them, he held out a hand and said, "Pax?"

Her lips twitched. "The goat-herd and the pig went off to sleep in the straw. Sounds like a fairy-tale."

"Let's just hope we find a happy ending."

"Christ, I wouldn't know where to look."

But she took his hand, and clung to it as he turned the light off and they left the flat.

Fenner was woken at six, by the revving engine of a lorry. Milk-bottles chimed below the window like a haphazard clock. He lay still, wondering why he hadn't slept through the noise, as usual; then he felt the ominous tightness of his chest, and knew.

Rolling to the edge of the bed, he reached under the low table beside it. His fingers found the shelf, a glass bottle, two plastic ones – and nothing else. He clenched his teeth, drawing a slow, determined breath as he swung his legs down onto the floor and sat up. He checked the shelf again, then dropped to his knees and ran his hands over the carpet beneath and behind the table, while he peered under the bed in the half-light. He found cigarette butts and matches from spilled ash-trays, two books, a dirty mug; but not the inhaler he was looking for.

Finally he remembered that he'd been prescribed a fresh one just the week before they'd moved to Wales. It had seemed silly to leave that one here and bother a new doctor for a new prescription, so he'd taken it with him to the cottage. And he'd had no trouble all summer, so he simply hadn't thought about it when they had been throwing essentials together for the journey back to the city.

Which meant that he was stranded without medication, with an asthma attack coming on.

Any hopes of fighting it off were stillborn that moment, as the breath caught in the back of his throat, and a tickling irritation deep in one lung set him coughing. It was a thin, dry cough, and its edges scratched his throat without shifting the irritation; and when he tried to breathe again, the room filled with the rasping, whistling sounds of an asthmatic in trouble.

Fenner stood up carefully and walked out of the bedroom, unhooking a towelling bathrobe from the back of the door as he passed. He knew from experience that without an inhaler, all he could do was keep his chest warm and sweat it out.

And he was starting to sweat already, fighting back the inevitable panic reaction as he struggled to force air into his frozen lungs. He hit the light-switch in the living-room and dropped onto the sofa, listening to the chaotic noises of his own breathing. His vision blurred and darkened as if even his eyes were focusing inward, on the only thing that mattered . . .

But then, through the roaring like wind in his ears, he heard the door open and close; and Tina stood in front of him in an old wool dressing-gown, looking anxious.

"What have you got up for, stupid?" he demanded, his voice only a strained whisper.

"How can a girl sleep, with you doing steam-train impersonations in the next room?" She knelt beside him on the sofa, pulling his head down onto her shoulder and slipping the other hand inside his bathrobe to rub his heaving, aching chest. Her lips touched his forehead lightly. "Poor Fenner, you're all sweaty. Where's your magic puffer?"

"In Wales."

"And you called me stupid?"

He bent forward in the grip of a long spasm of coughing; Tina pounded his back helplessly with both hands, then said, "Do you want a doctor?"

Fenner shook his head. "No. I'll live."

Tina blinked and looked away, hearing as he did an echo of Diana, perhaps remembering that people can die of asthma too, perhaps feeling a touch of fear, wondering if the words were ill-omened.

"It's awful," she said, "just sitting and watching you, not being able to do anything. I feel so useless."

"So why don't you go back to bed?" He battled to get the words out through a throat clenched as tightly as his fists. "Like you said, you can't help."

"Can't sleep, either." She punched him gently below the ribs. "You fuck off, mate. I'm not leaving you."

His mind was swimming too much to argue. It was easier just to find her hand and grip it as he fell back into the cushions, living one breath at a time.

The attack passed off after an hour or so, as he had known it would, leaving him fragile and hollow, remembering again how it felt to draw air freely and silently into his lungs, and blow it out like smoke.

"She's fine. Tired, but you'd expect that. No problems."

Tina appeared suddenly, sitting on Fenner's lap and wrestling the receiver away from him. "Mike? This is Tina. Has the baby come, or what?" She listened for a minute, then: "Oh, magic. Listen, if you're short of baby clothes, just say, won't you? I'll buy Fenner a pair of knitting needles." She listened again, and laughed. "Yeah, grans are like that. Okay, fair enough. Which hospital is Susan in? . . . Princess Mary. Right. I'll take her some flowers. See you, Mike."

She handed the receiver back to Fenner, who grinned and ruffled her hair, feeling a surge of gratitude. Then he heard Mike's voice, tinny and distant. "Are you still there, either of you, or are you having a quick snog, or what?"

"Sorry, Mike." Tina vanished into the kitchen, and Fenner felt his mood changing from light to dark, as suddenly as though a switch had been pressed. "Now listen, I was looking round Diana's flat last night, and . . ."

"How did you get in there?"

"I've got a key, of course. But you don't know that officially, okay?"

Malone hesitated, then said, "Okay. No point getting stroppy about it. Did you find anything?"

"I'm not sure. But there's a Samaritans bookmark by the phone; and I know it's a long shot, but she just might have phoned them in the days before she died, and if she did . . ."

". . . She might have said something relevant. Quite."

"You did chase it up, then?" Fenner tried to ignore the sharp bite of disappointment. It was part of the job, after all; you couldn't hope to win them all.

"Well, we tried. As far as I remember, we didn't get past first base. Hold on, I'll check the file."

Malone came back on the line a few minutes later. "Okay, here it is. We talked to the Director of the local branch, but he refused to help at all. They have a flat policy of never passing on information about their clients."

"Jesus, this client's bloody *dead.*"

"That's pretty much what we said. But it didn't get us anywhere. Worse than talking to a priest. The only thing he would say was that they don't keep detailed records of calls in any case, just brief notes which wouldn't be likely to tell us much."

"Anything's better than nothing."

"I know. But he still wouldn't cooperate. I'm sorry, Paul, we'll never get access to those files without a warrant; and I don't think the chance of finding something useful is worth the stink there'd be."

"It's a chance, for Christ's sake, Mike! And the whole bloody case stinks already. You can't get worse press than you've got so far."

"Want to bet? Anyway, it's the Chief's decision, not mine; and he's scrawled 'No Further Action' in red across the file. So that's it."

"Great. Bloody fantastic."

Tina perched on the kitchen table close to where he was gloomily nursing a coffee, so that her swinging leg nudged at his knee. "Maybe we could burgle them," she said cheerfully. "The Samaritans, I mean. Can't ask Mike to do it, he's far too upright, but two wicked dope-fiends like us, it'd be easy."

"How are you going to burgle a place that's occupied twenty-four hours a day?"

"Oh, that's no trouble. We just burst in there with stocking masks and bitten-off shotguns. Or use that sword-stick, that'd be enough to terrify anyone, and we haven't given it to Jude yet . . ."

Her nudging foot kicked him sharply, and he yelped. "Careful, girl!"

"Sorry, but I just had a thought. Jude. And Georgina."

He waited, then said, "Is there more? Or is that it?"

"Samaritans," she said impatiently. "It's one of the things they do, remember? We've got contacts on the inside. They'll help."

"How?"

"Sneak a look at the files, of course. They must have access, if they're training to be counsellors themselves. If we just tell them what to look for, they'll find Diana's file, if there is one."

Fenner was quiet for a minute; then he said, "We didn't bring Jude's presents up with us, did we? The hat and the stick?"

"No, forgot. They're still on top of the wardrobe."

He nodded, and pushed himself to his feet.

"Where are you off to now?" she demanded.

"Going to phone Huw – or Alan Morgan, if I can't find the lad. He's got a spare key to the cottage, hasn't he?"

"Yes, he always had one for Auntie, so I just told him to hang onto it. But—"

"But nothing. I want those presents coming up on the next train, Red Star. Then we can go to see the girls, and enlist them as a fifth column. I'll get Georgie an extra-special box of Thornton's, enough to bribe anyone. But don't you move," he added, dropping his hands onto her shoulders and rubbing gently. "Because as soon as I've finished phoning, I'm going to carry you into the bedroom and fool around with you to your heart's content. Okay?"

"Oh, yummy," she said. "Oats."

21 *The Fifth Column*

"Well, go on," Georgina said. "Get your penguin suit on. You can't wear a top-hat with a baggy sweatshirt and dirty jeans."

"Come and tie my tie for me," Jude demanded, spinning the hat on the end of the sword-stick.

"I'm busy."

"Doing what?"

"Making coffee, obviously. You get the right clothes on, to go with your present; and I make the drinks to go with mine."

"Okay – but that tie's going to be dirty grey by the time I've finished messing around with it."

"You could always wash your hands first," Fenner suggested, chuckling. It won him a glare from Jude and a muttered, "Up yours, mate," as she left the room.

"Such a sweet child," Georgina murmured, running a selective eye over the vast box of chocolates that they'd bought her. She picked one out, then spoke around it as she headed for the kitchen. "Do make yourselves comfy, won't you? I may be some time, the coffee machine needs *very* careful nursing."

"Great, aren't they?" Tina said, laughing as Georgina swept out of the room. Then she looked around, and added, "I like this place."

"You would."

Two of the walls had been painted a rich purple, and the other two green. A Chinese varnished-paper umbrella hung open from the ceiling, doing service as a lampshade. There was a full-length mirror in one alcove, a standard lamp in the other. The walls were hung with a white lace tablecloth, a crocheted silk shawl and a black mantilla. There was no furniture at all apart from a long, low table, painted matt black; otherwise, the bare varnished floor was simply heaped with cushions and bean-bags. Fenner and Tina built themselves a nest below the window, and sat quietly and comfortably together until Jude came back in full evening dress, with the top-hat tilted at a rakish angle on her dark head and the sword-stick swinging in her hand. The white tie round her neck was formed into a perfect bow.

Jude examined herself in the mirror for a full minute; then she swung round and said, "All right, Tina. On your feet. Or do I have to jab you?" She half-drew the sword, and Tina stood hurriedly.

"I'm up, I'm up! But what for?"

"How could I hug you down there?" Jude pulled her close and kissed her; Tina laughed, and returned the kiss.

"Do I get one of those?" Fenner asked plaintively. "After all, it was my idea . . ."

"Come on, then." As Fenner got to his feet, she tapped him on the chest with the stick's silver head. "No liberties, mind. I know you men."

"Pure and chaste as the driven snow," Fenner promised; and laid his fingertips lightly on her shoulders and touched his lips to her cheek.

"I am not," Jude said disgustedly, "made of tissue-paper." Then she smiled, wrapped her arms round his chest and hugged him hard.

"Is this a private cuddle, or can anyone join in?" Georgina was just behind them, putting coffees down on the table and taking another chocolate. Jude leapt away from Fenner, drew the sword and threatened Georgina with it.

"So, my pretty maid, you have discovered us! But you will live to regret your spying . . ."

"Oh, I shouldn't think so." Georgina steadied the sword's point between finger and thumb, and stuck her chocolate onto it like a button. "There you are. It's a lollipop. Eat it now; but watch your tongue, okay?"

"You watch your figure," Jude growled, glancing at the depleted box. "You'll get bloat."

"Do you two think you could sit down and shut up for two minutes?" Tina asked suddenly. "We want to talk to you. Serious stuff."

Georgina dropped where she was, sitting cross-legged by the table; Jude squatted against the far wall, where she could still sneak glances at the mirror.

"Speak," Georgina said. "I'm all ears."

"They are big, aren't they?"

"Shut up, Jude. And take your hat off."

"A lady," Jude said, "always keeps her hat on indoors."

"Not when she's playing hostess. Ask my mother."

"Your bloody mother wouldn't tell me. We don't speak, remember? She cut me dead at your cousin's wedding."

Tina flung a cushion across the room. "Put a sock in it, Jude love. Please?"

Jude shrugged, and smiled. "All right, if you want to be boring. What is it?"

"We want you to do something for us, Or, no, we want to ask if you will do it; but no pressure, okay?"

"Sure. What are you after?"

Tina hesitated, and looked at Fenner. "You tell them, mister. It's your dirty work."

"Your idea, though." But he didn't mind; he could understand Tina's discomfort. So, looking at his hands because that was easier than meeting eyes he couldn't read, he said, "You both know why we came back. What we're doing here."

(Or not doing. Thrashing around in darkness, caught in webs and shadows while the Butcher walks cleanly in the sun.)

"Yes." A simple confirmation from Georgina, to save him having to say it all out loud. He gave her a quick, grateful smile, and went on.

"Well, there's a chance we may be onto something. It's only a slim one; we're just clutching at straws, really, but it's all we've got. Thing is, though, if there is any information we could use, it's buried in the files at the local Samaritans office; and they won't let us get at it."

"How do you mean?" All the joking was gone from Jude's voice and face as she leant forward, her fingers absently playing with the stick in her hands.

"It's just possible that Diana phoned the Samaritans in the week before she died. Maybe even her last night, we don't know. But if she did, there'll be a report of the call filed away; and she just might have said something useful. Mentioned the places she was going, perhaps, or new people she was seeing. Maybe even a name. For all we know, the Butcher might spend days chatting up his victims before he finally lures them out and kills them. He's not been seen at it, but that doesn't mean much. So they could have his bloody name there on paper, and they won't let us look through the files to find it."

"Of course they won't," Jude said flatly. "No one'd trust us if we let outsiders look at the records. It's the main thing we've got going for us, that we're utterly confidential."

"Yeah, sure, I do take the point. But—"

"But nothing. It's the sort of rule people have got to feel a hundred per cent sure about. Which means no Samaritan is going to break it. Ever."

"Even if breaking it could save someone's *life*? This guy's killed half a dozen times already, and he could kill a dozen more before we catch him. If we ever do. And all it'd need would be a couple of discreet men in plain clothes let in the back door for a couple of hours. No one's going to broadcast it."

"Except a journalist," Georgina pointed out. "It'd be headline news if it ever did get out. But what are you shouting at us for, anyway? We can't change anybody's mind for you, if the Director's already said no. And I don't think I'd try."

"Me neither," Jude said definitely. "Even if it was all kept dead quiet, it'd still be a betrayal of trust."

"Some betrayals are necessary," Fenner said quietly. "But I'm sorry, I didn't mean to shout. I just feel so bloody frustrated . . ."

"It's all right, Paul," Georgina said gently, as Tina took his hand and squeezed. "You're entitled to get worked up. But you still haven't told us what you wanted us to do."

"Not much point now, if you feel that strongly about things. I'd been afraid you might, but there was always the chance . . ."

"Chance of what?" Jude demanded.

He shrugged. "That you'd sneak a look through the files for me, and see if you could spot Diana's. I was presuming that you'd have access to them."

Jude nodded. "We do – though it's not exactly random access. We're not supposed to go snooping out of curiosity. But we might be able to contrive, mightn't we, Gee?"

"I don't see why not," Georgina said. "If we're careful. If it's only a week or so we've got to check up on, I think we could manage it without being spotted. Maybe not all in one night, but . . ."

"Hang on a sec." Fenner was frowning. "You mean you'll do it?"

"Yes, of course, stupid," Jude said roughly. "We won't let you see it, mind; but we'll have a look ourselves, if you tell us what to check for."

"It's the least we can do, really," Georgina said, smiling as she reached for another chocolate. "You've supplied so much bribery, it's practically our duty to furnish a little corruption . . ."

With something finally to focus on, one vague chance of finding something concrete – perhaps even of forcing the first thin crack in the Butcher's wall of anonymity – Fenner lost the will to search for more. It was as if this were his only hope, as if he had been told that there would be just one chance, and this was it.

The worst of it was that it was out of his hands now; he could do nothing but trust his agents. He reminded himself a dozen times a day that Jude and Georgina were both intelligent and well-briefed, that they could spot anything significant as easily as he could; but he didn't really believe it. He'd never enjoyed delegating any work he thought of as crucial, and it made him anxious and irritable now to have the crux of this search taken out of his control and given over to two inexperienced and untrained amateurs who lacked his own desperate need to uncover a solution and ultimately a name. To be forced into inactivity, with nothing to do but wait.

"You're smoking too much."

This was on the fifth day, and Tina threw it at him from across the room, just as he tore the Cellophane off a fresh pack.

"Get off my back, will you?"

"No, I bloody won't." She smiled, trying to twist it away from the raw emotions that threatened like a storm in the air around them, trying to turn it back into their normal banter. "It's my rightful place. Just like the Old Man of the Sea. You're my cock horse, and I'm going to ride you."

"Bloody right. You never stop riding me, do you? First the drink, now cigarettes . . . You don't want to go over the top, Tina, or you might turn round one day and find I'm not there any more. I can only be pushed so far."

"What's that supposed to be, some kind of threat?" Her fingers lay very still on the table-top, as though the slightest movement might shatter the increasingly fragile web that bound her to Fenner. "Would you rather I'd left you alone, and just let you drink yourself to death? You've still got the option, you know. You can start again, any time. Just so long as you tell me beforehand, so that I know to get out of the way, because I don't want to watch it, okay? Like I don't want to watch you smoking yourself stupid" – and now at last she moved, one hand sweeping savagely across the table to send a full ash-tray spinning through the air, smashing against the kitchen door, falling to the floor in splinters – "just because you can't think of anything else to do with your fucking fingers!"

Beat.

And the drummer was back again; but this time he tapped for them, stick rapping on a hollow log to call them into his destructive winter.

Keeping his face straight and still and his voice impassive, Fenner glanced from Tina to the broken glass and the scattered ash and cigarette-ends. "Messy brat."

"Just – just don't expect me to clear it up." She caught his mood instantly, and he could tell that she was trying as hard as he was, scrabbling back from a precipice that had opened suddenly and terrifyingly under her feet.

"I'll rub your face in it, if you're not careful."

"You just try it. See what happens."

"Got to housetrain you somehow."

But it was Fenner who went for the dustpan and brush, and knelt on the carpet to sweep up. Tina watched, until he had finished; then she went to him, leaning her head on his shoulder in mute apology.

"I just wish you weren't so bloody stupid," she said, after a while. "You don't know what's important, you don't understand."

"Yeah? What is?"

"This." Her hand pressed against his chest, so that he could feel his own heartbeat against her palm. "You and me. People. Being alive." She paused for a moment, then went on before he could speak. "Remember the day we left, when Diana found that dead cat in the back yard? What I said to her then?"

"What?"

"That the cat was dead, and it wasn't hurting any more. That's what dead is, Fenner, it's the end of all the hurting. The end of dying. And that's what Diana is now. Dead. Dying's the bad bit, but it always stops. Diana had a foul one, but it doesn't matter to her any more, it can't; so why should it matter to us?"

"Because it does." She made a small, impatient movement and he held her tighter, to keep her where she was. "No, listen. You can try and logic it away as much as you like, but that won't stop your emotions coming at you with broken bottles. It would've been different if it had been the cancer that got her, but—"

"Why?" Tina demanded. "She'd have been dead, just the same. You would've accepted that, so why can't you accept this? I mean, you wouldn't have thrown all your time into trying to find a cure for cancer, would you?"

"No, because I don't know anything about cancer," Fenner said patiently. "I do know something about this job, and I'm fucked if I'm going to turn my back on it while the Butcher's still laughing. It'd be okay if they'd caught him, I could handle that. But he's still free; and if I can help, I've got to try."

Tina pulled away, frowning. "That's it, isn't it? That really is it. It's just your sodding male ego that's doing this. It's like the Butcher killed Diana as a personal challenge to you, and you've got to be the one who nabs him."

"*No!*" He buried his face in his hands, closing his eyes, trying to keep that idea right outside his head. "No, that's not true!" Please. "I don't care who puts his finger on him, as long as someone does. But it could be me. The chance is there, and I can't waste it. He's not going to stop at Diana. He's going to go on and on . . ."

"So's every other psychopath in the world. They're not all your responsibility, so why should this one be?" He didn't answer that; so she came close again and started punching him in the ribs, while tears leaked from her eyes. "Fuck you, Fenner, why can't you just be selfish for a change?"

His arms enfolded her, but his eyes were staring far out across her shoulder, past the walls of the flat to the city beyond. "I don't know, love. I wish I could."

(But there's a drummer out there somewhere, and he drums with bones on a bleached skull. And as long as he's out there, calling people into his dance, I can't sit still. Not till the last dance is over. Not till the laughing stops.)

22 True Confessions

"May I speak to Mr Paul Fenner, please? Or to Miss Tina Blake?" This was at ten o'clock in the morning, with Fenner still trying to shake the sleep from his head as he answered the phone.

"I'm Paul Fenner. What can I do for you?"

"My name's Ross, Mr Fenner. I'm the junior partner at Fingal, Lammerty and Ross."

Solicitors. Fenner remembered the names gold-lettered along a row of windows in the city centre; and they were familiar too from his police days.

"We represented Mrs Trumbull before her death," Ross went on, "and she named us as executors in her will. We've been trying to trace you for some weeks now, but we had only an address in Wales, for both you and Miss Blake."

"We do live in Wales, but we haven't been home for a while," Fenner said, thinking, why are you chasing us? What's it to do with us, that you're Diana's executors?

And then thinking, maybe it's nothing to do with Diana being murdered. Maybe it's only because she's dead . . .

"Yes, so we were told this morning," Ross said smoothly.

"I've been trying to get in touch with you by telephone, since we had no acknowledgement of our letter; and this morning, I finally got through. A Welsh lad answered the phone, and told me that you were here in Newcastle."

Huw. Up at the cottage early, to milk the goats – or had he perhaps been there all night, with Steph? Fenner grinned secretly as he said, "Well, here we are. What's it all about?"

There was really only one thing it could be about, by now; but even so it was a shock when Ross said, "Did you not know? Yourself and Miss Blake are named jointly in the will, as sole beneficiaries. The whole estate is to be divided equally between you."

"No." Take a breath, a deep one. And bless you, Di. "No, I didn't know that. She never told us."

"Ah. Well. Sometimes people don't like to talk about these things." Ross plunged swiftly on to safer ground, the details of the will. "It's not a fortune, of course. But on the other hand, the value of the property is by no means negligible. There is her own flat and the one above, where I believe you yourself hold the tenancy. Then there are six more flats through the city, all on short-term furnished leases to students. Mrs Trumbull's personal property would be of no great commercial value, but there is also a sum of money amounting to several thousand pounds, the bulk of it invested in unit trusts and government securities. The will must be probated first, of course, and that may take some months; but if you and Miss Blake would care to call into my office here at some point, we can discuss the estate in detail, and make arrangements for probate."

"Yes," Fenner said vaguely. "Yes, of course."

"Just make an appointment with the receptionist. I'll look forward to meeting you, Mr Fenner."

"Yeah, right. Goodbye . . ."

Fenner hung up, and walked slowly back to the bedroom. Tina frowned at him from under the covers.

"Who was that?"

"Di's solicitor. About her will." Fenner shook his head, scratched it, looked at Tina. "She's left everything to us, love. All of it."

Tina stared for a second; then she closed her eyes and turned away. When Fenner touched her shoulder, he could feel her trembling. He kissed the soft skin lightly and left her alone, going to make her a coffee. Giving her time.

They were still talking about it, trying to find out what it was going to mean to them now and in the future, how it would change things, when the phone rang again. Fenner answered it, as he had answered every call for a week; and this time, it was Jude.

"Hullo, Paul. Have you got a moment?"

"As long as it takes, for you. You know that." He reached for a pen and notepad. "What have you got for me, anything?"

"No – or not what you're waiting for, anyway. This time we want to ask you a favour."

"Sure. What's up?"

"We're in trouble. Or we may be."

"Yes, but how?"

"We got caught." Jude paused; and Fenner could hear Georgina behind her, giving an appreciative little chuckle to applaud the drama of the moment. He could almost hear the scowl that Jude gave her before going on, "At least, someone got very curious about why we were nosing around in the files so much. And this stupid cow here has to go and *confess* . . ."

"Oh, God." Fenner ran a hand through his hair and groaned softly. "Couldn't she just have made up some excuse?"

"That's what I said, afterwards," Jude told him disgustedly. "We had this cover story all worked out. If she'd stuck to that, everything would have been fine. But the thing is, this bloke who got inquisitive about what we were up to, he's the same guy that Georgie talked to last year when she was all screwed up about things. I think she's got a crush on him, or something. Anyway, she's just gone all Little Miss Innocent on me, wandering around saying she couldn't possibly have lied to him."

Fenner heard Georgina's voice, distant and fuzzy: "Well, I couldn't, darling. It's those eyes of his." He cut in quickly, "Okay. If it's happened, it's happened. You didn't find anything before you got fingered?"

"Not a thing."

"All right, then. So what happens now? Do you get thrown out, or what?"

"We're not sure; it's all up in the air at the moment. David says we ought to be slung out on our ears – breach of confidence, and all that. He says if we do it for you, how does he know we won't do it for anyone else who asks? But he says he does understand that it's a bit of a special case, and he's not going to report us to the Director yet, anyway. Not till he's talked to you."

"Me?" Fenner blinked.

"Yes, that's the big favour we want to ask you. Will you meet him? He just wants to get your angle on everything, and find out why you asked us to do it. Then he'll decide. Please, Paul?" Jude went on, more uncertain than he'd ever heard her. "He's a decent bloke, and it really is important to us, to go on working there . . ."

"Yeah, I know, love. It's okay, of course I'll talk to him. Where and when?"

They met on neutral ground, a coffee-house in town. Fenner got there a few minutes late, delayed by the heavy rain that was falling outside; and he found Georgina at a table by the door, talking quietly with a man. They both stood up as Fenner joined them, and Georgina smiled at him edgily.

"Hi, Paul." She touched his sleeve lightly – to wish him luck, Fenner wondered? Or perhaps to draw luck from him, like rubbing a rabbit's foot? "This is David Linden. David, Paul Fenner. The famous one. Did I warn you about that?"

"No, but Jude did. In graphic detail. I think she was trying to frighten me." He held out his hand and Fenner shook it, smiling in response and at the same time scrutinising his man carefully. Falling back on an old technique which had served him well in one career and was proving likely to do the same in his new one. "Listening to what they look like," his old CID sergeant had called it, "as well as what they say."

David Linden was a big man, an inch or two taller than Fenner's six foot. He was well built with it, and the strength of his grip suggested that none of it was flab. He looked to be in his early forties now; but with his rich black hair and near-perfect teeth, his pale complexion and above all his deep, grey-green eyes, Fenner put him down as one of those men who had been beautiful as a boy and would still be stunningly attractive at eighty.

"Sit down, Paul," Georgina said, nudging him towards a chair. "I'll fetch you a coffee."

"No, it's all right, Gina, I'll get them." He fished in his pocket for change, but she made an exasperated noise and pushed him into a chair.

"Shut up and sit down, darling. Talk to David, it's what you're here for."

Linden sat down opposite him, another smile quirking his lips. "Strong-minded young woman, isn't she?"

"They both are," Fenner responded feelingly. "I suppose they'd have to be, to live the kind of life they do."

"Even to get into it, in the first place. Weaker types would have given up fighting, long since. And ended up working out their aggressions on someone else's washing-up, as like as not."

Fenner smiled. "You may be right." He sat back, eyes wandering round the walls, wondering how to lead into the subject they were both here to discuss. In the end, he fell back on the easy approach, small-talk. "What do you do, Mr Linden? In your private life, I mean?"

"I work in a bank – but that's my public life. Working for the Samaritans is what I do in private. And please call me David, by the way. I'll call you Paul, if I may."

"Fine. I'd appreciate it. So how long have you been a Samaritan?"

"Forever," Georgina said, arriving back with two black coffees. She put them down on the table, and said, "Right. Consider yourselves waited on. That's all the pampering you're getting from me tonight." She picked her bag up from the seat beside Fenner's and sketched a wave with her hand.

"You're not going, are you, Georgie?"

"You bet I am, darling. I'm hardly going to sit here and listen while you two fight about our future. Anyway, I've got to go and hold Jude's hands, or she'll start chewing her nails and just not stop until she reaches her elbows. You two have a nice gossip, and then one of you come and tell us the verdict, eh?"

She smiled, as if it all meant less to her than the milk-bill, and walked quickly out onto the street.

"So," Linden said, while Fenner's eyes were still following Georgina through the plate-glass window, "why are you trying to subvert two of my favourite Sams? Or more to the point, how did you manage it?"

"Is that more to the point?" Fenner asked.

"I'm not sure, but it may well be. A lot of people would probably like access to our files, for one reason or another; but we always say no, unless they're asking for the reports on one specific client, and we have that client's permission to pass them on. We certainly don't smuggle information out to satisfy a friend's curiosity."

"This isn't curiosity." Fenner fought down a surge of anger. "You could have the name of a mass-murderer hidden in those files of yours. You might save a lot more lives by letting someone go through them, than you ever will by talking people out of suicide."

Linden nodded slowly. "Forgive me," he said. "I didn't mean to sound disparaging. Or rather, I did – but only to see how you'd react. I wanted to be sure you weren't just doing this in a dilettante sort of way, to keep busy. I do have faith in the girls' judgement – but I wanted to see for myself, all the same." He shrugged and smiled again, disarming Fenner's anger as easily as he had sparked it. "Sorry again. Don't run away with the idea that I'm playing with you; this is no game to me. To answer your question, I've been a Samaritan for twelve years now; and in that time it's become one of the principles I live by, that the Sams' files are sacred and must remain so."

"I can understand that," Fenner said. "But circumstances alter cases – or at least they ought to. And this isn't just important, it's vital. It's all we've got, and it could be all we ever get. If it's anything at all."

Linden nodded. "So tell me about it. I've followed the newspaper stories about the Butcher, of course, and the girls told me roughly what line you're pursuing, and why. But give me all the circumstances. I want to understand, that's why I'm here."

"It's a long story," Fenner said. "If you want it all."

Linden smiled. "That's all right. I'm a good listener."

So Fenner told him. He talked about himself, and therefore about Tina; and he talked about Diana, and how she had died. He talked in detail about the investigation, and how it was getting nowhere: how all the alleys he'd followed had been blind, and how the police were doing no better. How they didn't dare to waste the smallest chance of finding a thread to follow; and how, if Diana had indeed phoned the Samaritans, what she had said then might give them that thread.

"I couldn't let the chance slip, at any rate. Not with contacts on the inside. So that's why I talked the girls into looking around for me." He looked at Linden anxiously. "I don't think you need to be seriously concerned about the sanctity of your files. I don't believe they'd do it for any lesser reason than they had this time; and the chances of this kind of thing cropping up again must be pretty remote."

"No, I think you're right." Linden steepled his fingers together, rubbed them slowly down the line of his nose, and nodded. "It's all right, I won't take it any further. I think they have at least learned not to start something like this on their own initiative; and that's enough. Besides, as I said before, I trust their judgement. So as far as I'm concerned, they can go on working for us."

Fenner felt a tension leave him; but Linden was going on. "That doesn't help you, though, does it? You're no closer than you were, to finding out whether your friend did indeed phone us, let alone what she may or may not have said."

Fenner shrugged. "Right, but there's no help for that now, with my fifth column exposed. Your Director's already refused to let an outsider look through your files and see what he could find."

"You shouldn't give up so easily," Linden taunted him gently. "Okay, so your first two moles are out on parole, and won't do any more digging; but there's always me."

"What?" Fenner shook his head, staring. "You're not serious."

"Yes, I am." Linden's smile faded, and he leaned forward across the table till his hands and head were almost touching Fenner's. "Circumstances alter cases, as you said yourself. I came here prepared to be convinced, and I have been. If I didn't think the girls had been right to let you persuade them, I'd be taking the whole story to the Director right now, and they'd be out on their ears. But I do think they were right; I think this is an exception where our rules should be set aside for the general good. And believing that, what can I do but take up where the girls left off? I won't let them carry on, in case they run into trouble with someone else; they're far more vulnerable than I am, and it wouldn't be fair to them. But I'll do it myself, gladly. As you say, I could save more lives that way than by spending a lifetime as a Samaritan."

Fenner looked at him helplessly. "I don't know what to say."

"Then don't say anything. Far the best thing." Linden slid a notebook and a pen across the table. "Just write your address in there, and a phone number where I can find you. Oh, and the dates you're interested in – I think you said the critical period was about a week? I'll be in touch as soon as I can, whether I find anything or not. And do me a favour, would you? Don't tell the girls. I'd rather not have conspiratorial glances flashing at me across the room. And it's better for discipline, too, if they think their former activities are being furiously frowned on, and only overlooked out of the kindness of my heart."

Fenner nodded, and scribbled down his address, deciding not to tell even Tina. It might leave her feeling awkward, to keep a secret from her friends; and besides, he was learning that there were some hopes that were best cherished in silence, in private places, where they could root and grow and, if necessary, die with no one else being any the wiser.

"Would you like another coffee?" Linden asked, taking the notebook back. "Or are you in a hurry?"

Fenner shook his head. "No hurry. And I'd love another."

They were spending a couple of days with his parents, in Hexham; but Tina had gone on ahead in the train, and they were expecting him to be late.

When Linden came back with the coffees, Fenner said, "Tell me something, David. Why did you join the Samaritans in the first place? I think I understand why Jude and Georgina got involved, but I imagine your motives must have been different, and I'm curious."

Linden smiled. "Not that different, perhaps. It's not easy to explain, actually; but I'll try." He paused for a moment, then went on, "I had an unhappy childhood, in many ways. My mother left home when I was still a baby, she simply packed a bag one day and disappeared. I had a sister, Anne, but she was only five at the time, and my father was no kind of man to be entrusted with the care of young children. I suppose he could have put us into care, but he was too proud to accept that; he saw it as his duty to raise us himself. He was very strong on duty. That was the atmosphere we were brought up in, duty and discipline; there was no affection, apart from the bonds that developed between Anne and myself. My father left me very much in her care as soon as she was old enough, so that she became a surrogate mother to me as well as being a sister and a friend. But she died . . ."

His face and voice had a distant quality, focused on something very far away. Fenner said nothing; and after a sip of coffee, Linden continued.

"I found her body; and that broke me. I was fourteen, you see, and very immature, and suddenly I'd lost the only person I'd ever loved. I had a complete breakdown at that point, and it took me three years to recover. To begin to make sense of my life again. I managed, in the end; I found a room and a job, and built myself a new stability. But it was an empty kind of life, living only for myself. Gradually I realised that I needed something more, I needed to involve myself with others somehow. And I wanted to help people if I could, to stop them going through the same hells that I had. So I started looking around; and finally I found the Samaritans. Found my crusade, if you like."

"And they weren't concerned about your past?" Fenner asked quietly. "A breakdown, you said – did you mean literally?"

"Oh, yes. Three years in a psychiatric hospital. But the Samaritans would never turn anyone down on those grounds, provided they were satisfied that you were stable now. The selection procedure is quite rigorous in that respect, particularly if you do have a history of disturbance. But once they are satisfied, it can be an advantage, in a way. It's easier to understand what the callers are going through, if you've been there yourself. And it makes you want to help. As I say, that's basically why I joined; and you'd be surprised how many of our volunteers start by calling the Samaritans themselves."

Fenner nodded. "Like Georgie."

"Ah, she told you? Good, that saves me having to be discreet. Just so long as you don't ask me what we talked about."

"Wouldn't dream of it." The two men smiled at each other; and went on to talk about other things: Linden's slow, steady progress from clerk to Assistant Manager, taking in three different banks and a half a dozen cities; Fenner's writing, and Tina's painting; and of course mutual friends. And at last—

"Really, I'd better go." Fenner pushed himself to his feet, and peeled his wet jacket from the back of the chair. "I've still got to drive to Hexham tonight; and anyway, discipline or no discipline, it's not fair on those kids to keep them waiting any longer. Do you want to tell them they're okay, or shall I?"

"No, leave it to me." Linden smiled, and held out a hand. "I'll read them the riot act, just a little, before I let them off the hook. Drive carefully, Paul – and I'll be in touch as soon as I can, about those records."

Fenner looked for the words to thank him, and couldn't find them; so in the end he just nodded, shook Linden's hand warmly, and left.

23 Colours in Moonlight

"What I reckon," Tina said a week later, tapping the papers spread out in front of them, "is that we should sell the lot, this one included. Use some of the money to improve the cottage, and just stick the rest in the bank to keep us going until you make us rich and famous."

He nodded, and shifted her slightly on his knee. "I had a feeling you'd say something like that. But I'm not sure, love, I'm really not. Even after all the maintenance costs we can expect, we'd still be getting a bigger income from the rented flats than we would from selling them and investing the money."

They'd been to see the solicitor Ross that morning, and he'd given them written details of the whole estate, including estimated values of all the property. They'd spent the afternoon getting away from everything, leaping on a Metro to the coast and playing at being children, paddling and building sandcastles; but now, back in the city and the flat, they were talking futures and trying to make plans.

"That's better." Tina ran her fingers through his hair, then tilted his face up and kissed him carefully. "Don't do that to me again, eh? I was scared."

"Sorry." He smiled at her weakly, and got a fierce hug in return.

After a minute, Fenner felt her hand slipping inside his bathrobe again, sliding over his stomach to his groin. "Hey, mister. Want to fool around?"

He thought of the day ahead, and said, "No. I just want to hold you. Do you mind?"

She sighed heavily. "I can live with it. Who needs oats, anyway?"

"Horses. And Scots."

"And Quakers. Do they still quake, d'you know? The Quakers?"

"Don't think they ever did, really. Pity, but there you go."

They talked or were silent, kissed and touched or simply sat, as the moment required. Tina scrambled some eggs, when they grew hungry; then Fenner put the radio on and they listened to news of other people's lives, and other countries. And at half-past nine, Fenner lifted the phone and dialled the police station.

"Incident Room." It was a young man's voice, unfamiliar.

"Is Inspector Malone there?" Fenner asked. "It's Paul Fenner here."

"Just a minute, Mr Fenner. I'll see if he's . . ."

There was an explosive grunt, and the clatter of a chair falling; then Malone's voice said, "Paul. Why the hell aren't you in bed, this time of the morning?"

"Why the hell aren't you?" Fenner threw back. "You sound dead, man."

"Yeah. Been up all night. But it was worth it."

Fenner felt hope quickening inside him. "What, are you onto something?"

"No, nothing like that. I've been with Susan. I'm a father, Paul."

"Jesus. How does it feel?"

"Feels great. It's a girl, seven pounds five. Ugly little brat, I reckon, but she's healthy as shit. And the midwife told me she was a beautiful baby, and she should know."

"Congratulations. How's Susan?"

"Yes, of course we would – but who wants to be a landlord?" Tina demanded. "Especially an absentee landlord. They're a horrible breed. Maybe you don't know, you've never been a student; but honestly, students *always* hate their landlords. And I don't want to be hated like that, it's not fun."

"I don't think anyone could have hated Di," Fenner pointed out quietly.

"Okay, so maybe she was an exception – but even then, you can't tell. Some students just hate their landlords on principle. And honestly, Fenner, it'd be a hell of a hassle if we were trying to let flats here and live in Wales. They'd tie us down no end. I think we should just get free of them. Take the money and run."

She reached for the pack of cigarettes by the ash-tray, shook it, and scowled. "You pig, you smoked the last of them. And that was my pack, too. Have you got a secret stash somewhere?"

He shook his head. "Sorry, I'm not that organised at the moment. Why do you think I was smoking yours?" He eased her off his knee onto the floor and stood up. "I'll go up to the newsagent before he shuts. That's if you've got any cash?"

"On the mantelpiece in the bedroom. There's a fiver in that carved wooden box. Go on, quick, or you'll have to go all the way to the garage."

Fenner grinned. "Take the money and run."

Coming out of the newsagent with two packs of Winston and some rolling-tobacco, wondering for the hundredth time just when he would hear from David Linden, Fenner saw him walking down the hill just ahead. For a moment it seemed too much of a coincidence to swallow; but all the same, it was so. Even from the back, his hair and build were unmistakable, as was the easy grace with which he moved.

Fenner quickened his pace until the two men were walking side by side. Linden glanced across sharply, then smiled. "Paul. Hullo. I was just coming to find you."

"That's what I was hoping." There was only one question on Fenner's tongue; but the answer would change things so irrevocably, whether it was yes or no, that he hesitated to ask it bluntly, here in the street. "Come on down, you can meet Tina."

Linden hesitated, then shook his head. "I'd rather not, if you don't mind. Not just now. It might be simpler if we went to find a pub, and talked there."

"Okay, then," Fenner said, "I'll introduce you to my local. Only I'd better drop some of this through the letter-box first, or Tina'll kill me when I get home."

So Fenner posted cigarettes through his door, and rattled the knocker to let Tina know they were there. Then he and Linden went on down, towards the river and the Green Man.

They made their way into the lounge bar, and Linden said, "Look, there's a table over there in the corner. You go and claim it, while I get the drinks. What are you having?"

"Just a tomato juice, please." Fenner was already moving towards the table. "And a box of matches, if you don't mind."

"Have something a bit stronger than that," Linden suggested quietly. "You'll want it, I warn you."

Which was the first definite indication that the news might be bad. Fenner noted it; but there would be time enough soon to pursue that. "No, I mean it, thanks. Just a tomato juice. I don't drink."

"Really?" Linden looked surprised. Fenner smiled, at a sudden memory of Tina's flailing hand sending a glass smashing into a wall, scattering every surface with an amber dew.

"I'm not allowed to," he said, and headed for the table.

It took Linden a few minutes to get served; watching him, Fenner thought that perhaps they had done this the wrong way round. Karen the barmaid had known him for years, since the old days, when he was in here every night that he wasn't working, putting away endless pints and double Scotches. He could have caught her eye in a moment.

When Linden did finally get Karen's attention, Fenner was surprised to see some kind of altercation between them. As she poured the tomato juice, Karen shook her head vehemently, glanced across the bar at Fenner and said something to Linden in a sharp undertone. He shrugged and paid her, then picked up Fenner's drink and his own pint of lager and carried them over.

He seemed to have forgotten the matches. As he sat down,

Fenner decided not to say anything, and to try to get through the session without smoking. If it ran to a second round of drinks, he could buy matches himself at the bar.

But just at that moment, Linden drew the fresh pack of cigarettes on the table. "Oh, damn. I didn't get your matches, did I? Here." He took a box of Swan from his jacket pocket, and slid it across.

Fenner started to tear open the Cellophane around the cigarettes, saying, "I didn't think you smoked?"

"I don't," Linden said. "Why?"

"Just that I've never met a non-smoker who carried matches around. Not regularly, anyway."

"Comes of working for the Sams," Linden said, smiling. "You really do learn to be prepared. I usually have cigarettes too, when I'm on emergency duty, just in case I'm asked for them."

"Not wanting to be facetious – but how do you pass cigarettes down the phone?"

"You don't. But many clients we meet face to face, eventually. We do try to arrange meetings in advance, but sometimes a client wants to meet right there and then, so we have a Flying Squad. Those are the times when you're most likely to have someone demanding a fag, or just a light. It's funny how many people will buy cigarettes and then run out of matches."

"No, it isn't," Fenner said, remembering times when he'd had to light cigarettes on an electric fire, for that very reason. "It's not funny at all. But listen, while we're talking about the Samaritans, let's have it. Did you find anything?"

"I'm sorry," said Linden. "I didn't. I don't believe there's anything to be found."

Fenner nodded, watching his fingers take a match from the box and strike it. He lit a cigarette as Linden went on, "I checked back on every call we had, between the dates you gave me; and there was nothing that accorded with what you told me of Diana. I'm afraid that she must just have had the number for reference, in case a time came when she couldn't cope any longer. She certainly didn't ring us, under her own name or any other."

"Okay," Fenner said heavily. "I'll just have to look somewhere else. If there's anywhere else to look. But thanks anyway, David. I appreciate your help."

"You're welcome," Linden said. "I'm only sorry I couldn't find anything for you. But listen, do get in touch if there's anything else I can do, won't you? And don't get too downhearted . . ."

Fenner smiled, and shook his head. Linden drained his pint, stood up and said goodnight, and was gone. Fenner sat still for a few minutes, trying to come to terms with this sudden destruction of hope; then he got abruptly to his feet and headed towards the door.

As he passed the bar, Karen called out to him. "Hey, Paul – who was that guy?"

"Hullo, love." Fenner grinned at her. "He's just someone I met, that's all. Why, are you getting lusty?"

She shook her head, refusing to smile. "It's not that. I just – well, I thought I ought to warn you, that's all. If you make a habit of drinking with him."

"I don't. But warn me of what?"

"He asked me to slip a vodka into your drink, on the quiet. I didn't do it, of course; but he might try it again, some place where the bar staff don't know you."

For a second Fenner's mouth was warm with the remembered taste of a Bloody Mary, innocently tomato, with the spirit hidden like a stiletto beneath the surface. He thought of the damage that even one drink could do to him now, of how precarious his safety was; and a shiver shook his body.

"Well," he said weakly, "you can't blame him, really. He was probably just trying to cheer me up. He knew I'd be depressed by the news he had for me. And I told him I'd stopped drinking, but I didn't tell him why. He can't have known . . ."

But you did know. Didn't you, David? You knew, all right. You'd read his book.

And you're feeling rather disappointed, as you walk slowly home. It would have been a new and novel way to destroy a man, pushing him off down the slope into alcoholism. Slower than anything you'd tried before, of course, but that's not important. He'd be no threat, once you'd started him drinking again. You're sure of that. He might have fought his way back up that slope once, but no one could do it twice.

It's a failure that niggles at you; you should have realised that the barmaid might know him. You should have been prepared for that.

But still, it doesn't matter. Not in the long run. There'll be other chances, other days. Or other nights: because you're a creature of the night, and always have been. Some colours only show in moonlight.

Part Four

Violent Ends

First things first – and for you at least, first things are the strongest. Memory's like a river, slow as time; caught on the same current, your childhood truths drift always in the corners of your eye, too close to be ignored or abandoned, too far off to be clung to.

Truths like this:

David sits under the table, waiting for Anne.

He knows she'll come. She always comes. He'll hear her footsteps quick in the hall, and the door opening; and then perhaps a giggle, before she lifts the corner of the hanging lace tablecloth and peers beneath. She'll make found-you noises, and he'll crawl out and take her hand; and they'll go into the kitchen together. She'll wash his face and hands, and cook their tea. Then she'll play with him, and maybe it'll be bath-night before bed, hot water and slippery soap, warm towels and hugging him and laughing . . .

So he waits in his private place until he hears a noise, which is the front door closing; and thinks this is Anne coming in. But the footsteps are slower and heavier, coming to the drawing-room door, coming in; and David is very still, only his eyes moving as they follow his father's movements through the holes in the lace.

Chair-springs creak and settle out of his sight, paper rustles, his father coughs lightly. He'll see, if Anne comes for David now. He'll be angry. *Little boys are not to play in the drawing-room, is that understood?*

But he didn't close the hall door before he sat down; and it's not far to the door from where David is. Perhaps, if he's very careful and very quiet, he can crawl out and not be noticed, and wait for Anne in the kitchen . . .

David edges one hand out into the light, and the other after it. He huddles close to the wall, letting the lace cloth slide back over his left shoulder as he inches towards the door. His father is turned away from him, reading a newspaper; David moves a little faster, seeing his path clear through to the hall. He doesn't notice as the dangling lace tangles itself with the buckle of his shoe. He crawls one step and another; and feels something check his foot for a moment. He glances back, but jerks his leg hard at the same time, to free it.

And sees the tablecloth sliding off the well-polished wood, taking with it three small porcelain bowls and a hand-painted figurine.

Still silent, he watches them fall and listens to their breaking; then he looks round, to face his father.

A big man, he looks bigger than ever now, rising to see. Light flashes across his spectacles, hiding his stone-grey eyes behind blank glass. Like David, he says nothing; his anger, like David's fear, is expressed in silence.

David is still crouched on hands and knees, frozen. His father crosses the room in three strides, and picks him up by the waistband of his shorts. The lace cloth hangs ridiculously from his foot. His father tears it free, and lets it fall; then drops David lengthwise along the back of a stout armchair, arms and legs straddling it. David digs his fingers into the fabric and screws his eyes shut, hearing his father unbuckle the narrow belt he wears.

Dimly, as the thin leather bites across his shoulders, David hears the front door quietly closing. A thin whimper slips from him as he turns his head. That, and the hiss of the belt cutting the air, are warning enough; when Anne appears in the doorway, she knows already what she will see. As silent as the others, she stands with one hand resting on the jamb. Her eyes find David's, and her face counts the blows.

After nine strokes David is sobbing and choking, his skin burning where the leather has marked it. His father drops him on the carpet and turns to Anne.

"Well, miss? Have I not told you again and again that I hold you responsible for your brother's behaviour?"

"Yes, father." Anne's voice is quiet and dull, like someone who has lived with fear too long.

He doubles the belt over, and slaps it into his palm. "Fetch a chair from the hall. And pull that dress down off your shoulders."

At nearly nine years old, she is too tall to be thrown across the back of an easy-chair. She must kneel and bend over the seat of an upright, her face dropped and hidden by lank blonde hair, only her knuckles for David to watch, rhythmically turning white as they clench on the struts of the chair-back, as the belt sears across her shoulders.

Truths like this:

And afterwards there are still no words for them, only a shuddering relief as he locks them into the tiny back bedroom. They will go hungry now until the morning, but they are used to that; and it is no punishment for them to be alone together. He has locked himself out, and they are safe for the night.

David has a truckle-bed set across the end wall, at the foot of his sister's. He perches on the edge of the horsehair mattress, pale and shaking, his face blotched with crying. Everything hurts.

He watches Anne sink down onto her own bed. Her dress is still pulled down to her waist, and he can see blood on her shoulders, where the belt has broken the skin. She buries her face in her hands, to be private for a minute; then she looks up and holds out her hand to him.

He goes over to stand in front of her, the first steps of a familiar dance. Slowly and carefully she undresses him, leaving his shirt until last, peeling it gently away from his back. He flinches, and she kisses him, patting his bare leg.

"Brave boy," she whispers; and that's as good as a kiss, or better.

She motions for him to lie on her bed, face-down. He hears the click of a cupboard door and squirms slightly, anticipating the cold touch of the cream she keeps there for nights like this.

She rubs it in lightly, not pressing hard enough to hurt; and he feels the fire dying out of his skin. Then she pulls her own clothes off, and rubs the cream into her shoulders, her face showing nothing when her fingers come away streaked with pink and red.

She wipes her hands on an old towel and lies down beside David, slipping one arm under his head for comfort. He puts his own small hand onto her arm and they stare into each other's eyes, sharing pain and warmth and silence. Glad that it's summer, and the nights hot enough not to need blankets;

even a sheet would keep them painfully awake tonight. Glad that another day is over, they're a day older and a day stronger, perhaps even a day closer to the end of it, if shadow can have an end. Glad that they have the night, the whole night and the silence of it.

Glad that they're not alone.

25 *Going Back*

"Well, that's it then, isn't it?"

"Is it?"

They faced each other across the kitchen table; and it might as well have been barbed wire that stood between them, they were so brutally divided.

"Come on, Fenner. Face the facts for a change, why don't you? It's over; even you can't kid yourself any more. You've tried, and you've failed like the rest of them. So why don't we stop tearing ourselves to bits over it all, and just go home?"

When he said nothing, she reached out slowly to touch his arm. "Please, Fenner. You've done everything you can; Diana would have nothing to blame you for. You did try. But it'd be stupid to go on and on, smashing yourself against a brick wall for nothing. You're never going to find anything now, it's all too long ago."

"Maybe. Maybe it is too late now. But it isn't over, Tina. It won't be over as long as that guy is still out there, running free." Tina snorted, and he went on quickly. "No, listen. This isn't a personal crusade any more; I've paid my debt to Diana. But to the Butcher there wasn't anything special about Diana's murder, the way there was to us. For him, she was just one more body in a line – and he hasn't reached the end of that line yet. He hasn't finished."

Tina opened her mouth, hesitated – then shrugged, and said it anyway. "So what? It's not your concern. You're not a part of this any more, you can just up and leave it, any time. You've *got* to, Fenner . . ."

"But I can't. I've made myself a part of it again; and it's a part of me too, now. If we go back to Wales tomorrow, I won't leave the Butcher behind me. He'll come with us, looking over my shoulder and laughing all the way. And when he kills again, next week or next month or next year, whenever, d'you think I'll just be able to read about it in the paper, and shrug, and go out and feed the fucking goats like nothing has happened? Nothing that touched me at all?"

"You might have to, in the end," she suggested quietly. "The way he's going, this guy could beat you all."

"He's human," Fenner snapped. "He'll make a mistake sometime."

"And you're just going to sit around and wait till he does, is that it? Wait for his next murder, and the next, and the one after that?"

"For Christ's sake, Tina, I don't *know*! But – the way I feel at the moment, yes. If I have to. When he does make a mistake, then the more people there are looking for it, the better our chances of spotting it. I could still find something that Mike and the others had missed. And that'd make it worth the waiting, however long it takes."

"Would it?" Tina asked. "If you wait that long, you'll be waiting alone. I won't be here. Will it still be worth it then?"

He looked at her, and didn't have an answer.

After a long minute, she got up and left the kitchen. He heard her walking slowly and deliberately through the flat; heard her pause on the landing, heard the rustle of her jacket as she pulled it on; heard her run down the stairs and out. He could even hear the effort she made, not to slam the door behind her.

Making a sudden decision, Fenner phoned the station, only to be told that Malone had gone home for the night.

"Well, thank God for that, anyway," he grunted, remembering the exhausted shadows on Mike's face the last time he'd seen him. "At least he hasn't forgotten that he's got a home. How long since he left?"

"About twenty minutes, sir."

Fenner rung off, and started to dial Mike's number; but he stopped after two digits, and cradled the receiver. If he spoke to Mike on the phone, then in ten or fifteen minutes he would hang up and be alone again, having to face the empty flat, to find some way of facing it down until Tina chose to come back . . .

A minute later he was clattering down the stairs with the car-keys in his hand. He'd left a note under the handle of the kettle, where she'd be sure to find it when she came in. *Gone to Mike's; back whenever. Thanks for coming home. Love, F.*

And under the scrawled initial he'd put two crosses, two kisses. Just to remind her – or perhaps to remind himself. But he was still thinking about that last question of hers, as he left the flat and unlocked the car; and he still didn't have an answer.

Mike answered his knock almost immediately, and led him through to the kitchen. He made Fenner a coffee, and got a beer for himself, moving with the sharp jerkiness of great fatigue, and talking nonstop, as if that were the only thing that stopped him falling asleep there and then.

". . . Susan's still awake, she's upstairs in bed, reading. I don't know if she'll come down, but I'll take you up, if not. You must say hullo to Flick, while you're here."

"Hullo to *who*?"

"Flick." Mike grinned. "Felicity-Anne, to her grandmother; but we're going to call her Flick. We figured she was bound to shorten it to something outrageous as soon as she was old enough, so we thought we'd get in first. Don't you like it?"

"As a matter of fact I do, in a funny sort of way. But listen, Mike, just in case Susan does come down, can we get something out of the way first?"

Mike sighed, and nodded. "Yeah, sure. You want to know how we're doing, right? Well, the computer's still whizzing away, but it hasn't told us anything yet. If you ask me, it's one big bloody waste of time; but the Chief's completely sold on it. I think he's hoping to blind the public with science – like, if he keeps shouting loud enough about modern technology, nobody'll notice that the cells are still empty. Or if they do notice, they won't think it's his fault. I mean, anyone who can hide from a computer must be some kind of supervillain, right? Except it isn't true. A computer's just a fancy filing system, and it's useless without something relevant to file." He took a slow swig of his beer, and scowled. "The Chief's got us running round on a giant PR exercise, that's all. It's not getting us anywhere, and I'm sick to death of the whole caper.

I'd jack it in, if there was anything else I was fit for. But what are you up to, still snooping?"

Fenner nodded. "I've been checking up on the Samaritans connection. Digging a bit deeper, to see if anything turned up."

"How did you manage that?" Mike asked, interested.

"Contacts. Friends of Tina's." That was as far as Fenner would go; he wouldn't share names and details, even with Mike. He felt that he owed it to Linden and the girls to keep their involvement secret. "But it was just one more waste of time. Not even worth putting in your computer. It's as sure as anything can be, that Diana didn't phone them."

"Right." Mike absorbed that, then said, "Why don't you go home, Paul? Back to Wales?"

"Not you, too!" Fenner exploded. "Tina stormed out on me tonight, because I said no to that."

"So why don't you listen to her? It doesn't make sense, you hanging on like this. The chances are you'll never find anything but dead ends. Why not cut your losses and get the hell out of it? It's not your fight, Paul, it never was."

"I've made it mine. And at least I'm fighting. You said it yourself, all you're doing is working a PR exercise to save the Chief's neck. Look, this Samaritans lead didn't come to anything, okay – but suppose it had? You'd have missed it anyway, because you let yourselves be fobbed off by some pillock with a rulebook. But I would've found it. And as long as there's a chance of that happening again, I can't just up and leave. Can I? *Can I?*"

Mike sighed, and drained his glass. "All right, I don't suppose you can. But what are you going to do now? Where the hell are you going to look?"

Fenner didn't have any answer to that one, either. But then Susan came in, wearing an embroidered Chinese dressing-gown and clutching a crying baby.

"Hullo, Paul." She gave him a tired smile, and turned to Mike. "Sorry, love, but she needs changing again. If you do that, then I'll feed her and we can put her down for the night."

It was a sudden and startling shift of focus; and somehow that question and everything else got forgotten, overshadowed by the chaotic demands of young Felicity-Anne. Fenner watched Mike in a new and strange role, as he cleaned and changed her; then he talked quietly to Susan while the baby fed at her breast. That was strange too, something once erotic turned purely functional; and the process was fascinating to watch, and oddly reassuring. That he could sit and watch Susan's baby suckling at Susan's breast, and feel neither bitterness nor desire, but only a warm fondness and an unfocused wish that they might always be as content as they were at that moment; it meant, or it seemed to mean, that the last cold ashes of his marriage had finally fallen away, leaving him free to build something new with Susan. Something good, that would hold nothing over from the past – neither the sexual attraction that had brought and tied them together, nor the jealousies and mistrust that had torn them apart.

"Here Paul – be a good uncle and hold her for a minute?"

He took the baby cheerfully, and made rude noises at her while her mother went to the toilet and her father laughed; and shortly after that he left them, seeing that they both needed sleep more than company, and knowing that Felicity-Anne wasn't likely to give them more than a few hours undisturbed.

The flat was dark and still when he got in, with no sign of Tina. His note was still where he had left it, under the handle of the kettle; there was an ironic twist now to the simple faith that underlay it, the *Thanks for coming home*, that made him shiver as he destroyed it.

He put a record on and went to bed, leaving the doors open so that he could hear the music and listen out for Tina at the same time.

She came back sooner than he'd expected; and after moving restlessly around the flat for a minute, she appeared in the doorway, still with her jacket on.

"Fenner? You awake?"

The sudden flare of his cigarette should have been answer enough, as he inhaled; but he took it from his lips and said, "Yes."

"Good. I – I want to talk to you . . ."

"Why don't you clean your teeth, and get rid of all that gear?" Fenner suggested quietly. "I'm not going to fall asleep on you, and if we've got to talk we might as well do it friendly."

"No." Her voice was determined in the darkness. "This is serious, Fenner. I'm not fooling."

"Christ." His voice was oddly dull to his own ears, as he absorbed an unexpected hurt. "Have things got that bad between us, then? That you can't even talk to me without barriers between us, covers and clothes and God knows what else?"

"That wasn't what I *meant*, Fenner! I just, I don't want to be distracted, that's all . . . And anyway, after I've said, you might not be feeling that friendly; and I just thought, maybe it might be easier if one of us could just get up and go away for a bit . . ."

Fenner didn't say anything, he just lay there and let her listen to herself; and after a pause she whispered, "Oh, *bugger* you!"

She wrenched her boots off and flung them across the room. The rest of her clothes followed, with the sharp sound of fabric tearing. She was breathing fast and angry, and when she tumbled under the duvet Fenner could feel the tension in her muscles before he so much as touched her.

"Happy now?" she demanded abruptly, lying stiffly next to him in the wide bed.

"You didn't clean your teeth." He was testing her mood, to see how fragile this defensive anger was; when she made no reply, he reached out and pulled her closer, till her head was nestled on his shoulder. "Friendly, I said; and friendly it is. Right?"

"All right." She relaxed a little, resting one hand on his chest; but he could still feel the tautness inside her, like sprung steel ready to snap.

"Right. So where did you go tonight?" He was trying to help her, to give her an easy way in, and she knew it. Her lips nuzzled his collar-bone briefly, gratefully, before she said, "Jude and Georgina's. Where else?"

Right. Where else. "And?"

"And, well, we talked about things, and . . ." He felt finger-nails scrape his skin, as her hand clenched into a fist. "And, damn it, Fenner, I want to go home! Now, this weekend I want to get back where we belong."

"I know you do," he said wearily. "But it doesn't work like that, Tina. I told you. Part of me belongs here, until this thing's cleared up."

"Only because you want it to. But anyway," she went on hurriedly, as he stirred impatiently beneath her, "I don't want to argue about that, it's not the point. What it is, is that I *don't* belong here. This isn't my life, and I don't want to live it." There was a short silence, and Fenner stamped down hard on his spinning mind, refusing to second-guess her. Refusing to see the obvious until she actually said it.

"I'm going back." With his eyes closed, Fenner pictured her whispered words as something physical, like writing on a steamed-up window, or letters drawn in dust. Barely real, but all the more threatening because of that. Shadow-words, with a shadow-world close behind them. "Whether you come or not."

"So soon?" This was what she'd threatened, only a few hours earlier; but now it was suddenly here, lying between them like an extra layer of skin, cold and dead to the touch.

"Yes. We've got to face it sometime, Fenner, and it might as well be now." Her voice became harder and tougher, and Fenner could almost hear Jude talking behind her, giving her the words. "I've stuck it out this long, for your sake; now it's your turn. You choose. You stay here, or you come with me."

A straight choice it might be, but it was blackmail too. If she went, he'd be left with the shadows; and he might never find a way out, back to her. She was throwing everything they had into his hands, all the love and trust and surety they'd found together, risking it all to try to drag him back with her. If they separated now, there'd be little or nothing left of it by the time they came together again; it would drip between his fingers like water, and lose itself in dryness.

Quite unconsciously, Fenner's hands had cupped together in the small of Tina's back, the fingers pressing tightly against each other as if trying to contain something liquid and precious. But she was using their love as a weapon against him; and a brief flicker of anger made him spread his fingers wide, while his eyes saw water in the darkness, draining into hot sand.

"Sorry," he said, "I'm staying."

That was Wednesday. From then till the weekend, both he and Tina seemed to spend their time waiting and hoping for something to happen, to change either her mind or his. But the days followed each other like mechanical soldiers, each of them in step, with nothing new to offer; and then it was

Saturday, and she was standing on the platform with a ticket in her hand.

And he was a couple of yards away, just looking at her; and his hands were empty.

Jude and Georgina had come too, to see her off. They talked a little between themselves, and watched for the train. It came before any of them were ready; and in the chaotic hustle of passengers getting off and passengers boarding, of greetings and partings and panics, Fenner seemed to be the only one standing still, with nothing to say or do. The girls helped Tina get her luggage on, and claim a seat with her jacket; then they got off, and she came with them to say goodbye. She hugged Jude, and kissed Georgina; but when she turned to Fenner, it was more than either of them could stand, to touch each other.

"Goodbye, then," was all she said; and he nodded.

"Phone me."

"I will. But – give me a week or two, eh?"

"Yeah," he said; and felt the same relief he could see on her face. It would feel like stirring dull coals to life with his bare hand, or maybe like dying again, as he was dying now; and tomorrow is always a better day to die.

Then a guard was slamming doors at the other end of the train, and they both knew time had run out on them. Her eyes held him for a moment longer; but when Jude touched her elbow lightly, she turned and climbed into the train without looking back. The sun was shining on the windows, so that he could only dimly see her through glass that reflected his own haggard face.

Then the train jerked, and ran smoothly out; and he couldn't see her at all.

26 Turn and Turn, and Turn Again

Fear of your father, love of your sister.

If anyone's life can be founded on and sustained by two things, woven from two facts, two feelings – two truths – then yours was, David. Anne made you warm, and your father made you cold again; and you were turned from one to the other as easily and as often as a coin is turned in someone's pocket.

Coins only have two faces to meet the world with, and so did you. But the world expects – requires – more than that of its citizens, even of its children. And you didn't understand that, did you? You didn't know what to do with other people; so you just did what you could.

You turned.

Outside the gate after school, outside the wire, there is always a line of mothers waiting; and inside always a pack of children jostling and running down the slight slope of the tarmac playground to the gate. With their eyes watching through the wire, and perhaps one gloved hand curled through the links, the mothers talk and laugh amongst themselves while they wait; the children fight or shout or simply run, with news or needs too urgent for delay.

Behind the pack, David follows on alone, hands in pockets and eyes on the ground, with no one to look for or reach for and no reason to hurry. Anne is in the primary school on the other side of the wall; her classes end twenty minutes after his, and he must stay inside the gates until she comes for him, tall and ten years old. He doesn't mind that twenty minutes' lag, any more than he minds the whole day's lag before it. Every minute apart is a minute wasted, a minute of nothing; but he has learned not to count them. Unlike his classmates who live in an immediate world and need everything now, he has learned to wait.

(Like a coin balanced on its edge, empty of purpose, caught between being and being. Waiting to be pushed, to fall one way or the other, into fear or into love.)

So, waiting, David sits on the wall inside the wire as the last of the mothers disperse with their sons and daughters. Waiting is a slow thing, and it takes him a minute or two to notice that one boy, a face he knows from his own class, is still there by the gate, his hands hooked through the wire as his eyes stare down the road and his cheeks shake. This is a boy who has never learned David's lessons, who tries to weave a familiar figure from every inconsequent shadow, every trick of the light.

Soon, the boy comes to stand beside David. He sighs heavily, which fails to draw more than a quick glance; so he does it again, then nudges David, needing to talk.

"Is your mum late too?" And even as he says it he looks again up the road, just in case. And misses David's brief shake of the head. Waits a second, and says, "Is she?"

"No."

"Why're you waiting, then?"

David hesitates, reluctant to share even this much of his private truth with someone who doesn't belong; then, unwillingly, "For my sister."

"In the big school?" The boy's eyes move to the red-tiled roofs that can be seen above the dividing wall.

"Yes."

The boy nods; he's heard that the big children aren't let out till later. But: "Why doesn't your mum come for you, then?"

"I haven't got a mum."

The boy stares, forgetting for a moment even that he does have a mother, and she's late. "Why not?"

"She ran away," David says,

(because your father didn't even have the humanity to lie to you, and you'd never learned to lie on your own account)

"when I was one."

"Who looks after you, then?" A mother is part of the necessary order of things, and the boy's imagination falters at the notion of life without.

"My sister. Anne."

(And the thought of her and the sound of her name on your own lips were enough to topple you like a balanced coin falling, to stop you waiting and start you needing. Your hands clenched impotently on nothing, wishing they gripped her wrists. The taste and touch of urgency was hot in the back of your throat, and hot down between your legs; you wanted to cry, you wanted to go to the toilet. You wanted Anne, the hands and voice and smell of her tight around you, the two of you alone and the world locked out.)

And now the boy's mother comes suddenly, hurrying, running with straight legs to bring him kisses and apologies, and leads him away by the hand almost without noticing David, entirely without speaking to him. And the boy goes with her barely hearing what she says as he thinks of what he'll say to his best friend tomorrow – how he talked to that strange boy, the thin one who never talks to anyone. How the thin boy's mother ran away, which makes him doubly strange.

The boy glances back once through the wire; but he can only see David's back swaying restlessly from side to side, and that's not enough, he can't interpret it. He'd need to see the tears wet on David's pale cheeks, and the way he crosses his legs, recrosses them, shuffles his feet on the tarmac. Looks towards the toilets on the far side of the playground, looks back down the road to see if the big children are coming out yet, if Anne is coming. Hears a door slam, voices, sees teachers coming out of the school building; and is suddenly on his feet and running, rubbing his arm across his eyes as he dashes to the toilet.

Unable to wait.

And you turned:

On the fourth day of Anne's sickness, she gets out of bed and smiles weakly at David.

"See?" she says, a thin sweat like dew on her temples. "I feel fine this morning. You'd better get dressed and hurry off to school. Seven years old is big enough to go by yourself."

"No." David's voice is quiet, and definite. He hasn't left her alone since the illness took her; and he doesn't mean to until he's sure that she's well again. School counts for nothing.

"David, you *must*. It's the law." She looks anxious, reaching out to pull him close, so that he nestles against her, his hands clutching at the thick stuff of her dressing-gown. "They'll come to see father if you don't, and make trouble for him. And you know what'll happen to us then."

He shivers, feeling the burn of leather on his skin. She holds him tighter, and turns his face up to her. "You will go, won't you, love? For me?"

And it's that appeal that sends him down the road to school. It's knowing that the belt would cut her too, that there would be blood on her skin and that it would be for him that she was bleeding.

At register, Miss Moore the teacher glances up when she calls David's name, and hears him answer. "You've been away for three days, David. Why was that?"

"I was at home, Miss Moore."

Someone giggles, and the teacher frowns. "Yes, but why? Were you ill?"

"No, Miss Moore."

Miss Moore's frown is deeper now. "Have you brought a note from . . . from your father" – as, just in time, she remembers what she knows of his circumstances and bites back the word 'mother' – "to explain why you were away?"

"No, Miss Moore."

She hesitates, then asks softly, "David, does your father know you weren't at school for those three days?"

"No, Miss Moore." His father asks no questions; obedience to his own and other adult authority is simply assumed, until disobedience can be proven. Then it is punished. David believes that his father is barely aware of Anne's illness, let alone of David's nursing.

Miss Moore sighs shortly. "Very well, then." She says nothing further to David, merely making a mark against his name and moving on down the register.

But when the class moves through to the hall for assembly, David sees her have a word with the headmaster, sees him bend to listen, nod, and throw a frowning glance in David's direction. And after the hymn and prayers, after school announcements, the headmaster picks up a stout ruler from the lectern and says, "I've talked to you children already this term about the word truancy, and what it means. If you've been away from school, even for one morning, you *must* bring a note from your parents to explain why. I have told you this; and I have told you that anyone who fails to bring such a note will be punished. Come out here, David Linden."

Already expecting this, David doesn't jump at the sound of his name, though his legs are trembling as he walks to the front of the hall. For once he has to put into words what is usually only a feeling, reminding himself fiercely that it doesn't matter what happens to him here at school.

(And by giving it words, of course, you made it untrue; and you knew that, didn't you? Even then you knew it. You could feel the balance shifting, the coin beginning to fall.)

The headmaster is a tall man, almost as tall as David's father; and looking at him, at eyes hidden behind black-rimmed spectacles, David sees only his father's coldness, the same icy anger at being flouted and the same intention to punish.

(Which was when the coin spun down to fall with a clatter in your head, loud enough to drown your own tongue and all the world but his. Because looking at him, you saw your father; and you only had one face to show your father.)

"David, you have been absent for the last three days. Have you brought a note?"

Stillness and silence are all that David's fear leaves him with; so he stands and says nothing, not even waiting now, only afraid.

"Well?" Silence seems to anger the headmaster more, makes him colder, more like David's father. David is too scared now even to believe that there might be a difference, that they might at least live and breathe in two separate bodies. "If you tell me where you were, and why you didn't come to school . . ."

It is a last chance offered; but David doesn't even recognise it as such. All he knows now is that his father has taken a grip on this unlife at school, and made it real. Made it bad. And Anne is far away, beyond call or comfort . . .

"Very well, then, boy. If you will be stubborn. Hold out your hands." David holds out his hands palm upwards, as he has seen other children do for other crimes. The ruler whistles through an arc, and slashes across the soft pads of his fingers. David whimpers, and the ruler rises for another stroke.

After three blows on each hand, the ruler is returned to the lectern.

"Go back to your place, boy. And be warned. If this happens again, I shan't simply punish you myself. I will also write to your father."

David looks at his red, throbbing hands, and thinks, *You are my father.*

And you turned again.

"No, Stuart, forty-three is wrong, too. You're not concentrating. Who thinks they've got the right answer?"

She looks between the waving hands, and says, "David? What do you think the answer is?"

David's hands are both lying flat on the desk-top, volunteering nothing. He blinks at her, and says, "Thirty-seven, Miss Collinson."

"That's quite right. Thirty-seven." She turns to write it on the board, then looks back at him over her shoulder. "David? Why didn't you have your hand up?"

He says nothing, hoping to baffle her with silence; but Miss Collinson is persistent. "David? Answer me, please. You knew your answer was right, didn't you?"

"Yes, Miss Collinson." It had been easy, like all the work she gave them. Like schoolwork always had been.

"Then why didn't you put your hand up, to tell me? You've been here long enough, you know what you're supposed to do."

"Yes, Miss Collinson."

She frowns, beginning to be irritated by the blank wall of his replies. But a glance at the clock reminds her that there is not much time left, and several more sums to be looked at. "Well, I'll expect you to join in in future, please. Put your hand up even if you only think you know. It's no disgrace to be wrong."

"Yes, Miss Collinson."

She almost snaps at him; but bites it back in time, and looks down at her book. "Number seven, then." Hands thrust immediately into the air; David's is not one of them. She bites her lip, and says, "No, put your hands down. Stuart, let's see if you had better luck with this one."

"Er, twenty-one, miss?" But Stuart's only guessing. Again Miss Collinson ignores the hands of the willing and looks to David in the corner.

"Twenty-three, Miss Collinson."

"That's right, David." She essays a smile. "You see, it doesn't hurt, does it? Put your hand up if you know the answer, please."

There are three more questions; and for each of them, she asks Stuart first and then David. Each of them Stuart gets wrong, and David right. And not once does David raise his hand, to offer an answer.

After the lesson, she calls both boys over to her desk. When the rest of the class has scattered, she turns to Stuart, who is staring at his feet and shuffling.

"You simply weren't trying, were you? All those sums were

easy, if you'd only thought about what you were doing. You didn't get a single one right; and that's not good enough. I shall set you a special test tomorrow, that I want you to do during playtime; and if you don't do better then, there will be trouble. Is that understood?"

Stuart mumbles something.

"Very well, then. Off you go." He clatters out of the room, and she moves her attention to David. "Now then, David. Why did you deliberately disobey me? You knew all those answers; I think you always do know the answers, don't you? And I always have to ask you. I've never seen you with your hand up, all the weeks you've been in my class. I told you to join in today, and I might as well have said nothing, for all the notice you took."

A silence, which her breathing and David's only make the louder. "Well?" she says at last. "I'm waiting for an explanation."

David shrugs helplessly. How to explain that none of this is real to him – that she herself isn't real? That nothing about school is real except in moments, and that the less he involves himself the less real it seems? He hasn't even got the words to explain it to himself, let alone to her. It's just one of his truths.

"I – I don't know," he stammers at last, helpless in the grip of something greater than he can describe.

"And it isn't just my class, is it? It isn't just me. I've talked to the other teachers about you; and Miss Moore and Mrs Cowley both said that you were just the same with them. I know you're shy, but it's not that difficult, is it? To put your hand up, when you know the answer to a question?"

David fidgets with his fingers, thinking, *I just want to be left alone*. Knowing that he can't say it – and, because that's all of the truth that he can put into words, having nothing to say.

At last she lets him go, with a warning that in future she will punish his holding back as she would punish any other blatant disobedience.

Outside, in the playground, Stuart is waiting for him, and three of Stuart's friends.

(And you knew what they were waiting for, didn't you, David? As soon as you saw them, you knew. This too was punishment.)

"Hey, weirdie," Stuart says, shoving him back against the wall. "Do you think you're smart, then?"

There are two answers to that question, and both are fatal. So as usual, David falls back on silence, looking over Stuart's shoulder, hoping to catch a glimpse of Anne through the fence. David's three inches taller than the other boy, heavy-boned but perilously thin. He'd be no match for the stocky Stuart even if he knew anything about fighting; and all he knows is pain, and how to be hurt.

"D'you think it was smart, to make me look stupid like you did?" Stuart demands, his face mottled with anger as he gives David another shove. His friends are moving all the time, watching, enjoying the entertainment but keeping an eye out for teachers or parents coming to intervene.

"Just – just leave me alone, will you?" David tries to push past, but Stuart grabs his arm and pulls him back.

"I've had enough of you, weirdie," he says. "I'm going to teach you a lesson. And if you sneak about who it was done this to you, you'll catch it twice as bad tomorrow. Right?"

David just looks at him, not afraid,

(because it wasn't pain that frightened you, not ever. It was your father and the anger of him, the cold anger. Not the pain)

just wishing that Anne would come and it would all be over.

Goaded by David's detached silence, Stuart finally stops talking and swings his fist. David ducks, and it catches him on the side of the head. He tries to hit back, but it's only a gesture, a feeble wave of the fist. Then Stuart comes in with both hands and his anger blazing,

(and it wasn't Stuart's kind of anger, hot and immediate, that frightened you either. Only your father's, and the ice you saw in other men that made them like your father)

hitting David on the face and body and the face again, hitting and hitting until finally David stumbles and falls onto the damp tarmac. Looking down, Stuart can see blood and tears mingling on David's cheeks. He lashes out once with his foot, to show his friends that he's not afraid of anything, even breaking the rules; then they run off down the slope to the gate and away.

David moans, and pulls his legs up to his chest. He doesn't even try to stand; he just curls up tight, and waits for Anne to come. In his head, he's still spinning – spinning and falling, coming down like a coin on its face. Love is the same thing as need; and he needs Anne, and he needs her to come now.

He needs to stop waiting.

27 *Fountains of Distress*

In the three weeks that followed his talk with Fenner, David Linden watched the papers more carefully even than usual. Coincidence and lucky chance had brought Fenner much closer than ever the police had come; and while David wasn't particularly anxious, he was more alert than he had been for some time. He had grown complacent, this last year; and he had just been shown that complacency was dangerous. Careful preparation and luck had covered up for him this time – but luck could change sides at any moment.

So he gave the papers a lot of attention, using all his experience to read between the lines and try to decipher where their theories were leading the police, and how much help their computer was giving them. And still he could find no hint or smell of danger. Fenner was solidly and he hoped permanently blocked; and the police were chasing shadows. David would maintain his vigilance, just in case, but he was already sure that it was redundant.

The Wednesday of the fourth week was his duty night at the Samaritans. Home from work before six, he changed into shorts and tracksuit and went running easily down past the allotments. He wasn't due at the office until ten, but it was important to feel fresh and relaxed when he arrived. So he would have a lazy, leisurely evening, running just a single five-mile lap of the moor, spending an hour in a hot bath and then making himself a light supper before driving into town.

Sometimes it seemed to him that running was literally what he lived for now. It was more important to him even than the killing, because it was available any time he chose. And the pleasure of it was a lasting thing, a sweetness that settled on his shoulders with every step he ran and stayed with him for a long time afterwards. He'd read somewhere about the endorphins which the body produces during stressful physical exercise, and the drug-like high they can give afterwards; but there was more to it than that for David. Running was all he had left now, his only link back to the good times, his only link with Anne,

(except for the killings, of course; but they were links of a different chain, forged of a different need)

and for that he cherished it. When he ran, he left the world and his life behind, his age and status as well as his possessions, all the memories and muck that had accumulated since he came out of hospital. He might be fourteen again and barely started on his long run, only a few hundred miles gone under his feet. He might be fourteen and living in two worlds, the daylight and the dark. He might have his old beliefs back, knowing what was real and what was true; and he might have his sister back, and his love.

And if he were fourteen again and loving, a brother and beloved, then that might be his sister at the far end of the footbridge, waiting for him, Anne with her pale hair and nervous fingers which were only ever still when she was holding him . . .

. . . But it wasn't Anne, of course it wasn't. It was Jill, his neighbours' daughter: sixteen now, and a friend of his in a way that her parents were not. He had a smile ready for her, and his hand half-raised to wave; but she walked away from the rail she'd been leaning on, watching him closely. Waiting for him to stop.

"Hullo, Jill."

"Mr Linden. Please . . . Can I talk to you?"

"Yes, of course. That's what I'm for." Among other things – but he was all Samaritan now, his training elbowing quickly in between them as he saw the tight way she held her body, and the fidgeting of her hands.

"You – you won't tell my parents?"

He smiled. "I promise. I won't tell your parents."

She nodded, taking his word and trusting him; but still she stood awkwardly silent, watching her feet shuffle on the concrete. After a minute, he said, "Shall we walk for a bit? It's a cold night for standing around."

"Yeah. Sure." But as he took a step along the bridge, she

said, "Only I'm not supposed to go on the moor after dark, it's not safe . . ."

No parental diktat could have put that smile into her voice. David leapt lightly to a conclusion, and whistled softly, the chorus from "Take Good Care of Yourself". From the look on her face, Jill took the point.

"Come on," he said, chuckling. "You'll be safe with me, I can promise you that." And chuckled again. "We'll stick to the footpath, where the lights are. And while we're walking, you can tell me all about him. What's his name, and what does he do?"

That was all the encouragement she needed. She talked about her Peter, his hopes and dreams and ambitions; and finally, she talked about her problem. It was sex, of course; or rather contraception, an old family doctor who'd be sure to tell her father if she went to him for the Pill. And because she was a friend, because this wasn't after all the Samaritans, David broke the rules and gave her practical advice, telling her simply to change doctors.

"Say that it's really awkward for you, trying to discuss personal problems with someone who's such a close friend of your dad's. Every girl has secrets she doesn't want her father to know. You could say that it'll be difficult for Dr Marshall too, knowing things about you that your father doesn't. You don't want to put a strain on their friendship, or his professional integrity. So you think it'd be best all round if you just get another doctor, someone neutral. How's that?"

"Brilliant!" She slipped an impulsive hand under his arm, and gripped his elbow warmly. "Thanks ever so much, Mr Linden. I'll do that. I've been dead worried, this last week or so. I mean, maybe one time we would've run out of Durex, or we just couldn't be bothered about it or something, and I might've got pregnant. And that's really scary, even to think about . . . Are you cold?" she asked suddenly. "Your hand's trembling."

"I am, a bit. I'm not dressed for talking. I'll walk you back to the road and then leave you, if that's all right."

"Yeah, fine."

They came to the gate, with the ring-road beyond and the footbridge over; and he said, "I'll see you around, Jill. Let me know how it goes – and bring Peter round sometime, why don't you? I'll welcome him, even if your parents don't. I'm sorry to leave you like this, but I'm on duty at the Sams tonight, I've got to run."

She made a face at the pun, then stood quickly up on tiptoe to kiss his cheek. "G'night, Mr Linden. And thanks . . ."

And it was Jill who ran, sprinting up the ramp onto the bridge while he stood by the gate and watched her, while memories burnt him like hot sand on the wind.

Halfway through milking, Tina had found a sore spot on Sylvia's udder. She'd gone into the cottage to fetch some cream for it; and coming out again, she saw the Red Baron balanced on the bucket's rim, leaning carefully inside to drink. With a flare of temper, Tina picked up a stone and flung it, missed the cat and knocked the bucket over. The Red Baron vanished into the hedge, with a hurt glance over his shoulder.

Tina walked moodily down the garden, set the bucket upright and squatted down beside it, pressing her head against the goat's warm flank.

"Goddam it, Sylvia . . ."

It would have been funny, with Fenner here; but without him it was just one more frustration, fresh evidence that living alone made her impossible to live with, even for herself.

"I really love that bastard, that's what it is," she confided to the ruminative goat. "But he's there and I'm here, and I don't know what the fuck to do about it . . ."

Sylvia looked over her shoulder and snorted gently, as if in sympathy; and Tina saw herself reflected in the odd, slitted eyes. Herself alone in darkness . . .

"And no one to talk to except a fucking goat," she snarled, picking up the bucket and swinging round so violently that half the remaining milk was spilled. "Oh, *fuck* it!"

With the milk strained into a jug and the bucket washed, Tina walked down the lane to where Monty was grazing the verge. His life saved by Diana's death, he was as big as his mother now; but there was no longer any thought of taking him to the slaughterhouse. Things were different now, and there was no room for killing. She hadn't cooked or eaten meat since she came back from the city.

She pulled free the peg that held Monty's tether, and led him back to the cottage to shut him up for the night. Standing outside the shed, she looked at the bright kitchen, and thought of the evening that was waiting for her, alone with the radio and her temper; then she turned impulsively and walked back down to the lane.

There were figures coming up from the village, which resolved slowly into Huw and Steph.

"Hi, gang."

"Hullo, Tina." As usual Steph said nothing, offering only a smile for greeting. "I was just wondering if I could borrow your bike," Huw went on, "to run Steph home? I'll be back in half an hour."

"You'll have a job," Tina said. "The carb's flooded. Just another of the little disasters that make life interesting. Tell you what, why don't you take it apart and clean it up? It'll be good practice for you, if you've never done it before. I'm going out for a bit, but you both know your way around. Make yourselves at home, okay?"

And she left them before they could reply, her legs too impatient to wait, needing to walk, to carry her towards some kind of solution she knew she'd never find in the cottage.

"Tina! Come in, come in."

"I'm not disturbing you, am I?"

"Yes, but that's what I'm here for. That, and disturbing others. That's what I'm trying to do at the moment, writing a sermon about cosiness, but it doesn't want to happen. You don't know any good Bible verses about the benefits of getting up and doing something, do you? Applauding the adventurous spirit?"

"Well, there's all that about the talents, isn't there? Going out and turning money into lots more money? The rich getting richer. But I'm not into it myself. Why don't you try it the other way for a change, and push the idea that it isn't actually sinful just to be happy? Just to sit still and appreciate what's happening to you, rather than buggering off and trying to be a knight on a white fucking charger . . ."

It was no surprise that Tina's walk had brought her eventually to Alan Morgan's door. He was perhaps her closest friend in the village, and the person she could talk to most easily. He had an uncanny knack of finding his way quickly to the root of a problem; but even so, she hadn't expected to find herself confronted with the crux of it all, the fount of her distress, the minute she walked through the door.

Nor, clearly, had Alan anticipated his casual query being taken so personally. "Oh dear, have I touched a button?" he asked, ushering her into his small study.

"Yeah, you have, a bit. But don't worry, it's what I came here for. To have my buttons punched."

"Ah, and there was me thinking it was simply for the pleasure of my company."

She smiled, and dropped onto the rag rug in front of the open fire. He took two glasses from the cabinet she'd given him, which now had pride of place on one wall, and poured out generous measures of whisky.

"Straight, isn't it?"

"Please, Alan. Thanks."

He passed her down the glass and an ashtray from his desk, and settled back in an old leather armchair on the other side of the fire. "All right, then, girl. Tell me about it."

"I don't know if I can, really. I mean, nothing's happened. Nothing's changed. I just don't think I can stand it any more."

"You're talking about Paul, I suppose?"

"Yeah, that's right. Paul bloody Fenner. Supercop to his friends. But strictly on a freelance basis, of course. Like the rest of his life. Like me, by the look of it." They were bitter words, but she spoke them without bitterness. Her voice had the flat tone of a despair that had burned itself out. "It's all so *stupid*! That's what gets me most. I wouldn't mind so much if he was really doing some good. If there was any *chance* of him doing some good. I would've stayed with him, even. But he's just kicking at shadows, wasting his time. Wasting *our* time. And that's all we've got . . ."

"Have you spoken to him about it?" Alan asked. "Since you came back?"

"Not properly. We've rung each other up a few times, but we just end up yelling. Or rather, I yell and he goes all cold and quiet. I hate it when he's like that, it's not human. And it just makes me shout louder."

"Give him time," Alan said. "He's an intelligent man. Sooner or later he'll accept that he's not getting anywhere; and then he'll want to pick up the threads of his proper life again."

"Yeah, but it'll be too late, don't you see? It'll all be rotten by then, it'd fall apart. And I'd rather never see him again, than have everything turn bad on us." After a silence, she went on, "You've got to hang on to what you've got, and build on it – and at the moment, it's all slipping away. It – it scares me when I think about it, it really does. I need that guy – and I need him right here, right *now*."

"Perhaps you should tell him so."

Tina stared. "D'you think I haven't?"

"Yes, I do. I think you've told him over and over again that he's wasting his time doing what he's doing; but that's not enough. Life isn't easy for Paul at the moment, even disregarding this murder business. He needs a purpose; and if you want him back, you'll have to give him one."

"Six months ago, he would've said that I was his purpose."

"And meant it, yes, because it was true. It probably still is. He's a single-minded man, our Paul. He needs reminding, is all; he needs to be shown his own value, or he'll go on trying to find it in other places. Words down a telephone aren't much use; but if he could see you now, I think he'd come home tomorrow. So why don't you go and show him?" When Tina said nothing, he went on quietly, "He's probably just as bad, you know. I can picture the two of you both sitting and doing nothing, waiting each other out, determined not to be the first to break. Chicken's a foolish game to play, with so much at stake."

"I'm not!" Tina protested.

"Aren't you? Think about it."

She did, frowning against the distracting, sensuous insistence of whisky and smoke and the smell of applewood burning. And at last she said, "Well, maybe . . . In a way. But what are you saying, I should just admit defeat and walk over the road?"

"No. I'm saying you should abandon the game. It's pointless and dangerous, and selfish too. It distresses your friends, as much as it does you."

She looked at him, and laughed harshly. "Maybe you should go and talk to Fenner. You'd make a better job of it than I would."

But all the same, with the decision somehow made and the prospect of doing something definite before her, she was whistling cheerfully under her breath as she walked back through the village. Her route took her past the small pub;

and on impulse, she went in and bought a half-bottle of vodka.

Back at the cottage, she found Steph leaning against the table, laughing, watching Huw. He had all the parts of a dissected carburettor spread out on newspaper in front of him, and the baffled look of a doctor whose patient refuses to get better.

Tina grinned, and ruffled his hair. "Never mind, darling. It's always like that the first time, no matter what the book says. I'll fix it in the morning. Now shove all that lot out in the shed, and get cleaned up. We've got more important things to do." She pulled the vodka from her pocket and thumped it down on the table.

Huw looked at it wistfully. "I've got to take Steph home. And if the bike won't work, we'd better be off now."

"No way, Huw. Dammit, you're not running out on me tonight. You neither, Steph love. Can you ring your people, and say you're staying here?"

"Well, yes. If you're here."

"Good," she said, shamelessly bullying. "Do that, then, why don't you? You too, Huw. Then we won't have to worry about the time. You can have the double bed; I haven't been using it anyway, with Fenner away, and the springs'll be getting lazy." Steph's cheeks burned suddenly; and looking at Huw, Tina could see that he was just as embarrassed. "Sorry, kids," she chuckled. "Didn't mean to make you blush. But there's no need to, not with me. I'm on your side, remember?"

And later, after Steph had been introduced to neat vodka and coaxed into admitting that she liked it, Tina said, "Besides, I imagine that bed'll be seeing a lot of you over the next few days, so you may as well warm it up tonight."

"What are you babbling about now, Tina?" Vodka made Huw more forceful than usual, even a touch pompous. Tina grinned, and explained.

"I'm going off again. Not for long, this time – and I'm planning on bringing Fenner back with me. But if you could keep an eye on everything for a week or so, I'd appreciate it. And any time you want to make use of the, um, amenities, of course you're very welcome."

In the large Operations Room which was the living heart of the Samaritans, David Linden sat in a cubicle with wooden partitions on either side. In front of him was a work-surface that held a telephone, a notepad, a neat pile of blank report forms and a selection of pens. Above was a shelf with several folders and some reference books. Taped to the walls of the cubicle were lists of contacts and telephone numbers, to be passed on to clients who needed specialist help.

David had just finished writing a report on his last caller, a neurotic regular who phoned every month and always asked for David. If he'd called on the wrong day, he simply asked when David would be on duty next and hung up – which was the surest possible sign that he wasn't anywhere near as desperate as he liked to make out. Every time he phoned, David wondered again if he should simply be honest, say there was nothing he could do for the caller and ask him to stop ringing. But the man was certainly lonely, if he wasn't suicidal; and it didn't hurt the Samaritans to have the phone tied up for ten minutes once a month. So once again David let it slide, making no recommendations and leaving it to the Director to decide when enough was enough.

There were half a dozen things David might be doing now, all of them useful and needful; but instead he simply sat quietly in his cubicle, watching the wall. In the cubicle next to his he could hear Hilda, his companion for the night, talking softly to another caller. His face was still and peaceful, but behind the masking eyes memories were running rampant, like dark secrets released. Jill's face haunted him like a shop-window reflection, shining at him from every polished surface his eyes could find; looking too much like Anne, and making his body ache with a need almost thirty years unsatisfied.

The phone jarred him suddenly out of his world of half-dreams, with a sharpness that was something near to a blessing. He reached forward and lifted the receiver before the second ring was completed.

"The Samaritans – can I help you?"

In the brief pause that followed, the familiar moment when callers hesitate one last time before finally committing themselves, he glanced at his watch and jotted down the time, for his report. 12.07 am. The rush hour they called it, the period between twelve and one o'clock. Everyone waits till after midnight.

"Yeah," a voice said, husky and frightened. Male, and very

young. Seventeen, perhaps? "Yeah, can you gimme someone to talk to?"

"You can talk to me," David said. "Unless you'd rather have a woman?"

"Christ, no."

"Fair enough." Sex, then, was it – another adolescent with another hang-up? But he sounded too frightened, and not embarrassed enough. Instinct and experience were both telling David that this was serious. "Do you want to give me your name? You don't have to, but it helps if I have something to call you by. I'm David."

"Graham. Grey, my mates call me, just Grey."

"All right, so will I, then." But already he was being careful, not saying the name aloud, in case Hilda should overhear. She was still busy with her own caller, but he knew she'd have half an ear tuned to him, just as some small part of his own mind was continuously monitoring her. "What's the problem?" he asked, his voice quiet and professional, trained to sympathy.

"Christ, I don't know, I – I killed this bird tonight. I think. I didn't see, only there was so much fucking blood, she must've been . . ."

That nearly broke David; he had been remembering blood all evening, blood and Anne's face and the two together. Now suddenly he could smell it too, and his hand had to clench tight on the receiver to stop it shaking. "What happened? Tell me about it, it's all right. Take your time."

"Oh, fuck, well, I was in this car, see? Me and this piece. Julie. And I, well, I'd pinched it, hadn't I, this car?" He was breathing heavily, and talking quickly between breaths, spitting the words out as though they poisoned him. David was used to this, just as he was used to the slight hint of bragging that underlay the boy's fear. He might be scared out of his wits, but he still wanted people to think it was a pretty macho thing he'd done tonight. David went on listening, and watched as his fingers wrote 'Alice' on his notepad.

"And . . . I wasn't pissed, you know, not pissed, but I'd had a few, we both had. And Julie wanted a joy-ride, it was her really. I'd been telling her, see, how to hotwire a car and that, and she went on at me till I said yeah. So I pinched this Cortina, didn't I? Only we hadn't got far, and I come round this corner, and . . . And I don't know, we skidded, something. And, fuck, there was this bird, see? And we went right up onto the pavement, and she didn't move, stupid bitch just stood there. So I hit her, didn't I? Smashed her up against this wall, only she fell down again, over the bonnet. And there was all this blood, all over the windscreen and everything, and Julie was screaming, and I couldn't just sit there and wait for the filth, could I? So I just got the fuck out . . ."

Pips snapped the chain of his confession like a rotten string. David waited motionless until they stopped, and he heard the boy say, "You there, then?"

"Yes, I'm here."

"'Cos I've just put my last ten pence in, and – Christ, I don't know what to *do*! The filth'll be looking for me, so I can't go home. And my old man'd turn us in anyway. And I don't know nowhere else to go. Only I saw your poster in this window, and I thought, why not. Give it a try, anyway. But . . ."

His voice trailed away, and David said, "Listen, can you give me the number of the phone you're using? Then I'll call you back, and we can talk as long as you like."

"Nah, fat chance." The boy's voice sounded utterly defeated. "There's this old bag waiting, she'd never let me hang around while you ring back. And I don't like the way she's looking at me. They could've put my face up on the telly already, one of those photofit things. I've got to get moving . . ."

"No, wait," David said urgently. "If you can't stay on the phone, we could send someone out to talk to you."

"You'll send the filth."

"No. I swear it. We're only interested in helping you."

"Well . . . You come? Not some other guy."

"I'm not supposed to leave the phone. It's one of the rules."

"I'm not talking to some other guy," the boy said, defiantly loyal. "You come, or forget it."

"All right," David said quickly, wondering despite his determined atheism – as he always did wonder – if there weren't some force or fate pulling the strings. The boy could have saved himself a dozen different ways; but whether through chance or design, his own choices had made the decision inevitable now. "Where will I find you?"

"Come to the moor," the boy said. "That bit where the two paths cross."

"I know it." Both the main paths were lighted; anyone waiting at the crossroads could see quite clearly if he were being betrayed. Whether there was one man approaching, or a squad of policemen.

"That's where I'll be. But come quick, eh?"

"As soon as I can."

Then the pips broke in again, and they were cut off.

As David hung up, a hand touched his shoulder and a voice said, "Cup of tea?"

He jumped, then smiled at himself as he looked up. He'd forgotten that Georgina was here tonight, as part of her training.

"No thanks, love. I've got to dash."

"Dash where?" she asked, puzzled. "I'm not allowed to take calls yet, remember, and you can't leave Hilda to cope by herself. I'll go, if there's something you want . . ."

"Thanks, Gina, but this is a special case," he explained, getting to his feet. "Don't go shouting it around, because some of the rules are about to be broken."

Hilda's call had just finished, so he went round the partition and said, "We've got a problem. I've just had a caller, a woman, who wants someone to talk to right now – and I think she means it. Her husband's an alcoholic and a gambler, and she's been coping with it somehow for years; but they're both retired now, she's just found out that he's been draining their joint account on the quiet, and she can't handle it any more. Can't see any point in going on. You know the type – very quiet and controlled and sorry-to-bother-you, but if someone doesn't go to her she's a possible suicide."

Hilda nodded briskly. "Ring Joe, then, and get the okay to call out the Flying Squad. You're the senior out of us two, so it's your decision."

"That's the problem." David shrugged. "She doesn't want the Flying Squad, she wants me. I told her it was against the rules for someone on phone duty to go out on a call, but it didn't make any difference. She said she could talk to me – and that's the point, isn't it? That's what we're here for. I think I can get Joe to come in for a while, but can you hold the fort till he gets here? I know it's a lot to ask, but . . ."

Hilda's fingers drummed lightly on the desk-top for a

moment, then she nodded and pushed the phone towards him. "All right, I can cope. I've got Georgie for company, anyway. Ring Joe and see what he says."

"Who's Joe?" Georgina asked in his ear, as he dialled.

"Joe Adamson – he's the Leader on Home Service tonight. The last court of appeal for any problems. If you haven't met him yet, you will soon. Little guy, with a big moustache."

The phone rang just twice before it was picked up. David nodded approvingly. "Joe? David Linden. I'm on Night Watch, but I've just had a client on the line who wants to talk to me in person, right now . . ." Briefly he outlined the same story that he had given to Hilda. As he finished, there was a chuckle on the other end of the line.

"It's always you, isn't it, David? I remember the same thing happening a couple of years back. You must be a silver-tongued devil when you try. But the Director approved it last time, so I don't see why not. If you're sure she won't accept anyone else."

"I'm sure, yes. She was very definite about it. She said she couldn't talk face to face with a stranger. I don't know what that makes me, after five minutes on the phone, but . . ."

"A silver-tongued devil, I told you. Go, my son, go with my blessings. I'll be there in ten minutes. But it's strange, how clients have no respect for our rules. You'd think they'd have more consideration."

David laughed, and hung up. "That's okay, then. You'll only have to cope for ten minutes, Hilda; and with any luck, I shouldn't be out too long."

Beside him, Georgina said wistfully, "I wish I could come. I haven't been out on an emergency yet – and Jude would be so jealous, when I told her . . ."

"Not tonight, love," David said, thinking of what lay hidden and ready in the boot of his car. "When I break rules, I like to do it with the blessing of my superiors. And I'm not ringing Joe up again, to ask to take a passenger."

"I didn't mean that," Georgina said defensively. "I wasn't trying to cadge."

"I know." He half-lifted a hand to touch her, to reassure, but pulled away before his skin met hers. "Don't try to rush things, Gina – take your time. It's like doing anything that's important to you: you're always in a hurry when you're learning, and then suddenly you're on your own, and it's always too soon. You're never really ready for it."

"Go on, quick, before your little old lady does something drastic." Georgina put her hands on his chest and pushed him lightly towards the door. "What's her name, anyway?"

"Alice." He turned, and ran. "See you later . . ."

28 *Changes*

Earliest things are clearest; life was simple then, your two truths gripping you like magnets, pulling you from one pole to the other. You understood what you were, and what was happening to you; and you knew what you needed.

But that changed, sudden as a season. Certainties lost their focus, becoming smeared and vague as other things got in the way.

Blood, and other things . . .

With Anne at a senior school on the other side of town, David walks home alone now, and has half an hour to wait before the bus brings his sister to join him. His father is at work, keeping the accounts for a small engineering firm, and the house is empty; but David doesn't stay indoors. He has something to do now, a way to use the time. He's nine years old, in his second year at primary school; and he's tired of being a scapegoat and a punch-bag for the other boys. He's taller than anyone his age, taller than many of the older boys too; but there's no strength in him, and they all see him as a natural victim. Which perhaps he is, but he means to change it.

So, home from school, David drops his uniform on the bedroom floor and changes into vest and shorts, and plimsolls. Anne has bought him a book of fitness exercises by a retired Army sergeant, designed to 'Strengthen and Give Stamina'; and every morning, every evening, David exercises. After school – now – he runs.

He's been doing it for just a month, and so far he feels the difference mainly in sore muscles and stiffness; but the weighing-machine outside the chemist's puts him at two pounds heavier than he was four weeks ago, and he's a dogged boy. He'll keep going until he's satisfied. Until he's as strong as he wants to be.

He runs down the road and through the children's playground at the bottom, into the park proper. Following the fence all the way round, one circuit is slightly over the mile; and that's the course he runs.

As he runs, he thinks about Anne, wondering why he feels no urge to bring her running, to share this pleasant loneliness as he shares everything else. He thinks about it, and finds the answer – that if she were with him, he wouldn't be alone any more and it would all be different. Most things are better with Anne; but he's not sure that this would be, and he doesn't want to take the risk. He's frightened of spoiling it.

And he finds that strange, to think of Anne spoiling anything that's his . . .

He's still puzzling over it as he finishes his lap and comes back to the tarmac playground. He slows to a trot, to a walk, to a standstill beside the swings. He's breathing heavily now and his legs are tired, but he's not in any distress, and he knows he could go on and cover the same distance again before he had to stop.

But Anne has told him to be careful, not to overreach himself; and he won't. And she should be home by now, waiting for him, with the water hot for a bath and warm towels ready . . .

But – strange again – that thought doesn't send him jogging home to find her. At the moment he's content to sit on a swing and push himself gently back and forth, and feel good; and he almost labels himself traitor, for being however briefly happy without Anne.

When he does go home, with the sweat dried on his skin and all his muscles stiffening, nothing on his mind now except a long soak in the bath and Anne to soap him and towel him dry, she's not in the house. Panic fills his throat like a hard-rimmed bubble that he can't breathe around, until a movement through the window catches his eye, and he sees her down at the bottom of the garden.

He runs out, and finds her with a stick in her hand, poking at a smouldering something in the brick incinerator.

"What is it?"

"My nightie," she says, in an odd, tight voice. "The lace one, that I've been wearing this week."

He knows it well; and knows that she's fond of it. "Why are you burning it?"

"Father told me to. There was blood on it when I woke up this morning, and Father caught me trying to wash it off. He said to burn it, as soon as it was dry."

"I don't understand," David says, fear in his voice. "Why was there blood? Are you hurt?"

"I – I don't *know* why! He wouldn't say, he just said it would go on happening, every month now. But no, it doesn't hurt. It just scares me, that's all . . ."

Later, in their bedroom, she gives him the other news. The bad news.

"Father's told me to move into the spare bedroom, David. Today. We're not allowed to share any more . . ."

The spare room is just that, a room that's never used. A guest-room that's never seen a guest. To an observer it would seem to make sense to give a teenage girl a space of her own, and allow her brother too to be alone at night. But the shock of it leaves David numb, clinging desperately to her hand as his mind paints pictures of the room empty in the darkness, cold without her, loveless . . .

"I know, darling," she says helplessly, hugging him. "I *know*. But he's *told* me, and I can't say no, how can I?"

David shakes his head against her shoulder, giving consent to his own despair. Of course she can't say no.

Together, silently, they move her clothes into the big chest-of-drawers in her new room, make the bed, throw open the windows to let some air in. And together, back in the little bedroom, they push the little truckle-bed out of sight beneath its larger brother, and spread David's few things around in the tallboy to make it look less empty.

29 *Eyes in Moonlight*

David parked his car in a lay-by on the ring-road, close to the footbridge where he had said goodbye to Jill a few hours earlier. Inside the boot was an old sports bag that had been ready and lying there for weeks, waiting for a chance like tonight. David lifted it out, slammed the boot and walked quickly to the fence, vaulting over it rather than bothering to open the gate.

Ahead he could see the ill-lit path cutting straight across the moor to the western side of the city, and the lights of the other that crossed it, running north and south. It was too far to tell whether or not there was a figure waiting for him at the junction. He shifted the bag to his other hand and walked faster.

As he walked, he wondered again whether he should be doing this. He'd always been careful before, letting six months or more go past before even looking for an opportunity. And now, with pressures from the public and their own superiors driving the police to investigate the most unlikely of possibilities, with enquiries actually having been made at the Samaritans, perhaps he should lie low for a time, just sit still and let the world wash by him . . .

But the fever was on him, need and excitement burning deep in his bones, where no one could see. Even as he played with the idea, he knew that it was too late to stop. There was a limit, even to his self-control; he'd come too far, past the point where he could turn away and say no, not now, not yet. And it wasn't truly dangerous. Looking at it objectively, the hunt was no closer to him now than it ever had been. Fenner and the police were both convinced that the Samaritans lead was a dead end; so why should he worry? Another killing now, months before they would expect it, might even serve to baffle and confuse them still further . . .

(And maybe you were only justifying it to yourself, but you didn't care, did you, David? You wanted this boy; and that was enough. As it always had been.)

David came to the place where the two paths met, and stood looking, peering at the darker shadows beyond the pools of light. There was a figure perched on a stone water-trough some fifty yards from the path; David lifted a hand in greeting, and the boy gestured abruptly, a cigarette glowing fitfully between his fingers. David left the path and made his way across the rough turf to join him.

"You came, then." The boy eyed him suspiciously. "You the bloke I was talking to?"

"Yes, I'm David."

"David what?"

"I'm sorry, I can't tell you that." He settled himself on the cold rim of the trough. "We're not supposed to give our surnames. I'm a friend, is all – and you call a friend by his Christian name, don't you? Call me David, and I'll call you Graham. That's all we need."

"Grey. Just Grey."

"Fine. Grey, then." He looked about him. "It's a bit cold and windy for sitting, isn't it, out here? Why don't you come back to my car, where we can be warm?"

Grey shook his head violently. "No. No way. You could have a van-load of pigs back there for all I know, just waiting for me. I'm staying here, where no one can see."

"You can trust me," David said, not reproachfully, simply putting it forward as a proposition to be considered.

"Maybe – but even so, someone might see me. Recognise me." He got tightly to his feet, and started kicking his foot aimlessly against a rock. "Everyone's going to be looking, see? The whole fucking lot of 'em . . ." He swung round in a full circle, staring out across the moor; and for a moment David almost felt sorry for him. The city surrounded them like a ribbon, a thin circle of light between the dark, vast sky and the darker land; and whichever way the boy turned it was there, shining, waiting, the lights like eyes that never blinked.

"Come with me," David said, getting to his feet. "There's a place I know, a dip in the ground with trees around it. You'll be safer there anyway, further from the path; less chance of someone stumbling across us. We'll be able to talk, and figure out what's best for you to do."

Grey hesitated, then shrugged his thin shoulders. "All right. But no tricks, mind. If there's pigs there, waiting for me, I – I'll do you, I will."

"There won't be anyone there, Grey. I swear it."

"Right, then. Let's go."

They came to the hollow David had mentioned, almost a valley between two low hills, sheltered from view by the natural lie of the land abetted by a rough circle of trees. In the centre of the circle stood an older tree, riven by wind or lightning, its bark carved and christened with a hundred initials.

"Julie's sure to've told them," Grey was saying as he shuffled beside David, hands in pockets and shoulders hunched, eloquent of his bitter defeatism. "Who I am, where I live, everything. Every copper for twenty miles'll be looking for me. Christ, what'm I going to do? They'll send me down if they get me, but I don't want to spend the rest of me fucking life on the run . . ."

"Don't worry," David said, "we'll sort something out. Let's just talk for a while, shall we? There's a felled tree-trunk we can sit on, over there . . ."

They sat down, and David dropped the bag at his feet.

"What have you got in there, anyway?" Grey demanded.

"Food, mostly," David said, unzipping the bag. "And a flask of coffee. I thought you might be glad of something warm."

"Too right I would."

"Good." He reached into the bag, then checked. "Hullo – you're in luck. There's a fifty-pence just there, by your foot."

"Where?" Grey looked down quickly.

"In that tussock of grass. I saw it glinting in the moonlight. You'll have to feel for it . . ."

As the boy bent over to fumble his fingers through the grass, David lifted a fist and clubbed him brutally on the back of the head. Grey let out one soft groan as the air leaked from his lungs, and crumpled bonelessly at David's feet.

Methodical and unhurried, David took what he wanted from the bag. First, a large ball of soft rubber, which he crushed in his hand and forced into Grey's mouth, letting it expand again behind the boy's teeth. Then a length of new sheeting, again pushed behind the teeth and tied savagely tight at the back of the head. As a gag, this couldn't be bettered; the boy would be able to breathe, if with a little difficulty and a lot of discomfort, but he wouldn't utter a sound.

It took five minutes for David to peel off the boy's clothes and tie his hands behind his back with a leather thong. Grey stirred then, struggling back towards consciousness as the cold wind moved across his naked skin. David smiled, and took ten feet of chain from the bag. He had promised himself chain. He looped one end around a tree-root that thrust up at the base of the trunk, and held it fast with a padlock through the links; then the other end

(stirring memories which you can neither welcome nor ignore, but only hold like flaming coals in your head, accepting the pain of them for the pleasure's sake)

he fastened with another padlock, tight around the boy's scrawny neck.

Lastly he took a bulky pair of overalls from the bottom of the bag, and unfolded them carefully. Sharp edges glittered in the moonlight like blades, as he gripped the necks of two broken bottles and lifted them slowly, almost ritually towards the sky. He had taken a lot of trouble over these, spending an afternoon in his garage with a geological hammer and a couple of dozen empty wine and spirit bottles, discarding more than half of them before he had achieved the long spears of glass that he was seeking. Now they shone in his hands like cold flames leaping; and he was ready.

He drew a foot back and kicked Grey in the ribs, once and twice and a third time before the boy rolled awkwardly away and lifted his head like a bewildered dog.

"On your feet, boy," David said softly, almost caressingly. "Up you get, now."

He turned his back then, stepping into the overalls and pulling them up to cover his everyday clothes. When the last button had been carefully fastened, he picked up his weapons again and smiled, seeing the boy on his feet, wrists and shoulders twisting wildly as he struggled against the thong that bound him.

"That won't help you," David said matter-of-factly. "You'll

just tighten the knots even more if you fight them. They're designed that way."

He stepped forward, light-footed in his trainers, the bottles in his hand like cruel fingers sharp enough to make the air itself cut and bleed. Grey shook his head crazily, his eyes bulging, unbelieving; then, as David came on, he backed away slowly to the limit of the chain. For a full minute he fought it, hurling himself back, trying to break either the chain itself or the root it was locked around. David stood still and watched, smiling, until the boy's bare feet slipped on the damp grass and he went crashing to the ground.

Grey scrambled up again, facing David, his body half-crouched and every muscle in it tense and trembling.

"That's not the way," David said gently. "Your neck'll break before that chain does, or the root."

Then he stepped forward again, and Grey went backwards away from him, the chain forcing him to circle around the tree. After a few paces, David stopped, laughing.

"That's not the way either, lad. Twice round the trunk, and you'll end up with no slack at all. The tree'll be doing half my work for me, holding you still. You've only got one chance to get out of this. You'll have to fight me. Beat me, and you're away. You can cut your hands free on the glass, and you'll find the padlock keys in my pocket. Car keys too, and money. You could be anywhere by morning."

The boy's throat worked as he struggled to speak, to make any noise at all through the gag. His eyes flickered from David's face to the broken bottles in his hands, and back to his face again.

"Oh, I know, I know," David laughed. "But no one ever said life was fair, did they? And at that, I'm giving you a better chance than any of the others had. So come on, make the best of it . . ."

And at that moment the boy charged at him, as though the words were a trigger, head down, coming with frantic speed. David stepped easily outside him, to avoid the swinging chain; and as Grey passed, David ripped one of his bottles down across the boy's chest. Grey jerked upright, staring down at his ribs, seeing rough, jagged lines appear as blood welled out, black in the moonlight. Then David slashed him again, in the stomach this time, digging his blades in deeper.

When he twisted the bottle free, he saw a gobbet of flesh hanging loose.

Grey scuttled back and crouched against the tree-trunk, staring up at David, panic showing in his eyes, in his heaving, shaking body.

"Come on, then," David whispered enticingly. "Sitting still won't help. You've got to help yourself tonight . . ."

And the boy did come on again, in another rush, trying to get inside the swing of those deadly bottles. David ran lightly backwards, always keeping a yard away – always keeping his hands darting in and striking, cutting Grey from shoulder to thigh until he was clothed and coated in his own blood.

"Animal," David whispered, hearing it as an echo from his own past to match the clink of the chain and the smell of fear; and animal the boy was at last, standing slack and empty-eyed, shaking with shock and weakness but too numbed even to collapse in his surrender. David smiled, and laid a point of glass against the centre of Grey's forehead, and turned it slowly; and Grey never moved, never even winced. Too trapped in pain and terror to notice this latest prick, he watched David with the helpless stare of the acknowledged victim, only waiting to learn what was to be done to him.

It was that stare that cost him a little more even than David had intended. David heard his father's voice, mockingly out of reach inside his head, naming him animal; and ahead of him he saw the mute submissiveness of a boy he had himself made animal. In the boy's waiting, dependent eyes, moonlight showed him a reflection of his own face; and it was only to escape the mockery of that reflection, to try to destroy the memory with the evidence, that David drove spears of frozen light deep into each of Grey's eyes, to make them truly empty.

When he was finally done, David unlocked both padlocks, stowing them in the bag with the damp and sticky chain. The bottles went in too, and the rag and rubber ball he'd used as a gag. The boy's own clothes he left scattered across the muddy ground; and the boy he left hanging on the trunk of the tree, skewered by a tent-peg through his throat.

You moved to the grammar school, and Anne went on to training college, to learn shorthand and typing; your father would harbour no idlers in his house.

But nothing really changed, not where it mattered. One school was much like another; and your life outside the house was no more real than it had ever been. You were still only passing time, waiting to get back to the two things that counted, your love and your fear.

Because you were still just as afraid of your father as you ever had been.

You still had reason to be.

"You weren't trying."

They've trapped him after the match, catching him naked and dripping from the shower, pushing him into a corner of the changing-room. There are three of them, Parker, Johnson and Tattersall; and they're still wearing their rugby kit, shirts and shorts and the heavy studded boots. One of them, Johnson, was David's captain in today's game; and he's looking for a scapegoat to make the memory less painful.

"You weren't even *trying*!" he says again, shoving David back against the rows of pegs. "I didn't see you touch the ball once in the whole bloody game. Why didn't you tackle Colville, when he was running in for that last try? He came right past you, for crying out loud! And you're twice his size."

David shrugs. "I'm not interested, that's all. I don't see the point." He rubs his hand slowly down the wet skin of the other arm, not disturbed by being naked. "Can I get my towel, please? I'm cold."

"Cold out there, too, weren't you?" Parker sneers. "Cold feet, anyway. You were just scared, that's all."

"If you like." It doesn't matter what the other boys think of him. Nothing matters, here.

"I'll give you something to be scared of!" Parker swings his fist suddenly, catching David hard in the ribs.

David almost smiles, as he feels the pain and sees the anger on the other boy's face. It's three years now since he started to train, to be ready for the next fight he got caught up in. In fact, no one's so much as swatted at him

(except your father, of course – and he didn't count. Or rather, he was the only one who did)

from that day to this; but he still does the training. He's as fit now as a boy can be who runs five miles a day in just over the half-hour, who exercises night and morning with home-made weights,

(Anne's suggestion they had been, remember? Tins and bottles packed with sand. And for the last year, you'd been keeping the sand wet)

who'll swim a mile or two every chance he gets. And secretly, he's always been a little disappointed that no one's pushed him into a fight recently. He doesn't want just to be left alone; he wants to *teach* them to leave him alone.

So he's almost glad of the chance, now. He wouldn't have chosen odds of three to one, and he doesn't expect to win; but he means to hurt all three of them before the end.

He waits just for a moment, looking calmly into Parker's eyes, seeing uncertainty mix with the anger; then he lashes back with his left hand, straight at the boy's face. A cry of "Fight!" goes up behind him, as his fist lands squarely on Parker's nose, and he feels something give beneath his knuckles. He doesn't wait to see the damage, though; he hurls himself sideways at the silent Tattersall, and sends him sprawling over a bench onto the concrete floor.

David spins round to face Johnson, just in time to take a kick from one of those studded boots, high on his bare thigh. The leg buckles under him, and he can feel himself falling as Johnson draws back to kick again.

David lets himself drop, taking his weight on his arms; then thrusts himself forward under the captain's swinging boot to throw his body against the other leg. Onlookers jump out of the way with yells of encouragement, as Johnson crashes to the floor. David scrambles free of the savage, swinging legs; then someone drops on him from behind, knocking him flat and wrapping an arm chokingly tight around his throat. David twists sharply onto his side, gasping for breath; then he reaches behind him with his free hand, fingers hooked like claws, trying for the eyes.

The boy's hold relaxes for long enough for David to jerk free, and roll over. He has time to recognise Tattersall as he throws two vicious punches, left-handed again, into the boy's stomach. Tattersall stares at him, his face twisting; David raises his right arm and smashes him back-handed across the cheek.

Johnson comes back hard, wrapping his long arms round David's chest and dragging him back onto the damp concrete. The two of them wrestle clumsily, struggling for a hold; at last, David gets both his hands tight on the other boy's forearm. He twists it brutally against the shoulder-joint, and hears Johnson scream.

A voice hisses, "*Master!*", and the racket dies suddenly into silence as a tall figure pushes his way angrily through the pack. Looking round quickly, David can see Tattersall gagging and retching on the floor, blood running from his mouth, while Parker sits on a bench with his head down, watching a scarlet pool grow between his feet as blood drips relentlessly from his broken nose.

"Stop this at once, do you hear?" It is Mr Robson, the sports master. "*At once!* You, Linden, let go that boy's arm, and stand up, the pair of you."

David looks up at him, and something like a smile lifts the corners of his mouth as for the first time he uses all the strength in his arms and shoulders, throwing it into one quick, smooth wrench that snaps Johnson's arm like an icicle.

(*And you enjoyed it, didn't you, David? You enjoyed the pain and the panic on his face, as he felt his arm giving. You enjoyed the feeling beneath your fingers, the sudden jerk when the bone broke; and you enjoyed hearing him scream.*)

". . . He *meant* to do it, sir. It was deliberate, cold-blooded – downright vicious. The most shocking thing I've ever seen, in all my years of teaching . . ."

David watches the headmaster, Mr Carramore, and listens to himself being discussed; and he feels less involved than ever, as though he only imagines that he's here at all.

"Oh, come now, Mr Robson." The headmaster lifts both hands to his barrel chest and steeples the fingers thoughtfully together. "A twelve-year-old boy hardly goes into a fight with a strategy, does he? Or a plan of campaign? No, he doesn't, he simply goes in with his fists flying. Whatever happens to his opponents is almost invariably, ah, the result of misfortune or sheer happenstance."

"It wasn't like that, sir." Mr Robson sighs softly, as he tries to explain. "The fight was pretty well over. The other two were out of it, anyway. Linden had Johnson down on the floor, in some kind of wrestler's hold. I told them to break it up. Linden looked up at me, and I could see him thinking about it; then he smiled, and twisted Johnson's arm a bit more, and broke it. He was *smiling* at me, sir, as he did it . . ."

Mr Carramore pulls at his lower lip, once and then again; then he looks at David. "Is this true, Linden? Did you mean to break that boy's arm?"

And David, who's never learnt to lie, looks back at him and says, "Yes, sir."

The headmaster holds his eyes for a minute, then says, "Very well, then. Bend over the desk, if you please."

He goes to a coat-stand in the corner, and takes a cane from it. David bends across the desk, his hands gripping the edge of it, a little surprised to find himself biting back a smile.

If they only knew, he thinks, as the cane sobs through the air

(thinking of some of the punishments you've taken from your father, some of the things he'd thought of to do to you)

and cuts across his taut trousers, the slashing sting of it biting into his buttocks. David blinks. Five years ago, a beating like this would have brought tears to his eyes, maybe even had him sobbing if it went on long enough;

(two)

but not now. Not any more. Now he feels all the scorn of the professional victim for the amateur, the man who doesn't know what he's doing.

He wonders

(three)

what he'll say to Anne after his run. He'll have to tell her, of course; but he's not sure how to explain it all. He doesn't even

(four)

understand much of it himself. Why he wanted to break Johnson's arm, why it felt so good to do it.

Mr Carramore pauses, breathing heavily, laying the cane lightly across the small of David's back to hold him still.

"Four," says the headmaster, "for causing serious bodily harm to a brother pupil. And four more," the cane taps restlessly against the base of David's spine, as if impatient for the talking to stop, "for aggravated disobedience to Mr Robson."

Aggravated, David supposes, by the smile.

Mr Carramore's temper slips slowly out of his control now. The strokes come swifter and more savage, hard enough to make David gasp, and to damage that shell of detached contempt he shelters behind.

And when the eight are over, the headmaster flings his cane across the room, and strides back around his desk.

"Stand up, boy," he snaps. "And think yourself lucky you're getting away with eight. I won't have this sort of thuggery, do you hear? I won't have it!" He sits down, and takes a sheet of notepaper from a drawer. "I am writing to your father, to inform him of what you've done. I expect you to deliver this letter, unopened; and I warn you, I shall telephone Mr Linden this evening, to confirm that he has received it. I imagine that he will be as appalled as I am, by your behaviour. I am making it quite clear to him that you are exceedingly fortunate not to be suspended, or even expelled."

(And that's when you realised that the headmaster was wrong. You weren't getting away with eight. You weren't getting away with anything.)

David's father reads the letter carefully through. He glances up once at David, then back at the single sheet of notepaper. He reads it a second time and a third, folds it carefully and slips it back into its envelope.

David's hands clench briefly behind his back, but he gives no other sign of the fear that stirs thickly inside him like a fat worm, pale in darkness, knotted many times around itself.

"I see." His father's voice is quiet but not soft, the sound of rain on old iron. He takes off his heavy-framed spectacles and folds the ear-pieces in before resting them on the table beside the letter. As he does so, he says, "Did you so much as apologise for this," he pauses to select a word which his face says is already inadequate, "this outrage, David? Did you apologise to Mr Carramore, or to the boy you," another pause, "assaulted?"

David doesn't have to think about that one. He licks his lips quickly to separate them, to make them work, and says, "No, father."

"No." His father taps one finger lightly on the envelope. "I shall have to write to them, of course. To Mr Carramore, and to the boy's parents. To apologise for you. To do what you should have done. And to apologise on my own behalf, for having failed with you."

He stands up suddenly, and comes a pace closer. David would jump back, would run, even, if he could; but his fear holds him where he is, like a fly caught in amber.

(Remember that feeling, David? You should do, it was familiar enough once. It's the feeling you get when you meet the worst thing in the world. You daren't run away, because there are some things so terrible you just don't turn your back. And you daren't even back away, because for all you know it's behind you too, it surrounds you and grips you and somewhere inside your head there's something laughing, and that's it too. Remember?)

"It's strange," his father says musingly, looking him up and down. "You look human enough; and I did my best to bring you up human. To train you. But I failed, despite appearances. That letter says that I failed, and your attitude says that I failed." If a prefect or even a master at school had behaved this way, talking almost to himself and shaking his head with apparent distress at his own failure, he would only have been scoring points, to make a victim feel small. But David's father doesn't play games for points. He means it.

"You look human enough." He says it again. "But you're not. You're *animal*." His hand hooks into David's collar, and just the touch of him sets dark circles spinning inside David's head, and makes the floor unsteady beneath his feet. "Only an animal would behave the way you have done. Only an animal would do something like this for the simple vicious pleasure of it."

David doesn't squirm or wriggle, or reach to loosen the choking collar. He only stands there, breathing what air his gasping lungs can find. Passive, and afraid.

"And if you behave as an animal," his father says carefully, "then you must be punished as an animal. As the animal you are."

He flings David abruptly into a corner of the room, with one casual swing of his arm. "There's no point in hiding behind a uniform," he says. "Trying to masquerade as a human being, in civilised clothes. That game is over, you have betrayed yourself." And as David simply lies huddled on the carpet, he lifts his voice in a moment of frenzied anger. "Your clothes! Take them off, do you hear?"

David strips slowly, while his father watches. There's nothing new in this; it's part of Mr Linden's discipline to have his children strip before punishment. Being naked doesn't embarrass David, he's too used to it; and there's no place for something as pale as embarrassment in a life filled with the strong colours of fear and love. But his father has never shouted before. *Never*. That's one of the rules. And hearing him shout makes David think that whatever happens now, it's going to be very bad indeed . . .

His father's lip curls scornfully at the eight thin weals across David's buttocks. "Mr Carramore said that he had beaten you," he observes in his usual quiet tones. "*Beaten* was the word he used; but I think he should choose his words more carefully. He has won no victory over you, your attitude tells me that. He has punished you, I can see – but only as one would punish a human being. He wouldn't have been expecting an animal. Fortunately, I know you better."

He hesitates briefly, as if expecting an answer; then, given nothing but silence, he reaches out to grip David's neck. "Very well, then. Come with me. Animal."

Forcing David's head down so that the boy is almost doubled over, his father drags him through the house and out into the back garden.

Their way lies through the kitchen, where Anne is cooking; David hears his sister's stillness as they pass, and fear for her gives his thoughts a sudden coherence.

Don't say anything, Anne. Don't move, don't make a sound . . .

(And of course she didn't, did she, David? Didn't move, didn't make a sound. You'd both learned that – not to protest, hardly even to breathe while the other was being punished. It wouldn't have helped you, for her to share your pain. The

thought of her free of it was your only comfort; and the thought of her comfort afterwards your only hope.)

Hidden by a high hedge from the road and the neighbours, the garden is a box with no lid, an area of cropped grass and flowers in rows. They never come out here, except to weed and mow the lawn.

A coal-bunker adjoins the end wall of the kitchen, its fresh-painted wooden lid belying the fact that the house has gas heaters in every room and no open fireplaces. In fact, the brick bunker has been empty for longer than David has been alive. But his father finds a use for it now, tossing David face-down across the shallow slope of its lid.

"Stay there, animal," he grunts; and walks unhurriedly down the path to the shed. He doesn't even glance back, so sure is he that David won't move.

And David doesn't move. Fear breeds rebellion in some, but not in him. He lies on the awkward slope of the bunker with his eyes screwed shut, feeling the cool wood beneath him and the wind's tiptoe across his back. Feeling fear and the taste of it like brass in his mouth, bitter and oily, hearing it in his own body, racing his heart and pumping the blood in his ears. Hearing his father move in the shed, shifting things around; and that's fear too.

Finally, his father's footsteps come back up the path. David doesn't open his eyes, but he hears the noise that metal makes as it whispers against metal, and the scrape of it on the concrete path.

"Very well, then, animal," his father says – or breathes, rather, as though the words were the feelings and the feelings richer than oxygen. "Now, you will learn."

The air hisses abruptly with a thin tearing noise, as if it is being ripped apart; and something bites into David's back with the force of a great bird striking, driving the air from his lungs and even the fear from his mind, leaving a vacuum which pain rushes in to fill. Pain like long claws gripping and shaking him, pain which he can see behind his closed eyes as fierce streaks of red across murky brown, hungry to destroy. His body twists out of his control, and there's nothing to hold him to it except his father's iron hand heavy on his neck, to remind him of what is true. He draws one slow, sobbing breath – and it strikes again across his shoulders, again and again, with David retching and gasping until the air he is desperate for smashes like cold steel against his throat, until he can hardly distinguish between the pain that falls hard onto him like something solid, and the pain that swims inside him like a colour. Thicker than blood or water, it churns and eddies under his skin, turning all his flesh liquid, washing like acid against his bones. He is aware dimly of a warm stickiness between his belly and the wood he lies on, but doesn't know that that's his own urine, leaking from him as his body loses its identity; and there's a warm stickiness too between his back and the wind that blows across it, and he doesn't know that that's blood seeping out like sap.

Then he feels those rigid fingers shifting on his neck, feels another hand slide under his body; and he is lifted from the wood and tossed down onto the cold softness of the lawn and the rain-soaked earth beneath.

There is something rougher than grass twisted under his chest. He opens his eyes and moves slightly, enough to set the flames dancing in different patterns down his back, across his buttocks and legs. Now he can see a thin grey length against the grass; and after a moment, his mind gives it a name.

Rope. An old rope, grey with age, six or seven feet of it that hung on a nail in the shed and now lies dropped here with David sprawled on top of it. In his mind, David sees it coiled twice or three times and his father's hand gripping it. He sees the coils of it cutting through the air, hears the air screaming, feels the coils tearing again at his skin; and understands the pain that still shivers him, still swirls and burns and etches new pathways through his flesh.

He turns his head, and even that much movement hurts enough to set him screaming, if he had breath to scream with. Darkness blurs in from the edges of his vision, tugging at him, threatening to drown him; but now he can see his father, and watch what he does. David remembers those thin sounds of metal like a promise, and he knows that it isn't over yet.

His father has raised the lid of the coal-bunker, leaning it back against the kitchen wall; and David watches him screwing a heavy steel eye to the underside. A chain is already threaded onto the eye, running down the slope of the lid and hanging into the bunker.

David's father gives each screw a final testing turn, then leans his weight against the upright lid and tugs on the chain.

The loose end swings and rattles, but the eye stays firmly in the wood. A second tug, a grunt, a nod; and David's father turns and strides over, to stand above him.

"Up, animal. On your feet."

A hand closes around David's arm and pulls him up; but the pain tears him till he screams, and his legs fold shapelessly beneath him. His father grunts again, puts his other hand under David's thigh and lifts him smoothly, carrying him to the bunker and dropping him in on his knees.

"It should be a kennel for an animal like you," he says, pulling David's head up by the hair. "Or a cage. But this is all I have."

He picks up the free end of the dangling chain, loops it around David's throat and padlocks it at the back of his neck. David sees him silhouetted against the pale, bright sky, his face dark and unreadable. Then one hand lifts and blurs, and a vicious cuff across the head knocks David down onto the concrete floor of the bunker. Pain hacks at him, blunter now and more brutal, and he is hardly conscious of the lid slamming above him, and the sharp click of another padlock sealing him into the darkness.

Three different ways, your father locked you in. Cold steel on the outside, padlock and clasp; cold steel on the inside, a chain round your neck. They made two, and they were the visible locks, the sort that people look for and understand. But when he left you, he took time with him; and that was the third lock, and the worst. As long as you still had a finger on the pulse of time, as long as you could feel it passing, then you knew that everything had an end. You had that knowledge safe, and called it hope. But he took it away and left you swimming in darkness with no help and nothing to hold to, no contact with anything that you could not feel, taste or smell.

You could feel fear, and you could feel pain. They burned and shivered your body, as though bonded to you like an extra skin. But you could feel other things too, the grittiness of ancient coal under you, and the cold discomfort of the concrete beneath. You could feel cramped by the close walls of the bunker, uneasy with no room to stretch out and no light to see your prison by. And you could feel the chain around your neck. You could hear it as well, rustling quietly, sometimes two links striking together with a sharper sound when you stirred and stirred again. The lid was so low above your head that you had no room to sit up; you lay curled on one side, almost foetal, until cramps and the cold ache of your body forced you to move. You moved into pain and passed through it, and lay down again on your other side, careful not to touch your back or buttocks against the walls; and you lay still, your ears filled with the sound of your own breathing, until you had to move again.

You had no food or water, there was nothing for you to taste except coal-dust and dryness and the foul taste of fear. But you had plenty to smell, didn't you, David? Too weak and hurt even to edge around till your buttocks found a corner, you simply defecated where you lay. The warm, heavy smell of it filled the bunker like a mist rising, and hung like something solid in the stifling air; and when you turned over again, you hardly cared that you were lying in your own shit. It was soft for a while, and soothing against the raw skin on your hip; you felt it and treasured it, and were grateful.

And you turned, and lay still until the lying still hurt more than the turning would. So you turned, and it hurt more than the lying still had.

So you lay still.

When David hears a key turning in the padlock outside, it doesn't surprise him. He's too numb for anything so human. He squints his eyes against the dazzle as the lid is slowly lifted. He's not even wondering who is out there; he's just looking. Like an animal.

It's a slim figure that he sees shadowed against a shadowing sky. It's Anne's voice that he hears murmuring something unintelligible as she stares down at her father's work; and as the stench of him rises to meet her, it's Anne's hand that clutches the rim of the bunker while she drops to her knees beside it and is quietly sick.

David moves clumsily, getting onto his hands and knees, then grabbing the bunker's edge and pulling himself up. Every muscle screams at him; and left to himself he would have dropped down again and crawled out cautiously, limb by limb, like a sick or wary animal. But Anne is there, on her feet again, wiping the back of her hand across her mouth. It isn't pride that drives David agonisingly to his feet, half crippled with pain; these two have no secrets, and he doesn't have to impress her. She knows how strong he is, and how weak. But his father has called him animal and tried to make him so; and to behave like an animal now, to be anything less than human with Anne, would be to give him the victory. And David won't do that. He'll be an animal to his father, he'll be anything his father wants him to be; but to Anne he'll be David Linden and nothing else. If she looks at him even for a moment, and thinks "Animal," then he knows he will have lost.

Her hand reaches to touch his shoulder, as if the pressure of her fingers will stop it shaking.

"David," she whispers. "Oh, Davy love . . ."

His tongue touches automatically against his lips, but it is as dry as they are. He shapes her name, but no sound can find its way through the sour barrens of his throat.

He sees her mouth tighten as her stomach heaves again, but she swallows the nausea and bends around him, to fit a key fumblingly into the padlock at the back of his neck. He hears a dull click, feels the chain jerk and slide free, falling with a clatter against the upright lid of the bunker. Anne smashes the padlock down onto the path, and David can see the anger in her stiff body, even as the tears slide unnoticed down her cheeks. "How – how could he do this?" she whispers, more to herself than to David, touching his cheek with soft fingers that come away black with filth. "He's mad, he must be mad . . ."

David just looks at her, voiceless, his mind almost as dark and empty as the pit she has lifted him out from. She is his candle, offering him light and warmth; she has to burn, he has only to stand, and take what she gives him.

She fetches a bucket and cloth, and an old towel, and wipes gently at his face. The water is blood-warm, and it meets and moistens his thirsty skin like something miraculous. He sucks at the damp cloth as Anne wipes the dust and grit from his nose and lips, and the warm wetness of it chokes him for a moment.

The water in the bucket soon turns black, as Anne wrings the cloth out; but that doesn't matter. She can get him clean in the bath; at the moment she's only concerned with wiping the encrusted muck off his body – the thick layer of dust and grime that covers him like a blanket, and the caked excrement like a girdle around his hips.

Underneath, his skin is grey and dead. His back is a mess of scabs and raw, swollen welts. The scabs are black with coal-dust, and she can see a yellow pus forming in some of the wounds. She pats him lightly dry, wincing every time he flinches; then she drops the sodden towel, takes his hand and urges him into the house.

Your father was away, she said. He had left you for two days chained in that bunker, clutching at nothing, blind with pain and suffocating in the foetid air; and then he had gone away to a conference, leaving Anne with the keys and instructions to let you out and clean you up. With him out of the house, you could spend as long as you liked in the bath, changing the water time and again, soaking the dirt from your skin and the scabs from your back. It hurt, yes; but it was a clean and cleansing pain that was almost a pleasure. You sank back into it, welcoming the sharp bite of hot water on your bruised and brutalised flesh.

Anne brought you a glass of cold water, and you sipped it slowly, the clean taste of it pushing you close to tears. She asked if you wanted food; but after forty-eight hours in the pit, all you wanted was sleep. She dried you gently with a soft towel, and made sure that all your wounds were clean of grit and dirt; then she fetched iodine, and painted your back with it. You squirmed under the sting of it, and she laughed and called you a baby; then she cried, and took you to her own bed.

"We'll be safe together," she says, "with father away. And I – I don't want you to be alone, not tonight . . ."

He nods, and watches while she undresses. Talking is still painful, so he says nothing until he catches sight of the hard red lines across her shoulders. He grips her arm to hold her still, then lifts his other hand to touch the soft ridges.

"What for?" he asks, as she flinches.

Anne looks down, absorbed in undoing the fastening of her skirt. "I tried to threaten him," she mumbles. "Yesterday. I couldn't stand it any more, the thought of you out there, locked up in that horrible box. You could have been *dying* . . . So I told him that if he didn't let you out, I'd go to the police, and tell them."

"Anne . . ."

"I know, darling, it was stupid. But I was out of my mind, nearly." Naked now, she leaves her clothes scattered on the carpet and comes to him, slipping her hand into his. "For a minute, I thought he was going to put me in there with you. But he just beat me, and locked me in here. It's nothing, David. Honestly."

That's not true, though. She's broken one of the cardinal rules, not to stand between their father and his chosen victim; and they both know there will be repercussions lasting longer than a few weals.

They get into bed, and David rolls over to lie sprawled on top of her, needing to feel her body beneath his, to know for sure that she's there. She accepts him silently, easing his head down into the hollow of her shoulder, laying cool hands on his arms to save touching his back.

David breathes in once, relaxing as the soft, familiar smell of her permeates through his body, telling him that he's home. He holds the breath in for a moment, lets it out slowly and is asleep.

He wakes into darkness, with something tight around his neck. He draws one sharp, hard breath, thinking himself still in the hell his father built for him; but there's no cloying foulness in the air, only the sweet warm smell of Anne sleeping. Reassured, he remembers her freeing him, washing him, bringing him to bed. What he feels round his neck is only her arm, holding him protectively; and her body is still stretched beneath his like a willing sacrifice, a cushion against the harsh world.

He loves her because he has to love her, and again because he needs to, and again because he wants to. Caught in the rhapsody of that thrice-repeated love, he brushes her hair back onto the pillow, and moves his hand across the soft skin of her shoulder. He's always liked to touch her; but it's a pleasure oddly reinforced now, to feel the slight friction between his skin and hers as invisible strings pull his hand down to her breast. He strokes it lightly, folds his hand around it, slides his thumb towards the nipple.

Anne stirs under him, and opens her eyes. He smiles at her, and she touches a light kiss to his cheek.

Her nipple quivers and stiffens strangely as his fingertips brush against it. He closes his thumb and forefinger around it and squeezes gently, and feels her suck in a sharp breath. He glances quickly at her face, anxious that he's hurt her.

"It's all right, David," she whispers, kissing him again, her lips this time pressing warm against his. "It feels good."

So does being kissed, and holding her breast in his hand and her nipple between his fingers. So does the soft resilience of her body beneath his, the slight movements of her skin against his as she breathes. The pleasure of it all weaves itself into a cable of many strands that runs down through his chest and stomach, growing tighter even as he thinks about it, and melts to an odd tingling warmth in his groin.

David knows little or nothing about sex, only what he's heard other boys giggling about at school; and he barely associates their smirking confidences with the feelings that grip and possess him now. There's no time and no room for questions, anyway; he's overtaken by Anne's gentle, hesitant encouragement and his own explosive need. She guides him with fingers and whispered words, not even gasping as he enters her; they move together in a rhythm that builds and builds as his body dictates it; and for David it ends with a tearing inner violence that leaves him shuddering, emptied, inert.

Vaguely, he is aware of Anne's palm against his cheek, tender as a kiss. She shifts beneath him, settling them both more comfortably and pulling the abandoned covers over them again. Her cool hands touch and ease for a moment the great ache that is David's back; and he sees dark arms reaching out of darkness, to carry him down again into sleep.

31 Unravelling Threads

The phone woke Fenner, pulling him out of the wide bed and stumblingly through the flat before he was properly awake. The electronic clock on his desk read 7:53.

"Yeah?" He was too bitter to be polite, too tired to be vitriolic.

"Paul, it's Mike. I shouldn't be doing this, but get some clothes on and come down to the town moor, pronto."

"What? What's happened? Where on the moor?"

"Just follow the flashing lights. You'll find us."

Two clicks, a hum, the dialling tone; Fenner was alone again.

He got dressed and ran down to the car, without even stopping for a coffee; adrenaline would serve as well as caffeine, to give him the kick-start he needed in the mornings.

When he came to the moor, he found one of the wide gates in the fence standing open. He pulled onto the grass verge, and got out of the car.

They'd left one constable on the gate, but he was busy shooing back some curious cattle. Fenner walked through the open gate, and spotted the rectangular shape of a police Incident Unit van at the foot of a low hill half a mile away, with several patrol cars parked around. He was setting off to follow the tyre-tracks across the rough pasture when a voice called behind him.

"Excuse me, sir . . ."

He turned round, to see the constable abandoning his cows and trotting up to him.

"Sorry, sir. The moor's closed. You'll have to keep the other side of the fence, if you don't mind."

"No, I won't," Fenner said gently.

"Even if you're press, sir. There'll be a statement made later, but you can't come onto the moor."

"Yes, I can. Inspector Malone invited me along." Fenner waited for the name to sink in, then added another. "I'm Paul Fenner. And I don't know how well you remember your proverbs, but the grass always does look greener from the other side of the fence. At least, to a cow it does . . ."

The constable looked back, and let out a cry of dismay as he saw one of his bovine charges wandering idly through the gateway onto the verge of the main road. He ran off to herd her back; Fenner grinned, and carried on his way.

When he came near to the cluster of vehicles, he saw Mike standing beside one of the cars, leaning in at the open window, using the radio. Fenner waved, and a minute later Mike came to join him.

"Okay, so who was it this time?"

"A boy." Malone gestured with his head, and led him

between the vehicles. "A kid. Seventeen years old and running scared, and he has to run into the Butcher . . ."

There was an ambulance among the cars, a four-wheel-drive Range Rover. Must be the only kind they could be sure of, driving across the moor, Fenner thought; and, must be here for the body.

Okay – so where *was* the body? He could see a dozen people busy in the little hollow beyond the cars, measuring and photographing and picking things from the ground with tweezers, slipping them into plastic bags. But he didn't see the body, until Mike led him through the circle of trees and gestured at the old oak in the centre. A length of black plastic sheeting hung baggily down the trunk, shielding some slumped form . . .

"*There?*" Fenner whispered. "In God's name, how? *What holds him up?*"

"Steel spike of some sort. Through the throat. We – haven't been able to get it out, yet. We did try, but . . . I've got a man digging through a tool-box now, looking for something with more clout than pliers."

Fenner nodded inattentively. "Is that how he died, then?"

"No. He was dead already. The Butcher was just nailing his colours to the mast." Mike put a hand out to hold Fenner still. "Better not go any further. Been enough interference on the ground already, without two more sets of prints."

"How was he killed?" Fenner persisted.

"Not sure yet. The doc needs a chance to examine the body properly. Basically, though, his belly was ripped out." Mike shuddered. "It looks like some animal's been chewing at him, except the cuts are all too clean. Doctor says it was done with something jagged, a broken bottle, something like that. We'll know better later."

They were quiet for a time, both of them staring at the tree, trying not to see the body hanging obscenely on the trunk. Then Mike went on, "He took his eyes out, too. But not on the tree. There's blood all round it, bits of . . . bits of flesh. Can't be sure, but there's a theory says that the boy was roped or chained to the tree, and the Butcher just hunted him round it. Like a game of tag."

Another silence, longer, while Fenner took in this new information. Finally, he had a question.

"Running scared, you said. What did you mean?"

"We've got a preliminary identification. Not on the body, so it's not definite; but his pockets say that he's Graham McLaggan. And according to his girlfriend Graham McLaggan killed a woman on the streets last night. Drunk driving. We've been looking for him ever since."

"You reckon he was hiding out here?"

"Probably. It's a good spot if you're on the run. Only the Butcher found him first."

"So what was in his pockets?" Fenner asked. "Anything useful?"

Mike shook his head. "Not much. Wallet and driving licence, keys, pencil. Penknife. Usual junk you'd expect from a teenage boy. Oh, and a dozen girlie pics, cut out of a porn mag. Shoved into his inside jacket pocket, where his girlfriend wouldn't see them."

Fenner shrugged. "Who found the body?"

"Couple of early-morning joggers. Short-sighted types – had to come right up close for a good look, before they were sure what it was. That's one of our problems, sorting out their prints from the others. Oh, but that's the good news. Silly of me, I forgot to tell you. We *think* the Butcher *might* have a pair of size ten trainers."

"Patterned soles?" Half the population wore trainers; but every little helped, and from the pattern they could identify the make.

But Malone was shaking his head. "The grass is too thick to show it."

A uniformed sergeant came up to them, blinked at Fenner in hesitant recognition, then showed Malone a heavy-duty adjustable spanner.

"I reckon we can get it out with this, sir. With a bit of muscle."

"All right, John. Just get at it, will you? The sooner it's done and out of the way, the happier I'll be."

"Aye, sir."

Fenner and Malone talked desultorily of desultory things, rigor mortis and spiteful girlfriends, times of death and of discovery; but their eyes followed the sergeant's progress towards the tree and the shrouded corpse, with the spanner gripped business-like in his big fist. He lifted off the black plastic sheet, and let it drop; and Fenner took an unconscious pace forward. Malone's movement too was automatic, lifting a hand to touch his friend's elbow, in warning or something warmer.

Graham McLaggan's head dropped loosely towards one sagging shoulder, with the jaw twisted awry and the mouth half open. Thin dribbles of blood ran like unravelling threads from the dark sockets of his eyes; and there was a dark eye in his throat, too, with a silver glint to its heart. That must be the spike that held him floating there against the tree, his feet pointed like a dancer's a foot above the grass. His chest and shoulders were lacerated by jagged lines that showed black at this distance, clotted blood on a ground of blood; hips and legs were much the same, though marked more sparingly. But what joined them now was no human abdomen, nothing human at all, only a dark chaos that could have no name but death. Like a black hole, it seemed to suck the light; and caught in those currents, Fenner's eyes fixed themselves on it and stared, and stared.

It was movement that broke the horrible fixation. Fenner blinked, and saw the sergeant standing as far as he practicably could from the tree and the body, while he fitted the adjustable spanner to the head of the spike.

"One thing," Fenner grunted. "At least it isn't a sex thing, for the Butcher. He's never raped them, has he? Never even touched the genitals."

"Maybe that's his kind of sex thing," Malone replied. "Not to touch them. He's touched everything else."

"S'pose."

The sergeant was a burly man, but he was having problems. He was sweating and cursing under his breath, using all his weight to drag on the spike, stumbling and almost falling as the spanner slipped and came away. But he tried again, and a third time; and at last the spanner turned without losing its grip. The sergeant grunted in triumph, twisted the spike back and forth, and drew it smoothly out of the tree. The boy's body fell away, *rigor mortis* holding it stiff as it dropped against the sergeant's legs. His face worked for a moment, then some odd sense of decency made him turn away from the body a moment before he vomited.

And as the sergeant turned, so too did Fenner – turned as a cat turns suddenly for home, seeming to reverse itself inside its skin. He was suddenly sick to death of what was happening, sick of himself and of what he was doing. He stood as a partial and prejudiced observer on the sidelines, watching others fulfil their appointed roles: watching stretcher-bearers come forward for the body, watching Mike speak softly to the embarrassed sergeant. There was no part for him here, nothing to do but watch; and if he were useless here and now, with a new body and a new crime to give a fresh thrust and direction to the search, then he was useless altogether.

And more than that, the investigation was worse than useless to him. Already his involvement had damaged his relationship with Tina, perhaps beyond repair. Whether he still belonged with her, in Wales or anywhere else, he couldn't say; but he knew that he didn't belong here any more. Here they could offer him nothing but games played over the dead bodies of boys, trying to guess whodunit; and he didn't want to play any more.

So he walked quietly back between the cars, passing all but unnoticed through the hustle of activity.

He nodded to the constable at the gate, jingling his car-keys in his hand; but he walked past the car too, and went to the public phone-box beside the road.

He dialled the number of the cottage, leaning one shoulder against the cool iron framework of the booth while he waited for the connection to be made. There were no directories on the metal shelf, only a folded sheet of paper apparently torn from a glossy magazine. Fenner picked it up idly as the phone began to ring at the other end of the line. Unfolding it, he saw without surprise that it was a piece of clumsy soft porn, a young woman naked with her legs spread, exposing large breasts and a tangled bush of pubic hair. Someone had been using it as an *aide-memoire*; there was a number scribbled in pencil across her pale stomach . . .

. . . And it was a number he knew: 37373 – it was an easy figure to remember, deliberately so. That was the number the Samaritans advertised; he'd seen it on dozens of posters and leaflets, during his time in Newcastle.

He cradled the telephone receiver, without registering that it had been ringing at the other end for some time now, with no reply. He looked again at the photograph, and remembered Mike listing the contents of McLaggan's pockets. "*. . . driving licence, keys, pencil . . . Oh, and a dozen girlie pics, cut out of a porn mag . . .*"

Fenner folded the paper carefully along its original creases, leant his weight against the door of the phone-box to swing it open, walked out –

– and he turned again.

32 *Blood and Love*

After that first time, you went to bed with Anne whenever you could, whenever it was safe. But she was careful to explain the law to you, to make you see that if anyone found out, you'd never be allowed to share a bed again. Anne might even be taken away from you altogether. Or you might be taken from her.

So, of course, you told no one. Just as you'd never told anyone about your father, or tried to run away, for fear of being separated from Anne. You'd both read stories about families being split up, brothers and sisters sent to separate council or foster homes. That would have destroyed you, shutting you away from all that was real in your life, your fear and your love; so you kept quiet, and you kept them both.

You remember the feelings, and the physical symbols of those feelings – blood and sweat, tears and semen. But blood is what you remember most. What you see. Like a petrol-spill on a puddle, or rain slicking a window down: a thin wash of blood over everything. Blood damping and matting your hair, running into your eyes. Blood beneath your fingers, blood in the air – the taste and smell and touch of blood like smoke in your throat and lungs.

You were fourteen; and all your memories, like roads, lead you here, to the sudden knowledge of how it feels to breathe someone else's blood.

In his last year at school, David still takes it day by day, living only for Anne, and perhaps a little for his long runs alone. School is as it always has been, a thing to be endured, a time to be waited through. He watches the other pupils watching him, as secretly scornful of them as they are secretly of him.

No one has forgotten Johnson's arm; David never fights now, and that alone makes him different, and somehow fearful. The other boys steer well clear of him when they can, and only mock him behind his back, well out of earshot.

They mock him for what they see: a clever, silent boy who does his work and nothing else, who has the face and body of a Greek sculpture but uses neither to any purpose. They see a boy with no spirit in him, dull and unlovely, mocked by his own physical perfection: a rat trapped in the body of a lion. And the fools think that they see the truth; they never realise that what they're looking at is just a shadow of the true David, a hollow transparency only waiting for the night to flow into him and make him real.

Today school is perhaps harder to bear, because waiting is more difficult. David's father has gone away for three days on one of his regular business trips, leaving the house to his children; so the gates of their true world can swing open that much sooner, as soon as David is home and closing the front door behind him. All evening and all night they can be together and sharing, in the only way they want.

At last four o'clock strikes, the school bell rings, and he can hurry out, for once ahead of his class, ahead of the whole school as he sprints across the playground.

He runs home with the long, easy stride of the athlete in training. Their house is part of a small estate half a mile from the school; and he's there in under three minutes, his scudding feet sending gravel shooting from the drive onto the rose-beds. He fumbles for his latch-key, slides it into the lock, twists, pushes open the door –

– and entered nightmare. Didn't you, David? This is where it all ended, where it began. In a house of blood and love.

In that last dying moment of your innocence, you walked in –

– and briefly, the time between the end of one breath and the beginning of another, he thinks that nothing has changed.

Then he thinks that everything has changed.

Anne should have been here in the hall, waiting, as bubblingly eager as he is; but all that meets him is strangeness, a thin, rusty smell that catches at the back of his throat and a low liquid moaning.

Terror snatches at him with sharp fingers, pulling him running up the stairs, crying his sister's name.

At the sound of his voice, something moves in her bedroom. The door crashes open.

David screams.

It is a monster that comes shambling out onto the landing, a blood-swathed travesty of a human being. A Frankenstein creation, it moves as though moving is all that keeps it upright, as though only a precarious balance prevents it from falling apart. It staggers to a halt a yard away from where David is backed against the wall; it lifts feeble, drooping, reddened hands towards his face, and falls.

Looking down, David can see that the monster wears his sister's face, and dress.

"David . . ."

She calls to him with a voice like dead roses, blood-red and brittle; but his transfixed body will not, cannot move from the gripping wall, and his mind has no power to force it. Too great a change; he cannot encompass this.

"David!" She invokes him, as a sudden widow might invoke the body of her lover. David senses the wrongness; she is so nearly dead, he should be calling after her. But he has no voice to speak to her, or hands to help. He is all eyes.

"David." She coughs, and a little crimson leaks at the corner of her mouth. David's eyes trace the path of it across her streaked cheek, into her hair. "Help me. You must. In my room. There's a knife . . ."

But the knife has done too much already. He looks at her wrists, where she wears great scabs of clotted blood as bracelets; at her dress, splashed everywhere but soaked from the waist down; at the thin pool forming on the carpet, beside her hip.

And at last a question breaks out of his silence.

"Why?"

"Does it matter?" She speaks after a time-lag, as though there were a great distance between them; and then it's only to block his question with another, in the tired voice of the ultimately desperate.

"Yes." David drops to his knees beside her, tears streaming

down his cheeks, fighting revulsion as he stretches his hand out to touch her. To dabble his fingers in her blood. "*Yes!* It does . . . It does *matter.*" He spits the words out like something dirty – which they are, for David. He doesn't understand why they feel so foul, he doesn't understand anything at the moment; but they're like a confession that everything has changed, that all the good has gone out of his world. It's the first time that anything has mattered to him, and not to Anne: which says again that she's a long way from him now, and moving further.

Perhaps she feels it too, or perhaps it's only pain that twists her face momentarily into a stranger's. But her voice is still the same, grey and weary as if she were already dead, as she says, "I'm pregnant."

From the way she says it, that should be all the explanation that he needs. But he only shakes his head. It's nothing – or at least, it's not enough. Not enough to draw bracelets of blood around her wrists, to soak the skirt of her dress and make a monstrous nightmare of her.

"*David!*" It's almost a scream, and he almost doesn't recognise it as his name, coming from her lips without even an echo of love in it. "David, *think*!" She's having to fight now pushing the words out past a barrier of pain. Instinctively David reaches for her hand, feels the stickiness of clotting blood and pulls back. Both his hands are stained now, and he can feel the stain encroaching on his mind.

"I'm *pregnant*," she says again, each word a gasp like a scream in whispers. "With your child. I couldn't . . . I couldn't get rid of it, I don't know how. I don't know who to go to. And what would Father say, when he found out? What would he *do*?"

(You knew what he would do. He would name you animals, and punish. And go on punishing, and on and on, until he was proved right – until there was nothing human left, in either of you.)

But –

"Couldn't you have waited?" David sobs. His hand is back on her stomach, feeling the wide slash where she has ripped herself open, trying to hold it closed, to hold the blood in. Already, despite the pumping blood that trickles over his fingers, it feels more like raw meat

(dead meat)

than living tissue. "Couldn't you have told me? Talked to me?"

She shakes her head, but it's not an answer to his question. Her whole body moves with the violence of the gesture, as she tries to deny the whole world of questions and answers, fear and love, and pain. She's trying to turn her back, to tear free of it – to die.

"Help me," she grunts, as her legs push her across the carpet towards David. He backs away. "David, for God's sake . . . I tried, I tried to do it myself, I did try. I cut my wrists, but it clotted too quickly. So I stabbed . . . I wanted, I wanted to stab it, that seemed right, and I tried . . ."

(Tried to stab the foetus, your child, your enemy. You would have stabbed it, kicked it, crushed it under your foot. But neither she nor you could come at it, except through her.)

"David!" She shrieks it, but her voice breaks and bubbles before the end, and she coughs a gush of blood onto the carpet between them. "You've got to help me, Davy! I can't, I can't stand this. And I haven't got the strength any more." Her voice is briefly lucid, free of blood or pain and all the more terrible for being Anne's voice in the mouth of a monster. Terrible, too, for what it says. "Get the knife and finish it for me, Davy. Please? If you love me, do it now . . ."

David jumps to his feet, but not to fetch the knife. "No. No, don't ask me. I can't. I won't."

"You've got to. You can't leave me like this. If you *love* me, Davy . . .!"

"Don't say that! It's not fair . . ." David is caught at the top of the stairs, wanting to run, but unable to leave her, unable even to take his eyes off what his sister has become.

"Fair?" She repeats it like a dry red echo. "Nothing's fair. It's just real, Davy, that's all. It's what you've got to do . . ."

Her hand grips one of the wooden posts that support the banister rail, then hitches itself higher, leaving a ruddy stain on the paintwork.

"*Nooo!*" It's David that's shrieking now, throwing the refusal at her for as long as he has breath to hold it. Choking and sobbing, he shakes his head wildly, and pounds his fists on the wall behind him.

Anne looks up at him – or rather, Anne's eyes look up through the stained mask of pain she's wearing instead of a face – and slowly, impossibly, she pulls her ruined body up until she's standing, leaning heavily on the banister. Both her wrists are bleeding again, but she doesn't seem to notice.

"Coward," she says, her voice a hard rustle like the sound of dry petals falling. "You coward. You weak, snivelling little *coward*. It's all right when you're taking things, isn't it? That's what you think love is, just taking from me, taking and taking. But you've got to give something now, David. You owe me."

She lurches, blunders towards him, those dreadful, dripping hands held out like gifts. And all the time her voice goes on, accusing and demanding.

"It's no good running, David. You can't run forever. Not from me. I'm a part of you. Like Father's a part of us, like we could never run from him. There's only one way you can get away from me. Kill me, David. I'm dying anyway, finish it for me." He whimpers, and her face twists again. "You Christless coward. That's it, isn't it? You're scared of what'll happen, of what they'll do to you afterwards. You don't care a shit about me, you never did. It's just you, that's all you – "

David screams to blot out that terrible voice, and what it's saying. He closes his eyes, but he can still see her coming. He can smell the blood and the fear and the pain of her; and a moment later he feels her hands scrabbling against his chest. He gasps for air, and hears what she's saying –

". . . baby dressed up in a man's body, how could I ever have . . ."

– and almost of their own accord

(but not quite, because you wanted them to, God how you wanted them to)

David's hands fly up and find her throat, his thumbs pressing hard against the windpipe to choke back that voice and keep it in, somewhere where he doesn't have to hear it. His eyes open to see her still shaping words at him with an empty mouth; and he squeezes harder, and feels the soft flesh giving, feels the strength going out of her in a rush so that all her weight hangs from his grip on her neck. And

(remembering another time when someone was helpless in your hands, and remembering the pleasure of it)

he twists savagely to feel the flesh bruise and tear beneath the skin, and watches himself do it; and twists once more for the sharp snap of splintering bone.

And then, with his hands sated and his mind content, he lets go and watches her fall at his feet, and knows that she's dead –

and remembers that she's Anne, and that she loves him. Loved him, rather, because she's dead, and he killed her.

You killed her – and you enjoyed killing her. You felt her die beneath your fingers, tasted the moment of her dying as a soursweet thrill you'd never known before. The memory of it still shines for you, like fire in a grey landscape, a mirror among dust.

But then you had to learn to live without her; and that wasn't so easy.

Was it, David?

When they found you – when someone looked through the door you hadn't closed and saw you, and saw what you had made of your sister – you were crouching in a dark corner of the hall, moaning softly, your eyes glazed and vacant. Like an animal.

Licking blood from your fingers, like an animal.

33 Out and Away

Fenner vaulted over the fence and headed back at a run, ignoring the shout of the constable behind him. The Range-Rover ambulance was already pulling away from the group of parked vehicles, its blue light flashing; Fenner jogged past it, and located Malone.

"Mike . . . Listen, I think we've got something . . . Where's all the stuff you got out of his pockets?"

"Packed up," Mike said. "Ready to go back to the station. Why?"

"Let's find it."

Malone led him over to a car with an open boot. Inside the boot was a case, with its lid too standing open; and a plain-clothes detective was adding one more plastic bag to the collection in the box, while a constable noted it down on a list.

"Steel spike, Thomson, from the victim's throat. Bag number seven."

"Check."

"And if you like, you can put down that it looks a lot like a tent-peg to me. Maybe the Butcher's a boy scout." The detective reached up to shut the lid of the case, then spotted Malone and Fenner. "Hullo, chief. Something I can do for you?"

"Break out what he was carrying on him, will you, Bill? Paul's got an idea."

The bags were laid out on the car roof. Fenner picked one up, and nodded. "I couldn't be sure until I'd seen them; but I'm sure now."

"Sure about what?" Malone snapped. "You know the model, or something?"

Fenner put a hand into his pocket, and took out the page he'd found in the phone-booth. "It's from the same magazine, and you can see it was McLaggan's. Look, the creases match; and you might even get fingerprints if you're lucky, it's glossy enough."

"Where did you find it?"

"In the phone-box, by the road," Fenner said. And then, "It's real, Mike. It's a link. Look." He pointed at the scribbled number. "Recognise it?"

"No." Malone frowned. "Should I?"

"Not necessarily; but I do. It's the Samaritans."

"I don't get it," Malone said, staring at the photograph as if willing the model to come to life and talk. "You said the Samaritans thing didn't lead anywhere."

"It didn't. But it was only a faint chance then, that Diana had ever called them. This time we can be bloody nearly certain that McLaggan did."

"Unless he lost his nerve at the last minute. But suppose he did ring them, I still don't understand the link."

"Neither do I," Fenner admitted. "Maybe there isn't one. Maybe it's just coincidence. But it's the first possible connection that's turned up, right? Diana might have phoned the Samaritans, was certainly ready to do it if she felt the need; and McLaggan almost certainly did. Okay, they both had good reason to; Diana was dying, and the boy was on the run. Maybe that's all there is to it, but we've got to check."

"Yes, of course. But we didn't have much joy last time, remember; the branch director blocked us right from the start."

"I know," Fenner said with a thin smile. "And I imagine he'll block you again. That's why I'm going to sneak in the back way. You do what you can, okay? I'm going to find a friend of mine."

Linden lived just a couple of minutes from the moor, in a small cul-de-sac. Fenner drove round and found the house, a semi with a garden front and back, a garage and a gravel drive. Standing in the shelter of the wooden porch, he pressed the bell and heard the soft two-chime tone inside; and a minute later, David opened the door.

"Paul Fenner." He said the name carefully, as if tasting something unexpected. His eyes moved quickly past Fenner to the road, and back; then he smiled. "How did you know that I enjoy surprises? Come in."

He led Fenner through the hall to the kitchen. "What can I offer you? I lead an embarrassingly healthy life, but I do have real coffee, if you don't mind waiting while it percs. Other than that, it's herb teas or fruit-juice, I'm afraid."

"I'd love some coffee." Fenner's body was reminding him none too gently that he'd taken nothing at all since he got up, and that a man can only run on adrenaline for so long. "If it's not too much trouble."

"Not at all."

David made the coffee and found an ashtray, then took Fenner into the front room. He lit the gas fire, sat down and cocked one eyebrow in a consciously inquisitive gesture. "Well, Paul? You can't persuade me that this is simply a social visit; no one visits socially at half-past nine on a Saturday morning. And besides, you've got something burning inside you on a very short fuse, however hard you try to sit on it. So spit it out, why don't you?"

Fenner nodded. "I don't know if you've heard yet, on the radio or anything, but there's been another killing."

"No, I hadn't heard. Who was it?"

"A boy. Seventeen-year-old. Same kind of foul killing the

Butcher goes in for, so we assume it's the same guy again. But this is the thing: this kid was in trouble, and we're fairly sure that he phoned the Samaritans last night."

Fenner detailed what he'd found in the phone-box, and the conclusions he drew from it.

David listened intently, then said, "There's still no guarantee that he actually put the call through. A lot of people get the number and the right change and everything, and never quite find the courage to pick up the receiver and dial."

"Sure," Fenner conceded, "it's not solid; but the chances must be pretty high."

"Agreed," David nodded. "So what do you want me to do?"

"Snoop. Find out who was on duty last night, and who took the call. Get as much detail as you can, then ask if they'd be prepared to talk to me, or to the police."

"As it happens," David said, "I was there myself. I don't remember this lad calling; but I was out for an hour or so, on an emergency. It might have come in then, or on one of the other shifts. I'll certainly do my best for you."

"I'd appreciate it. The police are doing the job officially again, but they didn't get past your director last time, and I don't suppose his attitude will have changed much."

"Not much, no – though the coincidence might shake him a little." David looked up, frowning. "It is odd, you know, Paul. First Diana and now this boy, and both of them leading you to us."

Fenner shrugged. "Maybe it's not even coincidence; maybe there's a solid link somewhere. We just don't know enough to tell."

"I don't understand that," David said. "How could the Samaritans be a link between the two killings?"

"I don't know." He ran his hands hard over his face. "I don't understand it either. Maybe the Butcher listens in, maybe he has a tap on your telephone line. Or maybe he's telepathic, and he deliberately picks on people who are desperate enough to phone you lot. Hell, maybe he's one of you lot. Or maybe he's trying to close your organisation down by getting rid of the clientele."

"Easy, Paul."

"Yeah." Fenner breathed deeply a few times, fighting off

the trembling in his fingers; then he took a long swallow of coffee, and forced himself to relax. "Right. Sorry. I'm just getting a bit worked up. Chasing shadows gets to you, after a bit." He drained his mug and got up. "You will do that for me, then? Hunt around, and see what you come up with?"

"Yes, of course. Just give me the boy's name."

David wrote it on a scrap of paper, and slipped it into his wallet. "There. I won't forget; I'll go in tonight and raid the files. If he did call, he should be in there somewhere." He hesitated briefly, then went on, "Paul, have you told the police about me?"

"Not your name, of course not. Only that I have a fifth column in the organisation. Why?"

"I'd just sooner not be on *their* files, as a potential spy. I'll cooperate with you, because I think in this instance it's valuable and important; but my loyalty isn't generally up for grabs, and I don't want it thought that it might be."

"Don't worry," Fenner said. "I'm very discreet."

"Good, thank you. That's all that was worrying me. Why don't you sit down and have another coffee? You don't have to race off, I'm not busy."

"No, but I am," Fenner said regretfully. "This whole case has come alive again, and if I'm going to make myself at all useful there's a lot I've got to do first. You've still got my number, haven't you? I'll be in and out no end, but if you keep trying, you'll get me eventually."

"Right you are. By the way, how's your girlfriend? Tina, wasn't it?"

"Yeah, Tina. You didn't meet her, did you? Pity, you'd like her." Fenner shrugged helplessly. "She's in Wales. I don't know what's happening, whether we're still together, even. We both got ourselves into a state, and . . ."

"Do you want to talk about it?"

Fenner smiled thinly, and shook his head. "No, thanks. I haven't reached that stage yet – or else I've been through it, and gone beyond. Either way, I haven't got time at the moment. But thanks for the offer."

"It wasn't just professional courtesy," David said. "And it stands open, any time. If you need it."

Not knowing quite what to say, Fenner simply nodded and moved towards the door. David saw him out, and was still standing at the door watching as Fenner turned the car out of the cul-de-sac and towards the main road.

Just south of Lancaster, Tina pulled into a service station off the M6 for petrol. She'd been on the road since seven; her mouth was dry, and a growing irritability with other drivers told her that she needed a cigarette. It wouldn't hurt to take half an hour's break, have some coffee and a smoke. But now that she'd made the move, now that she was *moving*, there was a fierce urgency pulling at her; she felt an aching need to be with Fenner, to find an answer, any answer that would stop her being torn apart. She begrudged even the five minutes it took her to fill the tank and pay the attendant. If she took a break now she'd be restless and impatient with herself, hurrying, drinking the coffee too quickly and getting no relaxation from the cigarette. Better to go on, and let the next coffee be with Fenner, that bit sooner. Better by far to light her cigarette from a match he'd struck. And so much better to let his and not a stranger's be the next face she was close to . . .

Driving yet again along the moor road, Fenner pulled up where he had parked before, and whistled the constable over.

"Yes, sir, can I help . . . Oh. Inspector Fenner, is it, sir?"

"Not officially, but you've got the general idea. Listen, is DI Malone still on the moor?"

"No, sir. The Chief Superintendent came down for a look, and Inspector Malone went back to the station with him."

"All right. Thanks, constable."

Fenner went home and put a call through to the station.

"Good morning. Could you get a message to Inspector Malone for me, please? It's rather important. If you could just ask him to phone Paul Fenner, as soon as he can . . . Thank you, yes. He's got the number. You'll probably find him in the incident room . . . Thanks very much. Good-bye."

He made himself a coffee, then sat at his desk and doodled on a notepad, building triangles. The Samaritans at the apex, Diana at one of the lower corners and Graham McLaggan at the other. The game was to join them with arrows and find a place to fit the Butcher in, and have the whole make logical sense. He put the Butcher at the heart of the triangle, as a pivot which all three corners could turn around; he put him at the top, with the Samaritans; he put him outside the triangle altogether. And still nothing made sense.

He was crumpling up his fifth attempt when the phone rang.

"Yeah, hullo?"

"It's Mike, Paul. I got your message, but I've only just managed to get away."

"With the Chief, were you?"

"Too right," Mike groaned. "Team lecture for the lads."

Fenner chuckled. "I thought you might be in for something like that; that's why I didn't ask to be put straight through. I thought you'd rather not take a call from me with the Chief maybe listening in."

"He wouldn't have been very happy, certainly. He *isn't* very happy. Doesn't like the idea of a Samaritans connection at all."

"Why not? It's the only game in town."

"Yeah, but he doesn't want to play it with you. He tried to shunt the whole thing off as fanciful nonsense, only then the forensic report came through, that it was definitely McLaggan's picture, and the phone number was in his writing. *And* they found his prints on the phone. The Chief gave way a bit then; I am officially instructed to get hold of the branch director again, and see if I can get anything out of him. I can even lean on him a little, if I need to. Threats of subpoenas, withholding information, obstructing the police. That sort of thing."

"Good. Are you going now?"

"As soon as I've checked that the guy's available to talk to. Why?"

"I'd like to come. Can you manage?"

Malone chuckled. "Yeah. I'll just mumble the introductions, and he won't notice the 'ex-' I stick on your 'Inspector'. Shall I pick you up at your place, to avoid the reporters?"

"Thanks, I'd appreciate it. Now listen, have you still got those psychiatrists on the team? The guys who were trying to tell you what kind of a man the Butcher must be?"

"Yeah, we've still got them. They're as much use as a wet fart at a wedding, but they're around. What do you want them for?"

"Tell them to forget the Butcher for a bit. I want them to look back over the victims, see what they can figure out about their states of mind just before they died. Send 'em out to talk to relatives and friends, if they haven't enough to go on already."

"Yeah, sure – but what are they looking for?"

"I want their opinion on something. Whether they think it's likely that any of the other victims might have phoned the Samaritans before they were killed."

"Okay, will do." Mike's voice was hesitant. "Going to tell me why?"

"Just that we've either got a coincidence or a connection, Mike; and if it's a real connection it ought to run back further than Diana. If those guys are any good, they should be able to tell us whether to work on it or wipe it out."

"I suppose . . . Okay, Paul, I'll get them onto it. See you in a bit."

Half an hour later Mike arrived, in a police Fiesta driven by a WPC.

"This is Julie Johnson," Mike said, as Fenner got into the back. "She's like the car, only here to impress this Taggart man. You know how people go for blue lights and uniforms. But listen, Julie, Paul's not here at all, get it? He will not be mentioned in my report; and if you end up taking notes, then all the questions are coming from me."

"Aye, sir." She caught Fenner's eye in the mirror and smiled amiably. "He's the Invisible Man."

Three years in the Norton Bramley Psychiatric Hospital didn't teach you much, David; but you learned one thing quickly, because you had to. You learned to lie.

And when they released you, because both your truths were gone now, you learned to live a lie. One of the hospital trustees was the manager of a local bank; you lied to him, and he gave you a job as a counter clerk. You found a bedsit, and lived alone; and for a while you even lied to yourself. Telling yourself that you were normal now, that it was all behind you, that Anne was dead and everything was over.

But there was a mouse in your room, that feasted nightly on the crumbs in your carpet and scuttled quietly along the skirting-boards beneath your bed; and it was that mouse that reminded you of one truth, at least. Wasn't it, David?

You bought a trap from the ironmonger, thinking to bait it and leave it, and find the mouse dead in the morning. But when the time came, that wasn't what you did. Not quite.

You set the trap with a lump of dried cheese, and put it down beside the table; then you turned the light off and just sat quietly on the bed, waiting again. You waited, and waited; and at last the mouse came like a summoning, a dark shadow slipping over the floor towards its ending. The trap glittered in the faint light through the window, and sprang shut; and you heard the mouse scream.

And you smiled. Smiled as you tore its small body from the spike and held it, warm and still moving; smiled as you dug your thumbs into the rag of flesh, and ripped at it with your nails; smiled as you smelt the blood, and felt the creature die.

It was another beginning, a new birth for you; and for the second time you built yourself a secret life in darkness, and kept it hidden from the daylight world. For a long time you contented yourself with small deaths, stray cats, occasionally a dog; while the world only saw a quiet bachelor with an athlete's body, an intelligent man who worked hard in his chosen profession and spent his leisure time in training and solitary sports.

And you still lied to yourself as much as the world, believing that what you had now, what you took, would always be enough. You heard about the Samaritans and applied to join, lying to them too by telling them almost all the truth. They asked you to an assessment interview with a member psychiatrist; and you played it very quiet, very open and honest and vulnerable. Without the long years in hospital, you'd never have got away with it; but you know just what to say, how to act, what to give away. At the end, the psychiatrist congratulated you; he said it took a strong mind to regain stability after a trauma such as yours, and he was confident that you'd be a great asset to the organisation. And you smiled, and thanked him quietly, and said you hoped so. And at first you found genuine satisfaction in trying to help people who were mostly more fortunate than yourself. There are qualities of despair; and these people were rank amateurs by your standards. You listened to them night after night, the lonely and the suicidal, and were constantly reassured by their miseries. None of them could touch you, or even come close to it. You knew what had been done to you, and were truly glad never to hear it repeated in someone else's life.

So you listened, and helped when you could; and believed it to be enough.

Until the night you were on duty, and a woman wanted to speak to you in person. Because the situation was critical, because she was so close to suicide, you got permission to go alone, as she demanded; and you went with no other thought than to listen, to talk a little, to try to help.

But she met you with bitterness and laughter, called you a liar and laughed; and you wanted the death she was so close to, needed to feel it beneath your fingers, to share in it. So you took it; and knew in that moment that you had found a pathway back to Anne. Her life was gone, but you could find her death again, relive it over and over by recreating the pleasure you had found in it.

You were careful and clever, lying expertly to cover your tracks, killing with caution and imagination, and no conscience. Your victims were half dead already, dead inside; and Anne was dead and rotten, so what did it matter anyway, what could it matter?

You never expected to get away with it forever; but that didn't matter either. You made contingency plans, to stretch it out as long as you could; and promised yourself that if ever the police came close, you would act decisively. Whatever the consequences.

So when Fenner had gone, you didn't waste time cursing the luck that seemed to have left you. You stripped and changed, and went for a hard, driving run round the perimeter of the moor.

Home again, you did half an hour's weight training on the equipment in your garage, to burn up the last of the adrenaline in your system; then you had a long shower, put on a fresh track suit for comfort and made yourself some lunch.

After you'd eaten you went back into the garage, and took a heavy American hunting knife from its sheath. You found an oilstone and began to circle the blade lightly across the smooth grey block, bringing it to a razor sharpness, a killing edge.

Feeling the weight of it in your palm, cherishing in advance the driving danger of it, the feel of skin ripping like cloth and the soft flesh folding itself around the steel. Waiting for the warm flow of blood across the handle and your hand, and the stickiness of it as it dried . . .

Tina came to an abrupt stop in front of the flat, just behind Fenner's car. All things being equal, she might have taken these last yards more slowly, after hurrying for two hundred miles. She might have sat for some time astride the cooling bike, just looking at the door and wondering what decision and what futures lay behind it for her now. But all things were not equal; she hadn't stopped to find a toilet since she left Wales, and she was suddenly desperate.

It would make a great opening line for the big reunion, she thought, grinning to herself as she hauled the bike onto its stand and snatched the keys from the lock. "*Sorry, can't stop*," as she raced through the living-room, where Fenner would be sitting, staring, just starting to his feet. "*I'm dying for a piss*." It might even help to make things right again, turning what could have been a big melodramatic moment into a little domestic comedy.

She was enjoying it in advance, almost relishing the urgent pressure in her bladder as she unlocked the flat door and hurried up the stairs. But there were no lights burning, no response to her arrival or her yelling Fenner's name. Disappointment hit her like a slap in the face, brutally physical, leaving her with none of the nerves and the incipient laughter, none of the caring need to find solutions, only a thin resentment. She resented the smug furniture which mocked her with its emptiness, she resented her own unreasonableness in expecting to find him in when he didn't know she was coming; and of course she resented him for being out, for turning her entrance into hollow farce, solitaire showmanship, a tango for one.

Fenner's absence even took away her rush for the toilet. But she went anyway, then wandered back through the flat, checking it room by room. Just in case. Satisfied eventually that Fenner was neither hiding in the study nor lying dead in the bedroom, she filled the kettle and put the radio on, slipped off her leather jacket and sat down to unbuckle her boots, wondering what more long-term ways of filling time she might find. Wondering how much time there might be to fill, before Fenner came home.

"I'm not sure that I understand," Alex Taggart said, his fingers fidgeting with a Biro as they had done solidly for the last half-hour. He was an unprepossessing man to look at, Fenner thought, with his straggly curls and his buck teeth; but there was nothing wrong with his mind, and his voice was a soft, mellow tenor that was probably tailor-made to dispense comfort down a telephone line. "What is it you're trying to say?" he went on slowly. "That there is some connection between these last two murders, and that the connection comes through the Samaritans?"

"We don't know yet." Malone was endlessly patient when he needed to be; Fenner couldn't hear a hint of irritation or impatience in his friend's voice, though he knew the urgency that was burning beneath it. "It does seem possible, though; and if there is such a connection, we may well find that it goes further back, and touches all the Butcher's murders. It could give us the key to this case, if we can find what that connection is. Alternatively, of course, we may simply be looking at a coincidence; but even then it would help us to know if McLaggan did ring your organisation last night, and what was said if he did. Whichever is the case, we need information from your files and permission to interview some of your volunteers, if we're to get any further."

Taggart nodded, tapping the end of the Biro against his protruding teeth. "I am more disposed to help you this time than I was when you came to me before," he said at last. "However, I don't feel that I can make this decision alone. I should like to consider what you say, and then speak to my seniors at the national office in Slough, before coming to a decision."

"The longer you delay, the more you damage our chances," Malone said bluntly.

"Yes, I can see that – but you must look at it from my point of view. Our promise of confidentiality is absolute; the nearest parallel I know is that of the priest and what he hears in the confessional. He is forbidden by God and the church to break his trust; and I am forbidden by my conscience and the rules of my organisation. You must give me time to think, and to consult some of my colleagues. Let me ring you back this evening."

Seeing that that was as much as he was going to get, Malone nodded and rose to his feet. Fenner and the WPC followed suit, and a minute later had been politely ushered out of the house.

Fenner's eyes found Mike's, and saw his own sour cynicism reflected. "Well, quite," he said, with a shrug. "But there's no use brooding. Either they will or they won't – and if they don't, maybe you should think again about a warrant to seize their files."

"Never get it past the Chief."

"No, I suppose. But let's leave it for now and find some lunch, eh?"

"Better not. Too much to do. I can get a sandwich at the station."

"Sandwich, schmandwich. I said lunch." Fenner grabbed Malone's arm and frogmarched him to the car. "Open up, Julie. And listen, if you drive us anywhere near the station I'll put you both under citizen's arrest, get it? Take us somewhere we can get hot food in large quantities; pick a good one, and you might even get it bought for you."

Just after two o'clock, David Linden ran his car slowly down the hill to park a few yards behind Fenner's. For a wonder, the street was empty. Not that it mattered particularly; it would take a very sharp eye to see what Linden did, when Fenner opened the door. Any casual passer-by would see nothing more than a visitor stepping into a gentle hug with his friend, and the door swinging shut behind them.

David was still in his track suit; as he got out of the car, leaving the door unlocked and the keys in the ignition, he could feel the handle of the knife bumping his leg, shifting around in the deep pocket. He steadied it with his hand, gripping it inside the secrecy of its hiding place, smiling quietly.

There was a motorcycle beside the kerb, the engine ticking arhythmically as it cooled. He was aware of it as he was aware of everything, from the dirty litter and dogshit on the pavement to the cat on a wall opposite to the pale mackerel sky overhead. This sense of heightened perception, almost of heightened understanding, was nothing new; it happened every time before a kill, almost as though the world slowed down a little to give him more time to cherish each fragment of the way it was, to give him more to remember.

He knocked on the door, brisk but friendly, with his left hand; with his right he eased the blade from his pocket and stood with it pressed against the leg of his track suit. Every muscle was poised and ready. He heard footsteps coming unhurriedly down the stairs, and rose slightly onto his toes. He would strike hard as soon as the door opened, stepping forward at the same time to catch the slumping body and carry it back into the hallway, kicking the door shut behind him. It would only take a moment; and once the door was locked, he could have all the time he wanted. He'd make sure that Fenner was dead

(but not play with the body, David. Not this time. It mustn't look like the Butcher's work this time, remember?)

and then he'd go through the flat, check that Fenner didn't have his name written down or anything else that was relevant and dangerous. He'd mess everything up, make it look like vandals or burglars, or a fight – anything to throw the police off the scent.

But no more time to plan it, now it was happening. He heard the latch being turned back, saw the door start to open; and his hand swung the knife up for the single savage thrust below the ribcage that would shock the life out of his victim . . .

. . . and it wasn't Fenner. A tousle-haired girl was blinking, trying to adjust her eyes to the light, not even seeing him properly. His arm stiffened with shock, lost its momentum; but her eyes focused suddenly on the knife and he stabbed her anyway, having no choice now.

The knife took her in the abdomen, with only a fraction of the force it needed. He pushed the blade clumsily deeper and she folded forward and sideways, away from his grabbing left hand, so that he had to kick her back into the narrow hallway. He had just sufficient control left to step inside as he had meant to do, and push the door shut. Then he stood with the streaked blade hanging from his fingers, watching helplessly as a rim of bright blood oozed from beneath the girl's slumped body.

He could put a name to her, no trouble. She must be Fenner's Tina. She should have been in Wales; but there was no time now to wonder what had happened, what she was doing here. No time to wreck the flat, no time to do anything with Fenner alive and perhaps coming back any moment.

And Fenner blood-hot on his trail after this, Fenner possessed . . .

Wanting only to get out of there, to get somewhere where he could think, David backed out of the flat and slammed the door. Children's voices yelling up the street reminded him to thrust the knife into his pocket and walk steadily uphill to his car, doing nothing to attract attention and make them notice or remember him.

Into the car, turn the key, pull out, get out and away. Go home, yes – but only as the first step of a journey. Get out, get out and away . . .

34 Masks

Fenner had left Mike and the WPC to go back to the station alone. He'd walked home, with his mind chasing itself in circles; and now he pushed his key into the lock and turned it –

– and the door swung open under his hand, and Tina was there, lying in huddled stillness at the foot of the stairs, and there were damp, sticky patches on the carpet between them.

Fenner snatched at the door for support, as the solid world plunged and heaved about him. He closed his eyes, drew a deep, shuddering breath, felt a scream building in his chest, and . . .

Stop.

Breathe out.

Good.

Now in, and out.

Five times more.

Now open your eyes. Don't think. Just look.

(Tina's dead, and I –)

No. No names. It's a girl, that's all, and she's been hurt. Is she dead? Find out. Staring won't get you anywhere.

Move forward. It's all right, take it slowly. One foot at a time. Good. Now kneel down beside her. Never mind the blood. You know what to look for. Do it the way they trained you.

Stop shaking. It's not Tina, and you're not involved. It's a training exercise, that's all. A test. Mind you do the thing properly.

Put your hand under her jaw, that's right. Fingers on the pulse. Never mind that your hand knows the shape of that jaw, that you could tell her from a thousand women with your eyes shut, just by touching her here or anywhere else. Never mind that her skin feels cold and clammy and dead, just do it.

Don't panic, or you'll be feeling your own pulse in your fingers instead of hers. Breathe deeply, keep calm, and wait.

(feel nothing, nothing to feel)

Shift your fingers slightly, and try again. Don't panic.

(nothing)

Wait.

(there! it's weak, and it flutters like a moth in cupped hands, but it's there, she's not dead –)

Don't cry. Not yet.

(but what's she doing here anyway? and what the hell –)

No. No questions. Don't even think about it. It's just a test. Upstairs now, quick. Call an ambulance. Pull the quilt off the bed to keep her warm. Don't try to move her, just make sure she can breathe, tuck her up and leave her alone. The bleeding's stopped, and there's nothing else you can do.

And when that's done, back upstairs and put a call through to Mike before the ambulance comes.

David had fallen away quickly from the crescendo of sharp feeling that had been something close to panic

(and something close to welcome, because it touched you in a place where nothing touched you now, except the killing)

and was calm again, drinking orange-juice in his kitchen. However ill his luck went, he must have at least a little time in hand; but even so, he had to assume that from now on he was a hunted man.

He was ready for this, though; had been ready for years, ever since the first killing. There was a case packed and standing in the hall, containing all his immediate needs. He could pick it up and go; but while there was no panic in him, it might be best to make it look as if there were. The important thing was to confuse the trail as much as possible. So let them start off wrong-footed about his state of mind, as well as other things. He washed and dried his glass carefully, and put it back in the cupboard; then he ran noisily upstairs and wreaked a deliberate chaos in his bedroom. He pulled open all the drawers, and tossed clothes at random across the room. He left the wardrobe doors standing open, and swept half the suits from their hangers; then he clattered his way downstairs again and did much the same in the front room, knocking a few breakables off shelves – and making sure they broke – as he left cupboards wide open and threw books and papers onto the floor.

Fenner was never more grateful for his police training, which came up out of the shadows of memory and switched him to automatic pilot, keeping him functioning until they came to the hospital. There Tina was taken away from him and rushed into surgery for an emergency operation; and there was suddenly nothing left for him to do. Except wait, of course; and the training hadn't covered that.

He found a corner to sit in, and sat; and lit a cigarette with hands that felt like ill-fitting gloves, too numb even to tremble.

David came out of the house to the sound of protests and laughter. He looked across the hedge to see Jill perched astride a branch of the flourishing young horse-chestnut in the garden next door, while a boy leant against the trunk nonchalantly examining his finger-nails.

"Hey, Mr Linden!" Jill yelled. "Could you come over and help me down, *please*? This pig's just laughing at me!" And she swung a helpless leg towards the boy, who simply ducked and grinned up at her.

David paused instinctively, and almost agreed; then

(muddle the trail. Muddy the waters)

said, "You got yourself up, you stupid cunt. Get yourself down."

Her startled silence followed him as he ran to the car, threw his case onto the back seat and drove off. Glancing in the wing-mirror, he saw the boy reaching up to her, while she sat motionless, staring after him. Good; she would remember, when they came to ask questions.

Clocks held no meaning for Fenner now. He had been sitting here in this grey room, smoking this same cigarette, since the world was made; and he expected still to be here when the last trump was blown. As long as Tina lay unconscious under the knives, neither truly living nor truly dead, nothing else could move or change.

A detective-sergeant came to ask him questions; but there was no word from Mike Malone, who had been unavailable when Fenner called and was apparently still unavailable. Fenner told the sergeant what he wanted to know in a hard, detached voice, and when he was asked handed over the keys of his flat without protest, so that the fingerprint and forensic experts could have a look round. None of this seemed to matter. There was only one question now – life or death, hope or destruction. Everything else was waste.

Fenner drew on his cigarette, watching with dead eyes as the detective left. What was the point of wondering who had done it? The thing had been done, that was all that counted. As for whose hand had been on the knife, he only knew that it wasn't Tina's and it wasn't his own. It might have been anyone else – which meant that everyone else was equally suspect and equally guilty. It was the world outside that had attacked her, catching at her life as barbed wire catches at clothes and skin; but if she lived, he'd make her safe. He'd keep the world out, with its knives and hidden faces.

(And God, how ironic it was; a man with a knife and no face had brought her here, pushing her to the edge of death, and now men with masks on their faces and sharp steel in their hands were trying to bring her back from that edge.)

If she lived, he'd make her safe.

If she lived . . .

David parked in a side-street behind the bus-station, picked up his case and hurried away, leaving the car unlocked. Passing through the bus-station, he crossed the road, picking his way adventurously between the taxis, and entered the Palladian portico of the railway station.

After a quick glance at the electronic data-board, he took his place in the queue for tickets. When his turn came, he asked for a single to Edinburgh. As the clerk punched buttons on the cash-register and slipped the ticket in to be dated, David said, "Is Access okay?"

"Aye."

While the man filled in the details on the credit voucher, David glanced anxiously at his watch.

"You're all right, mate," the clerk said placidly. "Ten minutes yet, for the Edinburgh train."

He passed the voucher and his Biro under the grill, and David scrawled a signature, looking at his watch again while the man checked it against the signature on his card. Finally, card and ticket were handed over; David took them in one hand and his case in the other, and pushed through the crowd towards the platforms.

Tina had been in surgery for more than three hours before anyone came to give Fenner news of her; and even then the young doctor refused to commit himself.

"We believe the operation itself has been a success," he said, "though we can't be definite about it until we've seen how she goes on. There may be complications; her spleen was ruptured, and she lost a massive amount of blood before she was brought in. And then there's the shock factor . . . We're hopeful; but she must still be considered on the danger list, I'm afraid."

"When can I see her?" he demanded.

"Not tonight, at least; she's unconscious and in intensive care, and we don't have facilities for spectators. Tomorrow, perhaps – but not until the evening. Go home now, and try not to worry. We'll give you a ring if there are any developments."

Darkness settled on Fenner like a cloak, clouding his eyes and his reason. He walked slowly, quite at random, letting time slip past him as he watched his feet, playing old and childish games to keep at least the surface of his mind occupied.

(Walk on the squares, or the bears will get you. They're watching you, you know. They're always watching. And bears have knives today . . .

And if you tread on a line with your left foot, you have to do the same with your right, heel or toe or the ball or the arch of the foot, exactly the same. You have to stay symmetrical, that's the important thing.)

He passed an off-licence; then paused, and went back. Looking past the pyramids of beer-cans in the bright window he could see well-stocked shelves, malt and blended whiskies arrayed like skittles behind the counter.

Now there was a thing.

This was an emergency, after all, a special case. He'd never sleep tonight, and he'd go crazy without someone – or something – to lean on. Tina wouldn't blame him this once; and in any case, there was no reason why she should ever find out. One bottle, one night. Unless it snowballed, of course, you had to consider that. But if it did, even if it did, where was the harm? He'd stopped once with Tina's help, and he could do it again,

(unless she died, and then he wouldn't want to)

he was damn sure he could do it again. It'd be easier the second time, he'd know what to expect . . .

Hands in pockets, he stood looking in through the window without the strength of will to make a conscious decision either way. To give in and enter the shop was as definite an act as resisting; and he didn't have the power for definite action any more. So he stood unmoving, until somewhere behind his shoulder he heard a clock strike. The lights in the shop flickered out, and Fenner turned away neither grateful nor frustrated as someone inside locked the door.

He wandered slowly home, and pulled the key-ring from his pocket. He searched through the bunch three times before remembering that the detective had taken his flat keys from him in the hospital. Fenner hadn't really registered it at the time, but the man had also said something about could he find a friend to stay with tonight, as the forensic boys would want a second crack at it in the morning?

Fenner had mumbled agreement; but now he was confronted with it, he couldn't think of anywhere he wanted to go. He'd be welcome at Mike's, he supposed; but Mike was probably still working, and Fenner couldn't face telling Susan what had happened. He couldn't face telling *anyone* – which took Jude and Georgina out too, and the rest of Tina's friends.

He was thinking about settling down in the car, when he remembered that one of the keys he was still playing with would open Diana's door; he'd transferred it from Tina's bunch to his own, the night he searched the flat. And it was his door now, his flat, or would be when probate was granted. No one could object if he waited the night out in there.

He opened the door as quietly as he could, feeling like a stranger, and closed it carefully behind him before turning on the light. All the ghosts had been laid last time; there was nothing here to disturb him now. Besides, he was long past grieving for the properly, peacefully dead when Tina lay poised on the border, somewhere between that country and his own.

He went into the living-room, sat down on the sofa and let his eyes drift round the room; and saw a bottle of Teacher's on the sideboard, just where there had always been a bottle of Teacher's.

"Now there's a thing," Fenner murmured. He got to his feet, and hefted the bottle in one hand. Diana hadn't got through more than a quarter of it; Fenner chuckled, watching the whisky sloshing about as he rotated the bottle.

"Well, if I can't talk to anyone else," he said companionably, "I'll talk to you."

35 Not Another Killing

It was another hand that had whipped up Fenner's world and set it spinning; but his own that kept it on the tumble. He drank solemnly, almost stately, sometimes pouring a capful at a time and tossing it back, sometimes simply swigging from the bottle as he paced the flat. The whisky flickered through his throat and stomach like a light, like a flame on a candle-stub drawing everything up into itself. There could be no fooling himself now; he knew what he was doing, had known indeed since the first taste of it like blood and steel hot on his tongue. He took it as though it were poison – because for Fenner, it was poison. Even if it didn't kill him, this was still suicide. Which is why he wouldn't cry, why he fought hard against the easy maudlin of the drunk as the whisky closed velvet gloves around his mind. A man should keep his dignity, when he walks open-eyed into his own death. At the most, he should be angry; but Fenner wasn't ready even for that. He mourned a little, mourned himself and Tina as though they were both already dead, and their graves severed. No matter if the width of the world stood between them, or only the width of a city; they were apart, and that was another death.

So he drank to it; and to his own death, which lay in the drinking.

The first public lavatory David went into featured a random sample of Edinburgh youth arguing about football players. David put his case down where he could keep an eye on it, unzipped his trousers and stood at the urinal for a minute, then hurried out again.

The next was locked and barred; but finally, down a deserted side-street, he found one that was both open and empty. He bolted himself into a cubicle, set his case on the toilet seat and lifted the lid.

He was a little cramped for space, but there was no great hurry now. He stripped completely, dropping his track suit and underwear behind the toilet, out of the way. Then he put on the costume he'd collected from charity shops and jumble sales over the years: worn long-johns, a string vest over a cotton vest and a collarless shirt over that, darned trousers from a suit of cavalry twill that had probably been quite good twenty years ago, an ancient corduroy sports jacket and a heavy overcoat pulled on and belted with a length of fraying rope. Everything was dirty and foul-smelling, after being bundled up in the case for many months. There were thick socks for his feet, with clumsy darns in them, and old boots of stiff, cracked leather to give him a convincing hobble.

Hair was less easy to change; but the police would be looking for a man with black hair well off the ears and collar, and for the moment David was prepared to risk a well-made wig. He had searched theatrical costumiers in London three years ago, and had come home with a long, wispy wig of pale brown hair a little streaked with grey.

He fitted the wig, and pulled a stained and drooping trilby down over it. He took a miniature bottle of whisky from the case, used it as a mouthwash and gargle, then rubbed a drop into each of his eyes. It stung like fury, but he knew from previous rehearsals that his eyes would be red and slightly swollen for some hours afterwards.

There was a plastic bag full of his own cocktail of dust and earth, which he rubbed vigorously across his cheeks and chin to give himself a shadow, then more lightly onto the rest of his face and his hands. He dug his fists hard into handfuls of the mixture to work the grime well under his finger-nails and into the creases of his knuckles.

Another small bottle contained a dentists' preparation, which he shook vigorously then swilled around his mouth before spitting it out

(character, David. You have to act in character, even when you're alone – but you know that, don't you? You've done it most of your life)

onto the floor. It would stain black all the plaque around the edges of his teeth, and leave a thin film of dye like a veil across the white enamel. The effect was only temporary, but in the next few hours particularly it might help to be able to present a mouthful of blackened and rotting teeth to any curious policeman.

Finally, he took a railway ticket from a pocket in the lid of the case. This was the single detail of his sea-change which had cost him most in both money and time, but he had been sure all along that it would prove its own value. It was the return half of a second-class ticket from Edinburgh to Newcastle, valid three months from date of issue; and every three months he had replaced it, going to a different travel-agent every time. Forearmed with this, he needn't go near a ticket clerk or any other official at Waverley.

He put the ticket into the pocket of his overcoat, then threw the clothes he had discarded into the suitcase, along with the empty bottles and other paraphernalia. His credit card he broke into pieces and tossed into the lavatory, along with all the other identification he'd been carrying. He had to flush the lavatory twice, to get rid of it all.

A minute later, a shambling tramp with the smell of cheap whisky on his breath and clothes came stumblingly out of the public lavatory and crossed the road at a hesitant angle, making for the centre of town. He carried all his worldly belongings in an old suitcase, and as he walked he mumbled constantly to himself.

*

There was a knocking that wouldn't go away, and a voice shouting through the letter-box, calling his name; and eventually Fenner lost patience, and went to the door. Taking his bottle with him.

Dark uniform, gleaming buttons and white stripes: a police sergeant, straightening rapidly from his letter-box crouch as Fenner wrenched the door open.

"Mr Fenner, sir? Sorry about all the noise, but I tried next door and there wasn't any answer. Then I saw the lights on here, and heard you moving around, so . . ."

"Why the *fuck*"

(and here came the anger at last, too late to be useful; like spitting at a JCB)

"can't you bastards leave me alone?"

The sergeant's lips tightened, and his eyes touched momentarily on the bottle. "Sorry, sir. I know it's late, and you've got worries of your own; but Inspector Malone sent me to fetch you. It's important."

"Bullshit." How could it be? Nothing was, now, except the one thing. "Leave me alone."

"It wouldn't hurt you to come over for a few minutes, now would it, Mr Fenner? Take your mind off . . . things. And we'll bring you straight back, if that's what you want." His tone was placating enough; but the slight flare of his nostrils suggested that in his opinion, while it certainly wouldn't hurt Fenner, it wouldn't do much good for Malone. Fenner had reached that coherent but over-sensitive stage of drunkenness where the mildest insinuation is a gross insult; and a flaring nostril was enough to bring the anger rising again, burning the other way.

"Come on, then," he said, pushing past the sergeant and slamming the door behind him. "What the hell are you waiting for, Christmas?"

He walked neatly and accurately to the car, then lifted the bottle to his lips and swallowed convulsively.

"Wouldn't want it to spill, see," he explained, pulling his lips back in a snarl because he'd forgotten that a smile needed anything more. "And I've left the cap inside, haven't I?"

The sergeant said nothing, he just unlocked the door and walked round to the driver's side.

"This isn't the way to the station."

"That's right, sir." The sergeant was imperturbable. "We're

not going to the station. The Inspector's at a house in Jesmond. He wants to show you something."

"Not another killing?" He felt no emotion at the thought, except for a weary irritation with Mike's obtuseness. Did the man have no imagination? To suppose that Fenner would want to view or even hear about a body and a murder tonight . . .

But: "No, sir. Not another killing."

Fenner shrugged, turning a discontented shoulder to his driver and staring out of the side window. There was the moor again, dark beyond the street-lights; there the phone-box where he'd found a dirty picture and forgotten Tina. This was the way he had come that morning, to see David Linden. There was the entrance to the cul-de-sac – and oddly, that was the way they were turning now. Two police cars were parked by the kerb, blue lights flashing; and the door to Linden's house stood open. As he watched, a uniformed officer appeared in the doorway, using his radio. It made no sense, unless David had become another victim; and the sergeant had said that it wasn't that, that there hadn't been a killing.

On Waverley Station, a round-shouldered drunk stumbled up the steps into the Glasgow train, dribbling obscenities out of his mouth like saliva. He pushed his case into the luggage-space and moved slowly down the carriage, staring glass-eyed at the passengers already settled.

"Fucken non-smoker, innit? Where's a bloody smoker, then, a man needs a smoke . . ."

At the far end of the next carriage he got off the train and crossed the platform. Waiting at the other side was the next train to London King's Cross, calling at Newcastle and other stations on the way. The drunk boarded it, found his way to a smoking section and dropped into a window-seat, still muttering and cursing under his breath.

David was well pleased with himself. The case would be found at Glasgow, bearing large labels giving a fictitious address in the Netherlands; there was nothing to help them connect it with him.

He pulled an old and dented tobacco-tin from his pocket, opened it and began to roll a cigarette. This was a skill he had acquired slowly in the privacy of his house, as indeed was smoking the cigarette once it was rolled. He still hadn't learned to enjoy it; but David Linden was known never to have smoked in his life, and it was the details that would mean success or failure now.

He smoked with the lighted end inside his cupped fingers, as he had seen tramps smoke on benches beside the river, as if afraid someone might snatch it from him.

And while he smoked, he thought about Fenner.

The strange nonsense of bringing him to David Linden's house and filling it with policemen had reawakened some dusty shadow of Fenner's curiosity. He hurried up the path, pushed past the constable on the door and went straight in. Mike was in the hall, staring through a doorway into the front room, where broken china littered the carpet.

"Mike, what the hell's happening?" Fenner looked at the wreckage, then with a slight effort focused on Mike again. "Where's David?"

"Gone. But we'll – " Mike's face seemed to shift and change like a face behind water. "David? You said David . . . Do you *know* him?"

"Yes, of course I bloody know him!" Fenner lifted the almost-empty bottle to his lips, letting promises and good intentions slip for the sake of good theatre. "He's only my bloody contact at the Samaritans, isn't he?"

"Jesus Christ, Paul . . ."

"Well, what? I told you I had a bloody top dog for my fifth column, didn't I? Well, David Linden's it. He did ask me to keep it quiet, but . . ." The sudden incongruity of it all hit Fenner again, harder than before. "Where the fuck is he, anyway?"

"I wish I knew. Maybe you can help us find him. But – " Mike gestured angrily. "For Christ's sake get rid of the bottle, will you? I need you sober. I thought you'd given up, anyway."

"What the fuck do you expect?" Fenner snarled back. "Stiff upper lip and carry on regardless? Just let the dead bury their dead, okay? Tina and me are burying each other."

The two men glared at each other, friendships and old loyalties briefly forgotten. It was Malone who gave way first, perhaps recognising the depth of Fenner's suffering and allowing that he had the right to fail a little. At all events he shrugged and turned away, speaking in a flat, official voice.

"Alex Taggart got in touch with me this evening. He wouldn't give us access to the files, but he would go through them himself for what we wanted. He couldn't find any record of a Graham McLaggan calling last night, but he gave us the names and addresses of the volunteers on duty, in case the file had got lost or never made up for some reason. David Linden was one of the duty volunteers,"

(but Fenner knew that. David had said so, that morning. So what?)

"and apparently he broke one of the rules last night. They have a separate squad ready to go out to an emergency call; but Linden asked for – and got – permission to go himself. It's not the first time that's happened. I want to check back, for dates of the others. But that's hindsight. Anyway, we thought he might've taken the McLaggan call himself,"

(but he'd said not. Could've told you that, if you'd asked. Saved all this bother, smashing up his home when he's not here)

"and then not had a chance to write a report before the other call came in, the one he went out for. So we wanted to talk to him. I sent a man here with a car, and he found the house empty, no lights on and the car gone. He looked through the window, and saw the mess in here. So he asked around; and a kid next door says that he went out in a tearing hurry this afternoon, about two-thirty, and hasn't been back. He was carrying a suitcase, and she said there must've been something eating him, because he wasn't like himself at all. Swore at her, or something. So I got a warrant and came out to see. I reckon he's running, Paul. The place has been turned over, but it sure as hell wasn't burglars."

Fenner scowled, scratched his head, said, "What are you trying to say, for God's sake? You don't think he's the Butcher?"

"I don't know." Malone leant against the wall and looked at him helplessly. "It doesn't make a lot of sense, I know. A Samaritan, and all that. But why's he running?"

"Who says he's running? So okay, he had to go somewhere in a hurry. Maybe his mother's ill . . ."

A CID man came in, glancing uncertainly from Fenner to Malone. Mike nodded. "Yes, Jenkins?"

"Report just come through, sir – they've found Linden's car."

"Where?"

"Barratt Lane, sir – behind the bus-station. Parked illegally, and the driver's side wasn't locked." His eyes touched Fenner's again for a moment, before turning back to his superior. "The constable had a look inside – and he says there's a knife on the floor, like it might have fallen out of the driver's pocket. It's a heavy thing, proper Bowie knife or something like that. Hunter's weapon. And there are stains on the blade . . ."

Fenner was aware of Malone giving orders, rapid and confident – get the Super on the radio, get Alex Taggart on the phone, get a team down to look at the car and ask questions at the stations – but only as he might have been aware of a film on television, something interesting but ultimately unreal.

But knives, now, knives were real and bright. And in a world as small as Fenner's, shrunk to the size of a hospital bed and a single frail beat of life, there was no room for coincidence.

No room for David, either. Not yet. But Fenner drank, and drained the bottle; and promised himself that there would be.

36 Still Breathing

The telephone again, sounding like an alarm in Fenner's dreams; and then, as he opened bleary and unfocused eyes to stare into the corners of a strange room, a woman's voice, both oddly familiar and very, very wrong.

"Paul, are you awake? Mike's on the phone, he wants to talk to you . . ."

And with the mention of Mike's name things fell into place, as best they could in a shattered world. This was Mike's home, because he'd brought Fenner here sometime during the night. After he'd collapsed – after he'd finished the whisky, and there was suddenly nothing left to hold him up. And that was Susan outside, knocking and calling again; and Mike was at the station or off somewhere else, which is why he was phoning. And David had a knife in his car, and Tina had a wound in her belly, and . . .

"Paul?"

"Yeah," he mumbled. "I'm coming."

He sat up, and the sudden movement brought a sour sickness rising in his throat, and a rush of saliva as he swallowed, and swallowed again. He fumbled his way downstairs, one hand tight on the banister, and Susan pointed him towards the telephone in the hall.

"I'll make you some coffee, Paul."

"Thanks . . ." He sank into a chair beside the phone, and picked up the receiver. "Yeah, Mike? What have you got?"

"The Samaritans' files is what we've got. I bullied Taggart in the early hours – offered him the choice of two discreet lads going through them, or a magistrate's warrant and the whole lot being taken away. He caved in – and listen to this, Paul. Every night that the Butcher killed, David Linden was on duty. And every time, he got a caller who wanted to speak to him personally, face to face, and wouldn't accept anyone else. So he got the okay from that night's boss, and went off alone. Every single bloody time. And they never noticed . . ."

"Why should they?" Fenner asked dully. Some time during the night, while he slept, he seemed to have accepted what had been impossible before, that David was the Butcher: that he'd talked and smiled and shared a drink with the man who killed Diana, and had thought of him as a friend. "We never noticed that all the victims were in enough trouble to call the Samaritans."

"Yeah. Well, anyway. We're onto him now, and that's the main thing. Hindsight can wait."

"You haven't found him yet, then?"

"No," Mike said, "but he's left us an easy trail. He can't have been ready for this – or else he just panicked. We've got one witness already who saw him running down to the station with a case. And he bought a ticket to Edinburgh – with his credit card, for crying out loud!"

"Red herring," Fenner said immediately. "He's not that stupid."

"Except that the guard on the train remembers him well. He was definitely on that train, and he definitely got off at

Waverley. He might have changed there, or doubled back and gone on down to London, perhaps. Only we tried a photofit all around the station – no photographs, there wasn't one in the house. If he ever had any, he burnt 'em or took 'em with him. Anyway, a couple of people think they saw him leaving Waverley; and no one remembers him buying a ticket, or getting on a train. No one's identified him at the bus-stations either. We'll keep on looking, but I reckon he's still in the city, lying low there. The Chief's sending me up with a team to liaise with the Edinburgh force; but I wanted to let you know what was happening, first."

"Thanks, yeah. I appreciate it."

"Couple of things, Paul. Don't lose yourself today, will you? The Chief'll want you in to make a statement."

"Okay. I'll be around."

"Good. And that knife in Linden's car? Forensic say the blood on it's the same group as Tina's. And when we had a word with her – "

"You *what*?"

"Sorry, I should've told you that first, shouldn't I? She came round a couple of hours ago."

"Why the fuck didn't someone let me know?"

"You are being let know," Mike replied acidly. "If you mean why didn't the hospital call you, they didn't know where you were; and there wasn't any hurry, because you wouldn't have been allowed to see her anyway. I knew you were asleep, so I left it a bit. Listen, she's all right, get it? The hospital's being cautious, in case of complications, but she's a tough little thing and I reckon she'll pull through. Anyway, they let us talk to her for a minute, then they gave her something and she went to sleep again."

"What did she say?"

"Not much – just that a tall man knocked on the door, and when she answered it he stabbed her. She didn't see his face clearly, there wasn't time and the sun was behind him, but it could easily have been Linden. Certainly wearing a tracksuit; and that's enough for me."

"Yes, I suppose," Fenner muttered. Thinking that he might as well have stabbed Tina himself, or used her deliberately as a shield to protect himself.

"Don't worry, Paul, we'll get him. And if you ring the hospital later, they might let you see Tina this evening. Tell

Susan I'll call her tonight, will you? And look after Flick for me, there's a mate."

"Hullo, Mr Fenner."

Fenner looked up, and saw Andrew Jackson coming towards him down the hospital corridor. He grunted, and looked down again.

"Can I talk to you?" Jackson took the next chair, took out a notebook.

"If you like."

"Thanks. Obviously the first question is, how's Tina? The hospital won't tell me much."

"So what's new? They won't tell me much either. She's hanging on."

"That's good. But can you tell me why there's a police guard on her room? Are they expecting whoever attacked her to try again?"

"Why don't you ask them?"

"I have. They weren't very forthcoming." He paused, then went on, "Look, Mr Fenner. You've been in Newcastle for weeks, you've been seen with Inspector Malone, who's involved in the hunt for the Butcher. Fact number one. Fact number two, your girlfriend is attacked and nearly killed, for no apparent reason. Fact number three, the following morning the police issue the name, description and photofit picture of a man they want, in connection with the Butcher murders. Who's fooling who? I mean, it's not just coincidence, is it?"

"Work it out for yourself," Fenner said listlessly. "Everyone else has to, why shouldn't you?"

Jackson tried another tack. "Have they let you see Tina yet?"

"Yeah, I've seen her. For a couple of minutes, just now."

"Has she said anything about her attacker? Did she say anything to you?"

"What? No." He stared down at his hands. "No, she didn't say anything. I told you I'd seen her, that's all. We didn't talk. Christ, what can you say?"

"No one's saying very much," Jackson observed sourly. "The police won't even confirm that this Linden guy is wanted for the attack on Tina, as well as the Butcher killings. But I'll tell you what I reckon. I reckon he is – and that's why the guard, because she's the first one he's left alive. But I don't reckon that was his first mistake. Where he went wrong was attacking her in the first place. He was after you, wasn't he? Wasn't he, Mr Fenner?"

Fenner shivered, and took a half-bottle of whisky from his pocket. Jackson watched him drink and left him, satisfied.

"Hullo, Paul, it's me."

"Mike."

"Susan's got you answering the phone, has she?"

"She's cooking. I'll fetch her for you."

"Hang on a minute. How's Tina?"

"Out of danger, they say."

"Well, thank God for that, anyway."

"Yeah."

"You don't sound very sure, Paul."

"I don't like it. Nothing medical, I mean – they're the experts. But she's so quiet . . ."

"Best thing for her, at the moment. She'll recover that much quicker if she rests."

"That's not what I mean. Quiet inside, I mean. Like a house with all the curtains pulled, and nothing moving, no noise. She just lies there and looks at you, and her eyes don't move, even, she's that still."

"Be fair, Paul. It's only a couple of days since someone tried to kill her. She's bound to be shocked for a while."

"I suppose, yeah. But it scares me . . . Anyway. What's happening your end?"

"Nothing. Or plenty, rather, if you view a hundred policemen chasing their own tails as a happening. We go panting round in packs, like dogs on heat, but there's nothing to show for it. Except for one witness who saw Linden leaving the station, jogging up Waverley Steps like a man in a hurry, suitcase and all. He must've evaporated on Princes Street, because we haven't caught a whiff of him after that. He hasn't been seen again at the station, nor any of the bus terminals. No one admits to having given him a lift, or seen him walking out of the city. He sure as hell hasn't hired a car, or bought a pushbike; and if he stole either of 'em nobody saw which way he went. Personally, I don't think he went anywhere; he's either got a friend here or a place to hide up."

"If it was a friend, they could just as easily have taken

him to the other end of the country. You'd be none the wiser."

"I know. That's why I'm passionately believing in the hidey-hole idea. It's more likely, anyway. I can't believe that anyone would deliberately hide the Butcher, no matter how friendly they'd been up to now."

"I admire your confidence. But keep looking, mate. Listen, Susan's making faces at me from the kitchen. Do you want to talk to her?"

"Sounds good. But hang on a sec, Paul. Straight question, okay? Are you still drinking?"

"Are you still breathing? Here's Susan."

Leaving the house at seven thirty, Fenner heard a horn sound twice, just as he spotted a familiar van parked on the other side of the road.

He crossed quickly, and Georgina leant out of the driver's window.

"Are you going to the hospital, Paul?"

"That's right."

"Jump in, we'll give you a lift."

He might have refused, preferring to walk; but Georgina's voice had lost all its character, and beyond her Jude was sitting pale and distracted, like a weak watercolour of herself.

So he walked round and climbed in beside Jude. When he was settled, she touched his hand with all the nervousness of a child confronted by an adult in tears. "How is it?"

Questions without answers. He shrugged; but at least she cared enough to ask. His hand turned beneath hers, and their fingers linked for a moment, before he pulled gently away.

"How's Tina?" Georgina asked, edging out into the stream of traffic. "Really? We've seen the reports in the papers, but they just say she's 'making steady progress', whatever that means."

"It's true, though," Fenner said. "She's getting better. She was sitting up a bit, yesterday."

"Yeah? That's good." Jude tried a smile, but the visible effort spoiled the effect. "She'll be swinging from the curtain-rails tonight, if I know Tina."

"I don't think so. She's – not been very cheerful, since it happened."

"Is it right," Jude asked carefully, "that they're not letting anyone see her, except family? We did phone up, but that's what they said."

Fenner nodded. "Everyone's a bit worried, in case Linden tries to slip in. She's the only real witness, you see, everything else is circumstantial. So there's a police guard on her, and they're taking no chances at all."

"Yeah, but he's a man, for God's sake."

"Even so. They're just being careful, love."

"I suppose. But, fuck it, we've got to talk to her, Paul. If–if she wants to see us . . ."

That was where the trouble was, then; Jude's hesitation gave her away. Fenner decided to probe a little, and said, "Why shouldn't she?"

"Because it's our fault, isn't it? The whole bloody mess comes back to us. If we hadn't brought you and David together, he wouldn't ever have come near Tina."

And he might have gone on killing strangers slowly. That was the pragmatic answer, that put them ahead on points; but he couldn't say it. Maybe they had done the world a favour between them, maybe Tina was a useful sacrifice – but the idea burnt like acid, and would destroy them.

"That's ridiculous," he said slowly. "All right, it may be true, but it's no truer for you than for the rest of us. And you can't use hindsight like that, like a whip to beat yourselves with. Tina's not blaming you."

They took that in silence. "Look," he said, "why don't I ask her tonight, if she'd like to see you? I'm sure she'll say yes, and then we can arrange a special dispensation. I'll vouch for you, that should be enough."

"That we're not David Linden in disguise, you mean?" Jude sounded a little more cheerful, but Georgina's face was still closed in and bitter.

"We might as well have been."

"Stop it, Gina," Fenner said sharply. "Stop wallowing in it. You'll do Tina a lot more good by being reasonably cheerful when you see her. After all," he added with a quick smile, "at the moment she's having to put up with her parents every afternoon and me every evening. No wonder she's a bit gloomy."

Georgina pulled the van up suddenly, opposite the cemetery gates. "Won't be a minute."

Jude and Fenner watched through the window as she

checked the padlock on the gates, then scrambled instead over the iron railings.

"What the hell's she up to now?"

"God knows. But at least she's doing something." Jude glanced sideways at him. "It's been a lot worse for her, you know. She was really close to David – or thought she was. She hasn't been sleeping or anything. She just sits. Cries sometimes, or flies right off the handle for no reason. I don't know what to do."

"Just let her be, I would. Let her find her own way."

"Yeah, but that's the easy way, isn't it? The coward's way. And I want to be with her, I want to *share*; we always have before. But she won't let me, she won't say anything . . ."

Georgina's tall figure came back into view, striding between the gravestones; and Jude chuckled suddenly, seeing what she held in her hands. "Flowers. She's been pinching flowers off the graves."

"There you go," Georgina said, when she came back to the van. She dropped a double handful of carnations and daffodils into Fenner's lap. "Give her those, will you? With our love?"

"Yes, of course." He grinned at her. "And I just might tell her where they came from, too."

Georgina gave him a tentative smile back. "Thanks, darling."

Two days later he found Tina sitting up in bed, with the television on in the corner. The detective-sergeant on duty nodded and stood up; he would wait outside the door till Fenner left. Fenner noted the way his jacket hung open, and wondered if Tina knew that her guards were armed.

He threw his jacket onto an empty chair, and gestured at the television. "Do you mind if I turn that off?"

"If you like."

So he turned the television off, perched on the edge of the bed and reached for her hand, where it was lying on the covers. "So how are you?"

"Okay," she said, shrugging. "Sore."

He squeezed her hand gently, and smiled as he saw a jar of honey and a large tub of yoghurt on the bedside locker. "Jude and Georgina bring those, did they? They're never hospital issue."

Her lips flickered. "That's right. They've both been in hospital themselves, they know how awful the food is. Honest, Fenner, I couldn't eat more than half of it, even if I wanted to. Jude was threatening to bring quiches and salads and stuff, next time."

"She'll do it, too," Fenner grinned. "Tell you what, I'll phone Huw and tell him to send Sylvia up. We'll tether her in the corner there and feed her on the slops the hospital provides for you; then you can be totally self-sufficient."

"Idiot." There was a long-missed warmth behind her voice as she smiled; and even if it was only a nostalgia for happiness remembered, it was still a step forward.

They talked a little about neutral things; then Tina said, "My parents want me to go back with them, when I get out of here."

No surprise. All their prejudices and fears about Fenner had been confirmed, in a more brutal way than even they could have imagined; and they would be trying all they could to separate Tina from him. He couldn't resist that on his own; she would have to fight them herself. If she had the will.

"What do you want?" he asked, trying to keep his voice easy, to mask his tension. "That's what counts."

"I want to go back." A whisper, or maybe a prayer. "I want none of this ever to have happened. I want us to be living in Wales with all of it wiped out. Obliterated, not just forgotten. Never there."

"Can't do that, love." It was pathetic to see Tina, of all people, begging to be allowed to run away.

"We could try. Couldn't we? Go back to the cottage when I'm discharged, we could try to pick up all the threads again . . ."

But they couldn't, and he told her so straight. "Not while Linden's still free. We're not working in the dark any more; and I'm going to find him."

"For God's sake, Fenner." He felt her shiver, felt her drawing away from him again. "Can't you leave it alone, even now?"

"Tina. He killed Diana, he tried to kill you. I can't walk away from that. *He tried to kill you.*"

"And now you want to kill him. Yes?"

Fenner hesitated long enough to see the tremble in his fingers, and to want a drink; then he said, "Yes."

She turned away.

"Excuse me, sir."

The tramp was hunched and filthy with a week's grey stubble on his cheeks. He reeked of alcohol, and the student could see a large bottle of Newcastle Brown thrust into his coat pocket.

"Excuse me, sir." The voice was a thin whine, with a strong hint of Irish. The tramp's head and eyes moved in brief jerks, never quite facing the student as he talked. There was a blur of alcohol over it all, voice and eyes and movement; but the hands were remarkably strong, gripping the student's arm to hold him still. "Excuse me, sir, could you spare me just a minute of your time?"

"Well, what is it?" But the student was already fumbling in his trouser pocket, sorting through the small change. He was an easy touch, and he knew it.

"If you could just spare me a few pence, sir. A few pence to buy a cup of tea."

The student pressed coins into the tramp's greasy palm, without even looking at what he was giving away. "Here. I'm sorry, I can't manage any more."

"God bless you, sir. Thank you very much, sir . . . You've made an old man very happy." But the last sentence was whispered wickedly under his breath, as David released the boy and watched him hurrying away.

He added the coins to the considerable weight of cash about his person, and sank back down onto the bench. His eyes returned to the hospital gates on the other side of the road. There was a police station at his back; but he wasn't concerned with that. They might be looking for David Linden, but they wouldn't see him sitting on their doorstep. He smiled to himself, and pulled the bottle of ale from his pocket. He opened it with his teeth, and drank; but his gaze never left the hospital entrance.

He was watching for Paul Fenner.

37 *Killing Him Softly*

Tina shuffled slowly down the corridor towards the hospital exit, with her parents solicitously on either side. Fenner hung uselessly behind, knowing that there was no place for him in that trio; but he had had to come, if only to say goodbye.

The police guard had gone on ahead to check that no one was loitering suspiciously by the Blakes' car. The veil of security was still wrapped tight around Tina; which was why she was leaving now on her father's arm, going home to her parents rather than home to him. Linden knew too much about Fenner's life, both in Newcastle and Wales. No journalist or other curious eyes would see her leaving with her parents; some careful disinformation had resulted in the small crowd of reporters and photographers clustering at one exit, while Tina was slipped quietly out at another, with two unmarked police vehicles running interference in front and behind. Whether she would be allowed to stay at her parents' house would depend on a police reassessment of the risk, but for the moment that was where she was going. While Fenner remained in Newcastle with the Malones, all but dead to anything except David Linden and any whisper of his passing.

The car was only a few yards away, the detective beside it and the doors open. Briefly, Fenner thought that Tina was meaning to get in without even a glance back at him; but she stopped, and pulled her arm free of her father's.

"You two get in," she said. "I want to talk to Paul."

She came back to him; but suddenly face to face with their parting only moments, a few paces away, there seemed nothing to say.

Tina licked her lips. "Paul – take care, okay?"

He nodded. "You, too."

And that was all. Lacking the words, he lifted a hand towards her; but uncertainty held it hanging in the air between them a moment too long. She responded instinctively, holding out her own hand to meet it; and they parted with a gesture ludicrously, horribly like a formal handshake.

Around midday, while Fenner was sifting listlessly through some photocopied reports Mike had brought him on the quiet, with half his mind on the empty space where Tina should have been:

"Paul, why don't you forget all that and come shopping with me?" Susan was standing in the living-room door, belting her coat. Beyond her, Flick was making soft noises in the baby-buggy. "It'll do you good to get some air; and I'd enjoy the company."

"Would you?" It was hard to believe that anyone could have enjoyed being with him, the last few days; but with a sudden decision, Fenner swept the papers off his lap and stood up. "I'll come, Susan. I'd like to."

She smiled, and passed him his jacket. "I thought you might. It's one of the things we always did do together, remember? Back when."

"Yeah." Until things turned bad between them; and then he was glad to let her go alone, to have some time to himself. But the memories didn't hurt any more, except that he could remember hurting her. "Come on, then, lady. Let's do it."

As they left the house, a tramp foraging in a rubbish bin abandoned his search, and limped down the street in their wake.

The day was unexpectedly warm; by the time they reached the shops, Fenner had draped his jacket over the handle of the buggy, and Susan wore her coat hanging loose from her shoulders.

"Let's leave the brat out here," she said, in front of the supermarket. "She'll enjoy the sun."

"Is that safe?" Fenner asked anxiously. "People do snatch babies sometimes . . ."

"Not this baby." Susan grinned, and bent underneath the buggy. "You've heard of car alarms? Well, this spoiled creature has her very own pram alarm."

"You're kidding."

"Not a bit of it. It was a present from Mike's mother. She's totally neurotic about the safety of her darling granddaughter; but it's quite a clever little gadget, really. If anyone releases the brakes without disarming the thing first, it goes off like an American police-car. That sets the baby off, too; and exit thief stage left, as frantic mother enters stage right swinging handbag and yelling blue murder."

"Right." Fenner winked at Flick, who gave him a slow, contented smile; then he followed Susan into the supermarket.

"Disposable nappies, Paul – on your left. The ones with the blue wrapper . . . Paul?"

"Sorry. I was just watching – there was someone bending over Flick's buggy. A down-and-out, by the look of him. It's okay though, he hasn't pinched her. No alarums or excursions."

"You know, you're getting quite neurotic yourself about that baby. You'll be spoiling her rotten when she's a bit bigger."

"That's right. Devoted pseudo-uncle, me. Every baby should have one."

Coming out of the supermarket, they could hear Flick's screaming even above the noise of traffic.

"She ain't 'appy," Fenner observed.

"Probably missing her Uncle Paul dancing attendance at the foot of the buggy," Susan said drily.

"I dunno, it sounds a bit serious to me."

"No, she's just bored."

But they came to the buggy then, and looked down; and it was Fenner who first understood what they were seeing, dark stains on the coverlet and the baby's waving hands slicked with a vivid red in the sunlight, and a shining necklace among the spattered blood.

"Jesus . . ." Fenner snatched for the glinting metal string, and cursed again as a dozen fine teeth slashed his fingers. Beside him Susan moaned softly, and reached for her daughter.

"No, leave her," Fenner said sharply. "We'll get her to the hospital quicker if we just push, and run."

His foot kicked at the brake, and the air filled with the shrill ululation of the pram alarm as he wheeled it savagely around.

"Leave that, too," he yelled at Susan. "It'll clear the way for us a bit. With luck, it'll bring a cop down to help."

He started to run, charging the buggy along the pavement as curious shoppers crowded back out of his way. Susan ran beside him, her eyes wide and blinded with terror, showing her nothing but blood.

Later, in another waiting-room, Mike came to them. He and Susan clung to each other, both of them crying a little.

"The – the doctors say she's going to be all right, Mike. I mean, she's not going to die or anything, she didn't lose too much blood, or cut any arteries. Only her hands are going to be crippled . . ."

"He said that isn't definite," Fenner pointed out quietly. "He wasn't hiding anything, he did say it was probable; but it's too early to assess the full damage yet. And they're rushing a micro-surgeon up from somewhere down south, to have a look. There's a good chance he'll be able to improve on whatever they do here."

"Yeah." Mike sat down slowly, pulling Susan down beside him and keeping her close with an arm around her shoulders. "Forensics have got the buggy now, but there's no question what it was, that necklace. Straight razor-blades, ordinary safety blades, splintered and drilled and threaded together to catch a baby's eye."

"I feel sick," Susan muttered. There was a thin sheen of sweat across her forehead; and a moment later she was on her feet and running for the toilet down the corridor. A nurse came out of a side-door and gestured at the two men.

"It's all right, you stay there. I'll go."

They sank helplessly back into their seats. Fenner felt Mike's hand touch his shoulder, and knew there was more.

"Paul, listen. When they took all the bedding out of the buggy, down at the station . . ."

"Well, what?"

"They found a Samaritans bookmark tucked down the side of the mattress. Like a fucking calling-card. That down-and-out you saw, I know you couldn't give much of a description, but . . ."

"Yes," Fenner said, seeing the figure again behind his eyes. "Yes, it could have been Linden. It could have been anyone. Mike . . ."

But again, there weren't the words. He closed his eyes and leant back against the wall, with a familiar guilt grown heavier. This was reckoned to his account, as much as the attack on Tina. His hands began to tremble, and he lurched clumsily to his feet.

"Where are you going?"

Fenner ran a hand across his face. "I need a drink," he said bluntly. "Sorry, but I can't . . . I can't handle all of this. And listen, get my keys back, will you? For the flat? I can't stay with you two any more, or he'll come at you next. Or poor bloody Flick again."

He ran out, before Mike could say anything; and having begun, he kept on running.

The first thing David wanted was a bath. His body was rank with its own sour juices, and the only way to get the tramp out of both his skin and his skull would be by scrubbing. The municipal baths were out of the question, but he didn't anticipate any problem in obtaining the use of a private bathroom for an hour or two.

One delightful whimsy crossed his mind: it was safe to assume that the Malones and Fenner would be at the hospital for some time yet, and it would be a salutary threat for them to come back to find damp and filthy towels, hairs on the enamel and another Samaritans bookmark stuck to the mirror . . .

But security had a higher priority than anything, and there was too much of a risk attached. If the baby weren't badly damaged, or if Fenner couldn't handle the waiting, and came back . . . David had no plans to get that close to Paul Fenner. Not yet.

Instead he made his limping way to the house of a friend and fellow Samaritan. Justin and his wife Amanda would both be out at work all afternoon, there were no children to come bursting in early from school, and he knew where they kept a spare set of keys hidden. Also, there was a way out from the back garden as well as the front. No curious Neighbourhood Watcher behind a window would see a jogger coming out where a tramp had gone in . . .

He walked boldly in at the gate and around the side of the house, as though he had some honest errand there. The keys were where he expected, in the greenhouse; he let himself in by the back door, locked it again behind him and hurried straight upstairs, starting the bath filling while he peeled the tramp's clothes away from his body, layer by layer. He groaned aloud as he eased his feet out of the ancient boots, and tried not to look at the festering blisters that covered his toes and heels. He lowered himself slowly into the bath, sliding down and letting his head fall back until the scalding water lapped the corners of his mouth. He moaned again, hardly louder than a breath; and closed his eyes.

When he finally felt clean again, after two changes of water and half a bottle of Amanda's Body Shop shampoo, David climbed out of the bath and dried himself thoroughly, treating his feet with a cream he found in the bathroom cabinet. Then he dressed in the jogger's gear he had brought with him, tracksuit and ageing trainers picked up at jumble sales in the last week.

He clipped a few hairs from his beard with a pair of nail-scissors, and scattered them in the wash-basin; and left Justin's razor wet behind a tap, to let them think he had quit the house clean-shaven.

There was an old suitcase on the landing, stuffed with papers. David emptied it, and filled it again with his tramp's clothes and a good suit of Justin's. A check on the time, and then down to the kitchen for some hastily-made sandwiches. He took a pint of milk from the refrigerator and left the house, locking the door behind him and putting the key back where he had found it. Muddying the waters.

The back gate from the garden led onto a footpath beside a small river. David loaded the suitcase with broken bricks and flung it into the soft-bottomed stream beneath a bridge, where the murky liquid was in shadow most of the day. Then he jogged on down the path to the main road, numbing his mind to the pain in his brutalised feet; and joined the queue at a bus-stop for a local rural service.

He got off five miles north of Newcastle. When the bus was out of sight, he trotted through a narrow belt of woodland to reach another minor road, running east and west. It was no effort to limp convincingly on one foot; and every time a car passed he looked back hopefully, and stuck his thumb out.

His first lift was a short one, in an ancient Mini. The driver, a young teacher, apologised that she couldn't take him very far; she lived in a cottage on a farm only a mile or so along the road. David flexed his fingers thoughtfully; but she went on. "I don't know what kind of reception I'm going to get, or I'd ask you in and strap that ankle up for you. Only I had a row with my boyfriend before I left this morning, and things may still be a bit glacial. That's what the flowers are for, on the back seat there; sort of a peace offering. I always buy him flowers. He buys me bits for the car . . ."

David laid his hands restfully in his lap, and told lies about training for the Great North Run. She dropped him at the junction where she turned off into a narrow lane, and only found out a few days later how lucky she had been to have a boyfriend waiting.

David walked another two or three miles, limping in earnest. He was beginning to feel anxious in case the police put out a general call against suspicious characters on the road, when at last a car stopped. This was a large new Volvo, and the man who leant over to push open the passenger door was wearing a good business suit and a tie.

"How far are you going?" The voice was light and cultured, the manner friendly.

"As far as possible, towards the Lakes. Or any town where I can get a bus."

"You won't need one." The man gestured him into the car. "I'm going to Keswick myself, if that'll do you."

"That's marvellous, yes." David settled himself down with professional ease, to tempt the driver into talking.

His name was John Marston, he was unmarried and undivorced, he was managing director of his own small company: "Business is going to the dogs," he said cheerfully. "Import/export, that sort of nonsense. And with the pound and the dollar playing leapfrog, I haven't a clue whether I should be coming or going. So I thought I'd take a few days off, leave my partner to watch things fall apart."

David deduced that the business was a success – that Marston had a very accurate idea of what was happening in world markets, and that he had left precise instructions for his partner to follow.

"I have friends in Keswick," Marston went on. "I had thought of buying a cottage there myself; but these people have given me an open invitation, so why should I bother? I turn up when I can and leave when I have to, and it works marvellously well. I use it as a retreat, you see; even my partner doesn't know the address or the phone number. As a matter of fact, my friends don't even know I'm coming today; it was one of those sudden decisions. It won't put them out, though. That's what's so good about it, it's all so easy. I could even turn up with a friend, if I wanted; they wouldn't mind."

David smiled.

The light was gone before they reached Alston. Going across the moors towards Penrith, Marston pulled off the road and turned off the engine and the lights.

"Grey Nag to your right," he said. "Melmerby Fell to your left. Coffee in the flask behind your seat, if you don't mind sharing the cup."

"I don't mind sharing." But David didn't grope behind him for the flask. Instead, his hand moved to the back of Marston's neck, massaging it lightly between fingers and thumb.

Marston chuckled, and turned towards him. David's hand moved round a little, the other came up to meet it; his thumb closed over Marston's windpipe, felt the gristly projection of the Adam's apple, and thrust hard. The sound of Marston's breathing cut off with a hoarse, choking wheeze.

His eyes bulged, and his mouth hung foolishly open. He shook his head madly; David smiled, relaxed his grip for a moment – then dug his thumb brutally deeper, and felt cartilage snap.

Marston's arms flailed helplessly, his tongue tested the air, his skin mottled and he died. David searched his pockets and made a neat pile above the dashboard of wallet, driving licence, cheque-book and a few letters. Then he got out of the car, went round to the driver's side and manoeuvred Marston's body out of the driving seat onto the grass. He took the keys from the ignition and unlocked the boot, made space by lifting out Marston's suitcase and put his corpse in its place. The suitcase went onto the back seat.

David flicked on the courtesy light and spent a few minutes familiarising himself with the basic facts of Marston's life, memorising address and age, date of birth and car registration number. Just in case.

Satisfied, he put the documents into the glove compartment, started the engine and drove on into the evening, towards Penrith and the M6, and the quickest route to Wales. This morning's *Gazette* had reported that Tina was leaving hospital for an unnamed destination in the country; David had put two and two together, and arrived at a very satisfactory figure. Fenner's staying in Newcastle only served to confirm it, as a piece of subtle misdirection. David was confident of finding Tina convalescing in her cottage. There would no doubt be police protection, but he would find a way to get at her. Not for his own sake; he wasn't in the least concerned that she could identify him as her attacker.

He was doing this for Fenner.

A phone was ringing in the Incident Room. Mike Malone, who was nearest, picked up the receiver and tucked it between his shoulder and chin, while his hands leafed through the reports he held.

"Incident Room, DI Malone speaking."

"Good evening. My name is Linden." The reports dropped from Mike's fingers, and he grabbed the receiver in both hands as the voice went on, "Matthew Linden. From the reports I hear on the wireless, I think you are probably looking for my son."

Alan Morgan was walking home from the pub with a bottle of whisky under his arm, when a car door slammed on the other side of the street and he heard a voice calling. "Excuse me . . ." Looking round, he saw a tall, bearded man in a track suit trot across the road to join him.

"I wonder if you can help me?" the man said. "I'm trying to find Paul Fenner, or Tina Blake. I believe they have a cottage in the village somewhere."

"Yes, indeed they do. *Plas y Gwyn* it's called, the last cottage on the left as you go up the hill. Hardly a part of the village really, scowling down on the rest of us from a great height. But if you're looking for them tonight, I'm afraid you've had a wasted journey."

"Oh, really?" The stranger frowned.

"Yes, they're neither of them here at the moment. Paul's been away for months; then Tina went to join him, and . . . But you must know all this, surely? If you're a friend of theirs? The media have been dining out on it for weeks."

"I'm afraid I don't follow news events. What's happened to them?"

Alan put a hand lightly on the tall man's elbow. "Perhaps you'd better come with me, down to my house. If you've the time, that is. We can be more comfortable there, and I can give you the full story, or as much as I know of it."

The stranger's name was John Marston. Alan took him into the study and poured two whiskies while his guest looked curiously at the cups on the top shelf of his glass-fronted cabinet.

"Clay-pigeon shooting?"

"I used to do a lot when I was younger," Alan said. "It's only vanity, that makes me keep those things around; I still go shooting on the odd weekend, but simply for fun nowadays. I wouldn't have the trophies on display, only Tina and Paul gave me the cabinet, and I had to find something to put in it."

"Gave it?" Marston's eyebrows twitched with surprise, as his hands caressed the dark rosewood. "That was generous – or foolish."

"Generous. They knew it was valuable. I told them so myself." Alan swirled the whisky in his glass, and smiled at the memory.

"You're a close friend of theirs, then, would you say?"

Marston's question had an odd flavour to it, but Alan answered simply enough. "Yes. They're very important to me."

"And you to them?"

"I hope so, yes. I believe so."

"Good."

In that word the oddness was back, sharp and strong; but Alan had no time to puzzle over it. He saw Marston's hands close on opposite corners of his beloved cabinet, and wrench it from the wall with one fluent movement of the shoulders; and behind the shock, some belated trick of the light showed him another face beneath the beard, and he understood.

"You're the Butcher," he said stupidly.

David's lips turned briefly upwards. "My friends," he said, "call me the Samaritan."

Alan snatched at the telephone; and David threw the cabinet.

A corner caught Alan in the chest, with the hurtling force of a javelin. He toppled backwards, the cabinet fell on top of him, and David's foot came smashing down, splintering glass and wood together. The brutal shock of it slammed against Alan's ribs like a sledgehammer. Fear and pain filled him, like oil and water mixed.

He tried to roll away, to force himself to his feet; some last-minute miracle would come to interrupt this horror, it would have to, and he wanted to be standing up to meet it. But the killer's hands caught him round the throat, and dragged him across the floor towards the hearth. Half-strangled, aware only of the impossible strength in those hands and his own draining resistance, Alan lost his faith in miracles.

He was turned over onto his stomach as casually as a farmer turns a sheep; and saw the glowing coals of the fire a foot away from his face. He could feel the heat from it drawing the skin tight across his cheekbones. Fingers like grappling-irons closed on the back of his neck –

– and his head was thrust suddenly forward, deep into the hissing fury of the coals. This was hell, then, the choking smoke and grit and a burning like the Devil's fingers tearing at your face, your eyes and lips and all, flames embracing your skull like the arms of a lover, and the pain so much more than pain that you hardly knew it when it came –

– and he gasped a breath to scream with, but there was nothing but fire to breathe, searing and blistering his lungs, hurting more than anything; and

(JESUS!)

wasn't a prayer, it was a curse and an accusing. If there were really any Jesus to accuse, or any god at all; and in these last moments, peeling slowly away from his pain, Alan knew that by going into death with that spasm of doubt, he'd made a waste and a nonsense of all his adult life.

David pulled the body back, away from the fire, and smothered the bubbling, reeking head in the rag hearth-rug to kill any lingering flames. Then he took a bookmark from his pocket and tucked it carefully between soot-blackened teeth.

He went out into the hall to look for something, and found

it in a case inside a tall cupboard. When he was ready, he left the house and walked quickly down to the Volvo, not caring too much if anyone should see him now. No one was watching for strangers here. Not yet.

He put what he carried onto the back seat, started the engine and drove slowly up the hill. That the parson had known nothing meant just that – nothing. Tina was there, he was certain of it. She would come to where she felt safe.

And to prove it, there was a light in the cottage window when he found it. No sign of a guard outside, no cars in the lane. There would be a detective inside with her, then, and he was taking a risk; but no matter. The luck was riding him high tonight. He thought of Fenner, and had no second thoughts.

All evening, Fenner had been expecting Mike to call. He knew his friend wouldn't be happy at his being alone in the flat; he might even suggest that it would actually be safe for Susan and Flick if Fenner stayed with them, on the grounds that he at least would know what to look for.

That was nonsense, of course. The danger came with Fenner; and the best thing, the only thing he could do to help his friends was stay out of their way. So he sat in the flat and rehearsed his arguments; and eventually Mike did call. But it was like a scene from another play, meeting none of his expectations.

"Know where I am?" Mike said disgustedly. "Fucking Oxfordshire."

"Christ, Mike. Couldn't the bastards give you a rest?"

"That's what I said. But the Chief had set his heart on me. I talked to the guy first, see, so by the Chief's reckoning we have established a rapport and I am therefore indispensable. So I'm in fucking Oxfordshire, and I have to bloody phone Susan to find out how my baby is."

"Hang on," Fenner said desperately. "I didn't follow half of that – but first things first. How is Flick?"

"Okay. 'Satisfactory.' You know what that means."

"Yeah. I know. So," Fenner picked the thread up again before the silence became impossible to break, "what are you talking about? What guy?"

"I had some files in the house, that had to go back to the station," Mike said. "So I took them in, and I was going to tell the Chief that he wouldn't be seeing me again for a bit. Only a phone rang as I passed it, and there was no one on the desk, so I have to go and pick it up, don't I? And you know who it is? It's only the bloody Butcher's father, that's all."

"*What?*"

"Yeah, I know. You thought he was dead. *We* thought he was dead. And why did we think he was dead? Because the local coppers told us he was dead. But the stupid bastards got it wrong, didn't they? Went chasing after the wrong Matthew Linden, or something. They're ever so sorry, you wouldn't believe how sorry they are. But they're obviously not *dependable*, the Chief can't *rely* on people who make mistakes like that. So a little troupe of us came galloping down the highway to talk to Mr Bones the Butcher's father – and who gets lead billing? The Chief himself, and poor bloody yours truly."

Fenner had a strong suspicion that poor bloody yours truly was drunk; but from the sound of it, he had a right to be.

"What's the guy like?" he asked.

"Sickening." Malone said it bluntly and without malice, which gave it all the more force. "Honest, Paul, if this is what the father's like it's no surprise that the son got twisted. I could almost feel sorry for the guy, now. Almost." The last word was said softly, but with a savage intensity that seemed turned more against Malone himself than anyone else, as if he were forcibly reminding himself of what David Linden had done to him.

"Tell me," Fenner said.

"Well, he's a big man to start with, hands like the shovel on a JCB; but it's not that. Like a tank – it's the guy inside that makes it dangerous, the guy who doesn't mind blasting buildings apart and crushing people under the treads. We've spent two hours talking to him – and Daddy-oh just sat there telling us what a little shit his son was. Always had been. He doesn't even rate the guy as human."

"Do you? After what he's done?"

"*Yes!* Okay, you can call him inhuman, call him a monster, but it's only words, Paul. You use the only words you've got; and you still see him as human. His father calls him an animal, and means it. He told us some of the things he'd done to David when he was a boy, as punishment . . . I'll show you the report, I can't even talk about it on the phone. But he was really enjoying himself, telling us all about it. Practically licking his bloody lips over it all."

"What, are you saying he's a sadist? Literally, I mean – getting a sexual kick out of it?"

"Can't be sure; there's no evidence, except for the bloody leer in his eyes. It'd help if we could talk to his wife, but she really has disappeared. Changed her name and gone. She might be dead, or out of the country; or else she's just lying very low. Whichever, we can't find her, to ask. I'd put money on it, though. With his own bloody kids, too . . . That's the funny thing about David, you know, Paul; that's what's missing. It's not just that he doesn't assault his victims, sexually. If you go through the file on him, the guy might as well have been a eunuch. As far as we know, he's never so much as touched a girl. Or a boy, for that matter."

"Except to kill them. That could be a sexual thing in itself. But listen, if the old man was that much of a bastard, David might go after him too, did you think of that?"

"If he can find him. It took us long enough, remember. But yes, we thought of it. Tried to warn him, but he wasn't having any. Even animals don't murder their fathers. I don't think it's dawned on him that David isn't scared of him any more. But frankly, I don't think I care a damn. Those two can tear each other apart, and welcome. The way I see it, the father butchered David, to make him what he is; and it's only poetic justice if he gets butchered back, isn't it?"

"Mike, you're drunk," Fenner said gently, "and you don't mean that. Or you won't in the morning, anyway. Get yourself some sleep, for God's sake – but tell the local CID to put a watch on Linden's house, right? Just in case?"

"Have done. Course we have. D'you think we're stupid, or what?"

"Yeah. G'night, Mike."

It was a shame to sleep, when it felt so good to stay awake. Huw felt a gentle lethargy washing over him, like being warm and underwater; but he didn't want to sleep. He was content to lie still and look at Steph in the soft light from the bedside lamp. Her face was just an inch away from his, too close to focus properly; but if he moved back he'd lose the touch of moist, warm air from her lungs as she breathed out. He liked to time his own breathing against hers, so that they shared a little of each other's air.

So he looked at her unfocused, which was just as good or better, when his thoughts were unfocused too. She was still a wonder to him, this girl, a godsend – only he wasn't sure he believed in God any more. Paul and Tina didn't, and they'd been around a lot more than he had, seen and done more and probably thought harder about it all. But then there was Pastor Morgan to set against them; he was a friend too, and absolutely certain. Huw just wasn't sure, but he went to chapel every Sunday anyway, with Steph if she'd come and thinking about her if she wouldn't. Sometimes when they were supposed to be praying he'd close his eyes and find her right there in his head, naked like she was now, with no shame in her, slender and beautiful and sexy enough to burn inside him from his throat to his thighs. And if there was a God he'd just have to take that any way he liked, because Huw wasn't going to feel any guilt about it. By his reckoning it was prayer enough, just to be grateful and glad and wildly in love with life and the world and a girl.

He didn't know what love was any more than God; but he knew what it did, and that was plenty. It woke something inside him that carried Steph's name and was like another life, sometimes sharp and painful, sometimes like fire and broken glass, sometimes like feathers. It lived in his body and in his mind; it pulled his strings and took his choices away, and it had brought him here where Steph was, bright and beautiful and loving him.

Her eyes opened, and she smiled hullo. He eased himself closer until he could feel the press of soft breasts against his chest. His arms circled her ribs and waist, and he marvelled again as he always did at how small she was against him. He moved one leg over to wrap it round hers, and moaned softly as she ran a finger slowly down his spine, counting off the vertebrae, the fleshy pad of her fingertip followed by the light scratching of the nail.

He was almost unbearably conscious of the rub of her skin against his as they nestled together, the thin prickle of sweat on his back and the dampness he could feel where his hands touched her, the sound of their breathing and the wind outside, a slight scrape of metal that might have been the door-latch rattling. Her teeth closed on his neck, oddly tender, barely nipping the flesh; he eased over, taking the lovely weight of her onto himself, and the world was a glistening, shrinking bubble with Steph and him at the heart of it –

– and the bedroom door smashed open and the bubble was gone and the real world with it, leaving them in television. The room was filled with noise, like an animal screaming, and a man with a long gun stood staring at them. Huw saw a dark beard and a tracksuit, and white teeth gleaming in an open mouth even after the scream cut off. Impossible to be afraid; this couldn't touch him and Steph, it couldn't be real . . .

But the man shrugged slightly, not an apology but something else, and lifted the gun to his shoulder. Huw saw the dull gleaming of two joined barrels, and his mind said *shotgun*. Before he could do more than stir himself wonderingly up onto one elbow, there was a double blast that shook everything, and filled the room with smoke and stink. He felt Steph falling away from him before he looked at her; and when he looked, it was a second or two before he could see her in the torn wet mess that lay slumped and soaking on the tossed-back duvet. But her head was still whole and hers, even though her face was hidden. He saw her fine, pale hair with the ends all scorched or splashed scarlet, and there could be no pretending now, no refusing to accept what was real.

Steph was dead. He would have known it without seeing and touching and smelling her death, he would have known it from the other side of the world; and the quiet singing was gone suddenly from his mind, and the living thing inside him that carried her name and called itself love was thrashing and crying and hurting like an animal wounded to death. That suffering filled him, possessed him and became him; and it was him now that was thrashing and screaming, kicking his legs free of the duvet and stumbling up. His own death was ordained and inevitable, he was dying already through Steph's death; but he'd have the man's eyes first, and his tongue too, tear them out with his fingers . . .

But he never got that far. The man reversed the shotgun in his hands and swung it like a club.

The blow shattered Huw's temple, and drove fragments of bone deep into his brain. Darkness reached for him while his eyes were still open; all the layers of his life folded in around him like the fading petals of a flower, leaving him closed in with a single image, a face turning to a word, a feeling that crumbled before he could name it, a momentary point of light.

It was after midnight when the phone rang again, after the bottle was empty. Fenner stumbled through to answer it, his speech as slurred as his feet.

"Yeah, who is it?"

The answer came back as another question, mocking and familiar, a pricking challenge his brain was too numb to feel. "Can I help you?"

"Look," Fenner said, "who is that?"

Again, no direct answer; but, "Hullo, the Samaritan, can I help you?"

Fenner shuddered, and felt suddenly sick. "*Linden?* Is that you?"

"Hullo, Paul."

"Oh, God." Fenner stared helplessly at the receiver. He had words to describe David Linden, but none to say to him.

"Just a status-report, Paul," David said evenly. "Just to keep you in touch."

"Where are you?" Fenner asked dully, hopelessly.

"Oh, round and about. What I think will interest you more is where I've been. And what I was doing there. You'd find out soon enough anyway, but I wanted to be the one to break it to you."

Tina. He couldn't say it, in case his simply admitting the possibility would allow the fact; but fear bled him white and grew fat on the blood.

"I was looking for Tina," David went on, sounding a little rueful, "only I must have been looking in the wrong place. Still not to worry. I'll find her eventually, you can be sure of that. She's mine now, more mine than yours. I've had some of her blood, and I'll be back for the rest. And after that, I'll come for you. When I'm ready."

"No," Fenner said; but even he wasn't sure what he was denying.

"Meantime," David said, "I've spent an interesting evening with some friends of yours. At least, I assume they were all friends. One said he was, and I don't think I ought to disbelieve him, do you? A man of the cloth, after all. The other two I can't be so sure about, I didn't stop to talk to them; but they were screwing each other silly in your bed, so I expect you know them. Unless they were squatters, of course. You haven't got squatters, have you? In that pretty little cottage of Tina's, up on the hill? A couple of kids, they hardly looked old enough for what they were up to . . ."

Alan, Huw, Steph. Fenner was crying now, choking sobs that ripped themselves from his chest and left the taste of bile and blood in his throat. "What . . . What have you . . ."

"Done to them?" David finished for him. "I think I'll leave you to find that out for yourself. There's nothing like positive action, is there? Something to keep you busy. Really, that's all I want to say. Just to let you know I haven't forgotten you. I'll come and see you soon; but not till I've found Tina. And there's a little private business of my own that comes before that, even."

Even smothered as he was by grief, Fenner wanted to lash back somehow, to damage a little of Linden's cool control; but the only weapon he had was a feeble one.

"Family affairs, you mean?" he said, swallowing, trying to come back hard. "How's your father?"

He heard a sharp, hissing breath; then the line went dead. Oddly, his words seemed to have struck home harder than he'd hoped; but he had no time to dwell on that now, with the ghosts of three loved friends standing behind him, just out of sight. He should go to the station and make a statement, soon, before his fuddled brain could forget the details of what Linden had said; but not yet. Not just yet, for God's sake . . .

He dropped his head onto his folded arms, and wept.

38 The End of all Songs

Fenner rattled the letter-flap, then shrugged off his hesitancy and rapped hard with his knuckles. If that didn't bring them down, he'd use his fist.

But he heard someone moving, slow footsteps on the stairs, and the door swung cautiously open.

"Hullo, Jude."

She was just that moment out of bed, wearing only a man's sweatshirt, hanging almost to her knees. She hitched the long sleeves back to her elbows and belted it around her waist with a striped tie; Fenner remembered Tina doing much the same with his own clothes, and shivered.

Jude looked up at him, rubbed her hands across her face and through her tangled hair, then beckoned him in with her head.

In the living-room, he dropped onto a cushion beside the fire while Jude went on into the bedroom. He heard murmured voices, and a minute later both girls came through together. Georgina was wearing a soft silk dressing-gown that brushed the floor as she walked, and using a hair-brush with a handle of mother-of-pearl.

"Morning, Paul." She touched his shoulder and smiled, before kicking a cushion over to join him. Jude went into the kitchen. Fenner heard her fill a kettle and light the gas; then she appeared in the doorway with a box of matches, and tossed it towards Georgina. She stretched out one hand, caught it and passed it to Fenner.

"Light the fire, would you? There's a love. Oh, and don't mind Jude. She doesn't talk in the mornings, she communicates by scowls. I'm used to it, but I know some people find it unnerving."

Fenner let the girls' morning rituals wash over him like a gentle, soothing rain; and when Jude came in with a loaded tray, he shared their breakfast.

Finally, Jude licked honey from her fingers, drained the last dregs of tea into her mug, and said, "What is it, then, Paul? Why the visit?"

"I . . . was walking," he said, "and I saw your van, and . . . I need your help."

"Go on, we're listening." Georgina passed him a saucer, as he lit a cigarette. He nodded, and put the dead match carefully in the centre.

"David Linden telephoned me last night." The name fell into the room like a dead weight, bringing silence with it. It was an effort to go on, a greater effort than it had been even to start; but he made the effort, and said, "He was gloating, mostly, or threatening. Playing games with me. He – he told me he was in Wales, or he'd just come from there. And he said he was going to go after Tina again. That's what he was doing in Wales, he thought she might be at the cottage. Only he found some friends of ours there instead . . ."

He dragged deeply on his cigarette, trying to kill the taste of bile in his throat. The girls just waited.

"I would have gone down myself," he said, "only I was drunk, I couldn't drive. So I just went to the police, and told them. They phoned through, and sent a team down to the village. Linden's killed our three closest friends there. The village pastor, and some kids he found in the cottage."

That was all he was going to tell the girls; but Fenner had seen, had insisted on seeing the detailed reports, and the photographs that were faxed through. And he'd learned that bloodbaths were different when you know the faces, when the blood comes from people you love and the bath is your own home. He had walked out of the room, made his way to the toilet and vomited; and the taste of it had been in his mouth ever since, and the threat of it again in his stomach.

"I should go there. Only, Linden said something else before he hung up. Something about having personal business to see to; and I think he meant his father. He's been warned, and the local CID is keeping an eye on him, but the old man won't buy it. If he isn't bloody careful, then David'll have him, police protection or not."

He paused again, feeling their eyes on him; but he didn't look up. Not yet. "I want to go and talk to him. Maybe I can make him listen; and if not, that's still where I reckon David Linden is going to be, sometime in the next day or two. And that's where I want to be, too. I might spot the bastard, you never know. Miracles have happened."

He was aware of the rising tone of hysteria in his voice, but didn't know how to prevent it; so he simply stopped talking for a minute. Georgina touched his hand. "Yes, but what do you want us to do, Paul? You said you needed help."

"Yeah. Drive me down? Please?" And now he lifted his head to meet their eyes, challenge them a little. "I can't go by myself, I daren't. You know I'm drinking again, and I wouldn't be safe on the road. I'll pay for the petrol, of course. And we can go in my car."

"No," Jude said immediately. "We'll go in the van, it's what we're used to. Okay, Georgie?"

"Sure," Georgina said, as if it had been a foregone conclusion all the time. "Give us ten minutes to get dressed, Paul. Tell you what, why don't you have a wash and a shave? There's a throwaway razor in the bathroom cabinet. You'll feel better; and believe me, darling, if you want to talk an old man into something, you'll get further if you don't look like death warmed up. I should know, I've had enough practice with my grandfather . . ."

Going down to the van, though, Jude said, "I don't know, Paul. You looked kind of romantic, with all the stubble; now you just look grey. Did you sleep at all last night?"

He laughed, a harsh croaking noise that ended with a cough. "Sleep? No, love, I didn't sleep. I was with the police till seven, then I just walked the streets till I wound up here."

"Well, listen, there's heaps of gear in the back of the van. Sleeping bags and stuff. Why don't you make yourself a nest and get some kip, while we drive?"

"No, I'll be okay, thanks."

"Of course you will. Once you've had some sleep." Georgina unlocked the side door of the van, and waved a hand at a deep pile of coats and sleeping-bags. "There you go, Paul, make yourself comfy. I daresay Jude'll tuck you in, if you ask her nicely."

"Don't you believe it," Jude said dourly. "The only time I ever tucked a bloke up in bed, he made attempts on my virtue."

"Did he achieve it?" Fenner asked, interested in spite of everything.

"No, he wasn't up to it."

Fenner smiled, and sank onto the soft heap of bedding. Perhaps they were right, perhaps he could sleep for an hour or two, perhaps he should . . .

He was aware of it when they stopped for petrol on the motorway, and the girls changed places; but he didn't try to break through the bubble of sleep that enfolded him, and soon slipped back to its dark centre.

He roused two or three times during the long run down through the Midlands, only to fall asleep again after a minute or two. It was the silence of the engine that woke him properly in mid-afternoon; he stirred, and felt an uncomfortable pressure in his bladder. The front seats were empty, and the doors standing wide; he made his way out, and found the girls stretching their legs in a garage forecourt.

Georgina smiled at him lazily. "Are you hungry? We saved you a pasty and a carton of orange."

"Later, maybe. What I want right now is a piss."

"Over there." She pointed out the toilets, and he crossed the tarmac at a fast walk.

A couple of minutes later, he joined Georgina in the garage shop, where she was buying toffees. "Are you two going to snap my head off if I smoke in the van?"

"Oh, I expect we can put up with it this once. So long as you don't look on it as a precedent."

"Thanks, Gina."

He bought cigarettes, and they moved to the door; and Fenner said, in a soft, savage undertone, "I wish these places sold booze."

"No, you don't. You've come down here to do a job, haven't you, Paul? Haven't you?" Her tone demanded some answer, so he gave her a nod. "And you can't do it if you're roaring drunk. So don't think about booze. Just don't think about it."

He laughed sourly. "Sounds like that tag people used to throw at me when I was a kid. *Try not to think of a white horse*."

(And that was whisky too, and it was no good trying not to think of it.)

"Tell you what," Georgina said. "Why don't you tell me about your friends in Wales?"

It was a cruel weapon, and her flat voice said that she knew it; but she went on more gently, "You can't hog all the guilt to yourself, Paul. If you claim it because it was through you that David found them, then I get a share automatically, because it was through me that David found you. I've a right to know about them, so that I can share it properly."

And clumsily, awkwardly, he told her: about Alan Morgan, and about Huw and Steph. And it was a long time before he thought again about a white horse, or a drink.

Finally, an hour after sunset, they came to a housing estate on the edge of a small town, and a bungalow on the estate.

For a while, Fenner only sat and looked at the lighted

windows. Behind them moved the man who had created David, and made him what he was; and it was easier to hate this unknown father now than it was to hate David. But he still felt a responsibility for the old man's life; there was no sense of just deserts in leaving him to David.

He pushed the passenger door partway open, and glanced sideways at the two girls. "Are you two going to be okay, just waiting? I could be some time, but I really don't think you ought to come in with me."

"Wouldn't want to, thanks," Jude said bluntly. "But don't worry about us. I mean, we actually get on quite well, you know, Georgie and me."

"Yeah. Right." Fenner grinned, and stepped quickly down onto the pavement. Before he slammed the door, he heard Georgina murmuring, "Good luck," while beyond her Jude gave him a thumbs-up.

He walked twenty yards down the road to the bungalow's front garden, and spotted a man in a parked car watching him attentively. Fenner hesitated briefly at the gate, then walked over to the car. The man wound down the window as he approached.

"CID?" Fenner asked

The detective looked startled, then nodded.

"My name's Paul Fenner. I'm tied in with this thing half a dozen ways; but if you're worried, check back with your station, and ask them to get in touch with Newcastle, okay? I'm just going to talk to the guy."

"That's all right, sir. We weren't expecting to see you here, but – well, we heard what happened last night." The detective looked helpless. "I'm sorry."

Fenner nodded, and turned away.

"I don't understand your involvement, Mr Fenner. Why exactly have you come to me?"

I'm trying to save your life, you old fool. Impossible to put it like that, though. Fenner hid his rising impatience, and tried to be reasonable. "As I told you, sir, your – David spoke to me on the telephone last night, and he gave me good reason to believe that he means to kill you."

Matthew Linden was easily identifiable as the father of his son. There were the same bones in his face, behind the black glasses and the white hair; and there was the same sense of physical power, though here it was a strength decaying with age and lack of exercise. But while David had kept his brutality and his workaday human face strictly segregated, in his father they were irrevocably mixed.

"And you've come to warn me? In your role of self-appointed do-gooder, would this be, Mr Fenner? An unofficial Samaritan, perhaps?"

You shit. You filthy shit. Linden knew everything he was implying with the comparison, and Fenner could feel his enjoyment as the implications struck home, too close to Fenner's own sense of guilt to be ignored.

But he had no time to respond, as Linden went smoothly on. "The police have already brought me a warning; and to put it simply, I find that it does not make me any the more gullible to hear it again from an unofficial source. I disowned my son a long time ago. There has been no contact between us since he was hospitalised; and if he had offered or asked for contact, I should have refused it. I fail to see why he should be so eager to kill me twenty-five years later."

Because he knows what you did to him. Because he hates you for it, as I do.

"He doesn't need any logical reason, Mr Linden. You have to remember that his first killings were all virtually random."

"By which reasoning I am in no more danger than any other member of the public. Why should I consent to having my house watched, and being followed wherever I go?"

"Because you're still alive; and to David, that makes you unfinished business. Which puts you very high on his list, Mr Linden . . ."

"Georgie, how much cash is there in the kitty?"

"What, the catastrophe money? About fifty quid, I think. Why, do you want to blow it?"

"Mind-reader."

Georgina looked up sharply. "I was joking."

"I'm not. Look, Paul's having a hell of a time at the moment, and he hasn't eaten today, hardly – so I was thinking, why don't we take him out for a meal somewhere? It's not going to help much, but we could make him laugh a bit, if we worked on it. And anything's got to be better than just letting him stew."

After a pause, Georgina said, "Jude love, how long have I known you?"

"Two years, near enough. Why?"

"Nothing. Just that I find I have not yet plumbed the depths of your wonder, and that surprises me a little, considering the amount of time I've spent splashing around in it." She pulled her lover close, and kissed her. "It's a marvellous idea. I'll dig the kitty out."

"Mind she doesn't scratch." Jude let her gaze wander over the chaos of boxes and clothes in the back of the van, and grinned suddenly. "Hey, we've still got all my gear in the back there, haven't we? The evening suit and the topper and all. We never unpacked it, from when we went down to London. Why don't I dress up for him?"

"Here he comes now."

Georgina was watching Fenner in the wing-mirror of the van, as he left the bungalow and came down to the road.

Jude tilted the top-hat to a rakish angle on her head, and put a hand on the ignition keys. "As soon as he gets in, we're off. Can't give him a chance to argue. You'll have to sit on him if he makes a fuss, I'll be too busy driving."

"Mmm. Long time since I sat on a fella's lap . . . Hang on. He's going the other way."

"What?"

"He is. He's walking off up the street."

"Shit. D'you think the moron's forgotten where we're parked? You'd think the van was big enough to spot."

"From the look of it, he's forgotten we're here at all. The rate he's moving, I'd say he's mad enough to spit."

"Great." Jude banged her fist on the steering-wheel. "So what do we do now?"

"Follow him, I think. He'll lose himself, given half a chance. We'd better leave the van, though – it's a bit obvious, sneaking along in a bloody noisy monster like this."

Jude nodded, and they jumped out of the van. Jude locked the door, then checked herself with a muttered oath and opened it again.

"What's the matter?" Georgina demanded, gazing after Fenner. "Hurry up, or we'll lose him."

Jude reached behind the seat, and drew out her sword-stick from its place on the floor. "May as well do the job properly."

The two of them walked quickly up the hill in Fenner's wake. As they passed Linden's bungalow, they both glanced inadvertently sideways, to see a burly figure standing four-square at a window. Neither noticed the detective in his car.

Fenner by this time was only a shadow, hurrying through pools of light with his head down and his shoulders hunched, never looking back.

Fenner's pace slowed gradually, and the girls could almost see the anger leave him, and depression move in. They hung back to keep a hundred yards or so behind him, and crossed to the other side of the street in case he glanced back. They were reluctant to intrude until they were sure he was ready for them.

Leaving the estate, Fenner turned along the main road, oblivious of both his surroundings and his followers.

A car door swung open a little way ahead of the girls, and a man in a tracksuit got out, walking away with quick, impatient strides.

"Silly bugger's asking to have his car pinched, leaving the door wide open like that," Jude grunted.

"Mmm. Looks like everyone's got something on their minds tonight."

Fenner was passing a church, with a large graveyard behind it. They saw him hesitate under a street-lamp, then walk through an open gateway onto the gravel path that led between the headstones.

The man in the track suit waited by the kerb until the road was clear, then crossed over to the church. The distant double note of a police siren made him turn his head as he passed under the light; and for the first time, Georgina saw his face.

She grabbed at Jude's arm, as the man disappeared after Fenner, into the dark graveyard.

"For God's sake, Jude, run and find a phone. Get the police, *quick*!"

"What the hell for?" But she was putting two and two together and finding an answer that turned her pale, even as Georgina told her.

"Didn't you *see*? That was David!"

Jude ran, with her top-hat in one hand and the sword-stick in the other. Georgina swallowed, bit down hard on one finger and began to recite a Buddhist mantra silently in her head to chase her fears down, as she followed David over the road and into the graveyard.

Fenner's feet scuffed gloomily at the gravel as he followed the path past the church. The graveyard ahead was as dark as his mood; only a little moonlight found its way between the branches of ancient yews to show him how the path ran a few yards ahead of his feet.

He went on unthinkingly; and never paused to wonder if the occasional soft noise behind him might mean that he was not after all alone.

Coarse ropes chafed David's skin beneath the track suit, and the mallet's head was an awkward weight below his ribs; but the discomfort was nothing compared with the convenience of having his hands free. And it meant that passers-by, like those fools in fancy dress who'd been behind him, could see nothing suspicious.

Fenner led the way down to the furthest corner of the graveyard, like any sacrificial victim treading a clear path of roses to the altar. David trod carefully behind him, his feet making scarcely any sound in the soft-soled trainers.

At last, though, Fenner must have heard something, or else felt David's presence with a sense not so easily named. He stopped, and half-turned to glance over his shoulder. David flung himself forward, two paces and a leap, to come crashing into Fenner. They hit the ground with David on top; and his fingers were already at Fenner's throat, feeling for the carotid arteries where a simple pressure would bring speedy unconsciousness. But after a single brief spasm, Fenner offered no resistance. His body lay limply beneath David's, his breathing shallow and irregular.

David lifted his weight off Fenner's chest, and Fenner still didn't move; so he checked with his hands, and found the sticky warmth of blood matting his victim's hair. Fenner must have hit his head as he fell, on the stone border surrounding the nearest grave. There was raised lettering on the border, a dark grey against the pale stone; and David took a moment to decipher it.

Some go the long road home;
others cross the fields.

"How true," he murmured, smiling. "And the stile's right here, Paul, and the signpost. Can I help you?"

Awareness came back to Fenner like bubbles bursting in a pool of mud. He rose into a bright moment of pain, and sank again; and rose, and knew the pain was in his head, and sank.

Two bubbles bursting at once, pain and movement; and a third, the knowledge of his head hanging low and arm trailing, his body folded over something moving. Then only the dark to drown in, the bottom of the pool.

When he rose again, pain was a constant singing in his head; and there was nothing else. No touch of earth beneath him. He was flying or falling, or floating. He moved by twisting, like a weed in water; but he hardly moved at all.

Eyes. Open your eyes.

(No. Last time there was a shadow coming at me like a nightmare, a bearded shadow with David's face under the beard. If I look he might be there again, or still there, still coming.)

Don't be a fool. D'you think he's hanging in mid-air, waiting?

(Why not? I am.)

Open your eyes.

– and he opened his eyes, and saw his naked body dwindling in perfect perspective, swaying gently above darkness –

(flying or falling, or floating)

– and then it changed. A hand seized his wrist and pulled the arm out horizontally. He felt a rough surface against the back of his hand, and a tightness gripping his forearm, holding it still.

No more flying tonight.

The first spasm of fear came with that thought, as he felt the strangeness abandon him. His mouth was full of something soft and treacherous; he tried to spit it out, and discovered the harsh discomfort of a gag stretching the corners of his mouth. So he turned his head, to look along his arm.

The first thing he saw was rope running across his shoulder and under his arm. That explained the flying. He could feel it now, the weight of his body making the ropes bite deep into his armpits. He looked behind his shoulder, and saw his arm stretched out against a long tree-branch. Another rope tight around the forearm, to hold it there; and hands still knotting that rope. He looked behind the hands and saw David Linden perched astride the branch.

"Paul." It was more than a greeting, almost a declaration of love. Dimly, Fenner remembered what David had said about Tina, on the phone: *She's mine now, more mine than yours.* Now the same warmth was claiming him, reaching to possess him, offering death in outstretched hands.

David gave a final tug to his knot, then stood up on the stout branch. He walked behind Fenner's head with a casual balance, and sat again on the other side. Fenner felt so listless, so much the victim of inevitability, he almost forgot to struggle. It was only a token defiance that made him swing his free arm across his body as Linden bent down for it, and fumble at the ropes that held the other fast. David only laughed, and leant a little further. His fingers closed over Fenner's elbow with a bruising strength, and wrenched it back.

"Don't be foolish, Paul," he said gently, clamping Fenner's wrist to the branch with one leg while he unwound a length of rope from his waist. "You can't escape me, you know that. You came too close."

Fenner tried one more time to break free; but the blow on the head had left him sick and shaking, and David's leg was as unyielding as another branch, trapping his hand against the dusty bark. There was nothing he could do but watch, as David tied this arm too to the branch. Watch – and listen.

"I suppose you couldn't help yourself," David said. "Could you? Like attracts like, it's very true. I couldn't have stayed away from you if I'd wanted to, I couldn't have let you go; and you couldn't let me go, either."

Fenner shook his head violently; and David laughed.

"Oh, we are, you know. We're very much alike. We think the same way. That's how I've kept ahead of you all this time – how I brought you down here when I was ready for you. And it's how you got as close to me as you did. Just a little too close for comfort." His voice softened to a whisper, sharpened to glass. "*Family affairs. How's-your-father*. Close enough to understand that much, weren't you, Paul? No one else ever did. And no one's mocked me for a long, long time . . ."

Fenner understood that less than anything; but answers didn't matter any more, only the mallet in David's hand, and the metal spike.

"You might recognise these," David said. "I took them from your garden shed, after I'd dealt with the goats. This one's for Anne, because you mocked her. The other one'll be for me."

He set the point of the spike against the soft inner surface of Fenner's wrist, where the veins run between the bones; heard Fenner's gasp of indrawn breath, and waited till he let it out again; and swung the mallet.

Pain splintered Fenner, rived him, ran through him from his wrist as cracks run through glass. Spasms arched his body and twisted it till the ropes tore at his skin; but his wrist never moved, and he heard the steady metronome of David's blows as he hammered the spike home, felt the beats of pain coursing through him, following nerve-paths like hot wires beneath his skin.

And then the asthma came to take him, riding on the back of agony. His lungs cramped and closed, he gasped for air through the soft obstruction in his mouth and found none. His own ribs were suffocating him, squeezing his lungs like sponges. He threw his head back against the branch, chest and stomach heaving, his skin sweating cold, his mind almost begging for the swimming darkness that threatened in the corners of his eyes. And as the walls of the world closed in around him, he felt the touch of David's hand like a benediction on his damp hair.

David took his weight on his hands for a moment, lifted his feet to the branch and stood up. He walked behind Fenner again, smiling down at his victim as he drew the second spike from his waistband and kissed it lightly. This one for himself, for the loss of his home and his life. He had sworn that Fenner should pay; and this was the final payment. Like a vampire he would set a tooth in each wrist, and suck Fenner's life in a slow crucifixion. He was still undecided whether to cut the ropes and let him hang only from the nails; it would be more painful, certainly, but it would also kill him more quickly. He would leave the ropes for the moment, at least; and perhaps cut them later, if dawn came and Fenner was still alive.

He was bending to sit again when he heard a noise, the soft rustle of footsteps through leaves. He straightened slowly, and a voice called up to him.

"David?"

She sounded tentative, almost in tears; but he knew her, and greeted her by name. "Georgina."

He couldn't afford the panic that grappled with him, threatening to take over eyes and mind and action. He put one hand out against the tree-trunk and waited, forcing her to speak.

"Please, David. Don't do this." It was like a child's plea against the world too cruel for understanding. "Just – just stop it, and go. I won't try to stop you, I swear. But don't kill him. Don't hurt him any more . . ."

David didn't respond in words. He stepped backwards off the branch; and ape-like held out a hand to catch it as he fell. For a moment the two men hung and swung side by side, David and Fenner; then David released his grip and dropped tidily to the ground.

Georgina was just a yard away, staring at him as a cat might stare at a king. He could see the fear and the tension in her body, and yet sense the hope that rested on nothing but their former friendship.

"Too bad, Georgie," he said; and dug his hand deep into her hair. He jerked her head viciously back, and showed her the spike that had been held concealed against his forearm –

– and then you plunged it into her eye, didn't you, David? You meant to write your name in her brain, with an iron nib; but the spike's tip grated on bone, and before you could gouge deeper her scream was echoed behind you. You let her fall, and turned; and as you turned, you heard the scrape of something metal.

What you saw was a dream, too strange for nightmare: a figure in top hat and tails neatly silhouetted against the rising moon, with a walking-cane clutched in one hand and a splinter of moonlight in the other.

You stared and stood amazed, and wondered what world you had fallen into; and before you could think or move the bright moonlight came stabbing towards you, while the figure moaned with a voice like the wind.

The moonlight split you between rib and rib, cold as a tongue of ice, a tooth to suck and a tongue to drink you –

Envoi

The Third Day

He listened to the radio all day. They'd put him on his own, so he didn't need earphones; and it was the easiest thing to do. At first he'd tried Radio Four, but words were too dangerous. Often and often something would be said to make his mind slip a gear and shudder him back to the bad times; and from there it was hard to regain the bland balance, the no-movement that they called rest. So he had done with words. He tuned to Radio Three, and lived in the music; and if they broadcast poems or a play, he turned it off and lived with nothing for a time.

His hand – his wrist – lay on the covers, and hurt. Sometimes his whole arm hurt, and through the shoulder to the neck; sometimes all his skin was alive and crawling with hot needles. But the hand, the wrist, never stopped hurting, no matter what they gave him. They said there was no permanent damage, and he didn't have the strength to disbelieve them; but for the moment it was eternal, the only constant.

So he lived with pain and music, and the rare visitors were only an interruption in that world. Mike came, and Susan; but they didn't bring their daughter, and to him that was an indictment. His parents came, frighteningly old and distressed. The Chief had come, and stayed too long. And today, now, Tina had come.

She pushed the door quietly open, and came to the foot of the bed; and he saw that though she was physically healed, she still walked on knives, like a mermaid learning the reality of land. Her shoulders were hunched and wary, she seemed nervous of the world; and that too was an indictment.

"Hullo, Paul." Oddly, because if anything he'd expected the reverse, she seemed younger than she was, younger than he had ever known her – like a child unsure of her welcome, looking for clues how to behave.

"Hi." He gestured with his good hand. She came to his bedside, and bent over to give him a quick, almost surreptitious kiss on the cheek.

"I, um, I brought you some flowers . . ."

"I noticed." He smiled at the daffodils. "If you ask the nurse, she'll lead you off by the hand and encumber you with vases."

"In a minute." She laid the flowers down on the bedside locker and stood empty-handed, the fingers of one hand resting lightly on the coverlet, a foot away from his own.

"Why don't you get yourself a drink?" he suggested. "Me too, while you're there."

She looked dubiously at the bottle. "Lucozade?"

"Whisky and water. Mike's idea. But don't tell the sister."

She smiled, and filled two glasses.

"You can smoke too, if you want. I told them I wasn't going to be dictated to, not in a private room."

She shook her head. "I've given up."

"Light one for me, then, would you? It's a little awkward, with the hand . . ."

He'd meant for her to pass him a cigarette and strike a match; but she did it the old way, lighting it for herself and passing it on.

"Thanks." He took it between his fingers, and waved it towards a chair. "Why don't you sit down?"

She hesitated, then perched on the edge of the bed. "How is it, Paul? The hand?"

"It hurts." He shrugged with one shoulder. "They say I'm in for weeks of that. But it's healing well enough. I shouldn't have any problems."

"That's good."

He smoked, and she watched him; and eventually she gave a swallowed moan, and her fingers fumbled over his for the cigarette.

"I don't know what they've told you," she said, "if they've been keeping you up to date . . ." He shook his head, and she went on. "Gina's going to be okay, they say. Apart from her eye, I mean. I saw her yesterday, and she – she was talking about getting a patch for it. Like a pirate . . ."

She smoked and spoke in jerks, her eyes fixed on the whiteness of the wall, watching her private procession of ghosts.

"They still haven't found Jude. They reckon she hung around with Gina till the ambulance came, then went off in whatever car David was using. But the chances are she's dumped that by now. I – I wish she'd come home. She must know she isn't in trouble, and I'm scared for her . . ."

"She'll turn up. A girl in a penguin-suit can't hide forever."

"Not from Gina, anyway. She said, she's going to find her . . ."

At last, Fenner asked the one question that was left. "What have they done with David?"

"They're cremating him, end of the week. Didn't they tell you? Don't tell me, you want to go."

"Why not? It'd make a day out, at least."

They snapped sullenly at each other, as if they were only doing it because it was expected. Then Tina said, "Jude must have stabbed him twice, did you know? They found him with the sword-stick skewering him to the ground, right through his spine, Mike said she must've been crazy-strong to do it. But he was dead already, she'd killed him . . . Clean through the heart . . ."

After a little, he noticed that she was crying. He took the dead cigarette from her fingers, and dropped it into the ashtray. She snatched at his hand and held it, lifted it to her face and rubbed her wet cheek against his palm.

"Oh, God, Fenner," she whispered. "What are we going to do?"

And because she put it like that, because she could at least find questions that involved the two of them together, he thought it might be worth it after all.

Pushed his fingers into her thick curls, and said, "I don't know, love. Something."

Author's Note

With a novel like this, it is necessary very loudly to state that the work is pure fiction. In particular, I would like to stress that the Samaritans have never to my knowledge harboured anyone of the name or character of David Linden. Also, those readers who know Newcastle will quickly become aware that I have callously redesigned the city to suit my own nefarious purposes; and to those readers I offer my profound and genuine apologies.

While I have your attention, I'd like to offer public thanks in vast quantities to everyone who helped me with this book, and also to all my friends, who had to put up with it and me for four years. Special gratitude is due to Dr P Ballichow (thanks, Prawn), Margaret, Pat, Ian, Jay, Lellie, Mike & Philippa, Nick, the 16s, the 25s, 38 and 130, the Immoral Terrace gang and half the population of Fenham. And also most especially to my agent, without whom this book would very definitely not have been written.

Chaz Brenchley, Newcastle on Tyne 1987